PENG

Josephine Moon was born and raised in Brisbane, and had a false start in environmental science before completing a Bachelor of Arts in communication and then a postgraduate degree in education. Twelve years and ten manuscripts later, her first novel, *The Tea Chest*, was picked up for publication and then shortlisted for an ABIA award. Her bestselling contemporary fiction is published internationally. Her books include *The Tea Chest, The Chocolate Promise, The Beekeeper's Secret, Three Gold Coins, The Gift of Life, The Cake Maker's Wish* and *The Jam Queens.*

In 2018, Josephine organised the 'Authors for Farmers' appeal, raising money to assist drought-affected farming communities. She is passionate about literacy, and is a proud sponsor of Story Dogs and The Smith Family.

She now lives on acreage in the beautiful Noosa hinterland with her husband and son, and a tribe of animals that seems to increase in size each year. She wouldn't have it any other way.

the Cake Maker's Wish

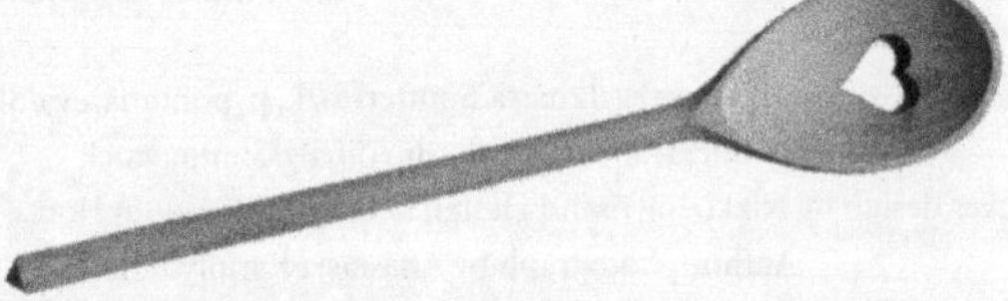

Josephine Moon

PENGUIN BOOKS

PENGUIN BOOKS

UK | USA | Canada | Ireland | Australia
India | New Zealand | South Africa | China

Penguin Books is part of the Penguin Random House group of companies whose addresses can be found at global.penguinrandomhouse.com

Penguin Random House Australia

First published by Michael Joseph in 2020
This edition published by Penguin Books in 2021

Cover photography by Baleika Tamara/Shutterstock, p_ponomareva/Shutterstock, lermont51/Shutterstock, zhu difeng/Shutterstock
Cover design by Nikki Townsend Design © Penguin Random House Australia
Author photograph by Anastasia Kariofyllidis
Typeset in Minion Pro by Midland Typesetters, Australia

Printed and bound in Australia by Griffin Press, part of Ovato, an accredited ISO AS/NZS 14001 Environmental Management Systems printer

NATIONAL LIBRARY OF AUSTRALIA
A catalogue record for this book is available from the National Library of Australia

ISBN 978 1 76104 188 4

penguin.com.au

FSC www.fsc.org
MIX
Paper from responsible sources
FSC® C009448

For Kate, for so much

1

It was November, three months after the awful day at the park when Olivia's life as she knew it had been blown apart. She looked around at the mountain of boxes tied with satin ribbons, filled with delicate latte-coloured macarons. Towers of the things teetered on the benches and the dining table, ready for the fundraising bake sale tomorrow at Darcy's school. It was possible, she observed, that she was channelling her grief into baking. This wasn't entirely a bad thing, given that she was a pastry chef. How much more complicated her life would be right now if her loss had manifested in an inability to bake. Instead, the windows of her cake shop in the main street of Richmond, Tasmania, were full of tempting treats, the aromas wafting out into the street to entice customers. She'd never been so busy.

Tonight, though, it was time to put the baking trays down. 'That'll do, pig,' she muttered to herself, echoing Farmer Hoggett from the movie *Babe*. She lifted her apron over her head and turned off the oven, quietening its hum. In the ensuing silence, she could hear her own heartbeat. The kitchen walls seemed to tick down like a cooling car, exhaling with relief after her whirlwind of activity. It was only nine o'clock, hours before she'd be tired enough for her busy mind to rest.

Darcy was asleep. She'd given him some paracetamol for the pain in his leg, and he'd drifted off in her arms. But for her, sleep had become an elusive thing. She was crippled by the silence, the emptiness, the stillness of Ma's absence. She was lonely, she realised with a shock. Lonely. A horrible word. A pathetic one. Thirty-three was too young to be lonely, surely? Yet Darcy was only six, and he was lonely too. They both missed Ma so much.

From inside her handbag, she retrieved the envelope and plucked out the black-and-white photograph she'd found at the back of a drawer in Ma's room. The photo must have been taken in England. There was Ma – Eleanora Kent – in a dark, fitted, sleeveless dress that came to just above the knee. It was impossible to tell what colour the dress was – navy blue, perhaps. Or green. She was a young woman, maybe twenty, and the expression on her face was one of secret delight, an expression Olivia was certain she'd never seen in a lifetime of living with her. Her hair was swept up high, and she clasped the handle of her bag with white gloves as she leant against a stone wall, smiling towards the photographer, or maybe someone nearby. On the back of the photo, in Ma's handwriting, was the year, *1966*, the same year she'd come to Australia as a ten-pound Pom with her parents, falling in love with Lawrence on the ship, marrying him as soon as they'd stepped onto shore, and having Olivia's mother, Laurie, the next year. Sadly, Olivia had never met Ma's much-loved Lawrence, who'd died not long after their marriage.

Olivia was fascinated by this image of Nora. It was Nora in a whole other world, a world Olivia had never experienced. She moved to the lounge room and flopped onto Ma's recliner, gazing at the photo. On a whim, she lifted her laptop from the coffee table onto her knees, and typed in *Stoneden, Cotswolds.* She was rewarded with breathtaking images of green fields and sparkling rivers, swans, stone cottages, gardens of lavender and roses. She skimmed through a site about the village's history, and then came upon a link to an article in the village's local paper, posted two months ago, that made her heart kick hard against her ribs.

Calls for descendants to rebuild dying village of Stoneden

After a controversial campaign, the Stoneden Renaissance Committee has pushed through its ambitious proposal to the district council to reinvigorate the village by inviting descendants of former residents to emigrate to Stoneden and contribute to its economic and social viability.

Although Stoneden's heritage charm has made it popular with Hollywood cinematographers, its population has been declining and its economy has suffered, with the closure of shops and other local businesses. The Renaissance Committee's president, Mr Clarence James, says the village needs an urgent revival if it is to remain a working village rather than 'just a museum'.

A similar project was previously launched in Italy, where over 100 castles, monasteries and farms were given away in return for their conversion into tourist destinations to boost local economies. The island of Arranmore in Ireland has also sought to reverse emigration by welcoming professionals from Australia and the US who are able to work remotely from the island and boost its declining population.

A trial phase of one year has been granted to Stoneden's Renaissance Committee, which now calls for applications from descendants of former residents of the village who have a profession or business and can demonstrate their ability to contribute to the local community and economy. Successful applicants will need to live and work in the village for a minimum of five years (pending final approval after the trial phase), and will receive financial assistance from the council for the transition. In the interests of building the population and securing a future for Stoneden, precedence will be given to families with school-aged children.

Anyone interested, from anywhere in the world, can visit the project's website to find out more and submit an application.

Olivia read the article, then read it again. She followed the link to the council's website and absorbed the information, excitement inching her towards the edge of the recliner, as if she could spring up and fly halfway around the world this instant. Stoneden was calling for people just like her, a professional pastry chef with her own business and a school-aged child. And what was there to keep Olivia and Darcy in Tasmania now that Ma was gone? They had no family left here, with Nora's parents gone at least twenty years and Olivia having lost her own mother when she was a small child. Darcy's father lived on the other side of the world, in Norway, known to his son only via the internet.

If she had just one wish, it was to have a family once more. Maybe this was the last chance for both her and Darcy to save what was left of their family, building a true relationship between Helge and Darcy, and maybe, just maybe, discovering the last remaining connections to Olivia's own family tree.

She clicked on the link to apply.

2

Ten months later

When the three sharp raps sounded on the front door of the cottage, Olivia's and Darcy's fingers were coated with butter and flour. It was twenty-four hours since they'd arrived in Stoneden, and the jet lag was knocking them around, but they were keen to get the apple crumble into the oven so they could head out for a leisurely stroll and explore the village's winding streets.

'A visitor already?' Olivia grinned at Darcy and wiped her hands on a tea towel. She hurried along the narrow hallway from the small kitchen to open the front door. It was barely ajar before an angry voice signalled that this might not be a charming English welcome to the neighbourhood after all.

'Thief,' the elderly woman accused, her finger pointing directly at Olivia's chest.

Olivia recoiled in surprise. 'What?'

'I saw you from my window,' the woman hissed, powdered make-up flinting away from her frown lines, her head wrapped tightly in a paisley-patterned scarf.

'Saw what?'

'Don't play the innocent with me. I watched you and that boy of yours stealing my apples. Cleaned up the whole lot, you did.'

Olivia's jet lagged mind took a moment to process this. 'But those apples were rotting on the ground.'

'It's my right to let my apples rot if I choose,' the woman said.

'But they were on our side of the hedgerow.' Olivia was genuinely confused.

'What sort of excuse is that?' The woman tapped the toe of her boot on the stone step. 'I planted them. I prune them. They're my apples.'

Olivia took a breath and smiled. 'Could we start this conversation again?' She held out her hand. 'I'm Olivia Kent. My son Darcy and I have just moved here and—'

The woman ignored her outstretched hand. 'I know who you are. You're one of the imports brought here by that devil-dealing Renaissance Committee.' She made a disgusted noise in her throat. 'They've sold you a good story, but you should know that half the village is livid about this and we don't want you here.'

Olivia turned this information over in her mind. 'That's interesting,' she said, feeling her nose twitch with concern. 'I'd like to hear more about that. Perhaps we could have a coffee and talk it through sometime in the next few days?'

'If you last that long.'

Olivia was rendered momentarily speechless by the woman's audacity, but rallied. 'Maybe we could just resolve the apple issue for now.'

'The apples you stole.'

'Mm, well, forgive me, but in Australia, if the fruit is on your side of the fence, it's considered yours.'

'Precisely what I would expect a convict to say,' her neighbour retorted.

To her dismay, Olivia burst into slightly hysterical laughter.

'Give me back my apples,' the woman demanded.

'I'd gladly do that, except that Darcy and I are making apple crumble. Your apples are all chopped up. You are, however, welcome to join us for afternoon tea to help us eat them.'

The woman's chin quivered and her eyes narrowed. 'This is not the end of the matter.' She spun on her heel and strode away down the drive, boots crunching over the pebbles.

With the apple crumble in the oven and the timer set, Olivia and Darcy ventured out the front door and down the driveway, past the second-hand van they'd picked up yesterday on their arrival in London. The early autumn weather was more comfortable than spring back in Tasmania, where the bitterly cold winter was hanging on. She put her arm around Darcy, pulling him close.

'I'm so happy we're finally here,' she said. Darcy didn't answer. She pointed out the iconic red English phone booth across the road, and the pretty stone cottages lining the grassy square. They headed down the hill towards town, and stopped outside the gate of the school where Darcy would start classes in a week's time. As she took in the squat buildings and concrete playground, Olivia felt a qualm. Where was the grass? Darcy seemed equally unimpressed, so she quickly guided him onwards, looking for something more picturesque to raise their spirits once more. They passed a graveyard, tufts of bright green grass sprouting up between wonky moss-covered headstones, and continued along the narrow footpath, spotting small birds nesting under the eaves of houses, ivy entwined around quaint rusted gates, and apple trees laden with fruit calling out to be picked. Olivia grimaced – lesson learnt. She hoped she'd soon mend that particular bridge with her new neighbour.

The row of houses ended at the River Fahn. White swans drifted serenely, and large trout, blushing pink around their necks and gently spotted, drifted lazily through the shallows. It was just like in the photos.

'Look at that!' Darcy pointed as a fish leapt out of the water to catch a dragonfly, then splashed back down on its belly and gobbled up its prize. 'Wow!'

His excitement helped to ease some of Olivia's tension. They continued, walking along the terrace of shopfronts. The smell of baking bread wafted out of the bakery. A stout woman spied them from behind her glossy black counter, grabbed two paper-wrapped loaves from the wicker baskets at her back and rushed to the doorway to meet them.

'Are you Olivia?' she asked in an Irish accent. 'You're the last one to arrive.'

'Yes – and this is my son, Darcy.'

'Fine lad. I'm Leanne, an import like you.' She beamed, gesturing to her shop. 'I'm the new baker. Here, these are for you.' She thrust the loaves into Olivia's arms.

'They smell incredible, thank you.'

'My pleasure,' Leanne said. 'I think we're going to have to stick together, us imports.' Coming so soon after the encounter with her hostile neighbour, Leanne's words made Olivia's scalp prickle uneasily.

'Right. Better get back to it. I'm still working out the temperament of my ovens. I've got three, each one with a distinct personality of its own and no desire to please me. Rather like cats, they are.'

Darcy giggled. The sun shone on his straw-coloured hair, almost giving him a halo. Olivia's heart squeezed at the preciousness of him.

Leanne waved goodbye, and they continued on to Olivia's new shop, the last of the buildings before the ivy-covered four-storey hotel. She'd identified the shop in passing when they drove into the village yesterday. Now she had the key nestled in the pocket of her jeans, and she itched to turn it in the lock and step inside.

Over the past two months, she'd studied floor plans and photos, and sent copious email instructions for the fit-out of the shop. She'd been in contact with both Clarence, the president of the Renaissance Committee, and Howard, its secretary and a retired builder who oversaw all the construction works for the new arrivals. The structural renovations were complete and the walls had been painted. Now, it was up to Olivia to finish the decor, with Darcy's help.

The freshly painted white wooden door had an ornate iron lock and handle. The shopfront was smart and glossy. The words *Rambling Rose Fine Cakes* arched across the large display window in pale pink and silver cursive script, above an image of a three-tiered cake overflowing with roses.

'What do you think?' she asked Darcy.

'It's bigger than the one back home,' Darcy said, referring to the tiny shop she'd leased in Richmond.

Olivia unlocked the door, and they were just about to step inside when a trio approached them, smiling – a woman with long, dark brown dreadlocks and a bearded man walking behind a girl of around Darcy's age. The girl was as blonde as her parents were dark.

'Hi,' Olivia said, waving at them.

'Are you an import with the Renaissance Project?' the woman asked. The young girl smiled shyly at Darcy.

Olivia made a rueful face. 'Is it that obvious?'

'Yes!' The woman laughed heartily, revealing two deep dimples. 'We are too. I'm Katrina, this is my husband, Russell, and our daughter, Eloise.'

Olivia introduced herself and Darcy. 'Are you from New Zealand?' she asked.

'Windwhistle, South Island. Is the accent that noticeable?' Katrina laughed.

'Maybe only to an Aussie.'

'I think we're going to have to stick together,' Russell said, rubbing at his beard. 'Apparently the locals don't want us here as much as we were led to believe.'

'So I've heard.' Olivia widened her eyes.

'What was your crime?' Katrina asked.

'Stealing apples from my neighbour's tree.'

Katrina snorted and rolled her eyes and Olivia decided she liked her very much. 'Yours?'

'Not sorting the recycling properly,' Russell said. 'It's a pretty intense system. At least four bins. I'll give you a lesson.'

'Excellent. I'm not sure I can afford to set my neighbour off again anytime soon.'

Darcy and Eloise had crossed the empty street to watch two swans on the river. Olivia noticed Darcy limping slightly, and winced with familiar guilt. The long-haul flight had probably aggravated his injury.

Although she was keen to start work on the shop, the sight of Darcy with a potential new friend made her pause. Right now, it was more important to help him settle in. 'I've got an apple crumble in the oven, made with stolen fruit,' she ventured. 'I don't suppose you'd like to come up and help us eat the evidence?'

'I've got to get back to the farm to fix a fence,' Russell said, apologetically.

'But Eloise and I would love to come over,' Katrina chimed in, and Olivia's heart lifted.

'Well, if you're going to go down for stealing apples then that was a great way to do it. I think that might be the best apple crumble I've ever had.' Katrina wiped up the last of the crumbs and cream with a fingertip, staring sadly at her empty bowl. She leant back in her chair, raised her coffee to her lips, sipped, and pulled a face.

'It's terrible, isn't it?' Olivia said, grinning.

'No, sorry, it's . . .' Katrina was obviously embarrassed to be caught out.

'It's fine, really, and it's not just you. Why's it so different?' Olivia said, staring sadly into the dark brew in her mug.

'Maybe it's the water?' Katrina said mournfully. 'We had rain-water tanks on the farm back home.'

Darcy and Eloise chattered happily in the lounge room, playing a card game version of Monopoly. Olivia was thrilled that Darcy had made a new friend so quickly, and one who would be starting school at the same time.

'Did you know your fridge is leaning to one side?' Katrina said, tilting her own head to the left.

'I almost pulled it on top of myself last night,' Olivia said. 'My fridge at home has a sticky door so I have to give it a good yank. I did that to this one and it staggered towards me like a drunken dance partner. Scared me half to death.'

The kitchen was a modern add-on to the original eighteenth-century cottage. Its floor sloped a bit, but the black-and-white chequered linoleum distracted the eye from the tilt. Ironically, the rest of the centuries-old cottage was possibly in better shape than the modern part.

'So, what made you decide to join in with this crazy Renaissance Project?' Katrina asked. Straight to the point – that was obviously Katrina's style. She'd already told Olivia that she was a nurse and would be working in the village's sole general practice. Olivia could totally see her in that role. With her warm, direct, no-nonsense manner, she was exactly the type of professional you'd want around in a crisis.

'There were a few reasons.' Olivia crossed one jeans-clad leg over the other. 'Darcy's dad lives in Oslo and they've never met in person – he's only spoken to Helge and his wife and kids via Skype. This seemed like a good opportunity for us to move closer.'

'Perfect,' Katrina enthused. 'That's only a short flight from London – a couple of hours?'

'Also,' Olivia leant forward and lowered her voice, 'there were some issues last year at Darcy's school, with the other kids, and everything imploded. And then my ma died.'

'Oh, I'm so sorry,' Katrina said, with a sympathetic grimace.

'She was actually my grandmother, but my own mother died in a horseriding accident when I was two, and I never knew my father, so *Grandma* just became *Ma* – she was the only mother I knew. When she died, I realised that I knew almost nothing of her life before she moved to Australia, and I was desperate to reclaim something of her past for us. I was terrified of forgetting her. When I saw the call for descendants to emigrate to Stoneden, it seemed like a chance to learn more about her and perhaps find some long-lost relatives.'

'That's a very good reason,' said Katrina.

They were quiet a moment, listening to the kids thump up the narrow spiral staircase to the bedrooms above, probably looking to ransack Darcy's luggage for something else to play with.

Olivia gathered up her long honey-blonde hair, piling it on top of her head while she thought. 'That's why I was so excited about the Renaissance Project, and why I want to save this place. The fact that it was Ma's home makes it a part of me too. This village is in my DNA. I want the chance to get to know it before it's too late.'

'Russell felt the same,' Katrina said. 'Both he and I have grandparents from around here. That's where Eloise gets her fair hair from, by the way. I promise you she is ours, though it's hard to tell by looking at her.' She laughed. 'My grandparents are still alive but they can't travel anymore. We're doing this for them as much as ourselves.'

Olivia gave an anxious grin. 'We just have to make sure we don't get kicked out before we've even started.'

'I suspect the committee has its work cut out for it,' Katrina said. 'While the project's in the trial phase, there's still a chance it could be shut down. There's already so much resistance to it. We had no idea.' She shook her head in dismay. 'We've upended our whole life for something that could be pulled out from under us at any moment.'

'We can't let that happen,' Olivia said, determinedly. 'Failure is not an option.'

3

Clarence held his *World's Best Grandpa* coffee mug in both hands and leant forward to peer over the deep pink orchid his daughter-in-law, Fallon, had given him last month for his birthday. It was doing well here on the kitchen windowsill, enjoying the morning light. Through the window, he could see clusters of children in the square getting to know each other, their parents chatting, a soccer ball being kicked around. On Monday, the school bell would ring and these imports would join the Stoneden natives, nearly doubling the number of children at the school.

Clarence's chest swelled with pride. He'd done this. He'd had the support of the other members of the Renaissance Committee, and of course Howard, his best friend since their own first day at that very same school almost seventy years ago. But it had been Clarence who had driven the project. He had pitched the idea to Howard over a mug of tea in Howard's garden more than two years ago. His friend had wavered a few moments, as Clarence had guessed his cautious friend would, but then rallied, as Clarence had known he would, always the one to back his plans. A grand plan it was – to bring the village back to life, to return it to the lively place they had known as youngsters. And now look! It was happening, right before his eyes.

He spotted Olivia Kent and her son heading down towards the high street, no doubt going to the cake shop. Olivia had been working hard this week, like all the business owners, readying their shops for the grand opening on Monday. He'd had to stop himself from running to Olivia and offering to help. There was something in the way she held her head high, just as her grandmother had once done. Olivia and Darcy were the only imports with such a direct connection to someone Clarence had known as a young lad. But he knew he couldn't be seen to be favouring any one new family in particular, even though he'd had a soft spot for this one from the start, something that had been a bone of contention between him and Howard, who'd argued a hairdresser might have been of more value to the village than a cake maker, particularly as they already had a baker.

Howard had been working for months to organise the renovations for the new businesses. Handyman jobs were Howard's domain. Not that Clarence was without maintenance skills; you didn't grow up in Stoneden in the 1950s without knowing how to wield a hammer. But whereas Howard had followed his father into the building trade, Clarence had gone on to be a white-collar man at the council, experience that had stood him in good stead during all the wheeling and dealing he'd needed to do to pull off the Renaissance Project, employing a mixture of practical negotiation, advocacy and charm. The charm rolled easily off his tongue, so it did, the proof of that in two ex-wives and a few other entanglements besides, which were quite enough for one lifetime.

He tipped the last of his coffee down the sink, pulled out his phone and messaged all the imports, reminding them about their first meeting tonight.

•

'Thank you all for coming,' Clarence said, standing in the centre of the circle of chairs.

Olivia gave Katrina an excited smile. This first gathering of the Renaissance Committee and the imports held an air of excitement and optimism – it was a brand-new start for them all. In honour of the evening, she'd pulled out her favourite dress – red with white polka dots, cinched at the waist and with a voluminous skirt. Her lips were painted red, and she'd taken the time to curl and style her hair. She was pleased she'd made the effort to dress up as 'Rambling Rose' tonight. It made her feel as though she was taking charge of her professional future, which was the one thing holding all her hopes and dreams together right now.

'Firstly, I want to thank Viola for hosting us down here in the cellar.' Clarence turned to pretty dark-eyed Viola, who was sitting next to Howard. 'The committee was most excited to receive Viola's application. She has come to us from Spain, with her husband and two children, and we're delighted to have her in the village, keeping us in fine wines. And I'm sure you'll all agree that she's done wonders with the space.'

There was a murmur of approval, lots of smiles and nods, and even a small whoop. To Olivia's great joy, the cellar of the Stoneden Hotel was entered via a large wooden trapdoor behind the piano in the ground-floor bar. Lanterns fixed to the stone walls guided visitors down the old stairs (painted with non-slip paint and fitted with modern handrails to meet safety standards, of course). At the bottom of the stairs, the room opened out into a long rectangle, with a stone floor, gentle lamp lighting, wooden barrels, and a wine rack extending the full length. It was utterly charming.

'Most of you have been here a week or so now, and you probably know each other a little, but it seemed the right time to gather as many of you here as we could manage.' Clarence beamed and held out his arms, the master of ceremonies. Olivia had to hand it to him: he had real presence and a smooth, easy voice, and she could see why he'd landed the role of president.

He introduced Howard next. Taller and thinner than Clarence, he had a gentle face and bushy eyebrows. Next to him sat Leanne, beaming her infectious smile.

'Leanne, please give my regards to your husband, Keith, and your four children,' Clarence said, then turned to address the rest of the group. 'I know many of you could only make it here tonight because your own children are right now at Leanne and Keith's home, eating fish and chips and learning how to play poker, I believe.'

'Jaysus, they'd better not be,' Leanne said, her body wobbling with chuckles.

Olivia had dropped Darcy off at Leanne's place on her way to the meeting. He was there with Eloise and several other kids who were starting school next week. It was a great chance for them all to get to know each other before their first day. She knew that all the other parents would be anxious about their young ones starting at a new school, but after everything that had happened to Darcy last year, she felt the pressure keenly. She hoped with all she had that it would be better this time around.

Next, Clarence introduced Elena and Newton, who were opening an Italian restaurant right next door to Rambling Rose. Olivia had been hoping to meet them while she was working in the shop today, but she and Darcy had had their hands full – painting the sandwich-board sign and an old-fashioned bicycle to sit on the footpath outside; sewing the red and white polka-dot bunting for the windows; and organising the sales dockets, cashbook, money float and Eftpos Square. She'd worked on her website at home, just a basic but pretty online placeholder for people to find her contact details.

On the other side of Newton was Lance, who came from Canada and would be running the greengrocer's and general shop. Olivia was surprised by his youth – he looked to be in his mid-twenties. But then, she'd finished her apprenticeship by the age of twenty-one and was running her own business at twenty-four. Lance was the only import without children, as far as she knew. Perhaps the committee was hoping he would one day marry someone in the village and raise a family here. Lance sat with his hands under his thighs and smiled but made no eye contact.

Next was Raj, who owned the toy and sweet shop. 'Lovely to meet you all,' he said in a strong regional English accent.

'As you can hear,' Clarence said, grinning, 'Raj hasn't come from very far away at all. He's from Manchester.'

'My mother's from India,' Raj explained, 'but my father's grandfather was born in Fahren Way, fifteen minutes' drive from here. My wife, Sally, is home with the kids tonight. We have two, and they started at the school last term. For any worried parents here, I can assure you they love it.'

'Lovely,' Katrina said, turning to express her relief to Olivia.

'Continuing around the circle,' Clarence said, 'we have Grayson.'

Olivia looked to her left just as Grayson's smiling gaze met hers. *My oh my.* He had wheat-coloured hair and denim-blue eyes. He was tall, too, as far as she could tell while he was sitting down, and his boots were large.

She whipped her gaze away, telling herself to get a grip. She'd only just arrived in the country; it was no time to be getting distracted by the first handsome man she saw. She focused her attention on Clarence, tapping the heel of one red pump.

'Grayson is a little different from the rest of you,' Clarence went on. 'He's not officially part of the Renaissance Project.' Intrigued, Olivia dared to glance over at the man once more. 'He used to be an optometrist, but two years ago he quit the city life and moved here from London, all by himself, and is a self-starting, first-generation dairy farmer.'

'Oh, well done,' Katrina said, 'one farmer to another.' She put a hand on her husband's thigh. 'Russell's a sheep farmer and has a position here in the village, working at the McCaffertys' place. We had a farm back home in New Zealand and we have loads of dairy farmer friends back there. We'd be happy to help you out in any way you need.'

Russell gave a manly nod in agreement, and Grayson smiled warmly. 'I might take you up on that. It's a steep learning curve.'

Now it was Olivia's turn. Clarence introduced her as 'an artisan who will keep us in fine cakes for every special moment of our lives,' and she felt her cheeks grow warm as she smiled around the room.

'Next, we have Katrina, an experienced nurse. Katrina is working with Doc Eli, who was born here and still serves the village.'

'And he's a great doctor too,' Katrina added.

Completing the circle, Clarence introduced Russell, Miguel, a Mexican man who ran the deli, Wilhelmina with her wool shop, and four members of the Renaissance Committee who were also present. As Viola poured wine and passed glasses around the circle, Clarence took a seat. He gratefully accepted a glass of red wine, and hesitated for a moment before continuing. 'While we're sure that the grand opening on Monday will be enthusiastically received by most Stoneden residents, the committee and I did think it was prudent to forewarn you about a small group of villagers who may not see this project for the great vision that it is.'

Olivia thought she saw Howard arch an eyebrow at that, though whether in gentle amusement at Clarence's use of the term 'great vision' to describe his own idea or to express disapproval of the villagers who railed against everything he and Clarence had worked so hard for, she couldn't tell.

'There are a few people – and I hasten to stress that they are in the minority – who oppose this project. They have, rather blandly, labelled themselves the Resistance Committee.' Clarence spoke the words with obvious derision.

'I've already met some of them,' Raj said, folding his arms.

'Us too,' said Russell. A chorus of agreement followed around the group.

Clarence nodded solemnly. 'To be fair, no one likes to be told what to do, especially through rules unexpectedly and swiftly handed down by their district council, and I admit that the project does limit people's financial freedom.'

Clarence rose to his feet again and began to walk around behind the chairs. 'The reality is this. Stoneden has been dying for decades. When Howard and I were boys, this was a self-sufficient village with a close, supportive community. All those cottages you now live in were filled with families. The lord and lady of the manor owned the whole village and we rented our cottages from them. We had jobs and we worked and we were happy. People don't understand this today. Everyone's so focused on themselves as individuals, proclaiming they have rights for this and rights for that. But when the manor and all the cottages were sold off, this village was sent into decline. Over the decades, we saw Londoners begin buying up properties as second homes and weekenders, driving up house prices. The very people who had made this village began selling their properties and moving away, the population declining, and the local economy collapsing.' His cheeks flushed with anger.

'The astronomically high prices the cottages were fetching created a false economy. Real estate prices were pushed out of reach of working families who wanted to buy here, and once the toffy blokes from London had bought their status cottage it sat empty for much of the year. Not enough people lived and worked in the village to keep it going. Residents had to keep moving further and further out to find employment, and they eventually moved for good. As a way to stop this, we asked the sitting council for a temporary freeze on house sales to give us a chance to get a foothold and halt the property drain. Understandably, some residents are unhappy.'

Just this afternoon Katrina had told Olivia about one of the older residents – Madeline McCarthy – who felt she was running out of chances to take care of her future, and that this project had ruined her options. Objections from residents like that must weigh heavily on the committee.

'But this project is about advancing the good of the whole community, rather than focusing narrowly on the rights of the individual,' Clarence said, his voice strengthening with conviction. 'That's an almost unheard-of concept in a Western, democratic, capitalist nation. It's brave and it's risky. In order to do the right thing for the majority, a few people may be inconvenienced. But it is all temporary. You here tonight are the future of Stoneden, the ones who will reverse the trend and build something bright for the future.'

In the bar upstairs, someone had started to play the piano, but down in the cellar you could have heard a pin drop between Clarence's words.

Clarence stopped behind Grayson's chair and put his free hand on the younger man's shoulder. 'Seeing Grayson move to the village and start something new was really what got Howard and me thinking and talking about the old times, and we decided we'd had enough. We pitched our plan to the district council and, eventually, we won.' He shook his head slowly and smiled, a tear glinting in his eye. 'Best day of our lives, so it was.' He gave Grayson one final clap on the shoulder, and walked on. Howard, clearly a man of few words, looked down at the hat in his hands.

'The ones who resist are those who want to sell their houses to the rich Londoners. They don't care if this part of the Cotswolds becomes nothing but a showpiece for tourist buses to drive through so visitors can take photos. But we care. We want a real, living, working village, and we're so happy to have you here. Some villagers might call you imports, but you are family, with your ancestral roots fixed deep in our earth.'

Family. The word trilled under Olivia's skin. That was why she was here.

'You're *our* family.' Clarence raised his glass in a toast.

'Hear, hear,' Howard said in a deep, rumbling voice. He too raised his glass, and everyone else followed suit.

Clarence tasted the wine and smacked his lips. 'So, if you do find yourself confronted by one of the resisters, remember that, to us, you're heroes. If we stand together we will overcome anything they can send our way.'

Olivia felt her chest swell with pride. She was proud to be helping to reclaim some of Ma's heritage. Clarence's rousing speech had got to her. He and Howard were visionaries such as were rarely seen these days. She jumped to her feet, holding her glass high. 'To the Renaissance Committee,' she said. The others stood up to do the same.

'And to a bloody fine grand opening on Monday,' Clarence added, grinning from ear to ear.

•

Madeline McCarthy took the milk bottle out of the fridge. The lovely young farmer, Grayson Levins, brought her fresh milk from his cows two or three times a week. If she was napping or didn't feel like talking that day, he left the bottles on the doorstep for her. And he never took a penny, either. Wouldn't take it, he said. It was his pleasure to deliver milk to someone who'd appreciate it. And appreciate it she did. Five bottles a week she went through, her tea half milk, her porridge swimming in the stuff, and her homemade yoghurt maturing on the mantle near the oil heater.

And then there was the saucer of milk she'd started to put out each day for the stray cat, the one living in the old shed. Madeline didn't mind if it took up residence there. It was likely feasting on the mice and rats. But even if it wasn't, she'd spent her whole life taking care of someone else, giving decades of dedication to her brother, so one little cat now was no bother.

She lifted a chipped bowl down from the cupboard, the peeling veneer on the door scratching her hand. It was the same bowl she'd used yesterday. That was the thing about living alone – you used a few dishes, washed them, dried them, put them away and then pulled out the exact same ones the next time around. Washing up was a rort. How many times had she washed up in her life? She did a rudimentary calculation of her age, the number of days in a year and the number of times a day she'd washed up, every day since she'd been big enough to stand on a step and lean over the sink. She shook her head. It didn't bear thinking about.

She opened the cupboard door again and looked at the stacks of plates and bowls that had accumulated over the decades. Burton had been in care for the past year. In all that time, she probably hadn't used more than the top quarter of each stack. It wasn't as though she entertained. It was just her and the stray cats that came through the shed.

Maybe she should stop washing up. It hurt her back anyway. Far easier to use the plates and throw them away, until she was down to a reasonable few that would serve out her time. It would save someone having to clear them all out at the end. And now that the blasted Renaissance Project had put a stop to her selling the house, she'd lost all enthusiasm and momentum for organising something as crass as a sale on the front lawn, with strangers, neighbours and various other nosy parkers picking through her possessions. What a ghastly thought. And you never got anywhere near what anything was worth, anyway. She'd rather burn it all.

Without the option to sell her house to fund her choice of aged care, who knew where she'd end up? It was depressing in the extreme. Selling a few plates wouldn't do it.

She fingered the chipped edge of the brown plate, one she must have had since the early 1980s. She thought she remembered using it to take an iced bundt cake to a church fete. She'd never liked it.

She stood on the lever at the base of the kitchen bin to flip open the lid, and dropped in the plate. A thrill ran through her, and she went to the glass display cabinet in the lounge room, which held the best china. She selected a bowl from the set with the delicate pink rose spray pattern, the porcelain so fine you could see through it when you held it up to a bulb. The stray cat could drink from this one tonight. She might as well give it all the good stuff to enjoy – no one else did.

4

I'll be there.

Olivia smiled at the text from Helge, confirming the time they'd arranged to Skype tomorrow. It was something they'd done countless times since Darcy was born, Helge getting to know his son from the other side of the world via a screen, yet it felt so much more important this time. The physical distance between them was so much less, the time difference only an hour. She could feel their worlds rushing towards each other. This time it would be so much more immediate, so much more real, and so much closer to the day when Helge and Darcy would meet face to face for the first time. It was exciting and wonderful and terrifying. It would be, without doubt, momentous.

'Darcy, time to go!' she called, slipping her phone back into the pocket of her jeans. The countdown to the grand opening was rushing towards them and she still had so much work to do in the shop.

'Coming!' Darcy thundered down the spiral staircase.

'Careful!' Olivia called, her stomach lurching. She'd almost slipped down the stairs herself this morning. The wooden treads were worn smooth with age. But Darcy didn't stop, jumping over the last four steps to land heavily on the carpet. She was just about to chide him for not listening when she noticed what he was wearing – a black vest and a pirate hat. He grinned at her.

'I didn't know you'd packed those,' she said.

Darcy just shrugged and said, 'Yeah.'

Olivia took the last bags of supplies out to the car and shut the boot. 'Ready?'

'*Arrr*, ready, me matey.' Darcy thrust his imaginary cutlass in the air, and she was pleased to see him so happy.

But once they got to Rambling Rose, he was unsettled and bored. She could hardly blame him. He'd been trailing around after her for days while she set up. Her mind raced to figure out how to handle this situation. Being a single parent meant it was a constant challenge to find another pair of hands when she needed them. Until last year, she'd had Ma to help. She'd also employed a baking assistant, allowing her to take the odd day off to spend with Darcy. But now they were here in Stoneden, it was just her.

'Come outside,' she said, hoping for some inspiration.

They stepped out onto the footpath just as Elena flung open the door of her restaurant next door, releasing the delicious aroma of frying onions and garlic. Seeing them, she smiled. 'Olivia and Captain Darcy! What are you up to this morning?'

It was impossible not to smile back at Elena, who exuded a nurturing, matriarchal energy. Olivia had learnt at the meeting in the wine cellar that Elena and Newton's daughter, son-in-law and grandchildren were set to move to Stoneden next year.

'I was just hoping to find something to occupy Darcy for a bit while I do some work,' Olivia explained now.

'Lucky for you that you did!' Elena clapped her hands. 'You will come in and help me cook, yes?' She bent down, grinning at Darcy. He giggled and spun on one foot, his pirate hat slipping over one eye. 'You will help me make sauce?' she said, straightening, hands on her white-aproned hips. 'You know how to use a knife?'

'Er . . .' Olivia frowned.

'Yes!' Darcy said, adjusting his hat and making a ninja *chop-chop* move.

'Don't worry about a thing,' Elena said, already guiding Darcy into the restaurant. Olivia hurried after them, wondering how she could tactfully suggest that sharp knives might not be the best thing to give to a seven-year-old.

They passed tables with red-and-white-checked tablecloths. Italian folk music played over the speakers. Behind the partition to the kitchen, crates of tomatoes, onions and garlic towered on stainless-steel benchtops, bunches of vibrant green basil, parsley and oregano sat in tubs of water, and pots bubbled on a six-burner gas stovetop.

Wiping her hands on her apron, Elena addressed Darcy. 'I'll teach you my grandmother's recipe. It will be the best sauce you have ever eaten.'

Darcy was agog. 'Okay.'

'Um—' Olivia opened her mouth to intervene, but Elena was already guiding Darcy towards the bench.

'You don't worry about a thing,' she sang again, waving Olivia away. 'Your boy will be a chef soon.' Then she leant in and whispered, 'I give him the small knife.' She patted Olivia's arm and shooed her back outside.

Olivia hastened off with guilty relief to start on her own preparations. She cleaned Rambling Rose from top to bottom. Just as she was pouring the last bucket of water down the drain, she heard the front door creak open. She looked up to see a young man with tousled dark hair standing in the doorway, wearing a plain white shirt beneath a loose all-weather jacket.

'Hi,' she said, slightly nervous until she knew if he was friend or foe.

'Olivia Kent?' he asked.

'Yes.'

'My name's Randolph Wilson. I'm a police officer from over in Fahren Way. I'm Gertrude's nephew.'

'Gertrude?' Olivia looked at him blankly.

'Gertrude Wilson. She lives next door to you.'

So that was the angry woman's name. 'This isn't about the apples, is it?'

Randolph nodded, squinting one eye apologetically.

'Gosh, what luck for her to have a member of the force in the family,' Olivia said sardonically.

Randolph cleared his throat and lowered his voice. 'Olivia Kent, it is my sorrowful duty to inform you that I am here to officially charge you with the theft of fruit from one Mrs Gertrude Wilson's property. We take these matters very seriously here in Stoneden. You'll need to come down to the station to give a formal statement, have your fingerprints taken and your passport confiscated until this matter appears before the courts.'

Olivia fumed. Her airfare had been paid for, her first year's rent paid by the committee, the cottage furnished, this shop put together exactly as she'd asked. The committee had tremendous faith in her, and a police matter so soon after her arrival would surely create a raft of ill feelings towards her. The last thing she wanted was to appear disloyal at best, and a bad investment at worst. Despite her hopes for a new life here, she'd been blindsided by the hostility lurking in this divided village, and to have something as petty as apples potentially ruin it all was infuriating. Darcy's happiness, too, was at stake – this was as much a new beginning for him as it was for her. She felt her nostrils flare, her jaw clench.

'Oh, bollocks,' Randolph said, holding up his hands. 'Forget everything I just said. I was just trying to be funny. Gertrude's got herself all in a knot about the apples, but no one's going to charge you. I just needed to chat with you so I could go back and tell her I'd done something. She's on the phone to me every other week reporting something or other that's happening in this village.'

Olivia stared at him in disbelief, then snorted. 'I see.'

'Forgive me?'

'Forgiven,' she said, feeling some of the tension releasing.

He nodded. 'Right, I'll get out of your hair. I'm sure you're snowed under with the opening on Monday. I'll come back then to show some support.'

'Great.'

'Just don't tell Gertrude,' he said, worriedly.

Olivia followed him out and waved goodbye. The local policeman was on the Renaissance Project's side. That could only be a good thing. She popped into the restaurant to check on Darcy and found him and Elena sitting at one of the tables, huge white napkins tucked into their shirt collars, competing to see who could suck up strands of spaghetti the fastest. Tomato sauce was splattered everywhere.

'Come and join us,' Elena said, dabbing at her cheeks with a napkin.

Darcy grinned at Olivia with saucy teeth and she kissed him on the head. 'I'd love to. It smells amazing in here! But I'm a bit behind with the shop, so I really need to keep moving.' That was true, though she was also keen not to overstay their welcome with Elena.

'I'll give you some sauce to take with you,' Elena said, creaking up slowly from the seat.

'No, you don't have to do that.'

Elena waved her protest away. 'It's my pleasure.'

'Thank you.'

Darcy arched back in his chair. 'Look how big my tummy is,' he said.

Olivia poked it gently. 'Yep, I think you're growing a pasta baby in there.' He laughed and swivelled easily out of his seat, picking up his pirate hat from the floor beside him.

Elena returned with a container of sauce and handed it to her. It was still warm. Olivia hugged her. 'Thank you so much. Let me know what I can do to return the favour.'

'Nonsense. I'm happy to help. That's what the village is all about.'

Back inside Rambling Rose, Olivia and Darcy got to work, setting out the small tables and chairs. Darcy stocked the pale blue bicycle's wicker basket with synthetic yellow daisies, then held the stepladder for Olivia while she hung up the red and white-spotted bunting inside the windows. Next, she used the hot glue gun to attach dark green plastic ivy vines to the walls.

'What do you think?' she asked Darcy, looking around.

'What about the cakes?' he asked. The long wooden counter had alternating panels of pastel pink, yellow and green. Glass cake domes and stands waited to display her freshly made creations.

She sighed happily. 'That's the easy part.'

Finally, they brought in the things for the children's corner. Olivia had asked Darcy to design it. 'You're the expert on being a kid,' she'd said. They attached more bunting to the walls above a kid-sized lounge chair and beanbags, and arranged a toy farmyard set on a low table. There were generous pots of chalk to use on a little blackboard, a crate of toys and a small box of books. The finishing touch was a small tent.

Darcy threw himself into the tent, turned and poked his head out through the flaps. 'This is so cool!'

Olivia nodded and looked around. It *was* cool. The shop was beautiful, with a real vintage 1950s feel about it, hopefully capturing the spirit of Stoneden in its heyday. All she needed was customers.

•

On Sunday, Olivia felt wired, and not only because of the grand opening the next day. It was partly due to thoughts of tonight's Skype session with Helge, just hours away. She'd been counting down to this for days, she realised, waiting for Helge to return from holidays with his family.

The grounds of the Stoneden trout farm were inviting on this sunny afternoon and, consequently, dozens of families were out to enjoy the mild weather at this family-friendly establishment. There were picnic rugs aplenty, squealing toddlers, and a few bored teenagers on their mobile phones. A couple of dads were fly-fishing in the practice pond, and an open-air grill was set up to cook the trout as they were plucked from the water.

Olivia and Darcy had found a spot a few metres back from a large pond. They waved as Katrina, Russell and Eloise arrived, along with Russell's new best mate, Grayson. The adults settled on the grass while Darcy and Eloise ran off to the play equipment nearby.

Grayson gave Olivia a friendly smile as he sat down. He wore jeans and a checked shirt, and his hair was tousled.

'Hi!' Olivia's greeting was a touch too exuberant. She hadn't realised he would be joining them.

After some general discussion about tomorrow's grand opening, Grayson and Russell became immersed in a detailed conversation about new treatments for footrot. Katrina and Olivia chatted as they watched Darcy and Eloise clamber over the wooden fort and slide, then start an easy, laughter-filled game of tag, which grew in size as more and more kids joined in. Darcy had barely stopped grinning since they'd arrived in Stoneden, and Olivia's heart soared to think that the trouble of last year was behind him. She fervently hoped that moving to Stoneden would turn out to be the best decision she could have made.

After a brief pause in their conversation, Katrina said carefully, 'I've noticed that Darcy occasionally limps a little bit.'

Olivia's heart squeezed. 'Yes.'

'What happened?' Katrina asked, gently.

Olivia closed her mind against memories of that day, against the scream she hadn't even known was hers at first, against the sirens, the smell of the hospital. 'He was hit by a car.'

Katrina sucked in air sharply through her teeth. 'When?'

'A year ago. He had crush fractures in both the tibia and fibula, at his knee.'

'Surgery? Plates? Pins?'

'All of the above,' Olivia said. 'As well as a post-surgery infection.'

Katrina groaned. 'Oh, love, that's terrible.'

'It was.' They watched Darcy and Eloise shrieking with laughter as they tumbled down the slide together. Olivia felt her anxiety about speaking with Helge grow; still, a year on, he didn't know the full story of what had happened that day. What would he think when she finally told him? 'He still gets pain in his knee and his hip. He has physiotherapy exercises he's supposed to do, though it's hard to get him to do them.'

Katrina adjusted the cotton scarf at her neck, releasing several long dreads that had got caught up. Perhaps sensing that Olivia didn't want to keep talking about Darcy's accident, she asked, 'Are you nervous about tomorrow?'

'Definitely.' Olivia felt the weight of expectation on her shoulders – the hopes and dreams of the Renaissance Committee and of all the other imports who'd upended their lives for a chance at a new start. Knowing that there were people in the village who didn't want them there didn't help.

'I'll be there,' Katrina said. 'Eli's blocked off the morning and we're not taking any patients – unless there's an emergency, of course. We'll be out and about to support the project, visiting each shop, so you'll see at least two friendly faces.'

'I'll be there too,' Grayson said, rejoining their conversation. 'So that makes three supporters.'

Olivia smiled at him gratefully.

At the practice pond, a man cheered as he reeled in a pink and grey fish. The poor thing. It wasn't like it had a sporting chance there in a closed pond. Russell wandered across to the playground to check on the kids. Darcy ran over to him, animatedly re-enacting his super-fast ride down the slide.

'How's the shop going?' Grayson asked Olivia. 'All ready for tomorrow?'

'I think so.'

'I've got some spare time in the morning, if you need any help,' he said.

'That's so kind, thank you.' She was genuinely touched by his offer.

'Until then, I've got wine,' Katrina said, pulling a bottle of red out of her picnic basket and cracking the top. 'Would you like a glass? It's from Viola's cellar. It's Spanish.'

'Love one.' Olivia set out plastic cups, while Grayson produced some crusty bread rolls, and homemade butter that he explained was made from his cows' milk. Russell returned from the playground, Eloise and Darcy trotting behind him, and they all settled down for a fabulous spread of dips, cured meats, olives and cheese from Miguel's deli. Olivia sipped her wine and gazed at Darcy's smiling face, and just for a while she let all her worries disappear into the sunny sky.

*

Olivia was sitting at the end of the dining table, her back to the thick iron-framed windows overlooking the village square, tapping on her laptop.

'Darcy, it's time,' she called, clicking on the Skype icon.

'Coming!' He ran down the stairs and jumped the last three, landing heavily, and she flinched. She really needed to stop him doing that. It couldn't be good for his leg. But she hated to remind him of his injury.

He came to the table, smiling.

'Er, what's that on your head?'

He touched the black velvet headband. 'Eloise gived it to me,' he said, grinning. 'And I gived her some of my Lego pieces.'

'*Gave* her,' she corrected.

'Gave her,' he repeated.

The exchange must have happened while they were playing at the trout farm. Darcy had always got on better with girls. Sports weren't really his thing. Eloise was lovely and he needed a friend. But there'd been times in the past when Helge had seen Darcy wearing a bracelet or with painted fingernails, and had been a bit stiff in his response. She didn't want today's conversation to be fraught with bickering or, worse, shaming.

'I'm glad you two are such good friends.' Olivia's mind raced, trying to think of a way to entice him to take off the headband without making him feel bad. 'But do you know what?'

'What?'

'I bet your little brother and sister would love to see you in your pirate costume! How about you put it on for them?'

He frowned. 'Okay,' he said, with just a tinge of disappointment. He pulled off the hairband and went upstairs. A few minutes later he came back down in his pirate vest, smiling again.

'You look gorgeous,' Olivia said, with a pang. She hated manipulating him.

She clicked on the tiny photo of Helge, blond, blue-eyed and stubbled, and Skype sang its little song while the call connected. She wrapped her arm around Darcy's slender waist, pulling him to her. Their heads were about the same height on the video box on the screen and they poked their tongues out at each other while they waited. When Helge answered, they were both smiling and laughing.

'*Hei!*' Olivia said.

'*Hallo*,' Helge replied, grinning, deep crinkles at the corners of his eyes. He wore a long-sleeved light-weave grey knit that clung to his toned shoulders and chest. Gosh, the man did take good care of himself.

'Hi,' Darcy said.

'You look tanned,' Olivia said.

'*V*e've been hiking a lot over summer,' he said. 'Darcy, look how much you've grown! Every time I see you, you have shot up, like sapling.'

'I'm a pirate,' Darcy said.

'You'll be able to sail across the *v*ater to come see me soon, *ha*?'

Darcy nodded uncertainly.

The beginning of a Skype session with Helge was always a little awkward. It felt to Olivia as though they were starting again from scratch each time. Helge had done the best he could, contributing financially and making sure they spoke at least once a month, but building solid relationships took time, and physical closeness. Again, she felt hope blossom that this move was the best thing she could have done for Darcy's relationship with his dad.

'*V*ot have . . . I mean, *what* have you been doing this weekend?' Olivia asked. It was so difficult not to imitate Helge's accent. She loved the way he spoke, she always had. If they'd been from the same country, who knew? Maybe it would be her with him and their three children right now.

Until last year, she'd thought she was doing okay in the single parent role. But when she told Helge about the accident she'd seen a different side of him. It was the only time she'd ever seen him truly angry. He'd lost his English for a few moments, lecturing her in Norwegian. Rightly so – his child could have been killed. But it had made her feel so alone, so vulnerable. And then Ma died, and Helge let go of his anger, showering her with sympathy instead.

Birgit approached the screen and ducked down to wave, her long hair falling in a dead-straight waterfall. '*Hei!*' She smiled warmly.

'Hi,' Darcy said shyly, leaning his weight further in to Olivia.

Then Helge and Birgit's children sidled into view, both with the same colouring as their parents. Three-year-old Elias stared, curious of the technology that allowed strangers into his lounge room, while four-year-old Regine was shy, half hiding behind her mother.

'*Arrr!*' Darcy roared, like a pirate.

Elias's eyes widened and he burst into tears.

'Oh.' Darcy's enthusiasm disappeared. 'Sorry,' he said quietly.

'It is all right,' Helge said, rubbing Elias's shoulder before Birgit picked him up for a cuddle and walked back a few steps so his piercing cries didn't deafen everyone.

Regine continued to stare at Olivia and Darcy as she whispered something to her dad. He replied in Norwegian, pulling her onto his lap.

'Regine wants to know where you are,' Helge explained. 'I said you were in a village in England. She wants to know if that's a long way away.'

'Is it?' Darcy asked, though Olivia had already explained this.

'Only about two hours on a plane,' Helge said.

'Amazing!' Olivia said, squeezing Darcy. 'After all this time, you'll finally get to meet your dad in person.'

Helge's face was pinched with sadness, or perhaps regret. 'I can't *v*ait.'

'Me either,' Olivia said. 'It will be so great to see you again, after so many years.'

Helge's eyes met hers and Olivia caught her breath. The intervening years seemed to vanish and she was back in the small airport in Hobart. She and Helge holding hands, both sniffing and wiping away tears. Olivia was two months pregnant. It had been a whirlwind holiday romance, but now Helge had to go back to Norway. It was a terrible wrench to be saying goodbye. But for Olivia, it was all too soon in their relationship to be turning her life upside down. They'd agreed marriage would be a rash and unwise thing to do, and Olivia didn't want to leave Ma and have a baby on the other side of the world with no family support. As well, she had her business to think of. Despite talking all around it, they couldn't come up with a vision that worked for everyone, and they'd said goodbye, with no idea how their future would play out, only knowing they'd be connected forever, one way or another.

Now, Helge blinked, perhaps shooing away the same memory. 'I'll come to you, on the weekend.'

Darcy bounced up and down with excitement.

'Wonderful,' Olivia said.

They finished their chat, and waved goodbye to Helge and Regine.

Helge waved back. '*Ha de bra*.'

'*Ha de bra*,' Olivia and Darcy replied. She felt light and happy for the first time that day. No matter what happened with the Renaissance Project and Olivia's business, it was all worth it, just to give Darcy the opportunity to hug his dad.

5

Olivia was up by five o'clock the next morning to shower and dress in soft, well-worn overalls. Her wardrobe was divided into three sections: slopping-around-the-house wear (mainly jeans and tracksuit pants), utilitarian overalls for baking, and 1950s-style dresses for serving, delivering, and promotional opportunities in newspapers or social media. She had already selected her outfit for the opening later that morning, laying everything carefully in a small bag, along with her make-up and hairbrush. But first she had to get Darcy off to his first day of school and then bake up a storm. Her heart was beating fast as she thought about everything she had to do.

Hair still dripping, she checked her phone. It was five-thirty. She had an hour before she had to get Darcy up. She blow-dried her hair and tied it up off her face in a topknot. Then she made Darcy's lunch. She'd packed the rest of his schoolbag last night, checking and double-checking the list of items he needed to bring with him, afraid she'd forget something. She desperately wanted his first day to go off without a hitch. At least he had Eloise to go with.

The plan was for Olivia to drop him at Katrina and Russell's place – on the other side of the square – at seven o'clock, to give her enough time to get down to the shop to start baking. Katrina would walk him and Eloise the two minutes down the hill to school. As of last night, Darcy seemed happy and excited about this plan, but Olivia was starting to question the sense of Clarence's decision to schedule the grand opening to coincide with the first day of school. In fairness, though, she was the only one who had a problem; of the shopkeepers, she was the only solo parent.

Clarence had explained that Mondays were slow tourist days in Stoneden, and most of the existing shops took the opportunity to shut on that day. After today, Olivia would shut Rambling Rose on Mondays too, just as she'd done with her shop back in Richmond, with weekends usually the busiest trading days. As the Renaissance Committee was intent on fostering good relations between the imports and the natives, they had decided that Monday would be a good day for all the new shops to make their debut – free of tourist buses, which often aggravated locals anyway, allowing residents time to visit each shop and get to know the owners. The shops had been given rolling opening times, encouraging the locals to move through the village on a 'shop crawl'. This was supposed to give the locals a sense of community ownership over the new ventures, or so the committee hoped.

Darcy creaked down the stairs around six, always a bit slower in the morning, a bit more prone to stiffness in his leg.

'Hey, baby, you're up early,' Olivia said, meeting him on the bottom step and wrapping him in a hug. Perhaps he was still adjusting to the time zone, or maybe her nervous energy had permeated the floorboards above and roused him from slumber. He was such a willing early-morning hugger, still sleepy, content to nestle in to her and just be. She held him for as long as he'd let her, kissing his head and rubbing his back.

'Morning,' he said quietly, then let go and stepped down. His bed hair was so spectacularly spiky that she'd need a wet brush to get it down. Maybe even some product. He flopped onto the couch and clicked on the television.

'Are you ready for breakfast?' she said. 'I've made porridge.'

'Not yet,' he said, his eyes glassy. She put a crocheted rug over his flannelette pyjamas and tucked it under his bare feet.

Her mobile phone *ting*ed from the kitchen. The message was from Helge.

> Wishing you all the best for
> a great day today. Looking
> forward to seeing you soon. x

Her mind jumped forward to the weekend, wondering. What would he be like so many years on? More importantly, how would he be with Darcy? Having an internet relationship was one thing; seeing each other in person would be something else entirely. What if he wasn't the kind of dad she'd imagined he would be? What if he was stern or bad-tempered? The potential for it to be a disaster was suddenly very real.

Perhaps worse, what if she felt the same attraction to him now, eight years on, as she'd felt when he left Australia?

She tossed her phone into her bag like a hot potato. This was the last thing she needed to be distracted by today.

Darcy did eat his porridge, followed by three pieces of toast and peanut butter. He didn't complain about his new yellow and navy uniform and black shoes, and he walked into Katrina and Russell's cottage as though it were his second home, immediately chatting and laughing with Eloise.

'Well, he looks super stressed,' Katrina said mildly, sipping on her mug of coffee.

'Do you think I should be worried?' asked Olivia. 'Do you think he's underestimated this big change? Or is in denial? Or is maybe so terrified that he's overcompensating?'

Katrina regarded her, amused. 'Only a mother would think that.'

'Am I nuts?'

'Only within the realms of normal, everyday parental anxiety. Trust me, he's fine.'

'Okay.' Olivia picked up her bag. 'Darcy, I've got to go now. Come and give me a hug goodbye.'

He raced over, threw his arms around her, then ran back to Eloise, who was making a paper plane.

'Well, that's that,' Olivia said, with a tinge of sadness that he wasn't more reluctant to leave her. She *was* crazy. 'I should go before I ruin this moment.'

Katrina laughed. 'I'll look after him, I promise. I won't leave until he looks settled.'

'Thank you.' Olivia hugged her.

'Go and show those snooty resistance villagers that you're the best cake maker in the whole world.'

The street fizzed with anticipation. Most shops displayed *Grand Opening* signs of some sort. Balloons waved in the breeze outside Raj's toy shop, and Lance had tied ribbons around wooden barrels of fruit on the footpath. A life-sized toy sheep sat in front of Wilhelmina's wool store, a *Welcome* sign hanging around its neck. Olivia sang hello and waved to each of the other shopkeepers as she made her way to Rambling Rose.

'Here we go,' she whispered, turning the old key in the lock.

She put the bicycle with its flower basket outside the door, along with her chalkboard sign saying *Grand Opening – Free Cake!* She turned on the downlights and set the music to a 1950s compilation – Bill Haley and His Comets, Chuck Berry, the Fontane Sisters, Frank Sinatra, Little Richard, June Valli, Fats Domino, Bo Diddley, Perry Como, Doris Day. She pulled out bowls, spatulas, spoons, scales, baking paper, beaters, trays and piping bags, filled the sink with hot water and suds, and turned on the oven. The butter was already set out on the bench – no need to refrigerate it here – with eggs and bags of sugar, flour and icing mixture. She collected vanilla powder, rosewater and orange blossom water, and allowed herself the luxury of taking a few moments to open each one, close her eyes and inhale the fragrances.

Olivia had big plans for today, including her showpiece, a triple-layered rosewater sponge with buttercream filling, covered with piped buttercream roses in three shades of pink, from pink champagne to a deeper cotton candy and rich magenta. She would display it prominently on a cake stand; visitors would first smell the delicious aromas, then be knocked out by its visual perfection. She went to the storeroom to make sure she had the right pieces for the piping bags.

As she opened the door, a shape moved across the floor. Olivia squealed.

Zipping across the narrow room, so close to her she nearly trod on it, was a large black rat. It ducked behind a tall bucket of icing mixture on the floor, but its pale, ropy tail was still visible.

After a moment, Olivia removed her hand from her mouth, where it had flown to silence her scream. She swore several times through her teeth, trying to think over the pounding of her heart. Where had the rat come from? Olivia had been here every day of the last week; she had cleaned and scrubbed and set up everything herself. There'd been absolutely no sign of rats – no droppings, no nests, no shredded paper or plastic, no smell. Why had one chosen today of all days to seek a home here?

Most importantly, no one else could see this. A rat in a cake shop, on grand opening day, in a divided village was a total disaster. Had she locked the door behind her when she came in? She didn't think so. Worse – she'd already put her sign out the front, advertising herself to everyone. She stood immobilised, staring at the tail, not wanting to take her eyes off it for a second lest it get away, but also desperate to stop anyone from popping in to the shop. There was only a curtain between the shop and the storeroom, so she couldn't even trap the rat inside. She was the only thing standing between it and the rest of the shop. She'd have to catch it, right now.

But . . . with her bare hands?

She shuddered. What if it bit her? Or ran up her body? Her eyes darted around the storeroom, assessing the available tools. There was a broom and a dustpan and brush. None were any use: she knew she didn't have it in her to bludgeon the creature to death, and she had no hope of capturing it in the dustpan. Then again, once the shop was full of people, surely it would be too scared to come out. Could she risk leaving it here, hoping for the best? It was a terrible option, but if she couldn't catch it, the only alternative was to report it, and news of such a serious breach of health laws would be a terrible blow, not just for her but for the whole project. No, she had to try to catch it.

To her left was a box full of paper goods – serviettes, paper towels, flat-packed cake boxes. It was nearly as wide as the storeroom door. With her eyes still focused on the rat's tail, she slowly bent forward and lifted the box, then carefully placed it against one side of the doorframe. As she did so, the rat's tail slid slowly out of view.

God, this was awful.

She picked up a tower of folded tea towels and shoved them into the gap between the box and the other side of the doorframe. It wasn't much of a barrier: the rat could easily scale the box and the tea towels. Still, she had to try. As far as she knew, the creature was still behind the bucket.

Once again she scanned the shelves, looking for something with a lid that she could use to catch it. There was nothing. On one shelf, though, she noticed two folded towels. Perhaps she could throw them over the rat like a net, then pick it up. Olivia shuddered, imagining the trapped animal writhing between her hands, its teeth or claws piercing the cloth.

Sweat beaded around her neck and she was vaguely aware of precious time ticking away as she stood there in a stand off with the rodent. She needed to be baking. She picked up the top towel, pale blue with white spots. Was it better to hold the towel open, with more surface area, or folded over to provide more protection from the rat's teeth? Somewhere in the back of her mind, a voice told her she would laugh about this one day. 'Yeah, right,' she said, under her breath.

Her heart pounding in her chest, her hands shaking, she inched towards the bucket. Was it better to approach from the side, or should she try going over the top? But the choice was taken away from her. The rat must have heard her footsteps, because it shot out of cover, towards the back wall. She squealed and leapt after it, holding out the towel. The rat veered left, and she followed, jarring her knee, then banged her head on the edge of a shelf. Reeling from the pain, she righted herself, and spun around to pursue the rat as it made for the door. Seeing the barrier ahead, it launched itself off the ground, seeming to walk on air as it ascended the side of the box.

'No!'

Olivia threw herself forward, getting the towel over the box, and then clutched at the rat's body. For a moment she felt it squirming beneath her fingers. But she hadn't grasped it firmly enough. The rat shot out from under the towel, leapt off the top of the box like a BASE-jumper from a skyscraper, hit the floor and shot through the shop.

'Shit, shit, shit!' Olivia stumbled over the box and out into the shop, but the rat had disappeared.

6

Clarence and Chester rose from their seats inside the Stoneden Hotel. For this difficult conversation, Clarence had chosen a snug, quiet spot near the fireplace, where the risk of being overheard was low. It was no secret to anyone who lived in the area that Clarence was not Chester Pepperworth's favourite person, but they didn't have to hear his contempt for themselves.

'Shall we?' Clarence said, as cordially as he could. He'd already sat through twenty minutes of Chester's smug, gleeful mocking of the Renaissance Project. The man had disgustedly inherited the project from the former council, whose demise was attributed to the divisive nature of the very project they'd approved.

'Let's get this over with,' his adversary said, putting on his hat. It was a homburg, just like the one Churchill was famous for, and Clarence was certain that Pepperworth wore it to give himself an air of authority that his five-foot-nothing stature would not have otherwise possessed. And then there was the baldness. The man might now have Clarence's second ex-wife and her family's millions, but he'd never have Clarence's height or his thick, luxuriant head of hair.

They stepped out into the crisp air, and Chester wound his cream cashmere scarf around his neck.

'For God's sake, man,' Clarence snapped. 'Could you smile? Or at least not look so dour? There are actual people who have moved here from other countries to build new lives. This is a big day for them.' He felt the breeze pick up his own hair and toss it about.

'Don't pretend for a second that this is about anything other than your own ego,' Pepperworth snarled, his expression unchanged. Droopy bloodhound eyes, that was what he had. Or maybe doleful eyes like Eeyore. Either way, the man couldn't be happy about anything. Clarence had no idea what Jean saw in him, except perhaps that Chester was the exact and complete opposite of Clarence.

They turned to walk up the narrow footpath along the high street. 'We'll start at the top end and work our way down,' Clarence said. As they passed Olivia's cake shop he cast a quick look inside. A pair of beaters whirred in her hands and he could see the light on inside the oven.

The men made their way along the row of shops. Across the road, the river burbled along gently, sparkling in the sunshine. One or two residents smiled at Chester as they passed, and he nodded and tipped his hat to them. The street was busier than usual for a Monday morning, many locals out for the opening. The lively atmosphere helped Clarence to regain some of his usual confidence and forget about Chester's ill humour.

'Doc Eli has closed the surgery this morning to attend the opening,' he said as they reached the last shopfront. Chester said nothing. Clarence guided him through the entrance of Miguel's delicatessen. Miguel stood behind his counter of smallgoods, wearing a white apron over tailored pants and a smart pale blue business shirt with a rainbow-coloured bow tie. He broke into a huge smile as Clarence and Chester entered.

'Morning, Miguel,' Clarence said.

'Welcome, friends!' Miguel called in his cheerful Mexican accent, his thick grey moustache dancing up and down. Miguel was alone in the village for now, waiting for his wife and children to arrive when they could.

'Miguel, this is Chester Pepperworth, the lead councillor, here to do the honours of welcoming everyone to our village,' Clarence said, smiling meaningfully down at Chester.

'Indeed,' Chester said, taking off his hat and tucking it under his arm. He reached out his hand to shake Miguel's over the cabinet, but Miguel waved it away, strode around the counter remarkably swiftly for such a big man, wrapped his tree-trunk arms around Chester and lifted him off the floor in a bear hug.

'Oh, my . . . *argh* . . .' Chester gasped, his face flushing red and his hands holding onto the tall man's shoulders for dear life. For good measure, Miguel swung the politician from side to side before dropping him back to the floor.

Clarence stared fixedly at the shelves of green olive oil and amber-coloured vinegar, squashing down the laughter he feared was about to burst out.

'Come, sit. What'll you have?' Miguel waved his two visitors towards a small bench seat and table that had been placed in the back corner for the occasional visitor who might like to stay and eat rather than take their purchases away. 'How about the tasting plate? A bit of everything?'

'Grand, Miguel, thank you,' Clarence said, answering for them both, as Chester seemed to have lost his voice. Perhaps he was winded. The small man pulled down his jacket and straightened his shoulders, looking discomposed. But he sat down. Guy and

Roger entered the deli, both wearing collared shirts and cable-knit jumpers, their trouser legs with perfect creases as always.

Clarence held up a hand in greeting, while preparing himself for trouble. Guy and Roger were out-and-out resisters: the two Londoners made no secret of the fact that they wanted to sell their cottage to the highest bidder as soon as possible so they could retire in the south of France. The men nodded curtly in reply.

Miguel placed an enormous tasting plate on the table for Clarence and Chester to share. Then he turned to the new arrivals, clapping his paws. 'Welcome, friends,' he boomed. 'Please, come and inspect the cabinet. The tasting plates are on the house today in celebration of our village's grand opening!'

He raised his arms and Clarence held his breath. *Oh, no, please don't hug them!*

But Miguel only landed a hand heavily on Guy's shoulder. Guy flinched and leant away. Miguel either didn't notice or didn't care, because he patted his captured visitor heartily, before doing the same to Roger.

Clarence picked up the small cheese knife and spread marinated feta onto a cracker and popped it in his mouth. He pushed the plate closer to Chester, signalling with his eyes to remind him to eat and enjoy. Only then did Guy and Roger notice the lead councillor and come over, smiling. They ignored Clarence, while Chester turned on the charm and complimented them both on their recent work on the community consultation committee for the development of culture and arts in the district. Clarence fixed a pleasant smile on his face, hoping they would be on their way soon.

'Why don't you join us?' Chester said, just as Miguel brought over another huge platter of food.

'We won't say no,' Guy said, sliding along the bench to cosy up to Chester, with Roger close behind.

Clarence looked up and gave Miguel a supportive smile as the shopkeeper shuffled awkwardly behind his cabinet, watching the unexpected assembly of resisters feasting on his food. To Clarence's dismay, the next arrivals through the door were Fern and Georgio, sniffing the air like dogs on the scent of a feral animal. Their actual dog, a chihuahua named Pixie, shivered in Fern's arms.

Miguel rushed over to greet them and pat the little dog, and Roger summoned them to join the group. Oh, this was terrible. Now there were five of the project's enemies here together. There was only one reason this group would be out and about today and that would be to cause difficulty.

Clarence sat stiffly, eyeing the door, waiting for someone, *anyone*, from the allies' side to arrive and save the day. And then someone did.

He got up, excusing himself, and strode across the parquetry floor to shake Grayson's hand. 'Good to see you,' he said fervently.

Grayson eyed the group of resistance fighters in the corner and raised his eyebrows at Clarence. 'Off to a good start, then?'

'Grayson,' Miguel said, coming to embrace the tall farmer. They were roughly the same height, though Miguel's bulk was superior.

'Hold on there, big guy,' Grayson wheezed, held in the vice-like arms. 'You'll crush the cheese.'

'Not the cheese!' Miguel bellowed. He took the paper bag from Grayson and extracted the creamy yellow and white blocks, murmuring appreciatively.

The front door opened again and Olivia burst in, her topknot askew and her shoulders stiff. A somewhat unhinged smile was plastered to her face. She pulled herself up suddenly, so as not to run into Clarence.

'Oh, hi,' she said, her wild eyes taking in the crowd, before turning to Miguel. 'Miguel, I know I didn't order any but I'm wondering if you might have some of your lovely edible flowers somewhere?' she asked, a bit breathlessly. She was harried, that was for sure. 'I changed my plan at the last minute, you know what we creatives are like.' She waved a hand frantically in the air.

'Everything okay?' Clarence asked.

'Yes, yes, fine!' she said, almost shouting.

'Just forget-me-nots, will that do?' Miguel said, matching her almost-shout.

'Perfect!' she shouted back.

He strode purposefully off to his cabinets once more, and squeezed himself down behind them to find what he was looking for.

'First-day nerves?' Clarence said, supportively.

'Oh, no, no, nothing like that.'

'Can I help?' Grayson asked. 'I know I'm not a baker or a pastry chef but I've got a bit of time. I could whip cream, or . . . chop things,' he said uncertainly.

Olivia's smile wobbled slightly, then she clapped her hands. 'You know what? That sounds perfect.'

Grayson gave a small smile and then bit it down. 'Okay.'

Olivia turned to receive a plastic container of pale blue flowers from Miguel's outstretched hands, before thanking him, waving enthusiastically and leaving, Grayson following close behind.

How very strange, Clarence thought, his worries intensified by Olivia's nerves. It hadn't been the smoothest start to the day but it could only improve, surely.

7

'Here.' Olivia passed Grayson the bags of powdered sugar. 'Use the scales to weigh out two kilos.'

'Two kilos?'

'Not a gram over.'

'Got it.'

She paused briefly to watch the muscles in Grayson's neck flicker as he lifted the heavy bags, then she continued peeling the paper off the blocks of butter. On the other side of Grayson's body, four dozen cupcakes sat cooling on racks along the steel bench. Half were vanilla, golden through the translucent papers, the other half chocolate. The chocolate ones would have Tia Maria icing with morello cherries and shaved curls of chocolate, while the white ones would have baby-pink icing scattered with Miguel's fresh blue flowers. The time she'd wasted hunting for the rat after it had escaped the storeroom had set her back, forcing her to abandon her plan to make the rosewater cake. For the hundredth time, she cast her eyes nervously around the shop, searching out the black furry body and long, scaly tail.

Please, please, stay hidden, she begged it.

'Two kilos exactly,' Grayson said, proud of himself.

'Now, pour that into the mixer bowl and set it to mix on the slowest setting for a few moments, to work out any lumps.'

She retied her apron around her waist and looked at his jeans and jacket. That wouldn't do. He looked clean enough, but still.

'What?' he asked, noticing her hesitation.

'I was just thinking that you should have an apron too.'

'Have you got a spare?'

'Um . . .'

'What?'

'Only these.' She pointed to the pile of frilly, floral and very feminine 1950s aprons on the lower bench.

He had to bend down to see where she was pointing. He caught sight of them and straightened again, smiling.

She held his gaze. 'It's just that it's a workplace health and safety thing,' she said as calmly as she could, trying not to think about the much larger hygiene issue that was lurking somewhere nearby. 'I just don't want to risk anything going wrong.'

Grayson squared his shoulders and nodded. 'Well, we can't have anything going wrong today. Lace me up.'

'Really?'

'I'm Team Renaissance. If we're going to go down it won't be because I wasn't prepared to wear a frilly apron.' He shrugged. 'No one's going to die. It's just an apron.'

'Exactly,' she said, breathing a sigh of relief at his pragmatic attitude. 'Which one would you like?'

'You choose,' he said.

She flicked through the neat pile and selected a black-and-white-striped apron with red and white-polka-dot trim; the pockets were red love hearts edged with frothy white lace. She handed it to him. 'Here you go.'

'Thank you,' he said, barely glancing at it as he shook it out. 'But I have no idea how to put it on. You'll have to do it for me.' He gave her a cheeky grin.

She considered telling him to work it out himself, but his willingness to jump in with both big boots did deserve some leeway. Taking the apron, she stood on tiptoe to place the neck strap over his head, catching a whiff of his fresh outdoor smell and lemony soap. He held out his arms like a tree while she moved behind him to do up the ties, her heart thumping at this unexpectedly intimate action.

'There you go,' she said, her voice a little croaky. She went back around to the front. 'You look quite the picture.'

'Thank you,' he said.

They smiled at each other a moment until she brought herself into line. What a morning she was having. 'Butter next.'

With Grayson's help, Olivia made up most of the time she'd lost due to the rat, and by eleven o'clock all the cupcakes were iced and dressed and arranged on tiered silver cake stands. Her look book – featuring photos of her previous commissions – sat out on display for visitors to peruse. She had plungers of coffee ready to go and teapots with cosies and teacups laid out. She'd even whipped up some scones with jam and cream, and these were presented in a basket with a chequered tea towel, buffet style.

Ten minutes before opening, she slipped into her storeroom to change into her carefully chosen outfit – a 1950s-style swing dress with a sweetheart neckline, in pale yellow and white vertical stripes, and adorned with big sunflower details. She wore it with a large yellow hairclip and green pumps. The dress showed just a tiny bit too much cleavage; Grayson quickly averted his eyes, and she covered up with a Dalmatian-patterned white apron.

A small crowd had gathered on the footpath outside, waiting for the doors to open.

'Ready?' Grayson asked, standing beside her. They both cast a final glance around the shop, Olivia seeking out the loaded missile waiting in a corner somewhere. She swallowed nervously. 'Let's do it.'

She opened the door, smiling brightly, and welcomed everyone inside. A number of people she didn't know came in, followed by Clarence, who beckoned in an unnerving grouping of grim faces behind him. He introduced them to Olivia as they entered – Fern, Georgio and Pixie, Guy and Roger, and Chester Pepperworth, whose name made Clarence's jaw twitch, she noticed.

Grayson wove between the customers with a plate of the cherry chocolate cupcakes. 'Nice apron,' Chester sneered.

Grayson nodded amiably. 'I think it's a good colour for me,' he replied, eyeing the red love-heart pockets.

As Chester brought the cupcake to his mouth, a cherry fell off the icing and slid down his jacket. Muttering impatiently to himself, he reached into his pocket for a folded handkerchief.

To Olivia's relief, Doc Eli was the next visitor through the door, accompanied by Katrina.

'Good morning, Olivia,' he said, holding out his papery hand for her to shake, his eyes kind and friendly behind his thick glasses. She'd seen him through the windows of his surgery but hadn't met him till now. Their eyes were level, his upper back slightly stooped, yet he exuded an assured presence. 'Congratulations. The shop looks amazing.'

'Thank you,' she said, returning his smile.

'Yes, many congratulations!' Katrina concurred, kissing Olivia on the cheek.

'Thank you. Please, help yourselves to cake, coffee, tea and scones.'

Katrina loaded up a plate with scones and poured herself tea with milk and went to chat to Grayson, teasing him about his apron. He gave her a catwalk twirl.

Leanne came in next, fresh from her own bakery opening.

'How did you go?' Olivia whispered.

'Aye, grand. A few grumpies around,' Leanne nodded surreptitiously to the resistance members Clarence had awkwardly ushered in, 'but I loaded them up on carbs and sugar for you, so they should be in a good mood.' She bit into one of the forget-me-not cupcakes. 'Oh, this is good,' she said, licking icing from her lips.

She was followed by more friendly faces – the vicar, Anthony Cabot, and his wife, Juliet, the local music teacher, who kissed Olivia on both cheeks and squeezed her arm. 'We're so excited about this project,' Juliet said, looking around the space with wide-eyed enthusiasm. 'The shop looks wonderful.'

'Well, I have Howard to thank,' Olivia said, just as the man himself entered, removing his cap. 'He did all the hard work.'

'Nothing to it, really,' he said, taking it all in. 'It's come up a treat, though, hasn't it?' He smiled at her proudly.

'I'm pleased,' Olivia said, ignoring the hammering of her heart. She wished she could sweep everyone out and get on with the business of laying a trap for that rat. But curious visitors continued to arrive, including her neighbour's nephew, policeman Randolph Wilson, and the other shopkeepers, until the little shop was full to bursting.

'Has everything been okay in here?' Howard asked her quietly.

'So far, so good,' she said tensely.

He gave her a questioning look, but she quickly shook her head and reattached her smile. 'Coffee?' she asked.

'Grand idea, thank you.' She saw him nod a greeting to Fern and Georgio across the room and thought it was generous of him, given their protests against the project.

Soon the shop couldn't accommodate any more people, and Olivia found herself ferrying plates of food out to the throng on the footpath. Her cheeks ached from smiling, and her belly bubbled with unease as time ticked on and she felt her luck with the rat must surely be running out.

She fielded countless enquiries: did she do wedding cakes? Birthdays, baby showers, engagements, dogs' birthdays, kids' birthdays, gay weddings, anniversaries, retirements and book launches?

'Yes, absolutely.' She flicked back and forth through her look book, and the guests pored over photo after photo of gorgeous cakes – tiered wedding cakes, with buttercream scraped semi-sheer around the sides to allow the cake to show through, adorned with fresh flowers; adorable unicorn cakes with gold horns and rainbow manes for a child's birthday; drippy triple-decker chocolate cakes with little bottles of Jack Daniel's bourbon on top for a man's birthday; pink or blue buttercream cakes with white flowers to celebrate a birth; and simple and elegant white cakes with bunches of roses made entirely of icing, each petal picture perfect. At twelve o'clock, Clarence announced that it was time for everyone to move on to the next venue – the wool shop, where Wilhelmina would give a spinning demonstration – and Olivia finally breathed a sigh of relief.

'Goodbye,' she sang, her shoulders beginning to drop away from her ears. 'Thank you for coming! Goodbye!'

She was almost clear and free.

Then a bloodcurdling scream rang out through the shop.

'Rat!'

People jumped and gasped. The scream had come from the corner next to the children's area, where Fern had climbed up onto a chair, holding Pixie high above her head while she shrieked and pointed. There, perched on top of the farmyard set, was the rat, staring out at the assembled villagers with a look of calm disdain.

•

The same group that had met in Viola's wine cellar the previous week now gathered in Clarence's lounge room, some perched on the arms of his sofas, while others leant against walls. Poor Olivia, stony-faced, sat on a dining chair, her legs crossed and her hands clasped at her knee.

Clarence stood near the fireplace, which smelt delightfully of ash from the first fire of the season last night. It hadn't been entirely necessary – the deep cold of winter was still months away – but he loved a roaring fire and a good whisky. Back in the day, he'd smoked a pipe. He'd since given it up, succumbing to pressure from the many women in his life who had harangued him about emphysema and other such horrors. But he missed it. Missed the feel of the brittle tobacco in his fingers as he filled the chamber. Those first few rapid puffs and the crackle as he lit the leaves. The rich, pungent aroma. The fireplace went a little way to replacing that – just a little.

Clarence's dog, Stuart, was asleep on the carpet at his feet. Howard sat on the deep brown sofa next to Grayson, who kept casting concerned glances towards Olivia. Clarence really should have seated Olivia in between them, he thought, rather than letting her perch out there on her own like an accused prisoner on trial.

'I know this isn't how we wanted the grand opening to go today,' Clarence said into the stiff air of the room. 'We all had high hopes for a perfect morning, some great publicity, community engagement. It hasn't gone the way we wanted, but we can bounce back from this.'

'Not if the health inspector shuts us all down,' Leanne muttered, with a glare in Olivia's direction. Olivia held her chin high.

'That's not going to happen,' Clarence said. 'As you would expect, the resisters have jumped on the incident and complaints have been lodged. Obviously, the council will have to do an assessment of Rambling Rose. But that doesn't mean they can shut down the whole project,' he was quick to add.

'Poor Olivia,' Elena soothed. 'Such bad, bad luck. It could have happened to any one of us,' she said pointedly to Leanne. 'None of us is immune to ill fortune.'

'True,' Wilhelmina said, her German accent faint, her arms crossed over her slight body, also smiling at Olivia.

'The place was spotless.' Grayson sat forward on the sofa, his elbows on his thighs. 'You're not to blame,' he told Olivia.

She gave him a small, grateful smile.

Howard cleared his throat and stared at Clarence meaningfully. Clarence sighed. 'Unfortunately, the complaint against Olivia is not the only one.' He held up a hand to silence the questions that rippled through the room. 'Fern and Georgio, whom I'm sure many of you met, didn't just lodge the complaint about the rat. They also registered a health and safety complaint about Miguel, stating that he patted their dog and then went to the cabinet to get the flowers for Olivia without washing his hands first.'

Miguel, who'd been leaning against the stone wall near the fireplace, pushed himself up straight, his mouth open. He looked as if he was about to protest, then something crossed his face, as he remembered the order of events perhaps. He shook his head in despair, eyes to the ceiling, muttering something in Spanish, to which Viola replied soothingly, also in Spanish. Olivia shared a grimace with him.

'Don't suppose we can keep this out of the papers, then,' Howard noted, stroking his comb-over (something he believed was a legitimate hairstyle, despite Clarence's advice to the contrary), patting it down just above his prominent ears. He'd always had big ears, even as a six-year-old, earning him the unimaginative nickname 'Wing Nuts'.

'I'll chat to Ryan Baker, the journalist with the local paper,' Clarence said. 'But either way, I don't want any of you to worry. It's only the first week. Things will settle down. And fortunately for us, the current health inspector is Rex Harrington.'

Howard raised his eyebrows in surprise. 'George's boy?'

'All grown up.'

George had been Clarence's supervisor at the council when he first started out, and Clarence had fast become his right-hand man. George had sold his house and moved away from Stoneden about ten years ago, like so many, relocating to an area with good aged-care services. It had been a sad parting.

'That's a bit of good fortune,' Howard said.

'I'll give him a call now,' Clarence said, reaching for his mobile phone.

'Wait,' Olivia said, speaking for the first time.

All eyes turned to her.

'I promise you, there was no way that rat was in the shop before this morning.' She paused. 'It might be worth us considering the possibility that this was a deliberate attempt to cause trouble.'

Viola gasped audibly.

'You mean . . .' Clarence's mind ticked over, the weight of her words settling heavily in his chest. 'You mean you think it was sabotage?'

Olivia shrugged. 'I don't want to cause any more trouble than I already have, but yes.'

A clamour broke out, everyone talking at once. Stuart woke with a start and looked around, wondering at the fuss.

'That makes so much sense,' Grayson said.

'We should tell the journalist straight away,' Leanne said. 'Clear our names as soon as possible.'

'Er . . .' Clarence once again held up a hand for calm, feeling a rising sense of panic. 'There are two ways we could go with this. The first is to tell Ryan this theory, perhaps buy ourselves back some individual credibility. But the downside is this – that sort of publicity could actually help the resisters' campaign to bring down the project in the trial phase. It would be proof, ammunition, that the community does not in fact support the Renaissance Project. I'm not certain that's the sort of publicity we need right now.'

'And the other option?' Grayson challenged. 'Let Olivia take the blame for something that's not her fault?'

Clarence turned to Olivia. 'I know it's hard to take,' he said, appealing to her sense of community. 'But it would be for the greater good.'

'Taking one for the team?' she said, wryly.

He winced. 'In a manner of speaking. Look, I'll talk to Rex Harrington. He'll come and see Rambling Rose, and I'm sure he'll find everything is in order, give you a warning, and all will be forgotten. Announcing to everyone that we have a saboteur on board—'

'My money's on Fern herself,' Leanne muttered.

'—would draw significantly more unwanted attention, perhaps even egg others on to do the same, become copycats. It could even turn dangerous.'

He watched Olivia processing this. If he were in her shoes, he didn't know which way he'd want to see this go. It was awful for her to take the fall for everyone, but publicly raising the possibility of sabotage could ignite a wildfire of fear and betrayal in the village.

Howard cleared his throat once more. Clarence turned towards him.

'I think we should call it sabotage now,' Howard said. 'It's like calling out a bully. The longer you let that sort of behaviour go in silence, the worse it gets.'

Clarence had to admit that Howard knew quite a bit about bullies. As a boy, he'd had an intense fear of rats. More than once during their childhood, Clarence had rescued him from Roy Hobson, the school bully, who liked to ambush Howard in the woodhouse, carrying dead rats by their tails, flinging them at him while he cowered and cried. Poor Howard's father was desperately ashamed of his eldest boy's fear of rats; Roy knew this and exploited it so that Howard suffered not just the humiliation but also a cuffing from his father. Nasty boy, that Hobson. It was a shame none of his descendants had applied to join the project; Clarence would have enjoyed personally turning them down.

'I agree,' said Grayson.

'Me too,' said Elena, as others nodded in support. 'Who knows who will be targeted next?'

Clarence swallowed. 'You have a point,' he said.

Olivia exhaled, her hand pressed to her belly. She was obviously relieved by the group's decision. 'Thank you,' she said.

Clarence fought to regain his air of authority. 'Right. First, I'll call Rex, then I'll call Ryan and tell him what we think has happened. If he agrees, he'll write an article letting everyone know that the Renaissance Project has been sabotaged.' He finished heavily, angry that this had happened but determined that whoever was targeting the project would not beat them.

8

'Olivia?'

She turned to see Grayson striding after her across the square. 'Hi.' She pushed her hands deep into the pockets of her coat.

He caught up to her and smiled. 'I just wanted to check that you're okay.'

She did a quick mental scan of her body, assessing how she felt. 'You know, I am.'

'Good.'

'Thank you for that, in there.' She nodded back towards Clarence's cottage. 'I expected everyone to hate me. It's good to know some don't.'

'No one hates you. I think everyone knows it wasn't your fault.'

'That rat, though.' She shuddered.

'It was huge,' he agreed, wrinkling his nose. 'I've got a trap at my place if you'd like it. It's a catch-and-release sort.'

She felt the corners of her mouth pull into a smile. 'Really?'

He lifted a shoulder and rubbed the back of his head self-consciously. 'What can I say? I don't much fancy killing things if I don't have to. Poisons are bad, because wild animals or dogs can eat the dead rats and then they die too. I'm not scared of rats, so I'm happy to release them out in the wild somewhere.'

'That would be great. I was going to pick up Darcy from school and head over to Fahren Way to buy a trap, but it would save me the trip out there.'

'Consider it done. I can go and set it for you, if you like, so you don't have to worry.'

'No, it's fine. Darcy and I will meet you at the shop.' She held his gaze a moment. 'Thank you.'

He grinned. 'It's the least I can do for someone who's come to the other side of the world to help save this village.'

She waved and headed down towards the school, smiling. He really was a sweetheart.

'Hello,' the young teacher sang as Olivia entered the classroom. She sat on the floor surrounded by enthusiastic pupils who were watching her robotic car, a mass of wheels and coloured leads. The bell had rung but the children were so interested in the robot that they hadn't moved.

Standing up, the teacher came to meet Olivia at the door, smoothing her culottes and cardigan and flicking back her long, dark, mermaid-like hair. 'I'm Cathy Finch,' she said, holding out her hand.

'Olivia. Lovely to meet you.'

'Mum!' Darcy flung his arms around Olivia and she rubbed his hair.

'How was your day?'

'Great,' he said, smiling and going to get his bag.

'Oh, Darcy, remember to bring your favourite book to share tomorrow,' Cathy said.

'Okay!' Darcy said, tucking his water bottle into the side pocket of his bag.

'Favourite book?' Olivia tried to picture what they had at home. They hadn't been able to bring many books from Australia. A year ago Darcy's favourite book had been *Frozen*, the storybook of the movie. He'd been *Frozen* mad, like most kids, but Olivia had given the book away not long after the accident. Now it was all about *How to Train Your Dragon*. They'd definitely brought that one with them. 'Gosh, I love your shoes,' she said, suddenly looking down.

Cathy pointed a toe to show off her glorious shoes. They had the rubber base of a sneaker but the uppers were made of woven raffia with pink and silver glittery flowers. 'They're Italian,' she said.

'They're fabulous.'

'And so comfortable,' Cathy said, sighing.

'Did the first day go well?' Olivia asked.

'He was fine, no problems at all. He's adorable,' Cathy gushed.

'Great.' Olivia smiled, grateful for her youthful enthusiasm. Other parents were hovering, waiting to talk to Cathy. 'Well, if anything comes up, or he has any problems with other kids or anything . . .' She trailed off, trying to sound like just another normal anxious parent, not one whose kid had almost died due to bullying.

'You'll be the first to know,' Cathy agreed.

'Thanks. Okay, I'll leave you to it.' Olivia took Darcy's bag. She said hi to Katrina and Eloise before heading back to the shop.

Darcy skipped beside her, telling her what they'd done in class. Olivia was thrilled that his first day had gone well. Seeing him so happy lifted her spirits after the business with the rat.

'Where are we going?' Darcy asked, as they headed down the hill towards the river.

'We need to pop back to the shop for a little bit. Do you remember Grayson from Sunday? He's going to help us catch a rat.'

'Whoa,' Darcy said, increasing his pace to match hers. 'Can we keep it?'

Olivia snorted. 'No, we can't keep the rat. The rat is definitely not part of the plan.'

That night, after Darcy had gone to bed and Olivia was tinkering with her website, she remembered that when she was eight, she'd woken in the middle of the night to find a rat on her bed, chewing the end of her blanket. She'd screamed and Ma had come running with a broom in her hand, ready to tackle an intruder. She snapped on the light, yelling 'Haaa!' in her loudest voice, and the rat had run for its life. Ma had been so brave to do that, Olivia reflected now, and it made her smile. She liked to think she'd inherited at least a little of Ma's strength, something that would hopefully be of benefit for the challenges that lay ahead. And like Ma, she wouldn't be running away from a rat any time soon.

After dropping Darcy at school the next morning, Olivia set out purposefully towards the shop, her head held high. While she strove for an appearance of quiet confidence, she hadn't slept very well the night before. She unlocked the door of Rambling Rose, and went straight through to the storeroom to check the rat trap. Fortunately – or unfortunately, depending on how you looked at it – the trap was empty.

She washed the floor and cleaned every surface she could reach, one eye on the clock, watching as it ticked down to 9 am, when Rex Harrington was due to arrive. If he was on time, and efficient, he would be gone by ten o'clock, when she was set to open the shop. But the extra time she spent making sure everything was shipshape for the health inspector meant that once again she would have to rely on small, easy-to-prepare items – cupcakes, custard tarts and scones. While she usually enjoyed rolling out buttery pastry and crumbling scone mixture between her fingers, watching it sprinkle down into the bowl like snowflakes, today she was distracted, half expecting protesters with signs and megaphones to appear on the footpath outside. She'd even made up a chant for them: *The rat baker has got to go! Hey, hey* (clap clap), *ho, ho* (clap clap).

Clarence sent her a message wishing her luck and saying he wouldn't come down because he didn't want to fuel any rumours that he was in cahoots with the health inspector, especially as the journalist – Ryan – was due to visit her for a statement too. Grayson also messaged, asking if the rat had made an appearance yet. And Katrina popped in with a bunch of flowers for her counter, giving her a supportive hug and promising her a stiff drink at the end of the day.

By the time Rex Harrington arrived, Olivia's imagined chant was playing on endless repeat in her mind. The bell *ting*ed as he entered the shop. She closed the oven door and turned to give him a nervous smile. 'Morning.'

He cleared his throat. 'Olivia Kent?'

'Yes.' Her heart hammered in her chest. She felt like she'd been hauled into the principal's office.

He handed his business card over the counter. 'I'm Rex Harrington, the local health inspector.'

She nodded. 'Thanks for coming so quickly.'

His lips twitched. 'Well, that makes a change from the greeting I normally receive.'

She shrugged. 'I have nothing to hide,' she said, sounding much more confident than she felt. Buddy Holly was singing too loudly for them to talk comfortably, so she excused herself to turn down the volume, by which time Rex had seated himself at one of the tables and pulled out a neat file. She approached the table and he indicated that she should also sit.

Rex was short, stocky and square-shouldered, with a helmet of dark hair. He reminded her of a Lego man. He wore a nice charcoal suit, though. Expensive. Very clean and tidy. His shoes were polished. He clearly prized cleanliness and order. She wondered what his home was like, if it had messy, sticky children in it, and if that drove him crazy.

'Here's your official warning, outlining the nature of the complaint, and the date and time when the breach occurred,' he said, passing over a piece of pale yellow paper. 'If you agree with those facts, sign at the bottom.' He held a pen out to her.

Olivia read the information. 'There's nothing here I can dispute,' she said. 'Yes, a rat was here on that date and at that time.'

Rex nodded, pleased, and he extended the pen further towards her.

'But there is no way that rat was here before yesterday,' Olivia went on. 'I cleaned this store from top to bottom and there was no evidence of rats at all. Someone planted it here,' she said emphatically.

'I understand,' Rex said, slightly impatiently, she thought. 'I have spoken to Mr James about this and I am aware of the tensions in the village surrounding the project.'

Olivia looked up to see Guy and Roger walking along the footpath, slowing noticeably to peer in the window. They clocked Rex and the paperwork in Olivia's hand and smirked – one might say triumphantly – before continuing on their walk.

'The thing is,' Rex went on, 'from a health and safety perspective, it matters not one jot how the rat got here. In all honesty, pests do just randomly turn up in otherwise clean environments with no warning. They are quite the nuisance, hence they are called "pests". From my department's perspective, we simply need to know that steps have been taken to remove the pest, that hygiene standards are what they need to be, and that any compromised food is thrown away. Once you sign that document, I will conduct an inspection of the shop, and if satisfied, I'll sign this form'—he tapped another official-looking sheet of paper in his folder—'to clear you to continue to trade.'

Olivia took in a resentful breath, but nodded her understanding. She signed the form.

With that, Rex pulled an iPad out of his briefcase and proceeded to wander through the shop, checking boxes on an electronic form and taking photos as he went. She knew he wouldn't find anything, but still it was difficult to watch. He was just finishing his inspection when another, younger man arrived, this one holding a notebook and pen. The journalist, Olivia assumed. 'Morning,' she said, tightly.

'Good morning, I'm Ryan Baker from the *Stoneden Times*.' He also extended a business card towards her. 'Clarence said you'd be expecting me. Is now a good time for a chat?' He glanced towards Rex.

Olivia rose from her chair, feeling flustered to have both the inspector and the journalist here at the same time. She reminded herself to calm down. Ryan was part of the Renaissance Committee, Clarence had told her, so he should be on her side.

But then, he was also a journalist. She wasn't sure what that meant in terms of his allegiances. If he stumbled upon a huge story, then surely he'd break it, wouldn't he? Wasn't that what they did – some kind of journalists' code or something? Then again, a rat in a shop was hardly a big story to break.

She realised she'd been twisting her fingers together, and made herself let go. 'Can I get you a tea or coffee?' she said brightly, moving to stand behind the counter. 'Scones are just about out of the oven, if you're feeling peckish.' She looked past him through the front door to see if anyone else was coming along to join him, like a cadet or a photographer. She spied her cheery bicycle through the window, a spot of brightness on an otherwise gloomy morning.

'No, thanks,' he said. 'I had a good breakfast this morning.'

Ryan was tall and lanky with bright ginger hair, his white skin dappled with freckles. If he lived in Australia he'd have a pelt of nearly joined-up freckles, for sure, and would probably be rolling up for twice-yearly skin cancer checks too. His forearms were sinewy, sporty looking. She wondered if he played cricket for the local club.

'Anyway, I'm here on business,' he said.

'The rat.'

'Yes, the rat.'

'It was sabotage,' Olivia said definitively, casting her eye towards Rex, who was still poking away diligently on the iPad.

'Yes, Clarence mentioned that was your belief.' Ryan narrowed his eyes at her for a moment. She held his gaze, trying to read him, but his expression was inscrutable. 'I'd like a statement from you about why you think it's sabotage. That's a big story, if it's true.'

Olivia felt her patience running thin. Who did these men think they were? Was it because she was a woman that they were so reluctant to believe her, or was it because she was a foreigner, an import? She was a millisecond away from telling them both to believe whatever they wanted to believe, but she managed to curb her anger. Like it or not, as an outsider she'd have to earn people's trust and respect here.

Rex joined them at the counter and the men shook hands. Then Olivia repeated her story, Ryan scribbling notes on his pad. The rat had absolutely not been in the shop before yesterday. The timing of its appearance was too suspicious to be a coincidence. She stopped short of pointing the finger at Fern, who was the one who'd spotted the rat, and was a known resister. If Ryan was clever – and she assumed he was – he would put two and two together.

'I'll need a statement from you too,' Ryan said to Rex.

'Of course. Naturally, the department takes complaints of this nature very seriously and acts expeditiously and thoroughly.

Today's inspection has found no areas of concern. This incident will, however, trigger an automatic increase in the frequency of inspections for Rambling Rose, including unannounced inspections, until I'm satisfied that the shop meets the required standards of cleanliness.'

Rex signed the form and handed it to Olivia. 'Thank you for your time, Miss Kent.' He nodded farewell to Ryan and left.

'I'll write this up today,' Ryan said, tapping his notepad on the counter. 'And I'll emphasise that Rambling Rose has been cleared to continue trading.'

'Thank you,' she said. 'Will you be mentioning the sabotage?'

'To be honest, it seems like a long bow to draw. I'm not sure how it would go down with readers. It might make you sound . . . defensive, even hostile, possibly ungrateful to the village that has invested a lot of money in bringing you here.'

Olivia registered his words, feeling wrong-footed. She was anything but ungrateful.

'Unless you have strong proof of deliberate interference, my gut feeling is that such a claim could do you more harm than good. It's your choice, of course, but my personal advice would be not to put your *hunch* on the record.'

Olivia wrestled with her choices. Say nothing, and she and her shop were tarred as dirty and unhygienic. Suggest sabotage and she risked being seen as spoilt, whiny and provocative, possibly even paranoid or hysterical. Neither option was good. She swallowed a hard, bitter lump in her throat. 'Fine. Let's say nothing.'

Ryan nodded slowly and pocketed his notebook. 'I'm sorry, I know this must be difficult for you.'

Alone once more, Olivia chewed over her frustration. She was still completely certain that the rat had been planted in her shop. But who would have done it? With a jolt, she wondered whether Ryan might have a hidden agenda for convincing her not to say anything in the newspaper about sabotage. Perhaps Fern and Georgio, and Guy and Roger, were too obvious as suspects. Was it possible that Ryan was a secret resister, acting as a mole inside the Renaissance Project while feeding information to the outside? Perhaps he was the saboteur? Or even Rex himself? It could be anyone, and that was the problem. Suddenly, everyone was a suspect. Either that, or she had made too big a leap in calling sabotage. Maybe a rat was just a rat. As Rex had pointed out, pests did sometimes simply turn up.

Hopefully time would reveal the truth. Just then, the oven timer went off and she reached for her mitts. The only thing she could do now was focus on what she did best: baking.

9

Olivia woke Wednesday morning to a text message from Helge.

Three more sleeps x

Apparently Helge was counting down the days till Saturday as eagerly as she was. Each message electrified her with excited butterflies.

After a promisingly steady morning of trade, serving cupcakes and pots of tea to friendly locals who either didn't know or didn't care about the rat, and one hungry busload of tourists, Olivia changed out of her frock and paisley apron and back into her overalls and sneakers. She was packing up half a dozen leftover cupcakes into a cake box when Clarence came through the door, wearing dark slacks and a white shirt under a smart navy blue woollen vest, and smiling like the cat that got the cream.

'You're in a fine mood,' Olivia observed.

'I am,' he agreed, rapping his knuckle on the countertop and admiring the vase of pretty white wildflowers Katrina had given her. 'I've been strolling through the village, enjoying the ambience of the new regime,' he said, a proud glint in his eye. 'It might be the sunshine gracing us with its presence but I am optimistic about the future of the village, despite the rocky start for you.' He motioned to his cable-knit vest. 'I just bought this from Wilhelmina to celebrate.'

'Good for you,' Olivia said. 'Ma's mother worked in the wool mills. I think it was one of the reasons they left, though, sadly. It was all coming to an end in the Sixties.'

Clarence's face fell. 'It was a difficult time for us all. We lost a lot of hard-working people during those years.'

'But their descendants are returning now,' she said.

'You are indeed.'

'Did you know her, my ma? Nora, I mean?'

His expression clouded a little. 'I knew her, of course. Everyone knew everyone. But I wouldn't say we were friends, exactly.'

She wanted to press him for more information, but she didn't have time right now. Rambling Rose closed at two and she needed to get Darcy at three, but first she had plans. She gestured to the box. 'I had the crazy idea that if I take some leftovers around to some of the more reluctant villagers I could break the ice, win them over with sugary treats and hope they ignore the gossip about the rat.'

'A clever idea,' he said approvingly.

'Could you tell me where Madeline McCarthy's house is?'

Clarence's chin raised a fraction. 'Madeline?'

'I'd like to start with her. I feel bad for her, in all honesty. I believe in what the Renaissance Committee is doing,' she rushed to assure him. 'But it can't be easy at her age, having her choices put on hold, even temporarily. Katrina told me about her brother and her lifetime of care for him.'

Clarence nodded slowly but said nothing, not blinking quite enough.

'Is that okay?' she asked. 'I have to confess, I was also hoping she might remember Ma. I think they would be around the same age. It might be another way for us to find some common ground.'

Clarence cleared his throat. 'Yes, quite right.' He tucked his hands into his pockets, looking significantly deflated after his earlier buoyant entrance.

'Does she live very far from here?'

'The thing is, Madeline is a bit . . . wary, I guess is the word. No, maybe not wary, but private.'

'Oh, I'll go gently,' Olivia said, picking up her shoulder bag and the box.

'Hm. Well, if you head across the bridge as if you were going to Fahren Way, go all the way past the trout farm, the professional suites – the solicitor and the dentist – past the old mill and the tourist information centre and take the next right, and continue all the way to the end, you'll find Madeline's farm on the left. Follow the dirt road up to the house. You'll know it because of all the thistles.'

'Thistles, got it. Okay, I'd better go now so I can be back in time to pick Darcy up from school.'

Clarence accompanied her to the door, oddly silent, and held the box of cakes while she locked up.

'Thanks,' she said, relieving him of the box. 'I'll see you soon.'

He dipped his head and walked away along the high street. For a moment she wondered what had triggered his change in mood, but then she brushed the thought aside, climbed into her car and headed over the bridge towards Madeline's house.

Following Clarence's directions, she found her way to the windswept entrance to Madeline's farm; as described, the land was covered with the collapsing skeletons of thistles. She steered carefully over the potholes in the driveway up to the stone home. It, too, was in a state of disrepair, with several slate tiles askew on the roof, and paint flaking off the window frames. As she neared the house, a small tabby cat streaked out from under a bush and dashed across the driveway, disappearing into an old milking shed. Olivia braked abruptly, then cut the engine. She collected her box, strode up to the front door and knocked on the flaking green paint.

'Hello?' she sang. 'Hello, Madeline?'

There was no sound from within. She considered walking around the side of the house, trying to convince herself this would be a neighbourly thing to do, showing concern for an elderly woman who lived alone, but she knew her real motivation was nosiness and a thirst for knowledge about Ma.

She tried again, leaning close to the door. 'Madeline? My name is Olivia Kent. I'm new in town.' She paused, listening. 'I'm a cake maker and I have some cakes here I made this morning. I thought you might enjoy them?'

The house remained silent. She nodded to herself and sighed with disappointment, then bent down to place the box on the doorstep. 'I'll just leave them here for you.' She straightened. Without any real hope of a response, she gave it one more go. 'My ma – well, my grandmother, actually – was Nora Kent. Eleanora Kent. Well, that was her name when she was young, then she got married and became Nora Oakley, but after her husband died, she went back to being a Kent. She grew up here in Stoneden and I was hoping you might remember her.' She turned, leaning back against the door, a wave of grief rising up her chest. 'She died last year and . . .' Her voice hitched, the ache of sorrow so strong. She let her watery gaze roam across the green and grey land to a paddock of cows.

Without warning, the door wrenched open behind her, and Olivia toppled backwards, landing hard on her bottom. Standing above her in the shadowy hallway was a wiry woman with two long steel-grey plaits, wearing overalls, just like her, except that Olivia's were newer and made of softer material than Madeline's hardy faded ones.

'Eleanora Kent, you say?'

Olivia smiled up at her, even as she wondered whether she'd broken her coccyx, or just bruised it. 'Yes!'

Madeline looked into the middle distance a moment, then back at Olivia. 'And cake?'

'Lots of cake.'

'Icing too?'

'Buttercream.'

Madeline grunted appreciatively. 'We'd better put the kettle on.'

•

Madeline lit the gas and placed the kettle on the hob.

Nora Kent. She hadn't heard that name in decades. It was amazing how gossip could ignite so quickly and subside almost as fast, especially when businesses kept failing and villagers kept packing up and moving away. The gossip changed rapidly from 'Did you hear about Matthew and the fire?' to 'Young James Beckham stole two sheep' and 'Have you heard the vicar's been making food drops to the Wentworths?' to 'Mary Crompton is in the family way.' Not to mention the awful years after the lord of the manor died and the inheritance and death duties were disputed and the eventual sale of practically the whole village – cut up and sold off for parts like a slaughtered lamb – which brought an end to the Stoneden she'd grown up in.

But gossip about Nora Kent was a different story. That was personal.

'I'm so pleased to meet you,' Olivia said, opening her box of cupcakes. 'I'm dying to find out more about Ma's life here, when she was young.'

Madeline went to the cabinet with the good crockery and pulled out two teacups, saucers and plates in a delicate bluebell pattern, their gently scalloped edges rimmed with gold. They had belonged to her grandmother and had to be at least a hundred years old. Lord knew how they'd survived all this time – probably simply because they were never used. She placed them on the table, the cups rattling gently.

'These are gorgeous,' Olivia said, hooking her finger through a cup's small handle and holding it up to admire the pattern.

Madeline took the opportunity to study her visitor. She couldn't see much of Nora in her, though she wasn't certain she could trust her memory to pull up an accurate image anyway. But she remembered Nora's dark hair. This girl was honey blonde, the colour of milky tea.

The kettle whistled and she extinguished the gas and poured boiling water into the plain white everyday teapot she'd had for thirty years. She placed it on the table near the cups.

'Which cake would you like?' Olivia asked. 'I've got white chocolate and raspberry or triple chocolate.'

'You can keep the raspberry. I've no time for white chocolate.'

The young woman selected a miniature chocolate cake piled with icing almost as high as the cake itself, and placed it on one of the antique plates.

'Do you take milk?' Madeline asked.

'Yes, thank you.'

Madeline pulled open the fridge door and took out a bottle of milk. 'It came fresh this morning. The farmer over there'—she inclined her head in the direction of the farm across the road—'brings me milk a few times a week. Never charges me for it, either. Grayson Levins, his name is.'

'Yes, I know him,' Olivia said, and if Madeline wasn't mistaken, her skin took on a rosy hue. 'He helped me get ready for my grand opening. I dressed him in an apron.'

'What an odd thing to do,' Madeline said. She liked Grayson very much and she wouldn't have anyone turning him into a spectacle.

'Oh, it was . . . nothing.' Olivia scratched self-consciously at her arm.

'I hear you had a rat,' Madeline said, eyeing her shrewdly.

Olivia cast her eyes to the ceiling, a frown line appearing between her brows. 'Yes.'

'That was quite a first day.'

'Sure was.'

Madeline poured the tea and for a few moments the only sounds to be heard were their forks on the plates and the sipping of tea.

'I'm very sorry to hear of your grandmother's death,' Madeline said, suddenly. The wave of sadness that came over her was ridiculous. Nora had never bothered to write to her after she left. After everything they'd been through together, to have it all end like that was devastating for them all. Yes, Madeline had been angry – furious, even. But to simply not hear from Nora again was another wound to deal with. They'd been best friends, once.

Olivia swallowed her tea. 'Thank you. Were you friends?'

Madeline took a breath. 'We were,' she said, carefully.

'Then I'm so glad I came over,' Olivia said, putting her teacup down a little too loudly on the plate. 'I'm hoping to find out more about her.'

'Obviously, it's more than fifty years since I saw Eleanora.'

'I wish Ma and I could have come here together. But you never expect the people you love to die,' her guest said flatly.

'No, you don't,' Madeline agreed. At her age she had seen most of the people from her past die. She watched Olivia, who had folded one arm across her body while the other supported her chin. She looked vulnerable, the grief still raw. She had the most remarkable indigo eyes and long lashes.

That was it. They were Nora's eyes.

A swooping sensation rushed through her, as she remembered Nora coming here, to this house, so they could all go to the dance together – Madeline, Nora and Burton, the trio about town. It was 1966 – the year Madeline would never be able to forget. Nora was wearing her deep-blue dress, sleeveless and impossibly short, leaving no doubt as to the length of her legs. She'd bought it a few months prior, wearing it to every dance since. Madeline had been slightly shocked when she'd first seen her in it. Miniskirts were the hottest thing in London, or so she'd read in the papers, but for Stoneden it was scandalous. What were Nora's parents thinking, letting her out of the house dressed like that? But that was Nora, always a few steps ahead of Madeline, always keen to try the new things, dragging a reluctant Madeline into the modern age.

Burton had approved of her dress, couldn't take his eyes off her.

It was summer. England had won the World Cup for the first time – and as it turned out, the only time – and spirits were still high. There was a sense of recklessness in the air, as if football fever had got under everyone's skin.

Olivia's voice brought her back from her memories. She was looking at Madeline expectantly.

'Pardon me, what did you say?'

'I was asking if you knew why Ma left here with her family. Was it just because of the economic collapse in the village?'

Madeline blinked, wondering how to answer this. 'I'm not sure I remember,' she lied.

'Oh.' Olivia's face fell. 'What a shame.'

Shame, thought Madeline. That was one word for it.

10

A thick fog embraced Saturday morning, as if trying to convince it to stay in bed a while longer. Olivia would have enjoyed a lie-in, but weekends were peak tourist times and she needed to be down at Rambling Rose early to prepare for customers.

Now, she was making scones again, as they were always a favourite, and she'd just finished laying the soft dough rounds out on the tray. Darcy was in the kids' corner, happily absorbed in moving farmyard animals around the stables and on trucks. Olivia didn't know how long his distraction would last. He was counting down the minutes till Helge arrived this afternoon. The song 'Summertime Blues' came through the speakers and he started singing along. She loved the fact that he enjoyed a wide variety of music. Perhaps she could look into getting some music lessons for him. Guitar, maybe? She wished she'd learnt to play something when she was young, and the guitar was such a social instrument, transportable and easy to sing along to. Knowing how to play might help him in social settings when he was older.

'Darcy, do you want to help me with the cupcakes?' she called, wiping her hands on her favourite apron – full-length and vintage yellow, with fussy details like reversible material on the pockets, hem and neckline, and flourishes of lace thrown in too. Today's cupcakes would be 'strawberry lemonade' – zesty, lemon-flavoured cakes topped with berry buttercream, all made with fresh fruit.

'Okay.' He jumped up and came to the bench.

She pulled over a wooden step for him to stand on. 'Here, you line the trays,' she said, handing him a stack of shiny silver papers. She weighed out the butter and sugar while he carefully separated each paper and tucked it into a hole of the patty cake pan.

'So, your first week at school went well.' Olivia spoke as casually as possible.

'Yeah,' Darcy said, with an upward inflection as if he was surprised by this too.

'We're doing okay here, aren't we?' she asked, wanting him to agree but nervous that he might say otherwise. She looked sideways at him: at his lovely unblemished skin, at the cute little snub nose, at his fair hair that never seemed to need washing, though she made sure he did, at the small curves of his shoulders and the slope of his back. She wanted so much to protect him, to never let anything hurt him again.

'I like it here,' he said.

Her heart bounced with relief as she set the mixer on low. 'And Pappa will be here this afternoon.'

'Yeah,' Darcy said again, and gave an impromptu hip wiggle. 'And Regine and Elias too?'

'Not this time, but you'll get to see them soon, I promise. Maybe we could take a trip to Norway to visit them for Christmas?'

He turned and grinned at her, his dimples deep. 'That would be epic. Could Eloise come too?'

'I'm not sure. We'll have to check with her mum and dad. But it's a while away yet, so let's just take it one day at a time.'

'How long is it till Christmas?'

'Still three months,' she said, switching off the mixer and releasing the beaters. She handed one to Darcy, who took it happily and began to lick.

'Is that long?' he asked, his words muffled.

'About ninety days or so.'

He frowned. 'Whoa.' She remembered that feeling as a child – every day seemed so long, time stretching out eternally before her.

She pulled out her microplane to zest the lemon, relishing the sharp fragrance of citrus oil that filled the air. 'But it's only a few hours till your pappa is here,' she said, bringing him back to more immediate joys.

He looked at the time on her phone. 'Yeah, three hundred and sixty-eight minutes to go.'

'He's here!' Darcy shrieked, thundering down the stairs at a tremendous pace.

Olivia heard the door of Helge's hire car clunk shut just as Darcy dragged open the front door. She hurried to his side, placing a trembling hand on his small shoulder. Darcy had been tightly wound all afternoon too, moping and whingeing one moment and smiling and chatting the next. 'I just can't wait any longer,' he'd moaned, at least twenty times.

Now he didn't have to wait a moment longer because Helge stepped into view. She'd forgotten how tall he was; these days she only ever saw him when he was sitting at the computer. His clothes were some sort of lightweight technical material, hiking gear perhaps, but somehow still managed to look like a bloody supermodel. He had a duffel bag slung over one shoulder and his fair hair was gently dishevelled. Another thing she'd forgotten was how intense and brooding he could look, with his thick eyebrows and that squint line between them. She remembered how intimidating he could appear until you got to know him.

'H-hi,' she said, smiling, feeling a hundred different things at once.

'Hi,' he said, his eyes flicking between her and Darcy. Under her hand, Darcy stood immobile, unsure what to do.

Helge hesitated, his eyes on his son, taking him in, and for a second she thought he might be about to cry. But then he crouched down till he was eye level with Darcy. 'Hi, mate,' he said, in his best Australian accent, which made Olivia burst out laughing, the release of pent-up nerves. Helge offered his hand, and Darcy cautiously shook it before falling back against Olivia's body.

'Come in, come in,' she beckoned, guiding Darcy out of the doorway to allow Helge to squeeze inside. She led him into the lounge room, then turned to face him. 'It's so good to see you,' she said.

'You too,' he said, and opened his arms to hug her. She laid her head against his chest, remembering what it felt like to fit her body against his, her arms around his back, feeling how strong and lean he was from all that hiking and skiing he did. She breathed in the smell of him – which was just a clean, fresh smell of nothing in particular but made her imagine big Nordic mountains and open green fields and endless skies – and unexpectedly burst into tears.

Embarrassed, she waved her hands at her face, trying to smile away the sudden overflow. He gave her a small, sad smile, his blue eyes piercing hers with their intensity, and there he was – the real Helge, the one she'd fallen so deeply in love with. Receiving his full attention was like being speared with a sunbeam – the rest of the world fell away, and she felt like the centre of his universe. She stared at him, swept away in memories, a terrible ache inside. Had she made the biggest mistake of her life in letting him go? If she had followed him to Norway, her whole life, and Darcy's too, would be completely different right now.

Darcy. He stood awkwardly to the side, clearly unsure what to do. Snapping out of her abstraction, Olivia moved shakily to sit on the couch, giving Darcy a reassuring smile. Helge, too, turned his attention to Darcy. He cleared his throat. 'I brought you something,' he said, dropping his bag to the floor and sitting down next to it.

'What is it?' Darcy said, venturing closer.

'You *v*ill have to open it and find out.' Helge pulled out a large box wrapped in red and silver paper and passed it to his son.

Darcy tore it open excitedly and pulled out the game Pie Face. 'Whoa,' he said, staring at the pictures on the box.

'Have you played it before?'

Darcy shook his head, grinning.

'*V*e *v*ill see who gets splat with the cream pie first, you or me.'

'I hope it's me,' Darcy said. 'Can we play now?'

Helge grinned at Olivia, clearly relieved to have broken the ice. 'Do you have any cream?' he asked her.

'Always.' She pulled herself off the couch and went to the kitchen, feeling a swirl of nerves and happiness and relief that Helge was finally here, in real life, finally part of Darcy's world, and they had got off to such a good start.

When she returned to the lounge room, carrying a bowl of whipped cream and a spoon, she found them both stretched out on the carpet on their tummies, propped up on their elbows, facing each other. The Pie Face apparatus was between them and Helge was showing Darcy how to play.

'First, you spin the *v*heel like this,' he said, flicking the spinner. 'Okay, I got four. Now, I put my face in here.' He angled himself to put his face through the mask. 'Then I turn the handle four times.' On the third click, the plastic hand flung up into the air, stopping just short of his face.

Darcy yelped.

'See. If there had been cream there I *v*ould be splat!'

'My turn!' Darcy said, pulling the spinner towards him.

'Here's the cream,' Olivia said, spooning a big dollop onto the waiting plastic hand.

'Spin the *v*heel,' Helge said. 'Let's see *v*ot you get.'

Darcy spun the wheel. 'Two!'

Olivia perched on the edge of the couch, watching them, enjoying seeing Darcy having so much fun, and also taking in the length of Helge's body, the smooth arch of his spine, the muscles of his arms. His legs were a bit too long for the space and his feet were shoved up against the dark wooden bookcase.

Darcy placed his head into the mask, squinting in anticipation.

'Turn the handle,' Helge said, already laughing.

'Okay. Oh boy.' Darcy turned the handle once. *Click.* He flinched, then yelped with tension. 'Oh no-o-o.' He turned the handle again, his eyes screwed up tightly. *Click.* Nothing happened. He groaned with a mixture of relief and disappointment and passed the spinner to Helge.

'My go.' Helge spun five. 'Uh-oh, I think I am done for now.'

Darcy shrieked with excitement and rolled over like an upside-down turtle, then sprang back up onto his knees to watch.

Helge turned the Pie Face around so he could put his face in it and gripped the handle. 'Are you ready?'

'Yes!' Darcy and Olivia both shouted.

'I am very nervous,' Helge said, hamming it up.

Click. Nothing happened. He turned it again. *Click.* Once more, nothing happened. Darcy jumped to his feet. The big dollop of cream was on the hand, like a gooey cloud, glistening under the lights in the room.

'I must be very close now,' Helge muttered. 'I'm about to be splat, yes?'

'Yes!' Darcy clapped his hands.

'Okay. Maybe this is it.' *Click*. Still nothing happened.

Olivia held her breath.

'Number four, then one more,' Helge said. He turned the wheel ever so slowly.

Click.

The hand flung up into the air, and whipped cream hit him between his eyebrows, splattering up into his hair and dripping down his nose.

Olivia and Darcy hooted with hilarity while Helge grinned that gorgeous smile of his. With fake disgust, he sat up on his haunches and wiped away a dollop of cream with one finger, then licked it off. 'Look at me! I am pie-faced.'

'You look so funny,' Darcy said, cackling, his smile so wide and his eyes so bright that Olivia wished she had her phone with her to snap a photo.

'Good cream, Livvy,' Helge said, still wiping away cream and licking it, and the effect that name had on her was like sinking into a deep, warm, perfumed, candlelit bath.

The next few hours were nothing short of magic. Helge and Darcy played more rounds of Pie Face until an actual pie – lemon meringue – was ready to eat, and then they polished off most of that. Afterwards they played with Lego and then kicked the soccer ball around on the small patch of grass behind the house, bordered by the vegetable patches and chicken coops of her neighbours, while Olivia prepared a simple dinner of lamb chops, mashed potato and greens. There was a lot of noise, and Darcy's spirits were so high she was afraid she'd never get him to sleep that night. But Helge read to him on the couch before bed and then hugged him, and the sight of Darcy's small body wrapped in Helge's arms almost brought her to tears again. Helge, too, had to look up to the ceiling and blink a few times, taking a deep breath to control his emotions, before releasing his child.

She placed a sympathetic hand on Helge's arm and then guided Darcy upstairs to lead him through the final settling phase before sleep. He eventually drifted off after two kids' meditations that Olivia played on her phone. She eased out of his bed and crept down the stairs slowly, avoiding the creakiest steps.

She found Helge at the dining table. 'I'm amazed he's asleep; he's so excited to have you here,' she said.

Helge looked up from his phone. He was messaging his family, Olivia guessed, wishing that *his family* actually meant *her family*. This reminder that Helge was only on loan to them burst the ridiculous bubble of hope and fantasy she'd allowed her mind to conjure throughout the day. A wave of sadness swallowed her and she moved towards the kitchen.

'It has been such a great day,' he said, shaking his head slowly as if he couldn't quite believe it himself.

'Would you like a cup of tea or coffee?' she asked, to give herself something to do as much as to be a good host. God, why was she feeling so confused by Helge? They'd been over for years. The problem was, though, that they hadn't broken up because they didn't love each other or because things had gone badly between them. It was just circumstances and timing that had forced them apart. All those feelings, all that chemistry, all that bound them together – especially Darcy – was still very much here.

At least, that was how it felt for her.

But Helge was married with two other children. He had an entire life that he was committed to back in Norway. Olivia wasn't in his future. In fact, the only reason she was in this picture at all was because of Darcy. Helge's connection was to Darcy, not her.

'Coffee, thanks,' he said, joining her in the kitchen. He slipped his phone into the pocket of his athleisure pants.

She looked up at him and snorted. 'You've still got cream in your fringe, like some sort of bad teenage hair product. It's all stuck together.'

He reached up to feel the dried cream in his hair. 'I'll try to vash some out,' he said, grimacing, then headed to the bathroom.

She finished making plunger coffee – determined not to imagine Helge potentially with his shirt off to avoid getting it wet – and served it in mugs, adding cream and brown sugar without even thinking. Then she stopped. 'Do you still take your coffee with cream and brown sugar?' she called.

He turned off the tap and appeared in the doorway, ducking his head under the lintel, rubbing at his hair with the green hand towel. He was still wearing his top, somewhat to her disappointment. His lips were raised at one corner in a half smile. 'Good memory,' he said, and his voice, she was sure, was dusted with nostalgia. All those mornings lying in bed, naked, tangled in sheets, sipping on coffee. Her skin erupted in tiny charged bumps.

She carried the mugs back into the lounge and set them down on the dining table, the stained-glass shade over the bulb casting the room in a rosy light.

'Did you get hold of your kids?' she asked, in an attempt to stop thinking about Helge in anything other than a platonic, co-parenting way, and remind herself – and him – of his priorities.

He eased down into the chair and wrapped his long fingers around the hot mug, his wet fringe scraped back from his face. The air had cooled outside; she could feel it pressing on the double-glazed windows. But the heating had kicked in and she still felt comfortable in jeans, socks and a light jumper. Or maybe it was the warmth she felt just being around Helge.

Seriously, what was wrong with her?

'I did. They're good. They've spent the day visiting Birgit's parents.'

She nodded, unsure what to say, imagining their happy little family, a family that didn't include Darcy.

Helge sipped his coffee, then tapped the side of the mug with a finger. 'Today has been . . .' He trailed off and sighed, looking at her as if she might have the word to finish his thought.

'Amazing,' she said.

'Yes, amazing.'

For lack of anything to say in that moment that wouldn't make her cry, she sipped her coffee too. She couldn't remember what she'd been expecting this weekend to be like, but the intensity of the feelings it had brought up had caught her off guard.

'Darcy is fantastic,' he said, and this time he didn't try to hide his emotion. 'You've done such a wonderful job with him.'

Her eyes welled up too, and her throat tightened. 'Thank you.' She resisted touching him; she was scared she might throw herself into his lap and hold him tight, united in their shared loss of what might have been.

'I *v*ish I could do it all over again. If I hadn't left . . . if I'd stayed . . . I didn't know *v*ot I was missing, not until I had Regine.'

She understood where he was coming from, having just been ruminating over the same thoughts herself. 'But you know, if you'd stayed longer, it might have been worse. It would have been so much harder to leave.'

'But he would have known me from the start. I could have held him, given him that early bonding, you know?'

'I know.' They sat in silence together, considering all the ways their lives might have been different – or at least that was what she was doing, imagining the roads not taken.

Helge's jaw worked a moment as he composed himself. He

scratched at the shadow of whiskers on his chin, then said, 'Can I stay the night?'

'W-what?'

'I have a room booked at the hotel, but I *v*ant to be here *v*hen he *v*akes up.'

'The only thing, though, is that I don't have a spare bed. The committee only organised beds for Darcy and me. We have a third room but there's not much in it and . . .'

Should she offer to share her bed? No! That would be terrible. There was no way she'd be able to keep her hands to herself. Or even if she did manage that, she'd never get a wink of sleep, trying not to touch him . . . not to fall in love with him all over again.

He's married, Olivia.

But this was the first time Helge had been around Darcy and naturally he wanted to spend time with his son, to take every moment he could with him. She couldn't deny him that.

'It's okay,' he quickly reassured her. 'I can sleep on the couch.' He gave her a cheeky smile, as though he'd been reading her thoughts, and she narrowed her eyes at him till they both laughed.

'No, the couch is awful,' she said. 'I can barely sit on that thing. Look, there are spare blankets and duvets in the linen cupboard. Why don't we lay them on top of each other to make a bit of a padded area to lie on.'

'Like a dog basket.'

'Something like that. You could sleep by the fireplace if you like.'

He craned his neck to study the fireplace. 'Do you have any *v*ood? It could be just like camping.'

'I do. It's in the little shed out the back.'

He nodded and pushed himself back from the table to stand. 'I'll get it.'

'It will be our first fire since we moved in,' she said, also rising. 'I almost want to wake Darcy up to see it.'

Helge raised his eyebrows. 'We could do that. He could sleep down here *v*ith me.'

She grinned at him, almost relenting. 'Let's not do it tonight, but maybe tomorrow night before you have to go home on Monday morning.'

A flicker of sadness crossed his face as he registered the going-home part, but then he rallied. 'Okay. This is a good plan. Tonight, he sleeps, tomorrow *v*e party all night.'

11

On her way to open the shop on Sunday morning, Olivia popped in to young Lance's greengrocer's shop to pick up apples. To mark the cooler weather, she had decided to make apple pies and individual pots of apple-blackberry crumble with crème-fraîche whip. In Rambling Rose's kitchen, she peeled apples and thought about Darcy and Helge. Darcy had put a beaded bracelet on his wrist before she left the house, and she'd stopped short of finding a way to get him to remove it, even though he'd made it along with the other kids in class this week, each colour representing a different fact about themselves. It was some kind of mathematical thing, Olivia had gathered. Still, she'd felt the need to explain it to Helge.

When Darcy was two, he'd loved *Dora the Explorer*, the animated TV show about a little Mexican girl who travels around and teaches kids to speak a bit of Spanish. Olivia had encouraged his enthusiasm, hoping that the show would spark an interest in different cultures, and especially different languages – after all, one day he might want or need to be able to speak Norwegian.

Darcy was so enchanted by the show that whenever they went to a department store he would beg Olivia to buy him Dora-themed clothing and underwear, all in pink and with bows and puffy sleeves. Olivia didn't want to tell him outright that he couldn't have these things because they were girls' clothes; instead she tried to gently distract him. But one day he wailed and begged so much that she gave in and bought him a Dora singlet. After all, what did it matter? He was at an age of exploration and experimentation. Besides, she didn't agree with strictly segregating colours, clothes or toys into 'girls' and 'boys' things. Darcy loved the singlet and wanted to wear it all the time – though Olivia made sure he only wore it at home. He also loved to dress up as a dinosaur, a pirate or a monster. At his age, kids imagined they could be anything or anyone. So what if he loved Dora? He also loved Thomas the Tank Engine and Fireman Sam.

Anyway, she couldn't blame him for liking girls' clothes – girls had more choices, prettier colours and more sparkly embellishments. Boys' clothes were mostly dark colours with images of trucks or dinosaurs or roaring tiger faces. No kittens or puppies or rainbows or unicorns. It was as if the world had to scream at these tiny people that they were *boys*, and so they needed to be hard and tough and dark. She couldn't understand it. Men wore pink business shirts. Male tennis players wore pink T-shirts on court. Surf lifesavers wore fluorescent pink tops while they muscled their way through the ocean and saved people's lives. How dangerous could it be to put a little boy in a pink shirt? It wasn't fair. Why couldn't Darcy have a pink shirt if he wanted one?

'Be careful,' Ma warned her one day, as Darcy sat on the couch in his Dora singlet.

'It's just a top,' Olivia argued. 'He's three. No one's going to die.'

'I know,' Ma said steadily, her pen hovering over the crossword. 'But people can be cruel.'

'So we're supposed to live in fear of other people?' Olivia countered, disgusted. 'Aren't we supposed to be teaching our children to accept others as they are? Isn't there enough violence in the world towards women and any man not considered masculine enough? Where does it end? Why must we polarise everyone? It certainly hasn't done society any favours.'

Ma merely nodded and raised her eyebrows. 'Just . . . be careful.'

The next time they were in a shop and Darcy asked for a plastic tiara and a wand, Olivia bought them for him. When she saw them, Ma opened her mouth to speak and then closed it again and left the room.

Darcy was all sorts of wonderful, quirks included. More than anything, Olivia wanted Helge to appreciate him for his gentleness and kindness and not be one of those dads who demanded that their boys 'toughen up', 'be a man'. She had assumed that it would be a fantastic thing for Darcy to get to know Helge, and they had certainly got off to a great start, but if Helge was the wrong kind of dad for Darcy, it could be a disaster. She really needed to know for sure that Helge would support his son. And, she reminded herself, she needed to tell him the whole truth about what had happened at Darcy's birthday party last year.

At around lunchtime, Helge and Darcy came into the shop, with red cheeks and wind-tossed hair, and both looking pleased with themselves.

'Hi, Mum.' Darcy marched around the counter and wrapped her in his arms. He was limping a little, she saw; Helge must have noticed too, because he winced and looked at her apologetically. She shook her head quickly to dismiss his worries and kissed Darcy's head.

'Hi, beautiful, how was your morning?'

'Good. We've been hiking and then we played down in reeds near the river and I caught fish and beetles.'

'Did you?'

'*V*e let them go again,' Helge was quick to add, his hands tucked into the pockets of his windcheater.

'Now we're starving!' Darcy said, scanning the cabinet for something to eat.

'Lucky for you I made quiches today,' Olivia said, picking up the mini chicken and asparagus quiches from a tray not long out of the oven.

'Come on, Pappa,' Darcy said, leading the way authoritatively between the full tables to the kids' corner.

Olivia paused, staring at Darcy as he limped away. She'd always referred to Helge as his pappa, and Darcy had once or twice tried out the word on Skype, but never so casually and confidently. She turned to Helge, who couldn't hide his proud smile as he joined Darcy on the floor at the blackboard, where they started up a game of noughts-and-crosses.

Just as she was plating the second quiche, Katrina and Eloise came in the door.

'Hello!' Katrina called.

'Well, hello to you too,' Olivia sang back, delighted to see them.

'Eloise!' Darcy stood up and waved her over. 'My pappa's here!' he all but shouted.

'Darcy,' Olivia shout-whispered, indicating the customers. 'Inside voice.'

Eloise skipped over to the kids' corner in her purple gumboots and Helge shook her hand in greeting.

Katrina leant over the counter. 'Oh my God, is that him? That's Helge?'

'Yes.'

'Far out, love.' She widened her eyes. 'He's gorgeous!' Thankfully, Katrina *was* using her inside voice.

Olivia sighed. 'I have to agree.'

They watched as Helge and the kids began using the chalk to draw scenes of robots and cars travelling over hills and shooting flames into the sky, accompanied by much laughter and bad acting from Helge as he was hit by a ball of fire, felling him to the ground.

'Explain to me again why you two broke up?' Katrina said, her brow wrinkled in disbelief.

Olivia groaned. 'I've been asking myself the same question since he arrived.'

'Did you come up with a good answer?'

'Only that it seemed like the right thing to do at the time.'

'And now?'

'And now he's married with two additional children.' Olivia lifted a shoulder and let it drop in defeat.

'Are you sure they're happily married?' Katrina asked, tapping her chunky silver rings on the countertop.

'Oh, stop. I can't go there or I'll make myself crazy.'

Her friend muttered, 'Such a shame.'

Olivia poured a coffee for Helge and added cream and brown sugar, stirring it thoughtfully. She glanced over at him, now balancing a teacup on his head, much to Eloise's delight.

'Have you told him?' Katrina whispered.

'What?'

'How you're feeling?'

Olivia gave her a look of horror, shaking her head.

'You never know, though,' Katrina persisted.

'Hm.' Olivia needed to change the subject, fast. 'Hey, would you like something to eat while you're here? Quiche?'

'God, yes. We've just been over in Fahren Way doing boring grocery shopping and we're famished.'

Olivia carried the plates of food, a coffee for Helge and hot chocolate for the kids to the last remaining free table and the three of them sat down together. Eloise gave Darcy her set of colourful plastic bracelets to try on as well, which he did, holding them up for Olivia to see. She nodded admiringly. Helge turned as if to catch her eye, but she gave him an easy smile and moved to serve a customer.

While Olivia tallied up the bill for a table of four, Katrina went over to introduce herself to Helge. Then she came back to the counter to eat her quiche and give Olivia her verdict. 'Yep, so hot you could smoke a pig over him.'

The first thing Darcy screeched at Olivia as she stepped into the house that afternoon was, 'Pappa's staying till tomorrow night!'

'What?' Backing into the entrance, she shook off her umbrella from the sudden downpour that had created gushing rivulets down the hill. As she speared the umbrella into the stand and hung up her jacket, she smelt the enticing aroma of something baking. She had a momentary time slip to a parallel life in which she came home from work and Helge had dinner ready for her.

'Pappa's staying till tomorrow night!' Darcy repeated.

Helge joined them in the hallway, looking a little anxious. 'I hope it's okay, but I changed my flight from tomorrow morning to tomorrow night. I didn't *v*ant to bother you *v*hile you *v*ere *v*orking but I . . .' he paused, 'I just *v*anted more time.'

'It's fine,' she assured him, following him to the kitchen. 'Was it okay with Birgit?'

He hesitated, grimacing a little. 'She is fine.'

Intriguing – but it wasn't really appropriate to dig into the state of his marriage. Instead she asked, 'What about work?'

'I have some flex time,' he said, easily.

She tried to remember what his current job title was, exactly. She thought it had something to do with planning community-engagement recreational activities for the local government. His titles seemed to change often.

He moved on quickly. 'I have made us macaroni and cheese,' he said, indicating the dish bubbling in the oven.

'*Makaroni og ost*,' Darcy said.

'Yes, you got it,' Helge said, beaming.

'*Makaroni og ost, makaroni og ost, makaroni og ost*,' Darcy repeated, delighting in the new Norwegian words.

'It smells amazing,' Olivia said, dumping her bag on the bench. The hems of her overalls were wet and clung uncomfortably around her ankles. 'It's such a treat to have someone make me dinner.'

'You are *v*elcome.' Helge gazed at her a moment, then stepped closer, slowly raising one hand to her face. She froze, her heartbeat leaping about in excited expectation. Was he about to take her face in his hand and kiss her? But instead he gently ran his thumb across her cheek, under her eye. 'Your mascara has run in the rain,' he said, his lips in a soft curl. His eyes held hers and she didn't move, until he suddenly seemed to come to his senses and stepped away. 'You go and put on something *v*arm and Darcy and I *v*ill serve dinner.'

'Yeah, Mum!' Darcy was already heading to the cupboard for bowls.

She was about to point out that it was only four in the afternoon, but the skies were dark and the rain was hitting the windowpanes, and suddenly macaroni and cheese was exactly what she felt like eating. 'Okay.'

Olivia skipped upstairs and fixed her make-up using the small washbasin and mirror in the corner of her room, then dragged her damp hair into a loose bun and slipped into soft bamboo pants and a long-sleeved tee. She padded carefully back down the treacherous stairs in thick woolly socks and took her place at the dining table, feeling nurtured. 'This looks fantastic,' she said, admiring the heaped bowl in front of her. 'Thank you both.'

'I grated the cheese,' Darcy said.

'I picked the *vine*,' Helge said, lifting a bottle of red. It was her favourite – cabernet merlot. He gave her a look that she interpreted to mean, *Do you remember the day* ve *spent tasting* vine *around the Tamar Valley?*

Oh, yes, she did; it might well have been the day Darcy was conceived. She smiled at him and proffered her glass for him to fill. 'Yum.'

They ate the pasta with much gusto, all three of them returning for second helpings, Helge going back for a third. They chatted about the day – about the ducks, swans, trout, turtles, beetles and small fish Helge and Darcy had seen. About the ice cream they'd had at Lance's shop. About the toy car set Helge had bought Darcy from Raj's toy shop, which Darcy then had to go and set up to show them over and over how the cars zoomed and went upside down.

When Darcy went to have a bath, taking several toy cars with him to line up around the edge, Olivia and Helge stacked the dishwasher. 'There's something I need to tell you,' she said, taking a rinsed bowl from him and slotting it into the tray.

'Hm?'

She looked up into his face, unable to hide her fear over what she had to say. His face fell and he put both his hands on her arms. '*V*ot is wrong?'

'It's about Darcy's birthday party last year. It was supposed to be fabulous.' Nerves made her voice tremble.

'Come. Sit.' Helge guided her to the small red kitchen table flush up against the wall. She sat down on one of the chairs, and he perched his tall frame on another. 'The accident *v*as not your fault,' he said.

'Yes, but . . .'

'I *v*as mad when you told me, but I realise I *v*as too hard on you.'

When she'd rung him to tell him what had happened, crying on the phone, he'd yelled at her. Why had she chosen to hold the party so close to a main road? Why wasn't she watching Darcy? What was she doing?

'It *v*asn't your fault,' he said, his voice deep. 'I'm sorry. I have kids too.' He stopped, looking stricken, and quickly added, '*Other* kids . . . kids I look after all the time . . . you know *v*ot I mean.'

'It's okay.'

'Things go wrong. Even *v*ith Birgit and me both *v*atching. The kids get hurt. I should have apologised sooner. You can't blame yourself.'

Now was the time to tell him all of it. She took a deep breath, readying herself. She should have told him at the time, but she was so ashamed, and so scared about Darcy's impending surgery. And Ma had had a stroke and was in intensive care. It was all too much to bear at once. The knowledge that she'd caused all of it had overwhelmed her. But now, it was time. This was one of the reasons she'd come to this village, to reconnect with Helge, and this was one secret she'd kept for too long. She opened her mouth to speak, but Helge got there first.

'Birgit and I are separated.'

They stared at each other for several seconds, neither of them speaking. A dozen alternative universes flashed through her mind. 'When? How? She was there, on Skype, just the other day.'

He nodded, rubbing at his forehead with the base of his hand. 'We broke up six months ago. She *v*as picking the kids up from me after our holiday away *v*hen you saw her on Skype. She has been staying with her parents. *V*e are sharing time with the kids, equally.'

'But you seemed so friendly.'

'*Ve* are. *Ve* have to be.'

'God, I'm so sorry.'

He took in a short, sharp breath, as though still getting used to this new state. 'It's okay. You know, not great. But okay.'

Olivia groaned. She'd never been married but she knew how difficult it had been for her to say goodbye to Helge. With two small children in the mix, a home, finances and an established life between them, it must have been that much harder for Helge and Birgit.

'Why did you break up? What happened?' She was genuinely trying to be supportive, to open a space for him to talk about it, but at the same time, she couldn't stop a part of her mind from leaping a hundred steps into the future, a future that might include the possibility of a second chance with him.

But then, why had they broken up? She'd never suspected any disharmony between them, not that she would, necessarily. She hoped very much that they hadn't broken up over infidelity. Could she be with someone who'd cheated on his wife? But then, did it matter? She and Helge would be a totally different proposition to Helge and Birgit and – oh my God, she had to stop her mind racing off in this wild direction.

'It *v*as just one of those things, you know? We grew apart.'

'Did you cheat on her?' Yep, she'd asked it out loud.

'No!' He looked aghast.

'Sorry, sorry. None of my business.' Olivia was standing. Funny, she didn't remember standing up.

'I'm not like that,' he said, and she believed him, and the relief was immense. He also rose to his feet. He was only inches away. She could cross that distance in a split second, be in his arms.

She could feel her pulse under her jaw. Was she having a heart attack?

Helge smiled and shook his head at her, reached out and enfolded her hands in his, steadying her.

'Why are you telling me this now?' she managed to ask.

'Maybe *ve* missed our chance the first time. Maybe now . . .'

The bathroom door burst open and Darcy emerged, still wet from the bath. Olivia and Helge leapt away from each other.

'The car even goes underwater,' Darcy was yelling.

'Wow,' Olivia said.

'Amazing,' Helge added, equally flatly.

Darcy looked between the two of them, his eyes narrowing a fraction as though picking up on some vibe he didn't understand, then headed to the lounge room. Olivia hurried to the sink and resumed rinsing plates. Helge came up behind her. She could feel the heat from his body, sense his height above her head. He placed his hands on her shoulders. She stopped what she was doing but didn't dare turn around.

'Sorry. I didn't mean to shock you. I just thought you should know.' He waited a moment, then followed Darcy into the lounge room.

Olivia kept tidying the kitchen until she'd calmed down, and then joined them in the lounge room till it was time for Darcy to go to bed. She went into the bathroom to supervise him cleaning his teeth, then all three of them went upstairs to his bedroom, because even though it was agreed that he and Helge were sleeping beside the fireplace, Helge had another surprise for Darcy.

'I brought you these.' He handed Darcy a packet of glow-in-the-dark stars.

'Cool!' Darcy tore open the packet and Helge helped him stick them to the wall and the ceiling. Then they turned off the lights and all three of them lay on the bed, Darcy in the middle, staring up at the galaxy of glowing green stars.

'Can we go to the moon one day?' Darcy asked, his small body wedged up against Helge's.

'Sure, *v*hy not?'

'How long will it take to get there?'

'Good question. Four days?' Olivia guessed.

Darcy laughed. 'No-o-o-o! It would take four years.'

'Sometime in the future they'll have some sort of super-fast rocket and *v*e'll all be able to jump on and go for a day trip.'

'Will they give us food?'

'Yes. Definitely. Martian moon cakes and alien asparagus,' Helge said.

'Asparagus!' Darcy slapped his hand to his forehead. 'I hate asparagus.'

'But you have to eat the asparagus or you can't get to the moon,' Helge countered.

'I can't do asparagus. It tastes like wee.'

'How do you know what wee tastes like?' Olivia asked.

'Um, I just do.'

'I tried it once,' Helge said, gravely.

Darcy squealed. 'You did not.'

'I did too.'

'Did not!' Darcy was laughing so hard that Olivia was mildly concerned he might vomit up his dinner, but she didn't have the heart to tell him to calm down. He was having too much fun.

'I had it *v*ith a t*v*ist of lime and a sprig of mint and I drank it out of a shoe. Mm . . . delicious.'

Darcy was in fits now and Olivia knew if she turned on the light he would be red in the face, his eyes scrunched up as his little body convulsed. *This.* Her son had missed out on so much of this with his father.

Was now their chance to change his future?

12

Heavy mist bloomed around the village the next morning, water droplets forming slowly on windows and dripping to the stone ledges below. The kitchen in the old stone cottage felt cosy and cocooned, and Olivia watched as Helge expertly made her a coffee. Today they were planning to take Darcy to Burford, about ten miles away, to visit the Cotswolds Wildlife Park and Gardens. But after what had happened the night before, Olivia was nervous about spending the whole day in Helge's company. She needed to slow things down, give herself some time to think.

Helge put a mug of coffee on the bench in front of her, his eyes lingering on her with a soft smile. Fortunately, at that moment Darcy raced into the kitchen. 'They have rhinos and giraffes and everything!' he shrieked, bouncing up and down and spilling his water on the kitchen floor. 'Oops.'

'I'm sure you're going to have a great day,' Olivia said, taking his cup and handing him a paper towel to wipe the floor.

'There's also lions, lemurs, meerkats and *v*olverines,' Helge said, packing a daypack with water bottles and scarves.

'I'm not sure I even know what a wolverine is,' Olivia said, smiling at Darcy. 'I've never seen one. You'll have to tell me all about them.'

'Ever heard of *X-Men*?' Helge said, with a cheeky grin.

'Oh, yeah.' She smiled back at him, and felt her belly flip. She had to shut this down, quickly. 'Plans have changed,' she said in her no-nonsense, no-arguments voice. 'I'm not coming today. I need to work, sorry.'

'No . . .' Helge gave her a pleading look.

'It's okay, really. You two will have lots of fun together.'

Darcy looked momentarily disappointed, but the prospect of a trip to the zoo with his dad was still a winning option and he began to tug at Helge's sleeve to hurry him along.

'Are you sure?' Helge asked, still looking downcast.

'I'll be here when you get home,' she said briskly, and pulled Darcy to her. 'You'll have a great time, baby.'

Darcy wrapped his arms around her waist and squeezed tightly. 'We will.'

'I'll see you when you get back, as long as you don't get eaten by a lion.'

Darcy laughed. 'I won't.' He skipped towards the front door.

She handed Darcy's weatherproof jacket to Helge and he tucked it under his arm. He gave her puppy-dog eyes. 'You won't change your mind?'

'No, really. It will be good for you both.'

'If it's about our talk last night . . .'

'Really, it's fine. Have fun.'

'Okay.' He slung the daypack over his shoulder and followed Darcy out the door.

After they'd gone, she walked down the hill to the school. Classes hadn't started yet, but Cathy Finch was already in the classroom, which for some reason was full of multicoloured lava lamps today. Olivia explained that Darcy was spending the day with his father but would be back tomorrow. Before she left, Cathy pressed a notice into her hand about a school bazaar to be held the following month. She explained that it was a fundraising event with a jumble sale, arts and crafts, home produce, penny auctions and a cake stall, and she'd already nominated Olivia to bring a full-sized cake.

'There'll be lots of slices and cupcakes but yours will be the show stopper!' the teacher said excitedly, her overly white teeth gleaming.

'No problem. I'd love to.' Olivia waved goodbye, with another bemused look at the lava lamps.

As she stepped out through the school gate, two cheery beeps made her look up. A muddied red ute pulled over, with Grayson in the driver's seat. He bobbed down his head to smile at her, and the passenger window descended.

'Morning!' He wore a brown puffer vest over a flannel shirt the same colour as his vehicle, but cleaner. 'I've just been delivering milk around the village. Can I give you a lift somewhere?'

She smiled. 'Thank you, but I was just heading home – it's literally two minutes up the hill.' She hadn't seen Grayson since last Monday, when he'd helped her set the rat trap, and she was surprised by how pleased she was at this chance encounter.

'Come on, indulge yourself,' he said, leaning over to pop open the door for her.

'You're mad,' she said, but climbed in anyway.

He grinned at her and shifted gears. They bumped down the hill, swung right around the graveyard and headed back up the hill, the gears crunching to get some oomph on the steep part.

'Any sign of your rat?' he asked.

'Nope. I think it's gone. I'll leave the trap there for a while, but hopefully all those people and all that screaming convinced the creature it would be better off elsewhere.'

'Let's hope so,' Grayson said, as Olivia indicated for him to pull up outside her house.

'Well, thanks for the lift,' she said. 'I really don't know how I would have made it up the hill on my own.'

'Are you opening your shop today?' He hadn't cut the engine and the vibration throbbed through her legs and back.

'No, Monday is my day off. I'm going to head out and explore. Raj told me there's a gate at the end of a laneway a few doors down and it leads to some public access pathways. I thought I'd check it out. If it's any good, I could take Darcy out for an early walk one weekend, before I have to be at the shop.'

He turned the key and the ute shuddered to stillness. 'That must be hard, working on weekends all the time.'

'It can be,' she admitted. 'I used to have my ma to help look after Darcy, but now it's just me. So far he hasn't complained about coming into the shop, but I'm sure he'll get tired of it. I'll just have to work things out as we go.'

He nodded thoughtfully, glancing up the street, and she took the opportunity to study the height of his cheekbones, the slight bump on the ridge of his nose, the stubble on his chin, the way his hair curled above his ears, the ruddy outdoorsy colour in his cheeks, those keen blue eyes.

'How about I come with you?' he said. 'I could use a walk. I've never tried those paths, but I've heard there's a whole circuit you can do.'

She scoffed. 'You're a farmer! I should think your daily step count would be just fine without adding a recreational stroll.'

He chuckled. 'It's not bad.' He looked down at the steering wheel then, as though biting down more words.

She realised her response must have sounded like a brush-off. Quickly, she said, 'Okay, let's go.'

He looked up, one side of his mouth working up to a smile. 'Yeah?'

'Why not?' She opened the door and he followed suit. She didn't bother going into the cottage, just led the way round the corner.

They found the laneway quickly enough, a long, flat stretch of nuclear-green grass with parallel tyre tracks running down to a wooden gate. On either side of the laneway were blackened stone walls overhung with tree branches, their leaves already turning bright orange and deep red. Piles of leaves on the ground created colourful picnic blankets. Olivia noticed several low wooden doors set into the walls: they were no more than four feet high, with iron handles.

'What are these?' she asked, pausing to stroke the wood of one of the doors. 'Were people very short in the past?'

'I've no idea what they were for,' Grayson said, and she admired him for that. In her experience, men often seemed to feel the need to provide answers even when they really had no idea, to make themselves appear knowledgeable. They didn't realise that it just made them dull, that it simply ended the conversation. To admit they didn't know opened the conversation up, giving scope for all sorts of imaginative possibilities and ideas that bounced back and forth.

'Tiny washerwomen?' she wondered.

'Hobbits, maybe.'

'Or child labour,' she said, the notion making her sad. She couldn't believe that children as young as Darcy had been sent out to do hard physical work in years gone by. Their bodies were still growing. They needed to play and sing and cuddle, not haul rocks and sweep chimneys, dying of lung diseases and malnutrition. It wasn't even that long ago, barely two hundred years.

'Portals to the past,' Grayson proposed, with an air of mystery.

'Oh, yes. Tunnels through time.'

'That's definitely it,' he agreed.

'I'll have to bring Darcy down to see this. He'll love it.' She gave the door a final pat and they continued on their way.

'What does Darcy like? I mean, what's he into?' Grayson asked, his long legs striding confidently, so Olivia was walking quite quickly to keep up. She slipped off her cream cotton scarf and shoved it into her jacket pocket.

'He's very kind, very funny. He makes me laugh all the time. He's a fantastic age right now. He's really into board games and card games, and we can while away hours playing. It's really special. He's a deep thinker, too. When he was five, he went through a stage of worrying about the world, wondering if it hurt the grass when he walked on it, or if the flowers minded being picked, or if lightning upset the clouds.'

They reached the end of the laneway, and Grayson slid the bolt across and held the gate for her to pass through. 'He sounds lovely.'

'He is.'

'The world needs more people like him.'

'I agree, though the world seems intent on knocking any kindness or sensitivity out of boys. We want them to grow up to be loving and caring men, but every time a little boy shows that side of himself society thinks it's their duty to tell him to stop *being a girl.*' She stopped, feeling the heat in her cheeks, taken aback by the sudden flash of fury. 'Sorry.'

Grayson locked the gate behind them and turned to face her, his gaze steady. 'Don't be. You're absolutely right. If the world wants men to treat women the right way, we have to show them how to do it from the start, not try to toughen them up first and then back-pedal to teach them to deal with their emotions instead of assaulting women.' A muscle twitched in his jaw, and there was an edge in his tone. 'I have sisters,' he said, carefully. 'One of them has been through some stuff.'

'Is she okay?'

'She's doing all right now, but it should never have happened.

All this Me Too stuff is showing us that we've been raising boys wrong for centuries.'

She swallowed. 'Exactly. Does it scare you, the Me Too movement?'

He shook his head. 'Not at all. Women have been abused for so long. The way I see it, their pain is like an abscess – it needs lancing.'

Olivia nodded in silent agreement. She wanted to ask more about his sister, but she feared to intrude on something that was clearly difficult for him. They turned right to follow a road that wound between fields dotted with sheep and yellow wildflowers holding on from summer, hedged with low stone walls.

'I can't believe how much stone there is in this village,' she said, feeling the need to change the subject. 'There must be one gigantic hole in the ground somewhere.'

'Incredible, isn't it? And it all would have been dug up and moved by hand and horse and cart.'

They walked in companionable silence for a few minutes. Low, dark clouds had moved into the sky above them. The road was flanked by tall trees, enclosing them intimately in the quiet, cool air. A few small birds – thrushes or robins? – flitted in the branches and twittered pleasantly. Grayson's boots made heavy, rhythmic strides on the bitumen of the empty road, while Olivia's sneakers made soft, squeaky sounds.

'So, what's your story, Farmer Grayson?' Olivia's curiosity was genuine. What experiences had produced this man?

'Ah, there's not much to tell, really.'

'Come on, you left a career and city life and came here on your own to have a crack at farming. That doesn't sound like nothing. What made you make the break?'

Grayson wrinkled up his nose. 'It's a bit embarrassing.'

'Go on. I won't laugh,' she promised, her hand on her heart.

He gave her a wry look. 'I'm the casualty of a very ordinary midlife crisis.'

'You're not old enough, surely?'

'I'm forty-two. I moved here two years ago. I'd just turned forty, had a bit of a do at the pub after work, looked around at the people who were there, listened to everything they were yammering on about and something snapped.' He pulled a face. 'It just struck me that half my life had gone and I was on the wrong side of it all now. I had friends and my mum and dad and sisters in London, but I'd also recently broken up with my long-term girlfriend and everything just seemed at a dead end.'

'You weren't enjoying optometry?'

His nose twitched as he thought about this. 'Not a lot, no.' He chuckled. 'I felt like I'd wasted my life on the wrong career.'

'Ouch.'

'Yeah.'

'So you chucked it all in and moved to the country.'

'Completely bonkers, I know.'

'Not really. I've done the same thing, haven't I? Packed up my whole life and come over here.'

'That's true.'

'Has it been working out for you? The move, that is.' She sniffed as quietly as she could; the cold air was making her nose run.

'It was hard at first, a total tree change. The pace of the village was a shock. Nothing opened till ten o'clock and shops would be shut on certain days. No cinema, a half-hour drive to a supermarket, just one pub. No friends. I even missed my work a bit, which I hadn't expected.' The road began to curve around a thicket of trees. 'It was probably just the social side of work, though, the general chatter and coffee breaks with others, just talking about nothing in particular. Everyone in this village was so . . . old.'

She smiled in sympathy.

'I got the cows and that gave me plenty to do, at least, but I was still wondering if I should go back to London with my tail between my legs when Clarence told me about his idea for the Renaissance Project. The vision was so inspiring. I joined the committee and suddenly felt like I had purpose again. It's a bit daft, I know.'

'No, it's not.'

They emerged from the cover of the trees, and Olivia gasped. Rolling out around them were acres of carefully tended emerald lawns, and what must have been the original manor house off in the distance.

'Oh my God.' Olivia whipped out her phone to take a photo. 'It's just like Downton Abbey.'

'Magnificent, isn't it? Seventeenth-century, I believe.'

The three-storey building had a long central axis with a wing on either side, one end covered with red and green ivy. There were at least six chimneys that she could see, dozens of windows, and in the centre of the circular driveway was a sculpture garden.

'Here,' Grayson said, holding out his hand. 'I'll take a photo of you in front of it.'

Olivia hesitated, suddenly shy. 'Okay, thanks.' She quickly ran her hands through her hair and straightened her shoulders, acutely conscious of him looking at her on the screen.

Grayson checked the photo before handing it back to her with a smile. 'There you go, you look great.'

She slipped the phone back into her pocket without looking at it. They continued along the road, heading towards a dense line of plane trees that seemed to be following a watercourse. 'Is that still the Fahn River up there?'

'Yes. It winds its way through many villages in the Cotswolds.'

As they walked, Olivia took more photographs – of an arched stone bridge beneath weeping willows over a stunning section of the Fahn, picturesque waterwheels, and several cottages and a scattering of tiny houses, which Grayson explained were in fact feed sheds and animal shelters.

'Why is everything empty?' Olivia asked, wondering why there were no people occupying these spaces. 'It's beautiful, but it's like a museum.'

'Too many people left,' Grayson said. 'It's hard to imagine now, but according to Clarence, when he and Howard were children there wouldn't have been a bedroom to spare in the village, let alone a whole building.'

Olivia paused to catch her breath as they ascended a steep hill. She estimated they'd walked for a couple of kilometres already. At the top of the hill, an empty field lay ahead of them.

'I think this should take us back to the main drag, up near the old flour mill,' Grayson said. 'It's all public access land, so we're fine to go on, if you feel up to it?'

By now she was guessing it would take them just as long to go back the way they'd come as it would to forge on. 'Let's go,' she said.

Light rain began to fall, blowing into their faces as they walked. Olivia lowered her head, hunching her shoulders as water gradually soaked through her clothing. Their conversation had slowed.

'Are we going the right way?' she asked, wiping the wet hair off her forehead and flicking a drip off the tip of her nose.

'I didn't think it would be this far,' Grayson admitted. 'But I still think we're heading in the right direction.'

She stopped and turned, squinting against the rain. She could hear machinery, but a long way off. All they could see in the apparently endless paddocks were sheep, and the occasional fence with a 'Warning: Bull in Field' sign. Oddly, in the middle of nowhere, they passed a cricket pitch.

Olivia's energy was flagging, and there was another issue that she'd been trying to ignore for the last half-hour but which had become increasingly pressing. Noticing a copse over a small rise, she finally spoke up. 'Um . . . I need to pee,' she said, feeling her face burning.

'Oh, right.' Grayson looked around, unfazed.

'I'm just going to pop over to those bushes,' Olivia said, trying to affect nonchalance. It wasn't like he didn't pee. Everyone peed. Still, it was unfortunate that she needed to go right now when they were on what could possibly be interpreted as an impromptu date, which was discombobulating enough given her conversation with Helge only last night.

'You keep walking. I'll catch up in a minute.' Olivia scurried over the rise and ducked behind the bushes, which were thornier than she'd expected. When she was completely sure that she'd hidden herself from view, she crouched down to take care of business, her cold hands fumbling with her zip. The rain chose that exact moment to come down harder. As soon as she'd finished and sorted out her clothes again, she was on her feet and jogging back to Grayson.

'We need to find some shelter,' he called as she joined him. The raindrops had hardened to pellets, and Olivia was thoroughly soaked now.

Running, Grayson led the way to a line of tall trees with overhanging branches, which provided some shelter from the driving rain. They sat side by side on the thick mossy trunk of a fallen tree. Panting, her hair plastered to her dripping face, Olivia caught Grayson's eye and they both burst out laughing. There was really nothing else to do: they were cold and wet, she'd just had to pee in a thornbush, and she was pretty sure they were now officially lost.

When they stopped laughing, Grayson said, 'Perhaps we should have gone back the way we came.'

Olivia's legs were aching. 'I can hear cars in the distance. Surely if we just keep going we'll run into a road eventually?'

He shrugged apologetically. 'I'm the local, I should be taking care of you, not getting you lost and possibly giving you consumption.'

'How very English of you,' she said, laughing some more, wiping away the rivulets running down her face. The air was thick with the smell of fresh rain and damp earth. 'Look, we're not in the outback, miles from anything. We'll be okay. We'll find something soon, someone's house or a road, and we'll be back on track.'

'All right. Maybe if we—' Grayson stopped abruptly, his eyes widening.

She'd heard it too, the swishing of grass along the barbed-wire fence behind them. They both turned their heads and were met with a low, loud growl from the biggest, blackest, shaggiest bull with the longest and pointiest horns Olivia had ever seen. Saliva dripped from his rubbery lips. Steam rose from his table-width back.

The bull charged with a deafening roar, apparently unconcerned that there was a fence between them.

They both screamed and propelled themselves off the fallen tree. Olivia ran blindly, not daring to look back to see if Mr Bull had broken through the fence. All she could hear were their footsteps pounding the earth and her own rasping breath. They found their way onto a grass vehicle track, which led them to the backs of houses, where they finally dared to slow down a little and take a peek behind them.

The bull wasn't there.

'Oh shit,' Grayson gasped, bending down with his hands on his knees, dragging in ragged breaths.

Olivia did the same, wheezing for air between helpless giggles. 'Come on,' she sputtered. 'He could still be looking for us.'

They alternated jogging and walking the rest of the way, occasionally stopping to gasp for breath between more fits of laughter, until they eventually found a fence with a wooden turnstile. It was rotted shut, though, so Grayson climbed over gingerly first, and then held out his hand for hers. Clutching his hand, she got one leg over the turnstile and then the other. She jumped to the ground, almost landing in his arms.

She looked up at him. 'Thanks,' she said, her cheeks aching from all the laughing. Her legs wobbled under her and she lurched to one side.

Grayson put his arm around her shoulder. 'Come on. I think I know where we are now. There's a pub just down the road. Let me be your brandy dog and buy you a warming shot.'

'I won't say no,' she said, still laughing, hardly able to believe the day she was having.

13

Helge crouched forlornly in front of Darcy, his backpack waiting next to the door. Darcy clutched his stuffed toy giraffe to his chest and his eyes welled. Olivia stood behind him, her hands on his small shoulders for support. Father and son had arrived back from the wildlife park soon after lunch, Darcy bubbling over with excitement about all the animals he'd seen. Olivia had got home an hour earlier, showered and dressed in warm clothes, and recovered from her drenching. But now Helge had to head to London for his flight home.

'I *v*ill see you again soon, yes?' he said.

Darcy nodded and wiped at his eye with the back of his wrist. Olivia, too, felt on the brink of tears standing there in the lounge room, about to watch Helge walk away, just as she'd done so many years before. Except this time everything was different – though no less confusing.

Helge hugged Darcy, who kept his arms wrapped tightly around the giraffe, then stood up to face Olivia. 'Thank you,' he said, putting his hand over his heart. 'This has been . . . incredible.'

She opened her arms impulsively, and they embraced with Darcy squashed between them.

'I still love you, you know,' he whispered into her ear, quietly enough that she knew Darcy wouldn't have heard.

What?

'*Ve vill* talk again soon, yes?'

She nodded, at a loss for words.

Helge released her and smiled down into her face. He raised his hand to touch her cheek momentarily, then picked up his bag, ruffled Darcy's hair once more, and was gone.

Sleep that night didn't come easily. Olivia remembered her walk with Grayson: his easy manner, his respect for women, the way they'd laughed while running in the rain, the way he'd stared intently at her in the pub over their glasses of brandy, as they'd dried off slowly by the fire. She liked him. He was easy to be with, easy to talk to, and with a natural generosity that saw him delivering milk to aged residents and jumping in to help her bake and catch rats.

Then there was Helge, his words in her mind. *I still love you.*

She imagined what it would be like to kiss him again, to feel his skin under her palms, his body pressed up against hers. She found herself imagining the three of them as a family, her, Helge and Darcy, the way it should have been, the way it could have been. Was this the real reason she'd come to England, because she'd known on some deep level that the timing was just right? They hadn't been able to make it work eight years ago, but now, maybe, they could.

She groaned and thumped the pillow again, trying to find a comfortable position. She tossed off the duvet to let the air cool her heated skin, then pulled it up again a few minutes later when she started to shiver. But sleep was still elusive. Clearly, she and Helge needed to talk.

For now, though, she let go of any idea of sleep and crept downstairs. She found the bottle of wine Helge had brought and poured the last of it into a glass, then retrieved her laptop and sat on the couch with it balanced on her knees, the wine on the coffee table beside her. She turned her attention away from Helge (and Grayson) and towards Ma instead. With everything that had been going on in the past weeks – moving country, setting up a new home, settling Darcy in to his new school, launching Rambling Rose, dealing with the rat problem, Helge's tumultuous visit, running the shop, her intriguing encounters with Grayson, and of course all the normal household things like cooking, cleaning, washing and mothering – she'd had no time to start looking for information about Ma's life here in Stoneden. There'd been no spare moment to visit a library or an information centre or sleuth through graveyards. Now, she did what any modern woman with a question might do and turned to Google.

She began by running a general search on why people had left Britain in the 1960s, but that proved fruitless. Next, she tried to find scanned online versions of historical newspapers from Stoneden in the 1960s but could only find a national archive of London papers, with a wickedly complicated filing system that made her eyes glaze over. Instead, she searched for *Eleanora Kent Stoneden*. To her surprise, the results included the same black-and-white photo of Ma leaning against the stone wall in her good dress. She wondered why the image would be in her own personal possession and online as well. It was tagged *Eleanora Kent* and the copyright was attributed to the photographer – Burton McCarthy. She clicked on it and found that it had been published in the social pages of the *Stoneden Times* in 1966. She'd been on her way to a dance. Olivia smiled, imagining Ma on the dance floor in some young man's arms. Maybe even that man, Burton McCarthy.

She wondered. McCarthy was Madeline's surname, but she didn't know if it was her maiden name or a married name. Either way, perhaps the photographer was related to her, by birth or marriage. Clapping her hands quietly in excitement, Olivia slugged back the last of the wine, shut her laptop, then fetched the original photo from a pocket in her suitcase and tucked it into her handbag. It was a great place to begin her search.

On Tuesday morning, Olivia finally had the time to make her show-stopping cake, the rosewater sponge. She went to the store-room – which remained mercifully rat-free – and opened the small wooden chest that held her prized collection of floral waters. Ma had given Olivia the chest for her twenty-first birthday. It was made of Huon pine, a rare and protected Tasmanian species: the wood could only be harvested from fallen trees. Prized for its durability and its own naturally occurring preserving oil, and with a distinctive earthy fragrance, the wood was perfect for food storage.

'Good to have you here, Ma,' she said, running her hand over the chest. Inside, it was lined with racks holding bottles of fragrant water, including versatile lavender, uplifting neroli orange blossom, earthy chamomile (perfect for banana bread), lilac, elderflower and, of course, Olivia's favourite, rose.

During her time as an apprentice, Olivia had visited a rose farm in the north of Tasmania that produced both essential oil and the delicate floral water. The farmers were of Iranian descent, and they harvested the roses and distilled the rosewater in the same way it had once been done in Iran – the world's largest producer of rosewater – before the factories were conquered by mass production. She'd joined the family and their workers in the fields just before dawn, donning long sleeves and thick gloves to protect herself against the chill and the thorns. Rose bushes grew in rows up to her shoulders, dark green leaves supporting delicate stems, with gentle pink buds just opening. A family member showed her how to pluck each bud along with a section of the stem, which held some of the scent, and drop it lightly into a cotton mesh bag tied around her waist. As they returned to the shed with their harvest, she sat in the back of the ute surrounded by mounds of cotton bags filled with soft pink roses, dizzy with the heavenly scent.

Fires at the shed had been stoked in readiness for their arrival. Three large copper pots filled with purified water sat on a long bench above three separate brick hearths. The roses were poured into the pots, where they floated on top of the simmering water, and then the lids were clamped down. With a steady, gentle heat to avoid cooking or burning the buds, the roses were coaxed to gradually release their fragrance into the water. The farm's small-scale, traditional operation meant that their products were expensive, but Olivia had never bought any other brand.

Now, she opened her bottle of Tasmanian-Iranian rosewater and inhaled. The aroma filled her nose and head, making her feel instantly joyful. The smell was also quintessentially romantic, which didn't help her confusion about Helge right now.

In the quiet of her store, more questions presented themselves. He'd said he loved her, but in what way – as a friend, as the mother of his child, or as something more?

'Just bake, Livvy,' she told herself. The sound of Helge's name for her made her smile.

She was piping the last pink buttercream rose onto the sponge, singing along to Buddy Holly's 'That'll Be the Day' blaring on the speakers when Juliet Cabot entered the shop with a cheery 'Hello!'

Olivia waved, hurrying to turn down the music. 'Sorry. I was totally lost in the song.'

'No need to apologise. I wish more people were as enthusiastic about music.' Juliet smiled, and Olivia remembered that she was a music teacher.

'Can I get you a cup of tea or coffee?' she asked, wiping her hands on her apron. 'It's only plunger coffee, but I've got some great vanilla cream I can put with it for a Vienna coffee if you'd like something a bit fancier?'

Juliet was a beautiful woman, with dark hair and brows, thick lashes and olive skin. She was immaculately put together, her blouse and long skirt entirely suitable for a vicar's wife. 'No, thank you anyway. I've just had coffee and I'm on my way to school for my music classes.'

'What instruments do you teach?' Olivia asked.

'Piano, cello, violin, viola, guitar and a little bit of flute and clarinet.'

'That's so impressive.'

'The wind instruments aren't my specialty. After a certain point I need to direct students over to Fahren Way to a colleague there. I had parents who valued music, but I see a lot of kids with real interest or talent whose parents aren't supportive.' Juliet shrugged, sadly, but her smile returned quickly. 'Anyway, I came in today to order a cake.'

'Of course. What sort of thing were you after?'

'Anthony and I have organised a wine and cheese event at the manor house Friday week.'

'I walked past it yesterday. It looks gorgeous! Does anyone live there?'

'Not anymore. It's now a hotel and function facility, extremely popular for weddings. We've kept the ticket prices low – we only want to cover costs. It will be good for people to feel like it's still a part of Stoneden, in some small way. I hope you'll be able to make it. It's part of our efforts to unite the community.' She clasped her hands together fervently. 'We firmly believe it's difficult to fear or hate people if you get to know them. And we'd like to order a large cake decorated with the words *Stoneden's bright future.*' She waved her hand across the air as she spoke the words.

'That sounds great. Just let me make some notes.' Olivia reached under the counter for a notebook and pen. 'How many people are you expecting?'

'We're hoping for a hundred.'

'Did you say next Friday?' Olivia frowned. 'Do you think you might need a bit more time to organise this?'

'Oh, no. This is Stoneden! The whole village will know by this afternoon. Anthony will promote it at church this weekend too. Plus I'm asking the schoolteachers to include some artworks from the kids as an art show – that always gets the parents and grandparents along. Tickets will sell out in no time. For the cake, I'm thinking something stylish and beautiful, like a three-tiered wedding cake. I'm hoping it will subconsciously communicate to everyone there that the Renaissance Project is a marriage of two big families and something worth celebrating, and that it will lead to new children, so to speak. But you get it – new beginnings, growth. Oh, and blooms! We must have lots of flowers to symbolise all this *blooming*.'

'Roses are my favourite,' Olivia said, nodding towards the rose-water cake on its stand.

Juliet bent forward to inhale the aroma, closing her eyes. 'That. Smells. Amazing.'

'Here, take a piece to try,' Olivia said, reaching for a knife and a takeaway box.

'Oh, no, no, no!' Juliet said, waving her hands. 'It's too beautiful to destroy.'

'Nonsense. It's nearly opening time. I'd be cutting it any minute now.' Olivia sliced into the cake, enjoying the sensation of the knife slipping through the cream roses, then the three sponge layers. The wedge plopped into the box with satisfying weight, and her own mouth watered. 'Here you go.'

'It's gorgeous. Thank you. I'll take it home and share it with Anthony,' Juliet said. 'Now, just let me know the cost when you're ready and we'll sort it out.'

'Any particular flavours or icing requests?' Olivia asked.

'No, absolutely not. This is your time to shine, so you make all the decisions. Whatever you choose will be perfect.'

Olivia closed her notebook. 'Leave it to me,' she said, already planning a cake in her mind.

'Bye for now,' Juliet sang, and swept out of the shop on her way to make children happy.

Two incoming customers passed Juliet in the doorway, and their eyes locked onto the rose cake. 'We'll have two pieces,' the first woman said, removing her gloves and anorak.

'And two coffees,' said the second, slipping the scarf off her head. 'Irish, preferably.'

'Coming right up,' Olivia said. She was happy to have customers, and dared to hope that the rat drama of last week was behind her and she could settle into some sort of normality. She'd just put down the two plates and coffees when she saw Grayson striding past the window. He smiled at her and she raised a finger, asking him to stop. She hurried to meet him at the door.

'Hi,' she said, noticing a definite tingle through her body, a self-consciousness. So, her business might be back on track, but her emotions were clearly all over the shop.

'Hi,' he said, giving her the warmest, loveliest smile, one that was so easy, offered so freely. She mentally compared this with Helge's demeanour – wary or brooding until the clouds passed, revealing the burning sun.

'I really enjoyed our walk yesterday,' she said.

'So did I,' he said. 'It's not every day I get chased by a bull. If I have another midlife crisis, maybe I could ditch the farming and become a rodeo clown and let bulls chase me for fun.'

'Oh no, don't ditch the farming. I actually wanted to ask if I could place a standing order with you for butter, cream, milk and cheese.'

He looked genuinely excited. 'Of course. I can deliver them to the shop each day.'

She felt her cheeks bunch up in a grin. 'Amazing. I've never had the opportunity to buy straight from the farmer before. I'd love to support you, and the village economy. And it means low food miles, I'd be choosing local and all that good stuff.' And then there was the added benefit of knowing she would see him every day . . .

He let his gaze rest on her a moment, and she felt herself grow warm despite the cold morning. 'I'd better get back inside,' she said, reluctantly.

Grayson inclined his head towards the ladies sitting at the table in the window. 'I think we have an audience,' he said quietly.

Olivia peeked around. One of the women looked between her and Grayson, then raised her cup to Olivia in a cheeky salute.

'First rule of small villages,' Grayson said. 'Everyone knows everything.'

Been thinking about what you said. Can we talk? x

Her text message flew off with a *whoosh*, destined for Helge's phone. Sitting on the garden seat, Olivia watched Darcy and Eloise kicking a soccer ball around on the square of lawn behind the cottage. She'd offered to bring Eloise home after school for a play date, and the kids were happily working up an appetite for dinner. Darcy kicked the ball to Eloise, who mistimed her return kick, toppling over onto her backside with her legs in the air. The ball flew off into Mrs Wilson's yard.

'Are you okay?' Olivia leant forward, about to run to her, but Darcy was already there, helping his friend up. Seeing that Eloise was shaking with silent guffaws, Olivia relaxed and left them to it. Giggling, re-enacting the event, they skipped around the row of apple trees and into Mrs Wilson's yard. Olivia winced, waiting for her neighbour to come out and yell at them, but the house remained silent. Hopefully, Mrs Wilson was not at home.

She watched the pair return with the ball. They were still in their school uniforms; Eloise wore a light cardigan against the chill, but Darcy had shrugged his off. 'Do you need your jumper, Darcy?' she called to him.

'I'm fine,' he said, kicking the ball again to Eloise, who was already laughing in anticipation. Her cheeks were bright red, whether from the cold, the exertion or the excitement, Olivia couldn't tell. She debated with herself whether to push the issue of a jumper with either child, but it wasn't as if they weren't used to cold weather. Tasmania and New Zealand both had their fair share of deep cold and snow.

She was so happy he'd made a friend in Eloise. Her heart positively sang. It was such a different story to his first year at school.

As a preschooler, Darcy had always made friends easily – at parks and playgrounds he happily chatted and played with other children. Yet when he started school, he struggled. The other boys were rough, loud and boisterous, where Darcy was reserved and thoughtful. He took his time to assess situations before jumping in, but that meant he was always a step behind.

'Who did you play with at lunchtime?' Olivia took to asking him when she picked him up from school.

'By myself,' he would say.

During the first term he often described being chased by a group of boys. His little brow furrowed and he looked at the ground, but when Olivia pushed him for more details he either couldn't or wouldn't give them. Olivia eventually told the teacher, who said she'd keep an eye on him in the playground. When he came home one day with a long red graze down his arm, she took photos of it to send to the school. 'A boy hit him with a wooden block,' she reported to the teacher, who was horrified and again said she would look out for him.

In the second term, the classroom seating arrangements changed. Darcy got on better with the boy he sat next to, and they sometimes hung out together at lunchtime. By term three, he still enjoyed the girls' company but they had begun to form cliques among themselves from which he was excluded. He was friendly with all of the kids, but had no close friends. He never teased or spoke cruelly to anyone, just accepted everyone and played with whoever was there at the time. The result, though, was that he simply flew under the radar and was overlooked again and again for play dates and birthday party invitations.

At first, Olivia brushed it aside. 'Not everyone can have a big party,' she explained to Darcy. 'Some people are only allowed to invite a few people.'

But another mum from school that she was friendly with would often complain, 'Oh, another bloody birthday party this weekend,' and Olivia would smile tightly and murmur in sympathy while Darcy went silent and his shoulders dropped. He would have given anything to have to go to a party.

Why could no one see how beautiful he was?

Then came the morning when she took Darcy to school and, as they stood waiting on the verandah with the other parents and children, one of the dads started handing out red envelopes with invitations to his daughter's birthday. The girls squealed and flashed their invites about. 'Shh! Just put them in your bags,' the dad said nervously. Olivia gave him a sympathetic smile, assuming that the party was just for the girls. But when he started giving invitations to the boys too, her heart fell to the floor. Darcy watched as boy after boy got an invitation. The man gave an envelope to Olivia's friend, for her son. 'I'm trying to keep it quiet,' he said. 'We only have room for twenty kids, so a couple need to miss out.' Olivia was mere inches away, but he avoided her gaze.

She stared straight ahead at her boy, with his huge eyes and his collapsing shoulders. She offered him a smile but he turned away and busied himself signing his name on the roll. There were twenty-two kids in the class, two had to miss out, and one of them was Darcy. He'd been rejected again.

When the classroom door opened, she got him settled at his desk, put his morning fruit snack in the bowl, his water bottle in the water crate and his homework bag on the pile on the spare desk, and kissed him goodbye. She barely made it through the classroom door before she burst into tears, feeling as though her own heart had been ripped in two.

When Katrina arrived at half-past five to pick up Eloise, she didn't look herself. She avoided Olivia's eye as she came through the front door, unwrapping the loose-knit purple scarf from around her neck. The tip of her nose was red, perhaps from the wind.

'Where's Russell?' asked Olivia, closing the door behind her.

'At the farm. A leaking water trough or something,' Katrina said, irritably.

'Ah, shame. And how are you?'

Katrina crossed her arms over her body and sniffed. 'All good, fine.' She still hadn't ventured past the coat rack.

Olivia put her hand on her friend's elbow. 'No, you're not,' she said gently. 'What's wrong?'

Katrina's drawn face suddenly twisted and she covered her eyes with her hands, taking a big gulp.

'Here, come into the kitchen. The kids are upstairs.'

'Oh God, sorry.' Katrina flapped her hands at her face.

'Don't be. Sit down, tell me what's happened.'

Katrina sat on one of the kitchen chairs and leant forward on her elbows, using both hands to wipe at the stream of tears falling from her eyes.

Olivia's mind raced with scenarios that might explain the loss of the tall, confident woman's usual demeanour. She lifted one of Katrina's long black dreadlocks and moved it behind her shoulder, revealing a Maori tattoo just below her ear.

'It's . . . I'm just . . . kind of homesick,' Katrina squeaked. She pulled the sleeves of her grey cardigan down over her hands and tucked them under her armpits, hugging herself tightly. 'My best friend, back home,' she clarified. 'We spoke on the phone before, and just hearing . . .'

'Her voice,' Olivia finished for her, nodding.

Katrina shook her head. '*His* voice. That's the problem,' she said, her tone hardening. 'No one understands.'

A double peal of laughter drifted down through the ceiling, and Katrina managed a small smile. Behind Olivia's back the oven whirred gently, browning shepherd's pie for dinner, warmth radiating through the small kitchen.

'Russell doesn't get it.' Katrina rolled her eyes in exasperation. 'He could never accept that Ian and I were just mates. We worked at the same hospital, both nurses, and just had a great, easy working relationship. We laughed so much.' Another tear slid down her face. 'I grew up with four brothers. I just get along with guys, I always have.'

'But Russell is jealous.'

Katrina nodded. 'It's a big part of why we moved here,' she said, her shoulders shaking as sobs burst up from her chest. 'I didn't really want to come, but Russell was so keen and I'm sure it was about getting me away from Ian, at least in part. I'm supportive of the project and I do like being able to reconnect with the English side of our family roots, but I do feel like I was pushed into it because if I fought too hard then it would have looked like I wanted to stay with Ian.'

'And you did?'

'Yes, but he's only my mate! My best friend just happens to be a man. On an average day, I spent more hours in Ian's company than Russell's.'

'That's so tricky.' Olivia got up to fetch a box of tissues from the sill. 'Is he married?'

Katrina nodded emphatically. 'Four kids. His wife is fine about us.'

Olivia wondered for a moment if that was true or if it was just what Ian had told her. But then, Olivia's own son was upstairs playing happily with a girl right now. Except that he was seven and didn't know anything about romance and attraction yet. His friendship with Eloise was pure and platonic and uncomplicated.

The oven timer went off and both women jumped at the harsh, intrusive buzz.

'I'm guessing you can't talk to Russell about how you're feeling.'

Katrina shook her head miserably, then her hand went to the greenstone carving on a leather strap around her neck, gripping it tightly as if for solace. 'Now Ian's cranky with me because I'm not talking to him as much as I used to,' she said, swallowing hard.

Olivia didn't like the sound of that. That didn't sound like a supportive friend; it sounded like a jealous lover. 'Maybe time will help,' she said, inadequately.

'Maybe,' Katrina echoed, but the word was barely audible.

'Come on, let's get some dinner. A good serve of hot shepherd's pie will do you wonders.'

Later that night, when Katrina and Eloise had left and Darcy was asleep, Helge called.

'Hi,' Olivia said, answering quickly so the ringtone wouldn't wake Darcy.

'Hi.' His voice held a smile in it.

'It was so good to have you here on the weekend,' she said, feeling suddenly sentimental.

'It *vas*.' He sounded amazed, as if he couldn't believe it had all happened.

'Did you mean what you said?' she asked in a rush. 'That you still love me?'

'Of course.'

She couldn't stop the smile that sprang to her lips, though she needed more. 'But . . . in what way? You know, *how* do you love me, exactly? Like a friend . . . or something else?'

Helge paused, and she heard him inhale. 'I don't know if I can choose the words, exactly. In Norwegian, there are many *vays* to express love.'

All right, this wasn't exactly what she'd hoped for, but she couldn't blame the guy for having translation issues. And she felt bad that she hadn't tried to learn more Norwegian herself. Waiting patiently, she could almost hear him going through words in his mind, and she felt a sudden regret at her own neediness. 'It's okay,' she said, with forced cheer. 'I didn't mean to put pressure on you. I was just wondering. Everything was so intense and—'

'I love you,' he butted in. 'And I *vould* like to come back soon. I *vould* like to take you on a date.'

She smiled with relief. 'That sounds great.'

14

Clarence would always remember that this Thursday in September was the day he knew for sure the Renaissance Project was in trouble. Darkness had already fallen, and the blackness of the river could barely be distinguished from that of the banks on either side. The streets were quiet, doors and windows closed against the cold, lights on inside while hot dinners were eaten and bedtime stories were read. Clarence met the shaking man on the narrow footpath in front of his store. He put his hand on Raj's trembling shoulder, both of them facing the glass frontage of the toy shop.

Inside the window, Raj had placed a stunning display of circus figurines beneath a red-and-white-striped tent with real fairy lights draped down its sides, illuminating the detail of each character – the ringmaster, the strong woman, the trapeze artist and her flying partner, the plate spinner, the dog trainer. It should have been delightful, a fantasy scene glowing brightly in the night. But sprayed across the window in ugly black paint were the words *Go home curry.*

'Raj, I'm so sorry,' Clarence mumbled. He couldn't think of anything more to say over the angry beating of his pulse in his ears. This was not the Stoneden he knew. Who would have done this?

'I was born in Manchester,' Raj said through gritted teeth, his fists at his sides. 'I lived there my whole life until coming here. I'm a British citizen.'

'It's not you. It's nothing to do with you, you understand?' Clarence said. 'You belong here. This town is in your blood.'

'I can't even work out how this happened. I'd only just shut the shop and left. They must have been waiting and . . . watching.' Raj's hand covered his mouth.

Clarence considered this. It was only luck that he'd strolled past now, on his way to the hotel for a quick pint. Whoever had done this was likely hoping the full impact would be felt in the morning, in broad daylight, witnessed by as many as possible.

'Have you called Sally?'

Raj took in a sharp breath, the idea of telling his wife obviously painful. He shook his head.

'Right. I want you to go home now.' Clarence took his hand off the man's shoulder.

'What?' Raj turned to face him, the lights from the shop window reflected in his glistening eyes.

'I will clean this up before anyone sees it. You go home to your wife and your lovely children and try to think no more of it.'

Raj opened his mouth to speak but the shock still held him immobile.

'I mean it now. On your way.' Clarence took the younger man by the shoulders and steered him away from the shops, already mentally running through a list of the tools he'd need to clean this up. 'I'll call you when it's done.'

Raj paused, turning for one last look at the racist slur on his shop and person. Then he sucked in his lips, his nostrils flaring as emotion threatened to spill over, nodded quickly and turned away towards home, his head lowered. Clarence watched his retreating back for a few moments, his gut twisting as Raj's shoulders sagged, leaning into the wind as he hurried home to Sally.

'Jesus,' he said into the night air. 'This is awful.'

•

Madeline McCarthy scrubbed at her nails over the kitchen sink. Even after several attempts, the black paint was wedged so deep into the quicks that she couldn't reach it. She sighed and snapped off the tap in frustration. Maybe she needed to soak in a bath. She hadn't done that in years. These days an orange stain drizzled from the tap fitting, but it was a good, deep bath, one she could practically float in.

She shivered, remembering what the one man she'd thought might change her life had once suggested to her about the usefulness of that bath as an easy way to release herself from the burden of caring for her brother.

Deep enough to drown in . . . if you fell asleep, he'd said, glancing across to Burton, who'd been sitting right over there on the couch, his hair sticking up, a napkin tucked into his shirt as he ate his dinner while watching Davy Jones singing on a stage with girls screaming below. The border collie was curled on the floor at Burton's feet, waiting for any spilt food. The man's words, said low and conspiratorially in her ear, had sent a bolt of fear down her spine.

Of course, his supposed concern had nothing to do with wanting to improve her welfare; it was about getting his hands on full ownership of the farm, which her father had left to her and Burton equally, and ridding himself of any ongoing responsibility for her brother.

What an awful man. She'd wanted to order him out in a flash, even opened her mouth to do so before realising that anyone who could suggest such a thing couldn't be trusted. Instead, she'd pretended to shrug it off and kissed him goodnight, then closed the door firmly and turned to Burton, who looked up at her quietly.

'Don't pay any attention to him,' she said. 'I'll be here for you, always.'

After that, she'd quite suddenly come down with a terribly contagious illness that meant she could see no one for at least three months. Oh, yes, it was a shame, she'd agreed, but he shouldn't wait for her, a young, good-looking man like him. He'd put up a show of concern, but lost interest quickly, as she knew he would, and last she'd heard of him he'd found someone else and they'd left the village for London. Sometimes she wondered what had become of that woman.

She'd realised that no man would ever take on her *and* Burton, and from then on she'd never let herself imagine a different life, not for one second. If times had been different, if they'd been what they are now, perhaps her life would have been easier, with some sort of funded assistance, giving her more freedom, more choices. But it wasn't to be. She didn't blame her brother. She'd promised him she'd never make him leave his home, a promise she'd kept right up till last year, when a combination of several falls, respiratory illnesses and increased confusion had become too much for her physically to deal with. She was ageing too, and it would do neither of them any good, Doc Eli had counselled, to have Burton fall on her and break her hip. It broke her heart to put him into the home, but Eli was right. After they'd both come to terms with it, he'd given her the most precious gift.

'Sell the house,' he'd said, his voice breathy and muffled through the oxygen mask.

She'd opened her mouth to protest, but he'd held up his mottled hand to silence her. So she'd nodded once, and covered his hand with hers, lowering it to his chest, and sat with him till the pain medication kicked in and he fell asleep.

And now the Renaissance Project and these imports had ruined her final chance for financial and personal freedom.

She scrubbed harder. She couldn't very well go into town with black-ringed fingernails. People round here always noticed anything different. Like her brother. In fairness, they'd been kind enough to him, for the most part, after his accident. And the older she and Burton had got, the more they just blended in to the heritage surrounds. Over a certain age and a certain number of grey hairs, everyone became at least a little invisible. But black paint would raise an eyebrow or two, start a whisper, and the last thing she wanted was anyone coming around just to 'check in on her' – especially if that person was Clarence James.

She went to the bathroom and turned on the tap for the bath. The ancient plug was stuck to the corner of the tub, and she had to lever it off before inserting it in the plughole. She poured a heap of shampoo in for some bubbles, then went back out to the kitchen. The tiny tabby with a white chest and white paws was meowing on the windowsill outside, only just visible in the darkness, the kitchen light catching her face.

'Hello there,' Madeline said, surprised to see the cat so close to the house. The little feline had been so wary up till now, hiding behind machinery in the shed when Madeline brought saucers of milk, then scooting out quickly to lap it up, looking around furtively while Madeline watched from the doorway. True, she'd become a little more trusting when Madeline started bringing her proper food – chicken scraps, boiled eggs and steak offcuts. The last time she was in town, Madeline had even found herself tossing tins of sardines into her shopping basket. There was something different about this little cat. She stood out from the many others who'd sheltered on the property. She was so small yet so determined.

Madeline opened the front door and poked her head out. A brisk evening wind rushed at her, making her pull her cardigan tighter. The cat watched her from the sill, her thin fur flattened against the breeze.

'I'll just leave the door open,' Madeline said, and retreated back inside.

She went to check on the water level in the bath. It still had a way to go, so she crept back into the lounge and peeked around the corner, yellowed wallpaper curling down like ribbons near her face. There was the cat, sitting on the mat just inside the door.

•

The next morning, Grayson arrived at Rambling Rose not long after Olivia had turned up to start the day's baking. He wore jeans and a khaki puffer jacket over a watermelon-pink wool jumper and carried a crate from which he unloaded his products. The butter was wrapped in waxed brown paper printed with a circular black and white logo with the words *Seven Cows* above a simple sketch of a cow standing in long grass with buttercups hanging out of her smiling mouth. The milk came in glass bottles, with screw-top metal lids, also with a matching brown-paper label, and the cheddar and cottage cheese were similarly adorned.

'These are gorgeous,' Olivia said, picking up each one. 'Who did the logo?'

Grayson smiled proudly. 'I did.'

'You're an artist too?'

'I wouldn't say that. But I didn't have a lot of money when I got here so I just did the best I could. I started with seven cows, hence the name. One of them, Ruby, is a bit of a character and would frolic around in the buttercups. I took a photo of her one day and then traced the outline and embellished it. It's pretty basic.'

'Don't undersell yourself. It's fabulous.' Olivia paused, admiring his work. 'I wanted to be an artist when I was at school. I was really into painting, mostly, but I loved clay work too.'

'What happened?'

She fiddled with the hook of her overalls. 'Ma convinced me there was no money in being an artist, which is fair enough, because generally that's true. But she still wanted me to be able to use my talents in my work, and she could see I loved baking, so she suggested I pursue cake making, but do it properly, with a pastry chef's apprenticeship.' She shrugged. 'She said I could always do my own art outside of that, but that every woman needs a career she can rely on. Her husband died early in their marriage and she had a baby and needed to work so she knew firsthand how tough it could be.'

'Sounds reasonable. Did you keep going with your art on the side?'

'No,' Olivia said sadly. 'I never seemed to have the space or time. She was right, though, I do get to use a lot of that creativity in my job. Moulding figurines out of fondant is not dissimilar to using clay.' In her time, she'd made yellow baby giraffes for christening cakes, entire farmyards of animals for kindergarten break-ups, Winnie the Pooh with his red vest, orange and black Tigger and old grey Eeyore, Alice in Wonderland in her blue and white dress, silver spaceships, pink-tutued ballerinas, glittery unicorns, pointy-nosed foxes and yellow Pokémon Pikachu, Peter Rabbit with his waistcoat, and several risqué pieces for hens' parties, to name a few.

There were also the characters from *Frozen*.

'It's not too late,' Grayson said encouragingly, perhaps noticing the sudden shift in her mood.

'True.' She made herself smile again. The *Frozen* incident was behind them now – she needed to put it out of her mind. 'You've inspired me. Once I'm on my feet here, I'll look into it. See if there's anything left inside me.'

'Good.' Grayson checked his watch. 'Ah, I've got to go, sorry. I have to get back to the farm. It's cheesemaking day, and I like to leave myself a lot of time because it doesn't always go to plan.' He pulled a face then laughed.

'I know how that works,' she said. 'Have fun. I'll see you tomorrow.'

He'd been gone a good five minutes before she realised she was still smiling, humming along to the music in the shop.

The smile snapped off her face a moment later, though, when she noticed a scattering of dirt in the corner the storeroom, which on closer inspection looked suspiciously like rat droppings. She tore off a piece of paper towel to pick them up, screwing up her nose in disgust. They appeared to be fresh – certainly they hadn't been there yesterday. The rat trap remained empty. She tossed the paper towel into the bin and scrubbed the floor, horrified at the possibility of an impromptu health inspection right at this moment. Then she checked her food stores. All the containers were perfectly sealed and there was no sign of chewing or crumbs. She very much hoped that meant the rat had since given up and gone on its way, though she'd be making regular checks throughout the day to make sure.

Fifteen minutes before opening time, Frank Sinatra's 'Love and Marriage' began to play. The song reminded Olivia of the most exciting thing she wanted to do that day – planning the cake for the wine and cheese event tomorrow. With the lemon cakes cooling on a rack and the scones baking, she pulled out her notebook and started to sketch.

She decided that the cake would have three round tiers, four, six and eight inches wide, of a moist vanilla sponge covered with fondant icing. Real pink roses would sit on top and greenery would trail down one side. She wanted to capture the feel of Rambling Rose as well as the village itself, with so many of its stone cottages adorned with climbing ivy. Maybe she could create a separate slab of chocolate art, too, mixing different shades of food colouring into white chocolate and using paintbrushes to create a village scene. Her conversation with Grayson had inspired her. She began to sketch out the scene: cottages beside the river with its ubiquitous swans.

When Olivia was nineteen and in the early stages of her apprenticeship, she'd entered a cake in the local show in the category 'Cottage Garden'. She'd iced a round sponge and then hand-painted it with coloured icing, replicating Monet's famous *Water Lilies* painting. She'd reproduced the swirling colours of the water and the lily pads floating on top. It had taken her two days to complete and Ma thought it was an amazing work of art, strikingly close to the original painting.

But it had placed last in show. Every other cake entered in the competition was covered with handcrafted icing flowers and leaves, super-traditional stuff. Hers had stood out all right, but clearly the judges hated it. Olivia was crushed.

Ma found her at home in the kitchen staring sadly at the cake on the bench. Olivia told her what had happened and Ma shook her head and grunted disapprovingly. Then she sighed. 'Unfortunately, people aren't always ready to see progressiveness when it appears before them,' she said. 'One day they'll catch up but, for now, you'll have to accept that you were ahead of your time.'

Olivia was struck dumb – it was unlike Ma to offer up her philosophy on life. Then Ma opened a drawer and took out the cake knife. 'More fool them. Let's enjoy this all to ourselves, every last crumb.'

The door opened and three white-haired tourists entered, the man in the lead booming, 'Mornin'!'

Olivia greeted them warmly, inviting them in out of the drizzle. On the street outside, a stream of people in colourful windcheaters and scarves were disembarking from a tall white bus with tinted windows. Seeing that she was about to be inundated with customers, she quickly tucked her notebook away.

One of the tourists announced that they were visiting from California and they were simply charmed to be in such a pretty town and they were famished and could she please bring them the menu and a pot of coffee and to keep it coming.

'No worries,' she said, directing them to the green table against the wall.

She continued like this all morning, barely keeping up with the influx of customers, who filled her small shop with their happy chatter and their damp coats slung over the backs of the chairs, and their locust-like ability to empty her cabinet and cake stands of food. Eventually, the bus outside tooted its horn to summon its passengers back. In the midst of the ensuing hubbub, Ryan Baker entered the shop.

Olivia eyed the journalist a little warily, wondering why he was there. Her good mood from the morning's solid trade ebbed away as she remembered his last, rat-inspired visit.

He nodded to her and waited till she'd finished tallying bills and accepting payments and the last of the tourists had shuffled out the door. Then he stepped up to the counter and fixed her with his gaze. 'There was an incident last night at Raj's store.'

Olivia frowned, resting her hands on the hips of her full skirt, perfect for twirling to jive music. 'What do you mean?'

'There was a graffiti attack on his shopfront.'

She drew in a sharp, shocked breath through her teeth. 'That's terrible. Poor Raj.' She thought for a moment. 'I didn't see it when I walked past this morning.'

'Clarence cleaned it up last night.'

'Any idea who did it?'

Ryan shook his head slowly. There was something about his watchful gaze that made her want to squirm away, as if he suspected that *she* was involved somehow and planned to trap her here until she confessed. 'Not at this stage. That's why I'm popping around to see everyone.'

'Would you call it sabotage?'

He shrugged. 'I still think that's a big leap.'

'Have the police been called?'

'No. Clarence wanted to keep it quiet. He removed the paint before any evidence could be taken.'

'Then . . . how did you find out?'

'I have my sources.'

She almost rolled her eyes at that. 'Why would they want to keep it quiet?'

'He thinks it will bring negative attention to the project.'

'You're on the committee, aren't you? Do you feel the same way?'

He hesitated. 'I'm still undecided. Yes, I – Ryan Baker, citizen of Stoneden – am obviously in favour of the project, but I'm also a journalist. My role is to be a neutral observer, simply reporting the facts. That's part of what's wrong with the media now – journalists are part of huge publicity machines, employed by mega corporations that have agendas the journalists are hired to push.'

'Right.' She was even more confused by Ryan now. 'Unfortunately, I don't know anything that would help. But I'm glad you stopped by to tell me. I'd hate to think of Raj going through this alone. Was it very awful, the graffiti?'

'Sadly, yes. It told him to leave, and included a racial slur.'

Olivia's mouth fell open.

'Look, I'll be on my way, but I also wanted to ask if I could write a feature story on you and Rambling Rose. Juliet mentioned that you're making a cake for the wine and cheese night next Friday. I thought that would be a timely angle for the paper.'

'Oh, sure,' Olivia said automatically. 'I'll be baking in the afternoon so it's nice and fresh.'

'I'll have to come in the morning in order to get my story submitted in time for Monday's delivery. Is that okay?'

'Absolutely.'

'I'll bring my photographer and we'll see you then.'

She breathed a sigh of relief as the door closed behind him, happy to be getting some good publicity from Ryan, then scanned her eyes across the counter to see what she had left to take to Raj and his family. It wasn't much, but she wanted to show some solidarity.

15

Clarence lay in the creaky iron-framed bed and watched the rain sluice down the window, which overlooked the rose garden, still frothing with pink roses. It was quite a downpour. A fair few of Marina's best blooms would be lost. Not that she cared right now, tucked up against him, her luxuriant curls tickling his cheek – oh, how he loved an older woman with long hair – her arm draped across his chest, her fingers absently stroking his chest hair, now white and thin, just like his pasty legs. She was soft against him, her flesh looser than it had been once but still lovely.

He'd planned on being home by now. Stuart would be wanting to go out for a wee and a walk, set on continuing his turf war with the neighbour's ginger cat, Rufus. Currently, Stuart was on top – he'd clawed back some ground with a few robust chasings through the bushes – but Clarence knew it wouldn't stay that way. The cat would reach his tolerance threshold soon enough and give Stuart a good walloping, the dog would scurry away yelping with his tail between his legs, and for the next week he'd shake in terror every time he saw Rufus, before he started to regain his confidence and it all began again.

These days, Clarence kept an indoor loo for the old boy, so he wasn't too worried about him. Besides, it was an hour's drive home, which he'd rather not do in this weather. And aside from all of that, he'd been enjoying his escape here with Marina today.

Ryan was writing an article on the graffiti, though Clarence had no idea how he knew about it. That was suspicious in itself. The article was sure to start an online war about the project when it came out next week.

Clarence's fingers stilled on Marina's skin. Was it possible that Pepperworth himself had orchestrated the rat and the graffiti? He wouldn't put it past him. The man would take any opportunity to stick it to Clarence.

'I can hear you thinking,' Marina said sleepily, then turned her head slightly and kissed his nipple.

He snorted in surprise and felt an instantaneous flicker down below the sheet.

'Do you want to stay for dinner?' she asked in her cut-glass accent. When they'd first met, early in the Thatcher era, she was a well-known politician. These days, no one batted an eyelid at her. But back then, when she was in the public eye, it was a different story. He'd been a fool to think he could keep their dalliance a secret; inevitably Bethan had been told.

He'd been a stupid man. His betrayal had put a wedge between him and his daughter, Anne; the only thing that had brought them a little closer was when she'd had Mikey. Now Anne was a grandmother herself, making him a great-grandfather, and he had no idea where the time had gone, fearing it was all too late now to ever repair the split between them. He should have walked away after the first time Bethan found out, when the guilt was savage.

They might have had a chance then. But he hadn't, and he'd ruined everything.

But then, he and Marina still had this – their arrangement – which suited them perfectly well and had done for nearly thirty years. Not for the first time, he wondered if he should have married Marina after his divorce from Bethan. Instead, he'd ended it with Marina, only to go on and marry Jean, before realising that it was in fact truly Marina he'd wanted all along. But she'd never wanted to marry, more than happy to be a free spirit, untethered by laws and domesticity. And he was a council man, someone who needed a steady home life to present to the world. It was all a facade, though. Marina was the one he loved more than any other. And there had been others. More than he'd like to count.

He'd always found it easy to get on with women, and as a young man he'd had plenty of fun along the way, living his life at every chance. For the most part he hadn't felt he needed to apologise for his actions. But there were one or two incidents he regretted . . . like Ellie. Until recently, she'd not have even crossed his mind. Now, though, remembering her made him feel uneasy. Their time together had been brief, yet the aftermath was life-changing. He pushed the memories aside. He couldn't be held responsible for the accident.

What he should really be atoning for was that he hadn't just ruined one marriage with his affair with Marina, but two. Whereas Bethan had bounced back from their split, finding it in her generous nature to forgive him and move forward together as parents of their children and grandchildren, Jean had been ruthless in her response. She'd thrown him out of the house. She'd used her family's money to hire the best legal team she could get and took him for everything he had. She told anyone and everyone she could about what a despicable man he was. Possibly the only good thing to come out of their separation was that they hadn't had children, so they never had to speak again.

Now she was married to that pompous, balding mole, Chester.

Marina sighed. 'Stop thinking about Pepperworth.'

'How do you do that?'

'Your jaw juts in a very specific way when you think of him. It nearly extends past your nose tip.' She mimicked his expression, and Clarence laughed. He kissed the top of her head and rolled towards her, the previous flicker under the sheet a firm high beam now.

'I love that you never take me seriously,' he said.

'I love that you never wear pants in my house.'

•

As soon as she'd closed the shop for the day, Olivia headed down to the surgery to visit Katrina. She brought a box of leftover apple turnovers, known in French as *chaussons aux pommes*, or 'apple slippers'. Olivia was partial to anything with apple in it, and she loved dipping her spoon into the cinnamon-spiced apple sauce while she was filling the pastry rounds, loved the way they magically puffed up and turned golden in the oven, loved watching how the dusting of icing sugar highlighted each ridge of the pattern she'd carefully scored into the pastry.

As she sidled through the surgery door, protecting her box of goodies, Katrina squealed at her from behind the counter. 'Have you heard?' She held her hands up and out to the side in excitement. Her dreads were twisted in a knot at the nape of her neck and a couple had come free, giving her a slightly mad look.

'Heard what?' Olivia placed the box carefully on the counter.

The waiting room held a few chairs and many aged framed pictures of thoroughbred horses and hunting dogs. It was slightly musty-smelling, the carpet a little threadbare.

'It's all over Facebook.' Katrina pulled out her phone and stabbed in her passcode, then swiped rapidly to find what she wanted. 'Look!' She held it out for Olivia to read.

There was no one else in the waiting room, so she stood beside Katrina and looked at the screen. A news alert read: *Ying Yue and Oden Eddie to Wed in the Cotswolds at Christmas.*

'Oh, wow,' Olivia breathed. 'That's a bit exciting!'

'I know it's not a royal wedding or anything, but it's still a bloody big celebrity wedding, isn't it?'

'It is!'

This was a major coup for the Cotswolds. Ying and Oden – or Yoden, as the tabloids had christened them – were front-page news in at least one newspaper or magazine each week. Katrina flicked through photos of the couple on red carpets around the world, she with her glossy, waist-length black hair, plunging Stella McCartney necklines and diamond-encrusted sky-high heels, and he with his perfect suits and impossibly chiselled jawline with varyingly styled facial hair. The pair of them in swimmers, frolicking in the waters of Barbados. Ying in a black Gucci suit, giving a speech about human rights violations. Oden in a film role, wearing medieval dress and astride a horse, holding an arrow poised in its bow. The couple out in New York, gazing adoringly at each other over coffee, with their fluffy dogs at their feet. They'd have been easy to hate if they weren't so passionate about saving the planet, speaking at United Nations conferences and visiting orphanages around the world.

'Wow,' Olivia said. 'I wonder where they'll hold the wedding.'

'People are placing bets already,' Katrina said, raising her eyebrows as she continued to scroll. 'Like, actual bets.'

'Do people really do that?' Olivia asked, incredulous.

'Apparently.' Her friend continued to search for more info. 'Here, the top pick at the moment is Upper Slaughter.'

'That sounds appealing,' Olivia said, dryly. 'Imagine having that on your marriage certificate.'

'A bit off, I agree. But it's widely considered one of the prettiest places around. Look.' They gazed at photos of a honey-toned manor house, Eyford, with its immaculately maintained lawn and gardens, and shots of the picturesque River Eye, which divided the villages of Upper and Lower Slaughter.

'Oh, look!' Olivia said, her shoulder bumping Katrina's as they peered at the small screen. 'There's a converted church that's now a holiday cottage. As soon as the date's announced we should book it so we can stay up there and catch a glimpse of the wedding!'

'That's a great idea,' Katrina said with a broad smile. Olivia was pleased to see that her homesickness seemed to have lifted. 'We can take the kids for an adventure.'

'Sounds perfect! Though I'm sure everyone else will have the same idea. People will be camping along the river just to catch a glimpse of them.'

They discussed the wedding for a few more minutes before Olivia asked, 'Are you feeling any better about Ian?'

Katrina's face fell. 'Yeah, I guess,' she said, flatly.

'Have you talked to Russell about it at all?'

She scoffed. 'God, no.'

'Well, you know my door is always open if you need to escape and chat, or have a cry, or just drink a lot.'

Katrina chuckled. 'Thanks. I might take you up on that.'

'I hope you do,' Olivia said, firmly. 'I know I'm not a replacement for your bestie but I'm sure I could patch a few holes here and there.'

Katrina threw her arms around her. 'You do a lot more than that.'

•

Madeline was walking down the hallway of Pine Forest Care Home on Saturday morning when she saw Blessing come out of Burton's room. The Nigerian woman was a qualified physiotherapist at home, but she was still awaiting registration in England; in the meantime she was working as a carer, for which Madeline felt guiltily grateful.

'Good morning, Blessing. How is he today?' she asked.

'He is irritable today,' Blessing said, shaking her head. She had so much hair piled high in a bun that Madeline always wondered if it strained her neck to carry it. 'Not enjoying the soft foods so much.'

'No, I can imagine. He was always a steak man.'

'But he cannot breathe enough to chew at the same time so is safer this way.'

'Yes, of course. Thank you, Blessing. I know you must be keen to move on from here, but you really have been a gift to us.'

Blessing beamed a toothy smile at her and placed her hand gently on Madeline's arm. 'This stage is very difficult,' she said.

'Yes, thank you.'

Blessing patted her arm and strode off, and Madeline stepped into Burton's room. He was propped up in a chair, a plastic sip cup with something that looked like apple juice next to him on the trolley table, and the racing paper open in front of him, held in his good hand. He looked up at her dully, then dropped his eyes back to the pages. He hadn't bet in years, but he still looked at the tables of wins and losses and track conditions and weather forecasts most days. He just liked following the horses.

'How are you, Burt?' she asked.

He wheezed and pointed a crooked finger at the list of names on the page.

'Oh, yes. Kingston's Dust, you think?' She didn't care for racing, never had. Before the accident, Burton had enjoyed listening to the races on the wireless while he worked in the shed, tinkering with the tractor. But he'd seldom laid out money. They'd rarely had enough money to risk losing it, and he'd been a sensible young man, right up until his reckless mistake, which had changed both their lives forever.

She still missed him, that older brother. The capable young man who'd helped her to lift the milk churns and dealt with the most difficult cows and never once made Madeline feel useless or less than him. In return, she'd tried to protect him from their father's mercurial moods, which she could see coming like clouds rolling in from the horizon, but which Burton was somehow oblivious to right up until a massive crack of thunder sounded over the house. Brother and sister looked out for each other, especially after their mother died and their father's moods darkened and became more protracted. And whenever they could escape, they went to the village dances, the two of them and Madeline's best friend, Nora Kent.

Madeline and Nora had been friends since their first day of primary school, when they'd been assigned to share a desk. Maddie had been tugging at the too-tight collar of her new dress and Nora had been trying to slip her feet from her too-tight shoes, and they'd distracted themselves by chatting to each other instead. Burton was three years older and paid no particular attention to Nora until the girls were in fifth form. He'd left school much earlier and worked on the farm. Now, whenever Nora came home with her after school, Maddie noticed that he'd started watching Nora from across the room, a look of wonder on his face. If he did have to speak to her, he looked away, his cheeks flushing.

By the summer of 1966, the girls were nineteen, Burton twenty-two. Now, his shoulders broad, his hair brushed down carefully, the smell of specially purchased Old Spice in the air, he took it upon himself to accompany them to the church dances. Officially he was there to chaperone his sister, but it was clear to Maddie that he wanted to get closer to Nora. When they danced, he held her as if she were a precious flower, and her smile lit up the room. He'd bought himself a camera and he took a photo of her outside the McCarthys' house one evening, leaning against the stone wall in her new short, sleeveless navy blue dress. A month later, after he'd had the film developed, he gave a copy to her as a gift. The attention he paid Nora no longer caused Maddie to lie awake at night dreaming of the day when Nora and Burt were married, so excited that her best friend would become her sister-in-law and the three of them would be together forever.

Madeline's reverie was broken by Burton's coughing fit. She passed him a handful of tissues as he gagged and wheezed, his eyes streaming, and waited for it to pass; it was all she could do. First there was the accident, leaving his brain unable to recover, now lung cancer. Her brother had never caught a break in his life. Now with Olivia here in the village, all those memories felt close once more, and she wished she'd reached out to her old friend, no matter how difficult it might have been.

16

Less than a week since Clarence's shoes had padded softly on the footpath as he headed down the hill in the dark to Raj's shop, here he was again, on his way to another incident. What the hell was going on in this village? His breath misted the air and the hairs on the back of his neck prickled like antennae. Beneath his jacket, his heart banged in his chest, not from fear but anger.

The village was quiet in these early hours of Tuesday morning, a time quite aptly referred to as the dead of night because so many people did in fact die during these hours. It was when people were at their weakest.

He shivered, clutching the screwdriver more tightly. He carried no torch, not wanting to attract attention. If he hadn't lived here for seventy years, if he hadn't walked these streets every day of his life, he might have worried about landing a foot incorrectly, about straying off the path and tumbling onto the road, something that could be hazardous for someone of his age. But this village was written into his every cell. It was why he had to protect it. He was part of it and it was part of him.

He hesitated, approaching the bakery. The door was ajar just as Leanne had said it was, her words sharp and breathy with shock. The policeman was on his way but he was coming for Fahren Way so Clarence had said he'd go now, rebuffing Leanne's protests.

'Not on my watch,' he'd said, reaching for his boots. The baker had run straight home again after finding the shop as it was. 'Stay where you are. I'll deal with it and let you know.'

Now, standing on the footpath, his eyes darting about, hunting for a perpetrator, the roots of his hair practically rattling in his scalp, he almost wished someone would appear, just so he could thump them.

Tentatively, he pushed open the black front door, and listened. There was nothing bar his own pulse in his ears. He pulled his mobile phone from his pocket and flicked on the torch, shining the beam into the store, sweeping over the black and white tiles and across the bread racks, before settling on the black wooden facade of the service bench.

His heart sank. There in white paint were the words *Go home imports.*

Hunched in a chair, Howard yawned and tugged at his ear, his other hand wrapped around a mug of black tea. Clarence felt a twinge of guilt for summoning his friend out of bed so early, especially with news of another incident relating to the Renaissance Project. Perhaps he should have left Howard to his sleep. But this was the way it had always been – Clarence and Howard, like Batman and Robin. Visionary, smooth-tongued Clarence, with quiet, knobbly-kneed Howard on hand to plug the gaps in his friend's grand plans.

Clarence shifted against the dove-grey linen cushions piled behind his back on the sofa. They were yet another gift from Fallon.

She'd always been like that – heavy-handed with the gifts. Over the years he'd felt embarrassed that she'd been spending money on him, but these days he wondered if she was trying to make up for the distance between him and Adrian.

'So she didn't see anyone?' Howard asked.

'No. She arrived at the bakery at three o'clock as always and the door was ajar.'

'Is it possible that she just didn't lock it properly?' As Howard frowned, the longer hairs that sprouted randomly from his bushy eyebrows bowed down in front of his eyes, as if they too were half asleep.

'It had been jemmied open. Randolph Wilson said it looked like the person had used a screwdriver. Besides, the graffiti is more the concern. Clearly an attack on our project and, I think, it now confirms what we were afraid of.'

'That we have a saboteur.'

'Yes.' Clarence yawned then too, as the adrenaline of being woken in the wee hours began to recede. He leant forward on the sofa, his hand dropping automatically to rub Stuart's head. The dog was gazing at him as though concerned, and thumped his tail in appreciation. 'Leanne's soldiered on, going back to bake and open at six as usual. Still, she's understandably rattled.'

'Shame,' Howard said, shaking his head.

His friend ran this thumb rhythmically in the webbing between his thumb and the first finger of his other hand, a tick Clarence knew meant his friend was anxious. 'Howard, you're not losing your water on me, are you?' he asked.

Howard met his eyes for a moment then looked up at the exposed timber beam in the ceiling and grunted.

'*Are* you?' Clarence's hand stilled on the dog's head. A fist had reached into his chest and squeezed his heart. This had been their dream – the two of them had built this whole project from the ground up, the boys who grew up here and knew how productive this village could be again, if it was only given the chance.

Howard's eyes dropped back to meet Clarence's. 'We expected people to be upset, I know that. But you ignored my concerns. You said once the imports were here, it would die down. It hasn't.'

Clarence couldn't speak. Howard was right, and he'd voiced Clarence's own worst fear, bringing it firmly to light: the conflict hadn't died down. The resisters' unrest had moved on from vocal taunts and sneering to concrete acts of mutiny. Howard *had* tried to warn him, that was true, but Clarence had forged on, believing that all the 'fuss' would just go away, believing it simply because he wanted to.

But what if it didn't go away? It seemed more likely now that the rat, the racial slur at Raj's shop, and now this break-in were all related.

It didn't help in the slightest that Ryan's story had gone out in yesterday's paper, starting fierce arguments in the comments section of the online version, mostly from anonymous commentators, many of whom felt comfortable enough to chime in, giving their voice to controversy. The story had caused enough of a storm that it had been picked up by *The Sun* online later in the day, spreading the debate across the whole country, where it had truly deteriorated into nasty comments, with accusations of the UK being overrun with 'curries and Muslims'. Some spoke in their defence, championing the values of humanitarianism and compassion, reminding people that the UK was a wealthy country with plenty for all, but this only ignited more vitriol. It had made Clarence physically sick, and Raj and Sally had even kept their kids home from school for the day, hoping to shelter them from any potential negativity.

Chester Pepperworth was clearly delighted, messaging Clarence to crow about the inevitable failure of the Renaissance Project.

More and more, Stoneden appeared to be a village divided, and people on both sides were fearful and angry. Tensions over land, jobs, opportunity, money and even race: these were the sorts of things that led to civil wars. Howard's words had just forced him to swallow his stupid delusions, and they burnt all the way down.

Hoping to offer more support to Leanne, Clarence ventured back down the hill to the bakery just after eight-thirty, when the school rush, such as it was, would have ebbed. But he encountered more people on the narrow footpath than he would have liked. He wove through the unexpectedly dense foot traffic, dodging flapping coats, umbrellas, dogs on leads, prams, and gloved hands on his elbow trying to force him to stop.

'Such terrible news!'

'Will the project survive?'

'Do you think they'll return?'

'Stoneden was always such a safe place. Now look what's happened!'

Time and again he smiled and nodded his head in greeting, or offered reassurance that everything was perfectly fine, it was all taken care of, and this was just a hiccup.

He was relieved to tumble into Leanne's bakery and close the damaged wooden door against the faces he felt were pursuing him. *Go home imports* was still there, a horrible insult to the hard-working woman behind the counter. In one corner of the shop sat Mrs Wilson, her heavy brocade coat tightly buttoned up and a silk scarf over her hair, eating a warm cinnamon bun. On one level he was pleased to see her here – a staunch resister if ever there was one – but her grimly set mouth and derisive sniff in response to his raised hand did little to soothe his jangled nerves. She picked up the remains of her bun and her basket of breadsticks, cast a concerned frown at the graffiti, and stepped out the door, letting it fall heavily closed behind her.

Leanne stood at the counter. Her bread baskets, usually full of fresh goods, were leaner today as she'd obviously not had as much time to bake. Her usually tight bun of hair – twisted like one of her fancy iced scrolls – was dishevelled, wisps sticking out in all directions. Against her white baker's shirt, buttoned to the neck, her pale skin had a tinge of grey. She looked as though she'd aged years in just five hours.

He stepped towards her. 'How are you feeling?'

'I've had better days,' she said, resting her hands on her hips in a resigned, fatigued sort of way. 'Keith had to see to a few horses this morning before the weather turns nasty but then he'll be down to help me clean off . . . that.' She gestured over the countertop to where the painted words sat, ugly and reproachful.

'Have you been very busy this morning?' he asked, wondering what sort of reaction she'd received from her customers.

'Aye. Lots of stickybeaks. But lots of good customers too. A lot of support.'

'I'm glad to hear it.'

'Keeping busy has been good, but as soon as a lull sets in, my mind starts racing. I keep looking over my shoulder and around corners,' she confessed. Her eyes brightened alarmingly, and she bit down on her trembling lower lip.

'I'm so sorry,' Clarence said. It was completely inadequate, but it needed to be said.

Leanne stared vacantly at the doorway, clearly still in shock.

'Please bring Keith and the kids down to the hotel tonight. I want to shout you all dinner by the fire. We can have a laugh and it might help you all relax a bit before you go to bed tonight.'

'You don't need to do that,' she said, frowning.

'I want to. Bring the family down at six? We'll get your spirits up again.'

She nodded, swallowing hard. 'All right then, thank you.'

He turned to leave, but she stopped him.

'Thank you, again, for taking my call this morning.'

Her gratitude warmed him. 'Of course – please call on me anytime. It's what community is all about.'

'You're a good man, Clarence.'

He lifted his chin, accepting her praise. 'I can meet you here at three o'clock tomorrow morning, happily. I want you to feel safe. This is your home now. I can bring Stuart to be our watchdog.'

She smiled briefly. 'Ah, get away. I . . . I should be fine.' But the hitch in her voice suggested otherwise.

'Well, we'll chat tonight. See you at six.'

He left the shop and forged back up the hill, full of motivation to fix this problem and, indeed, anything that wasn't right in his life, starting with the fact that he had a five-month-old great-granddaughter he'd only met once. Little Arionna and her parents lived in London. Her father, Clarence's grandson Mikey, worked in the City doing something technical that was beyond Clarence's scope of understanding – something to do with SEOs and cookies and content management – while his wife, Lillan, was a fashion designer. The little he'd seen of them together, he couldn't understand what they had in common, but now they had this gorgeous baby, maybe that would be enough.

Then again, it hadn't been enough to keep him and Bethan together. They'd had two of their own and he'd barely coped, and he wasn't even the one staying home with them. Bethan had done it all on her own. If he could impart one piece of wisdom to young couples today, it would be to get a nanny. Even if they didn't think they needed one, they did. Kids could ruin a marriage, snatching away every moment of spare time and peace and energy, putting a literal wedge between a couple who'd genuinely loved each other when they'd had the freedom to do so. Those tribes in the forests had it right – share the care of children between as many people as possible. Clarence should have been round to Mikey and Lillan's place, offering his help. It was just that the Renaissance Project had taken all of his time, every last minute, for the past year at least. He'd made it his whole focus, but now that his pride had copped a wallop or two, he realised that he'd done to Mikey and Lillan exactly what he'd done to Bethan and the kids all those years ago. He'd simply forgotten about them.

But he could change that today.

He phoned Mikey and Lillan's number, conscious that it was barely nine o'clock but also well aware that there was never a good time to call someone with a baby. You just had to take your chances. The phone rang four times.

'Hello?'

His smile faltered. 'Bethan?'

'Clarence? What a surprise.' She did indeed sound surprised, but pleasantly so.

'What are you doing there?' he asked, feeling himself on the back foot.

'Just doing great-granny time,' she said cheerfully. 'Honestly, I know we both said that having grandchildren was the best thing, but having a great-grandchild? My goodness. It was a gift I'd never even considered. I want to eat every one of her fingers and toes.'

He knew she wasn't trying to rub in the fact that she was there and he was not, but he suddenly felt keenly the loss of these precious months of Arionna's infancy. The sensation was accompanied by an odd, unexpected regret that he and Bethan hadn't made it to this point in their lives together.

These days, Bethan still lived on the north coast of Cornwall, where she volunteered her time as a costume designer for one of the local theatre companies. Apparently her talents were in high demand, as sewing skills were something largely lost to the generations that had grown up being able to buy clothes for less than it would cost to make them. Both of their kids and their families lived in Cornwall too, which was probably an inevitable outcome given that Bethan had taken sole custody of the kids when the marriage ended. Adrian had been fourteen and Anne twelve. Divorce was still fairly unusual back then, and the children had been happy to leave a tiny village where gossip was passed around like the collection plate in church, and to start a new life somewhere with beaches and shops and eateries.

Bethan had *relished* being a grandma. She and Clarence were friends on Facebook – how very modern of them – and he'd observed the scores of photos she put up of the grandkids (some in their teens and a couple in their twenties) with just a tinge of jealousy. Now Mikey and Lillan were in London with the scrumptiously pink baby with masses of fine dark hair and huge brown eyes, who loved to grab her toes and stare at them as if they were the most magical thing she'd ever seen, and whose enormous smile was breathtaking.

He cleared his throat. 'I was hoping Lillan might be there. I'd love to come down and see them all. I really need to give that baby a big cuddle.' He lifted his chin as he spoke, firming up his voice.

'I'm sure they'd love that,' Bethan said generously. 'Lillan is at yoga right now so I'm here with Arionna, who is smearing avocado around her highchair tray.'

'Onto solids, already?' he asked, riffling through his brain, trying to remember back to the stages of feeding their own kids.

'Oh, yes. The research changes all the time, but they're trying baby-led weaning, which basically just means that when the baby reaches for food, you give it to them. It encourages the baby to follow their natural instincts.'

'Right,' Clarence said uncertainly, suddenly feeling his optimism drain away. He had so much to catch up on. 'Well, if you could just let Lillan know I called.'

'I will.'

'Anytime she wants to get back to me is fine,' he said, feeling himself shrinking beneath his skin. 'I don't want to be a bother.'

'It won't be any bother at all. They'd love to see you.' Her voice was kind.

'Right. Well, I'll be off now. Lots of work to do.'

'Okay. Oh, wait! How is the village project going? I must come out for a drive to see all the new shops. Is it everything you hoped?'

'Everything and more,' he said with practised assurance.

'Congratulations. You should be proud. I can't wait to see the old village returned to new. And just think – you're building something your grandchildren and now your great-grandchildren will be able to experience too.'

'That's what it's all about,' he agreed, her faith in the project helping to restore his hopes for it once more.

17

On her way to Rambling Rose on Friday morning, Olivia took the time to stop in at each shop and say hi to her fellow shopkeepers. After the break-in at Leanne's bakery the other day, it was all the more important for them to support each other.

She started with Miguel, admiring his new stinky cheese from France and hearing about his wife's ongoing drama with the immigration paperwork to bring her and the three kids to England. 'Sorry to hear that,' she said.

'It's because she's my brother's wife,' he said miserably, leaning into the cabinet to rearrange his fancy cheese sprouting green froths of designer mould.

Olivia looked at him. 'She's . . . what?'

'My brother died. They had no one to look after them so I did what needed to be done to help them have a good life.'

'What do you mean?'

'She and the kids need this new start here. My brother was the victim of an armed hold-up gone wrong.'

'I'm sorry.'

'After that, Isadora was afraid. This is her chance to get away, to start over somewhere fresh, somewhere safe. But even though we are legally married, they are delaying her and the kids.'

'It sounds like an amazing thing you've done,' she said, in awe of Miguel's generosity and also intrigued that people still married for practical, honourable reasons rather than love.

'It's what you do for family,' he said, waving away her praise.

'Well, I hope it gets sorted soon. It must be awful to have your life in limbo.'

Miguel gave a final huff, but then his natural ebullience reasserted itself. 'At least we have these, look!' He held up a jar of something called *nopales*, with dull green strips the colour of pickles floating in liquid.

'What is it?'

'Cactus paddles,' he boomed, laughing, then kissed the jar. 'Now my liver will be healthy.' He patted his belly and grinned.

She left him to it and continued on to see how Leanne was feeling today.

'Aye, all good. Each morning, I've armed myself with a rolling pin ready to hit them over the head if they come back.'

'Excellent,' Olivia said. 'Glad to see you've got your spirits back.'

'Sure, even a black hen can lay a white egg,' Leanne said.

Olivia wasn't sure what that meant, but she was glad that Leanne's tone was upbeat.

She reached the door of Elena and Newton's restaurant and Elena beckoned her in, calling out to her from the kitchen. Olivia smiled and made her way between the tables towards the back of the restaurant.

'You know, I'm still angry about Leanne's shop!' Elena said, almost the second she saw Olivia. She was feeding dough through the pasta maker, long tendrils of fettuccine pouring out the other end, the subject obviously having been on her mind while she was working. Flour dust motes floated gently between the strands of fettuccine drying over wooden racks.

'Yes, me too.'

Elena tutted. 'It makes me worry, you know? Who will be next? It might be our restaurant.' She said this flatly, resignedly.

'It could be,' Olivia agreed, sadly. 'Maybe set some rat traps in advance, just in case.' She raised an unamused eyebrow at Elena. Of course, she hated that this had happened to Leanne, just as much as she hated that it had happened to Raj, but she was relieved that it gave her sabotage theory credibility. No one could deny the sentiment behind the words painted in the bakery.

'But they will not scare us away,' Elena said, punching the dough. She raised her chin, her dark eyes flashing defiantly at Olivia. 'We come from tough stock, Newton and I. Both our grandparents survived the war – mine with Mussolini, Hitler, spies, betrayals, while Newton's were surviving the Blitz in London. My mamma, God bless her, she was born *during* the war.' She shook her head. 'Their stories! *Mamma mia*. This is nothing,' she hissed. 'Whoever they are, they've chosen the wrong people to mess with. This is Newton's ancestors' village, not mine, but if it's in Newton's blood than it's in our children's and grandchildren's blood too and we're doing this for them. Do not let them get to you, *cara*. We will rise above this. You'll see.'

'Of course we will,' Olivia said. They had to. They had no choice.

Not long after she'd started the morning's baking, Grayson stepped through the door with a laden box of provisions. Olivia found herself self-consciously running her fingers through her ponytail, hoping she'd remembered to brush her hair this morning.

He presented the box with a satisfied sigh. 'Ruby sends her regards. She'd like to let you know that she worked really hard on the quality of her milk this morning.'

'What a sweetheart! I'll have to come and meet her one day to say thank you.' She spoke without thinking, and then bit her lip. Had she just invited herself over to his place?

He tilted his head at her and grinned, clearly delighted. 'Ruby would love that.'

Ducking down to hide her flushed face, she pulled a folder from her bag under the counter. 'I made this last night, just roughly.' She opened the folder and took out a small piece of paper on which she'd inserted the black and white logo from his website. On the edge of the logo's circle, she'd overlaid a small red heart, and at the bottom of the page she'd typed *Proudly supporting Stoneden's own Seven Cows dairy products.*

He reached for it, his smile widening.

'I'm going to put it in the window to help spread the word,' Olivia explained, feeling oddly shy. 'If you like it, I can send you the file and you could print it for your other customers until you're ready to have some window signs or stickers professionally made up.'

'I think it's perfect,' he said. 'I love this heart that you've added. Would it be okay if I keep that element in my logo from now on?'

'Sure.'

'Well, this delivery is on the house. Call it an artist's fee.'

She shrugged. 'It's nothing, really. I could, so I did.'

'It's not nothing,' he said, and the softness of his voice made her own mouth go dry.

Inspired by her artistic addition to Grayson's logo, and delighted that he liked it so much, Olivia spent the next ten minutes rolling out and cutting heart-shaped gingerbread cookies. When she took them out of the oven, they shimmered golden in a deliciously scented haze of cinnamon, ginger, nutmeg and cloves. After they'd cooled, she filled a small piping bag with peach-coloured icing and used the smallest nozzle to outline each biscuit. Then she piped the same icing, ever so slightly thinned with a few drops of water, inside the outline she'd created, and used the back of a spoon to spread it evenly before popping any air bubbles with a toothpick. While the icing set, she rolled out scones and popped them into the hot oven. That was one great thing about baking in a cold climate – she never needed to turn on the heating. Her shop was toasty warm.

Returning to the gingerbread cookies, the peach icing now smooth and shiny, she picked up a third piping bag and began drawing petals and leaves in white icing, before selecting a fine-tipped brush – just like the paintbrushes she'd used in art classes at school – to feather the shapes into waves and curves. Finally, she dropped little beads of the white icing, like tiny pearls, all around the outside of the biscuits. She straightened, stretching out her neck and shoulders, and sighed with satisfaction. There were many things she loved about her job, but this kind of fussy, delicate artwork was particularly satisfying.

Glancing at the clock, she realised it was two minutes to opening time. She rushed into the storeroom to change into a dress and apron. She emerged just as the front door opened and two tourists entered, looking around appreciatively and inhaling the rich aroma of gingerbread.

The stooped, white-haired man pulled out a chair for his equally white-haired wife and popped a red and white polka-dot cushion behind her back with such gentleness that Olivia smiled. She surreptitiously flicked through her playlist to select Frank Sinatra singing 'The Way You Look Tonight'. To her delight, the woman's eyes brightened and she reached across the table to take her husband's hand. He covered her hand with his and they gazed at each other a moment.

'Welcome to Rambling Rose,' Olivia said, bringing them a jug of water and two glasses. 'Are you in town for long?'

'Just for a day trip,' the woman said. 'We're from Stratford.'

'That's where Shakespeare's house is, right?'

'That's it, yes,' the woman said. 'We've read a lot about the Renaissance Project here in Stoneden and we think it's marvellous,' she added.

'Should be more initiatives like it,' her husband agreed. 'Are you an import, then?'

'Yes, my grandmother was born here.'

'Did she come with you?' the woman asked.

'No, sadly. She passed away last year.'

'Oh, I'm sorry to hear that. I'm sure she would have loved what they're doing here in the village. It would have been such a wonderful thing for her to see it come back to life as it had been in her day.'

'Yes, it would.' Olivia smiled.

Returning to the counter, she put four piping-hot scones in a small basket and wrapped them in a red and white tartan tea towel. After delivering them with pots of jam and cream to the delightfully romantic couple, she set about whipping up a batch of chocolate cupcakes, all the while thinking about the cake she needed to make for tonight's wine and cheese event. A group of four came into the shop, and they all ordered gingerbread hearts and pots of tea. No sooner had she settled them at the table near the window than Ryan stepped through the door. She'd completely forgotten that he was coming to interview her today. He was followed by a petite young woman carrying a rather large camera and wearing heavy eyeshadow and a purple hijab threaded with intricate gold stitching.

'Ryan, good morning!' Olivia greeted him. She held out her hand to the photographer. 'Hi, I'm Olivia.'

'Farzenah,' the woman said. She shook Olivia's hand, then lifted her camera. 'Here to take photo.'

'Perfect,' Olivia said. 'Can I get you some tea or coffee perhaps?'

'No, thanks,' Ryan said. 'Just a few questions and then some photos, if that's okay?'

'Sure thing. Come and have a seat,' she said, ushering them towards the yellow table by the counter.

'I take photos of shop,' Farzenah said.

'Go ahead.'

Farzenah headed back outside to aim her camera at the bicycle and the shopfront.

'As I might have mentioned,' Ryan began, taking out his notebook, 'I'm hoping to do profile pieces on all the new residents of the village over time. I thought today would be a good day to focus on you because I can combine it with coverage of tonight's event and make it a big, splashy piece with colour photos. Why don't you start by telling me what made you want to come here for this project?' he asked. 'Why leave your life in Australia for Stoneden?'

'Well . . .' Olivia mentally shifted gears, from baker to granddaughter. 'My grandmother – Nora Kent – was born here and moved to Australia in the Sixties. She always spoke so highly of the village.' Okay, that was stretching the truth. Nora rarely spoke of her life in England. Still, it sounded good and Olivia hoped that this small white lie might help to foster goodwill towards the project.

'Out of interest,' Ryan interrupted, 'did she get married? I'm wondering about her surname, and yours – Kent.'

'Oh.' The question threw her off track for a moment. 'She did marry, yes. She married Lawrence Oakley, an Englishman she met and fell in love with on the boat to Australia.' She smiled. 'Quite the whirlwind romance, I believe. She and Lawrence got married straight off the boat with her parents' blessing. Sadly, he died when their only daughter was five years old.' She spread her hands, trying to recall specific details, while Ryan scribbled notes. 'She always spoke highly of him, said he was a good man, even named their daughter Laurie out of respect for him. Some time after his passing, she went back to using her maiden name. It was the Seventies. Feminism was on the rise. I asked her about it once and she said it had simply not felt right to be an Oakley when she was born a Kent. She didn't make a big deal out of it.'

Ryan nodded, seemingly indifferent to this information, so she continued from where she'd left off before his question had interrupted her. 'Ma passed away last year, leaving a huge hole in my life and my son's life. I wanted to come here and make her proud, and to be close to her, to somehow get to know her better by seeing where she came from.'

Ryan scribbled notes and nodded approvingly. Apparently, she had given the 'right' answer.

'My son, Darcy, is seven, and it seemed like a good age for him to discover his heritage firsthand, and to show him more of the world.'

'Tell me about the cake you're making for tonight. Obviously we'll get pictures of the finished cake later, but maybe give me an idea of the thinking behind it.'

'I was honoured to be invited by Juliet Cabot to create the centrepiece for tonight's event. The Renaissance Committee is working hard to build strong community ties,' Olivia said. Ryan raised an eyebrow at that, though she wasn't sure if it was because of the recent bakery break-in or that he felt she was laying it on a bit too thick. 'I'm making a three-tiered wedding cake, to symbolise the new and established residents within the village coming together, and styling it with roses, as they're both the symbol of England and the signature flower of my business. I hope the cake will reflect this new life for the village.'

'Thanks.' He shut his notebook as Farzenah came back into the shop. 'Could we get a few shots of you working on the cake now?'

'I haven't had a chance to start it yet,' Olivia said, a bit flustered. 'I've been busy baking for today's trade. How long do you have?'

'Twenty minutes max,' Ryan said.

'How about I measure out some of the flour and sugar and you could get some shots of that, and the butter creaming, the trays out on the bench, that sort of thing? Then you can get the full thing tonight?' She prayed that would be enough.

'Yes, good,' Farzenah said. 'Also, these.' She snapped a few photos of the gingerbread hearts, murmuring in admiration. Olivia quickly started measuring out ingredients, and posed for Farzenah between serving customers. Before long, Ryan was checking his watch and they were leaving.

At half-past eleven, with no tourist buses arriving and the footpath outside quiet, Rambling Rose was empty. Olivia was relieved to have time to begin work on her cake. Pulling out her notebook, she studied her sketch of the tiered pieces, the delicate buttercream covering, the cascade of falling ivy, then read through her calculations of the ingredient quantities, checking them against what she'd already weighed out for the photos. She'd just pulled out the baking paper and set the first tin on top, tracing around it with a pencil, when her mobile phone sprang to life. It was the school. She dropped the pencil and snatched up the phone. 'Hello?'

'Olivia, this is Zoe from the school office. Darcy's had a fall.'

Olivia helped to support Darcy's weight as he limped into Doc Eli's surgery.

'Darcy, you poor love,' Katrina said, rising from behind the counter. Her worried eyes met Olivia's. 'Eli won't be long.'

'Thank you,' Olivia said. She was still shaken by the sight of Darcy's face twisted in pain when she'd arrived at the school sick bay, and also preoccupied with trying to solve the problem of how to bake the cake for tonight. She knew Juliet would understand if she couldn't deliver the cake as promised, but she really didn't want to let her down, especially since Ryan and Farzenah wanted to cover it so prominently in the paper. She sent Juliet a quick text to let her know that she was at the doctor's with Darcy and might be delayed in preparing the cake, but she still hoped to finish it on time.

A few minutes later, Eli came down the short hallway. He nodded to Olivia, then turned to Darcy. 'Now, are you able to walk down the hallway, young man?'

Darcy nodded. 'Yes,' he said quietly, a tremor in his voice. Olivia stood up with him, watching him anxiously. Her great fear was that one of the pins or plates might have been dislodged by his fall.

Katrina shot her a sympathetic smile. 'It's always the monkey bars.'

Olivia and Darcy followed Eli down the hall and into his examination room. Some children's drawings were taped to the filing cabinet next to his desk – made by his grandchildren, Olivia assumed.

Eli indicated for them both to sit down. 'Now, what have we done?' he asked, sitting at his desk and leaning forward so his face was level with Darcy's.

'I fell off the monkey bars.' Darcy's eyes were bright with unshed tears.

'I see. Well, you're not the first boy or girl to do that,' Eli said with a chuckle, 'and you won't be the last. Couldn't even hazard a guess how many broken bones I've seen in this room due to monkey bars.'

Darcy's eyes popped.

'It's a bit more complicated, I'm afraid,' Olivia said. 'There's an old injury.'

'Tell me all about it,' Eli said.

He took some notes as Olivia succinctly relayed the details of Darcy's accident and treatment last year. Then he helped Darcy to his feet and asked him to try putting his weight on the affected leg. Darcy grimaced, and Eli helped him back to his seat.

'He'll need an X-ray,' Eli said, scribbling a referral. 'The closest radiology clinic is in Fahren Way. It's open till five today, so you should have plenty of time.'

'Good luck,' Katrina said, as they passed the reception desk on the way out. 'Let me know how you go.'

In the van, Olivia tapped the address into her mobile phone's GPS. As they set off, she spoke reassuringly to Darcy while simultaneously trying to calculate how much time she needed to bake and decorate the cake for tonight. It was not yet one o'clock. If the X-ray was done quickly, she might just be able to get back and settle Darcy in the kids' corner while she whipped up the cake – though she wouldn't be able to paint her chocolate scene, that was for sure. Still, it might be possible to get the cake done, even if she didn't deliver it until midway through the evening.

But . . . what if Darcy had done real damage? What if he needed more surgery?

She was dismayed to find the clinic waiting room heaving with people. Gritting her teeth, she filled in forms and took a seat with Darcy, handing him her mobile phone to distract him with games while they waited. After ninety minutes had passed, she knew she'd never get the cake done in time.

'Darcy, I just need to make some phone calls. I'll give you back the phone when I'm finished.'

'Okay,' he said, taking a deep breath as though he'd forgotten to breathe while playing his racing game. She googled the names of cake makers within forty-five minutes' drive and then stepped out onto the damp footpath to make her calls. She didn't want to let Juliet down. If she couldn't make the cake herself, there was still a chance – admittedly slim – that she might be able to buy one.

'Hello,' Olivia said brightly when the first shopkeeper answered. This place was the closest, here in Fahren Way. 'I'm calling at the last minute because the cake I had planned for tonight has fallen through. I'm trying to find a formal cake, something with at least two layers but preferably three, along the lines of a wedding or engagement cake, to feed a hundred people but eighty at a pinch. I don't suppose you happen to have one spare this afternoon?'

There was a protracted pause. 'Are you serious?'

'I'm sorry, I know it's a long shot. As I said, it's an emergency.'

'There is no way we can do that this afternoon,' the woman said snippily.

'Of course, sorry to bother you.'

The second cake shop she tried was twenty-five minutes north of Fahren Way. When Olivia repeated her request, the man laughed rudely and then hung up on her.

Olivia gritted her teeth and called the third cake maker, a woman who answered the phone as Adele. Her shop was forty minutes away, in Stroud. With little hope, Olivia relayed her request again.

'Would you believe it, you're in luck,' Adele said. 'I've had a no-show on a triple-layer engagement cake this afternoon. I can't get hold of the person and I have to close my doors soon.'

'Oh, how rude,' Olivia said, feeling her frustration and disappointment.

'Yes, she'll lose her deposit, of course, but it's a shame to waste the cake. If you can get here by close of business, it's yours.'

'I'll be there,' Olivia agreed, with far more certainty than she felt.

She quickly texted Juliet to let her know that she had organised a replacement cake for the evening, then stepped back into the waiting room just as Darcy's name was called. As they followed the radiographer down the hall to the X-ray room, she squeezed his shoulder. 'You'll be okay,' she said to him, determined that it would be true.

'So, he's okay?' Helge asked, his voice tinny through the speaker of her mobile phone. Trying to tamp down her anxiety about being late, Olivia was driving the van carefully along the narrow, winding roads, tall hedges on either side obscuring her view as they approached intersections. The cake was on the back seat, next to Darcy.

'Yes, he'll be fine. There's no damage to the plates or pins, the X-ray guy said. I'm heading back to Stoneden now to see Doc Eli, but I'm guessing he'll say all Darcy needs is rest, icepacks, painkillers and to continue his physical therapy.'

'This is good,' Helge said, his voice carrying the frown of concern she was sure he was wearing between his brows. She wasn't sure why she'd called him, really. It wasn't an emergency, and if she'd been back in Australia she wouldn't have bothered. But she felt so much closer to Helge now, both physically and emotionally.

He offered some comforting words to Darcy and promised to come over again soon. Olivia ended the call feeling grateful for his support.

Now she needed to get back to Stoneden and to Doc Eli to discuss the results and talk about what to do for Darcy, then somehow get the cake to the manor house by five-thirty for the wine and cheese event.

18

The Jacobean mansion that she and Grayson had passed on their walk last week was already packed with people by the time Olivia and Darcy arrived that evening. During the week, Olivia had learnt that Father Anthony had persuaded the current owners of the manor to open the great hall for this event. The owners were known to be indifferent to the efforts of the Renaissance Committee to revive the village; they already made a mint from the tourist trade and saw no particular benefit to themselves from the project. But Anthony was a difficult man to resist, and presided over many weddings at the manor, so they'd agreed.

Olivia helped Darcy through the door and led him through the great hall to the children's art display at the end. Cathy Finch found him a comfy chair and a footrest to put his leg on, clucking over him while his classmates came to check on him.

'Is it okay if I leave him here for a little bit while I bring in the cake?' Olivia asked the teacher, running her fingers through

Darcy's hair. One day she knew he'd stop letting her do that; until then, she'd indulge herself.

'Of course,' Cathy assured her.

Eloise ran over and perched on the edge of Darcy's chair, offering to share her plate of food with him, and he immediately looked happier. Katrina followed her. 'We'll look after him, don't worry,' she said firmly to Olivia. 'Go do your cake thing. I can't believe you even got it done in time.'

'Oh, I . . .' Olivia started to explain that she'd had to purchase a cake from another baker, but she was interrupted by Clarence, who'd sauntered down this way to chat.

'Evening, ladies,' he said, nodding to them both.

'Hi, yourself. You're looking dapper,' Katrina said, motioning to his dinner jacket.

'Excuse me,' Olivia said, taking her chance to fetch the cake. She threaded her way back through the tightly packed crowd.

Hearing a snatch of music beneath the roar of voices, she glanced across and saw Juliet seated in a corner of the hall on a plush crimson wing-backed chair, her cello wedged between her velvet-clad legs. Juliet spotted her, and smiled with relief. Still playing her cello, she nodded towards a table nearby, which was covered with a white cloth and vases of pink roses, with a space for the cake.

Out in the cold evening air, Olivia ran across to her car. She carefully manoeuvred out the large cake box, then bumped the door closed with her hip. 'Excuse me, excuse me,' she said, re-entering the manor, stepping around Father Anthony and parting groups of guests clasping wineglasses and canapés.

Juliet took a break from playing to help her set it up on the table. 'Is Darcy okay?' she asked, standing back to take in the beautiful cake with its thick buttercream icing and a cluster of soft-petalled white roses neatly placed on top. It was more formal than Olivia's style; nonetheless, it was beautiful, and it did the job Juliet had wanted, that of suggesting union and marriage.

'He'll be okay, thanks. I'm sorry, again, for the terrible timing.'

'Don't waste another moment worrying about it. These things happen.'

'They do,' Olivia agreed. 'I'm only sorry Ryan won't be able to feature it in his newspaper piece now.'

'Hm.' Juliet pursed her lips, clearly disappointed.

'Is he here?'

'I haven't seen him yet,' Juliet said, craning her neck to survey the crowd. 'Anyway, I'd best get back to playing.' She gave Olivia a happy smile then resumed her seat.

Olivia gave the cake one last look-over, then glanced around at the beautiful floral arrangement on the table, the imperfect petals and large thorns clearly a sign they were from someone's garden. Suddenly inspired, she selected two pink roses from the back of one vase and pulled off the petals, then piled them on top of the cake, letting them fall down like snowflakes and land where they would; finally, she trailed a few individual petals strategically down the tiered cream sides. The addition of the blushing petals transformed the cake from elegant and formal to something warm and fresh. Olivia smiled, pleased that she'd been able to contribute her own talents towards the cake after all, and enjoying the gentle rose scent mingling with the vanilla and sugar.

Juliet looked across and smiled in surprise to see what she'd done. Catching Olivia's eye, she mouthed, 'Beautiful.'

Feeling much better about the cake, Olivia took a moment to catch her breath and take in her lavish surroundings. An enormous chandelier hung from the soaring ceiling with its ornate mouldings. A fire crackled energetically in a marble fireplace, warm light flickering over the rich, dark-red walls. Tall windows with velvet drapes overlooked darkened rolling fields. Guests sat on gilt-edged chairs and lounges. The very age of it all was mind-blowing. She couldn't fathom how one family had owned not only this museum of a building, but the entire estate, including the village. The little cottage where she and Darcy now lived had once been a worker's cottage. Generations of families had raised children there – probably three to a room downstairs and another four above – and paid rent to the lord of this manor.

Suddenly famished, she made her way across to the tables of food. 'That smells incredible,' she said to Leanne, who was slicing open freshly baked loaves. She turned at the sound of her name, called in a booming voice. A beaming Miguel was weaving through the sea of faces, a head taller than those around him, carrying boards of food high in the air.

'A little something I prepared earlier,' he said proudly, placing the boards onto the white tablecloths.

'This is amazing,' said Olivia. The grazing platters were a work of art, with six different cheeses, crostini, crackers, four different types of olives, sundried tomatoes, berries, beautifully cut fruit, rolled cured meats, marinated octopus and smoked fish. She helped herself to several pieces of cheese and meat, and added some buttered bread.

'I have the best cheese in the whole country.' Miguel hooked his thumbs under his rainbow-coloured braces and snapped them back against his chest.

'I'd say you do,' Olivia concurred, piling up a second plate with food to deliver to Darcy.

A large crowd of people arrived through the entrance then. Anthony rushed to welcome them, while Juliet picked up the pace of her cello music. Clarence, very dapper in a dinner suit, appeared to be taking a young couple on a tour of the room. Cathy Finch was directing people towards the art show, where the children's work hung on boards. She held a roll of sticky dots and a marker pen and was obviously trying to coax people to buy the pictures. Olivia had to hand it to her – the woman knew how to milk every last drop of goodwill out of her community. She caught Darcy's eye and gestured to the plate of food she was preparing for him. He gave her an eager thumbs up.

Viola arrived at the long serving table next to Olivia with much rattling and clinking of sparkling wine bottles in a large cardboard box. 'I underestimated how much people drank,' she puffed, wiping her forearm across her brow before straightening her white blouse, pulled to one side by the weight of the box.

Leanne dropped her bread knife and rushed to help her. Olivia put down her plates and did the same. Wordlessly, they pulled out bottles and opened them with much tearing of foil. Corks popped satisfyingly, and the three worked together to fill glasses. People thronged around.

'Exactly what I was looking for,' said a deep male voice. Olivia looked up and stared for a moment, jerking up the bottle in the nick of time to avoid spilling wine all over the table.

'Wow,' she said, taking in Grayson's attire, then laughed, embarrassed. Had she said that out loud? The tall farmer wore a maroon smoking jacket over a crisp white shirt and dark dress jeans, with formal black shoes instead of his usual farm boots. She had to admit, the man scrubbed up well.

He raised a hand to the lapel of his jacket. 'Too much?' he asked, but he was smiling at her.

'No, it's great. You look like you belong here.'

'I think I could handle a cigar and a balloon of brandy by the fire.'

'You could totally pull that off,' she agreed.

'You look sensational yourself,' he said, his gaze travelling appreciatively down her two-tone dove-grey dress. It wasn't what she'd intended to wear tonight, but she hadn't had a chance to change out of her Rambling Rose outfit. Belatedly, she realised that she must have looked quite the sight in the radiology clinic this afternoon.

She tried to suppress her smile, but failed. 'Drink?'

'Red, please.'

She turned to a crate behind her and retrieved the appropriate bottle, filling a glass. She handed it to him and he sipped appreciatively. The level of chatter in the drawing room had risen and it was getting harder to hear.

Katrina arrived at the table, a cluster of medieval-looking gold and silver bangles jangling as she walked. She greeted Grayson, then turned to Olivia. 'I just came to pick up Darcy's dinner plate,' she said.

'Oh God, sorry! I totally forgot.' Olivia picked up the plate she'd prepared for her son and passed it to Katrina. 'Sorry about that. What a day I've had. I'm not sure I've got any brains left at all.' She put a hand to her forehead, suddenly feeling bone-weary from all the stress of the day.

'Strong coffee for you tomorrow morning,' Katrina said, her eyebrows arched. Both of them agreed the village needed a fabulous barista as quickly as possible.

'If only I could find one,' Olivia said, her voice low so as not to offend anyone. Katrina laughed, lifted the plate in farewell and headed back to the art area where most of the kids were.

Grayson leant towards her, his breath warm on her cheek. 'I know where you can get a great coffee.'

She pulled back a fraction so she could see his face. 'Where?'

'I spent time in Italy at the beginning of my midlife crisis.' He rolled his eyes at himself. 'Now I own an authentic Italian espresso machine.'

'Really?' She was impressed.

He nodded sagely. 'And I have triple-filtered water. Maybe you and Darcy would like to come around tomorrow morning? I can make him a hot chocolate and you can say hello to Ruby. She's been dying to meet you.'

She felt herself grinning. 'We'd love that – though it will have to be early so I can get to work by nine at the latest.'

'Easy. I'm a farmer. I get up at four.'

'Then it's a date,' she said, noticing the chandelier light flickering in his eyes. 'Though we might come at seven, if that's okay. Four might be a smidge too early.'

'Seven it is.' He grinned at her.

She'd been so busy enjoying their little flirtation that she'd missed the arrival of Ryan and Farzenah. Now she caught sight of them over at the cake table, Farzenah's lens pointed at the Stroud baker's cake.

'Oh, sorry, I've got to go,' she said hastily. 'We'll see you in the morning.' Fighting her way through the crowd, she made as straight a line as possible towards the cake table. She needed to tell Ryan immediately that it wasn't her cake after all. As she approached, she saw that Ryan had positioned the little council man, Chester Pepperworth, next to the cake and Farzenah was taking his picture. Fern and Georgio – here with their little dog, in spite of the manor's 'no dogs' policy – rushed over to shake Chester's hand and get themselves photographed too.

'Excuse me,' Olivia kept repeating. She was just metres away now, but Ryan and Farzenah had finished up and were heading in the opposite direction. She made it to the cake table just as they were swallowed by the crowd. 'Shit.'

Juliet arrived at her side. 'Everything okay?'

'Ryan and Farzenah were taking photos of the cake, with Chester Pepperworth too. I need to tell Ryan it's not my cake.'

'Never mind. You have time. He won't file that story tonight,' Juliet said reassuringly.

Olivia nodded, still looking around to see if she could spot Ryan. Chester Pepperworth stood nearby, surrounded by a small group of resisters – Roger and Guy were there, and Mrs Wilson cast a disapproving look at Fern and Georgio with their chihuahua. Somehow the sight increased her unease.

Suddenly, a surge of excitement rippled through the room. Looking around, she saw several heads hunched over mobile phones. There were smiles and a few whoops.

'What's going on?' she asked Juliet, who shook her head, equally clueless.

Just then, Father Anthony came and positioned himself near the cake table, microphone in hand. 'Good evening,' he said. His face was flushed, and he pulled at the collar of his black shirt for a moment, waiting for the noise to die down. 'I'm here to officially welcome you to tonight's celebration of our new village, a community made up of many talented people from around the world, and all with deep historical ties to Stoneden.' There was some light applause at that, and a loud *hear, hear* from Clarence.

Someone called out, 'Tell them the news!' It was a woman's voice, though Olivia couldn't see her among the wall of people.

Anthony laughed. 'Okay, yes. I do have some news.' He held up a hand and a deep, expectant hush settled over the grand hall.

'Many of you would have heard that two of England's finest actors, Ying and Oden—'

'Yoden!' a few voices squealed, to snorts and laughter.

'—have announced that their impending nuptials will be held here in the Cotswolds.'

Excited chattering filled the room and Pixie the chihuahua barked along, her tail wagging frantically.

'Now, we've just found out'—he brandished his mobile phone high in the air—'that they have chosen Stoneden for the wedding!'

An enormous cheer reverberated through the room, accompanied by clapping and stomping feet. Olivia turned to Juliet, whose mouth had fallen open, her bright eyes fixed on her husband.

'And . . .' Anthony spoke into the microphone again, waiting for silence. 'There's more. Ying and Oden have stated that one of their reasons for choosing Stoneden is their support for the Renaissance Project. They are inspired and encouraged to see that a village such as ours can lead the way for community-driven change and revival!' His voice rose, sounding more like a Baptist minister than a solemn Anglican vicar, and the level of excitement in the room rose too. 'They believe in thinking globally but acting locally, and to that end . . .' he paused for effect, 'they will be using *only* local produce and services for this event!'

Juliet clasped Olivia's arm. Around the room, people hugged each other, clapped, whooped and stomped their feet. Olivia even saw Roger smile, until Guy elbowed him in the side. Chester's face conveyed controlled excitement, with a lifted chin, a tempered grin and bright eyes, while Mrs Wilson set her mouth in a grim line.

'This will well and truly put Stoneden on the map!' Anthony fist-pumped the air. Then he composed himself, as though suddenly remembering that he was a vicar and not a football fanatic. He turned to his wife, who was shaking her head in wonder and smiling at him. They gazed at each other adoringly, before he cleared his throat and went on, in a more measured voice.

'Tonight, we have come here to celebrate the union of the old village and the new arrivals, a union that is like a marriage in which two parties come together and create something new, something bigger than the sum of its parts. This beautiful cake here beside me, lovingly crafted by our own cake maker, Olivia Kent, symbolises this very real union.'

'Oh . . . oh no.' Any excitement that Olivia had been feeling was doused. She shook her head, stepping forward, but Juliet pulled her back sharply. Olivia frowned at her. 'But that's—'

'Shh!' Juliet commanded, sternly enough that Olivia was shocked into silence.

Anthony's excitement got the better of him once more. 'I can also confirm that Olivia, our one and only local cake maker, has been chosen to make the wedding cake, the most important piece of your professional career.' The whole room seemed to turn and stare at her as one.

'And looking at this beautiful cake,' Anthony said, 'I know you will be more than capable of meeting the challenge.'

Pixie yapped again, in time with a new round of applause.

Olivia swallowed hard, her heart pounding like a boxer going at a punching bag. Juliet threw her arms around her and whispered fiercely into her ear, 'Don't say a word.'

'What an honour,' Anthony went on, clearly enjoying the rapt attention – rather more enthusiastic than the usual response to his sermons. He almost looked as though he might cry. 'The world's eyes will be on Stoneden,' he said, shaking his head as if he'd just witnessed a miracle.

The world's eyes.

All around her, people were taking photos of Olivia and the cake, and she had the cold, sinking sensation that more images were being uploaded to social media by the second. She leant towards Juliet, panicked. 'I have to say something.'

'Now is not the time,' Juliet warned her.

'But—'

'Don't ruin this for the Renaissance Committee.'

'No, I—'

'Smile, Olivia, just smile.' Then she picked up Olivia's hand and thrust it triumphantly into the air, setting off a new wave of applause.

19

The sky was still a deep grey when Olivia drove herself and Darcy to Grayson's farm. She'd organised a meeting with Clarence and Juliet at Rambling Rose later this morning to discuss what to do, but for now she tried to push aside all her worries about what had happened last night; instead, she let herself enjoy the peaceful village streets, her headlights beaming through ghostly fog. As they turned down the same road that led to Madeline's place, the soft outlines of houses were replaced by a blanket of open fields.

She picked out Madeline's house in the dawn light, and just then a light came on in Madeline's kitchen. Olivia had a momentary urge to swing into her driveway to ask her about Ma's photo, but now she was already pressed for time, not having a lot to spare this morning.

'Are we there?' Darcy asked from the back seat. Olivia was relieved that the pain in his hip had diminished overnight with rest and anti-inflammatories. Still, he'd be having a quiet day, that was for sure.

'I think so,' she said, as they passed a rustic painted sign that read *Seven Cows Dairy.* She turned the car into the driveway, and several cows at the fence line lifted their heads, a few letting out querying moos. Darcy giggled.

Olivia pulled up in front of a large barn, lit up inside and out, and cut the engine. Grayson emerged from the L-shaped stone house, which had a peaked roof at each end, wearing jeans, jacket and boots, smiling.

'Morning!' he said, opening her door.

'Morning to you,' she said, sliding out of the car.

Then he went to Darcy's door and opened it for him. 'Hi, Darcy.'

'Hi,' Darcy said, smiling shyly.

'How's your leg this morning?'

Darcy shrugged. 'It's okay.'

The thumping of hooves made them all turn towards the paddock. Several caramel-coloured jersey cows trotted towards them, tails flicking in the air, like oversized dogs rushing over for dinner or belly rubs.

'Look at them!' Olivia laughed. The cows had reached the wooden fence and were mooing at Grayson. 'They seem to like you,' she said to him.

'It's crushing, really. They only want me for my grain. I've finished milking for the day, which is when they get their grain, but they're happy to act as if they're starving.'

Olivia and Darcy went over to the fence. Bells clanged musically on the cows' collars as they pushed and headbutted each other, trying to get to the front of the scrum.

'Hi,' Olivia said to a small cow at the front of the pack, and reached out tentatively to scratch her neck. The cow had big black eyes with long lashes, curved black horns, and wore a smart red collar.

'That's Ruby,' Grayson said affectionately, as the cow leant in to Olivia's hand. Darcy patted her nose, pulling an amused face at the wetness.

'Ruby, from your logo?'

'The one and only. She was my first cow, only a day old when I got her from a farmer nearby. I raised her by hand inside the house. Now she thinks she should be sleeping on my bed, and is most displeased to be banished to the paddock.'

'I'll bet. Why was she hand-raised?'

'Her mother died during calving.'

'That's so sad,' Olivia said.

Grayson scratched under Ruby's chin. The cow raised her head and closed her eyes blissfully, melting into the moment of being adored by three humans. She wasn't the only one melting. Olivia had visions of Grayson up in the middle of the night heating bottles to feed the calf by the fireplace, rocking her and singing to her.

Although that was ludicrous. Probably.

'All right, let's get you a coffee,' Grayson said, turning away from the fence. Ruby protested, then turned and shoved the neighbouring cow with her shoulder.

'I won't argue with that,' Olivia said.

'Ready for a hot chocolate, Darcy?'

'Have you got marshmallows?'

'I do.'

'Are they Pascall's?' Darcy asked, making Olivia snort with laughter.

'Not sure about that,' Grayson said, a smile tugging at the corner of his lips.

'It's okay,' Olivia rushed to reassure him. She gave Darcy a meaningful look. 'Darcy will be grateful for whatever you have, won't you?'

Darcy grinned at her. 'Yes.'

'Pascall's next time,' Grayson promised, and led them up the gravel footpath charmingly bordered with overgrown lavender bushes. Inside the warm house, they shimmied out of their coats, and Grayson took off his muddy boots and pulled on sheepskin indoor boots.

'Are they Uggs?' Olivia asked.

'They are. Authentic Aussie Uggs.'

'Nice one.'

He led the way into a large kitchen. At one end of the room was a red-tiled archway enclosing a wood-fired pizza oven. To its right sat a wood-fired stove, and on a bench to its left was an impressive red and silver espresso machine.

'I love this kitchen,' Olivia said. She and Darcy slid onto the bench seat at the table, which looked as if it had been handmade, sanded back and had a wisp of oil spread over it. All the room needed was a rusted bicycle hanging up in a corner, some cushions made of reused hessian coffee bags, industrial lights hanging from the ceiling and a bunch of wildflowers on the table, and it would be magazine-perfect. If she'd had the room, she would have loved to create a space like this in her shop.

She nodded to the espresso machine. 'And I love the sight of that machine enough to run away with it to a desert island for the rest of my life.'

'Well then, let's get down to business,' Grayson said, lifting a bag of coffee beans down from a shelf above the machine.

Olivia watched as he poured beans into a grinder and whizzed them to a fine powder; the aroma made her mouth water. He filled the metal coffee basket, hooked it into place on the espresso machine and pressed the button for steaming water to filter through it, dark liquid trickling into the red cups he'd placed below.

'What can I make you?' he asked. 'Cappuccino? Flat white? Long black?'

'A flat white would be perfect.' She put her hand on Darcy's knee and gave it a gentle squeeze. He leant in to her, still a little tired, and she wrapped her arm around him.

'Darcy, would you like something to eat?' Grayson asked. 'I can make you some fruit toast if you like? Or cinnamon toast? My mum used to make that for me when I was home sick from school, or if I'd come off my bike or something.'

'What do you think?' Olivia asked Darcy. 'Cinnamon toast sounds great to me.'

'Okay,' Darcy said, uncertainly.

'I've never made it for him,' she explained.

'I think you'll like it,' Grayson said, also sounding a little unsure. Olivia was touched by his thoughtfulness.

Moving comfortably around his kitchen, he pulled the bread from the breadbin, then flicked open the fridge door with two fingers and pulled out butter, then a glass bottle. 'As you've come to a working farm, you can even have fresh milk, straight from the cow.'

'Out of the cow?' Darcy asked, amazed. He peered through the window, trying to see the cows.

'Ah – technically, no,' Grayson corrected himself, 'not *straight* from the cow. We won't squirt it into your mouth.'

Darcy giggled.

'But close to it.' He held up the bottle. 'This came from the girls just an hour ago.'

They sat in silence for a moment as Grayson put bread in the toaster and poured fresh milk into a saucepan to heat for Darcy's hot chocolate. 'Have your feet touched the ground yet?' he asked.

Olivia was momentarily thrown, having been nestled in dreams of good coffee. 'Oh, right, the wedding. It's quite a trip,' she admitted, a knot balling in her belly.

'You're going to be the most sought-after cake maker in the world in a couple of months' time.' His words made her stomach clench. That was exactly why she needed to talk to Clarence and Juliet this morning.

Grayson heated some milk in a jug, the steam growling loudly. The toast popped up and he buttered four pieces, sprinkled over cinnamon and sugar and cut it into triangles. He offered the plate to Darcy first.

Darcy took a piece and bit into it. 'Mm, yum!' His eyes widened with pleasure.

Grayson added the milk to the coffees then delivered them to the table, setting them down carefully. 'Sugar?'

'Not for me, thanks.'

Grayson finished making Darcy's hot chocolate, adding two fluffy marshmallows and a dusting of chocolate powder. Then he joined them at the table.

Olivia sipped her coffee and felt the brew flood her system, every cell in her body singing with happiness. 'Oh my. You might be the best barista in Stoneden – and possibly the entire Cotswolds region.'

'I'm a man of many talents,' he said, with just the right amount of swagger. They were definitely in flirty territory now. Conscious of Darcy's listening presence, she changed the subject.

'Do you sleep during the day, after getting up so early to do the milking?'

Grayson stretched out his long legs, cupping his coffee in one work-hardened hand. 'Not anymore. I'm used to it now, and I rarely have time. There's always something that needs doing. I hit the hay pretty early each night though. What about you? You must get up early too.'

'During the week, not so much. Weekends have always been my busiest days, with all the weddings and parties. It's not uncommon for me to get up at three in the morning on those days.'

He whistled through his teeth. 'I thought four was early.'

'I'm used to it now. Besides,' she grinned at Darcy, 'once you've survived the sleep deprivation that comes with a baby, everything else pales in comparison.'

Grayson nodded. 'I'll bet it does.'

'My dad's in Norway,' Darcy said, eyes wide, top lip covered in chocolate and milk foam.

'Norway? That's a cool place.'

'You've been?' Olivia asked.

'Just once, for a week. I liked it there. I like all the Scandinavian countries.'

'We're going for Christmas,' Darcy said. 'We'll get snow!'

'Hopefully,' Olivia said. 'If it does snow, it'll be our first white Christmas.'

Grayson took all this in, nodding slowly. She wondered if he was curious about Darcy's father, and she suddenly felt awkward because she too had questions about Helge, questions she wasn't sure she could answer. He'd said he loved her. But did *she* want to start something up with Helge again? On the one hand, her attraction to him was still as strong as ever. It hadn't been the right time for them all those years ago, but maybe it was now. On the other hand, she'd just upended her whole life to move here, and Darcy was just settling after a tumultuous year; restarting her relationship with Helge would mean more upheaval. And what if they tried to make a go of it and it all fell apart? She and Helge were bound together for many more years yet through Darcy. For everyone's sakes, they needed to be on firm ground. Then again, she'd left Australia not knowing where she belonged. Stoneden had seemed like the right place, but perhaps it was Norway after all.

And then there was Grayson, sitting across from her. It was far too soon to be contemplating anything serious with him . . . they'd only known each other for a few weeks. Yet she liked him. She really did.

'You never know,' Grayson said, 'you might get a white Christmas here too. It happens every now and then.'

'I'd love to see that,' Olivia said, feeling more confused by the minute.

There was something so magical about beating egg whites and sugar and watching them grow and puff, silky smooth, pure white, like a big frothy wedding dress, able to be moulded into peaks and rounds. Olivia never grew tired of that. It was one of the simplest yet most satisfying parts of crafting her creations. Cooking was chemistry in action, and she often wondered who had first discovered these amazing tricks, the latent potential of food to be changed into an entirely different product with just a little knowledge and skill. She wondered, too, about all the things foods could do that humans were yet to learn.

This morning, she was making a flourless chocolate cake. She'd already melted the butter and dark chocolate together in the saucepan, forming a rich, thick sauce, and then she'd added her secret ingredient, a shot of espresso coffee, transported from Grayson's kitchen. Now she folded the egg whites into the melted chocolate in small batches, the key to preserving the air in the meringue, and carefully poured it all into a greased, cocoa-powdered tin, then slid it into the oven. It would rise and then fall, leaving a crusty outside and molten inside. She'd serve it with a scoop of ice cream and fresh raspberries dusted with icing sugar.

At quarter to ten, Clarence and Juliet walked in. Clarence smiled. 'Smells wonderful in here.'

'It sure does,' Juliet agreed. They both waved to Darcy, who was lying in a beanbag in the kids area, reading *The 117-Storey Treehouse*.

Olivia gave them a strained smile. 'Thanks for coming in early,' she said, eager to sort out the mix-up from last night. 'I feel really bad that people think that cake was mine.'

Clarence and Juliet exchanged a look and then Juliet gave her a reassuring smile. 'You have nothing to worry about,' she said.

Olivia bristled slightly. 'Yes, I do. Look, I know Anthony didn't realise that I'd bought that cake in Stroud, so I'm not blaming him, but now everyone thinks I made the cake. Ryan and Farzenah took photos of it. We have to fix this.'

Clarence ran a hand over his mouth, thinking. 'How could we do that now?'

'To start with, we need to tell Ryan so he doesn't let anything go to print that claims that cake is mine.'

Clarence cheered. 'Easy. I'll talk to him the moment we're done here.'

Juliet shifted her weight from one foot to the other. 'There's just one problem.'

Olivia braced herself. 'What is it?'

'Ying has already put a photo of the cake on her Instagram, tagging you, saying that she cannot wait to see the wedding cake. She's introduced you and your business to the whole world.'

As if on cue, people began to gather outside Rambling Rose, smiling and pointing at Olivia through the glass, and even taking selfies next to her signage.

Olivia felt a rush of panic. 'Well, we need to tell her the truth! What will Adele say when she finds out? She'll be furious. It was her cake!'

'Did you tell her who you were, where you were from?' Clarence asked.

Olivia tried to recall their conversation. 'I don't think so, but I can't be sure. It was all a big blur. I was so stressed.'

Clarence nodded and looked to Juliet. 'And didn't you say that the final cake looked quite different because of what Olivia had done to it with the rose petals?'

'Yes, it did,' Juliet said emphatically. 'It could have been a whole other cake.'

'That's not the point, though,' Olivia jumped in. '*I* know.'

'You really don't need to worry about this,' Juliet said sweetly, but a slight edge had entered her tone. 'This is a huge moment for the Renaissance Project and we *all* have to work together to make it a success. The driving ethos of the project is doing what's best for the group, not the individual. Anyway, no harm has been done to Adele here . . .'

'I disagree.'

'We can't do anything to risk jeopardising this wedding,' Juliet said, her eyes narrowing. 'The project is about working as a community, and this is your chance to do just that.'

Olivia was shocked into silence.

Clarence held up a hand in an attempt to quell the rising tension. 'Olivia, it speaks well of your character that you want to correct this misunderstanding. But last night's cake will be a flash in the media pan, gone by tomorrow.'

Olivia cast another glance through the window to the snaking queue forming at her door. She wasn't so sure.

Clarence went on soothingly, 'By tomorrow, or the next day, it will be forgotten. All anyone will want to talk about is the wedding and Stoneden's role in it.'

'I still feel bad, though,' Olivia said, and saw Juliet bite her lip.

'Everything will be okay,' Clarence said. 'As I said, I'll explain what's happened to Ryan and he'll make sure nothing false is printed. We can move forward from here with a clean slate.'

'Thank you,' Olivia said, relief washing over her. 'I don't want to build a reputation on lies.'

'But we do need to play this carefully,' Juliet cautioned. 'We can't do anything that will endanger the project. Remember, Clarence, we're still in the trial phase. There are those who would like to shut us down. Even the smallest scandal will play into their hands.'

Clarence put a conciliatory hand on her shoulder. 'Trust me. No one knows that better than I do,' he said, replacing his scarf as he led the way out the door. Juliet followed, and Olivia breathed a sigh of relief.

20

Clarence nosed his car into Madeline's driveway, the wheels bumping over the uneven ground. His day was tightly scheduled, beginning with the visit to Olivia's shop to discuss the misunderstanding about the cake. Last night's announcement from Yoden had also prompted him to renew his efforts to win over some of the project's known antagonists, such as Fern and Georgio, and Guy and Roger. He planned on catching Mrs Wilson at church tomorrow. He didn't really believe that any of them was capable of pulling off some sort of dreadful stunt – they all seemed more like paper warriors than genuine activists – yet the small but persistent incidents against the shops in the main street that had preceded last night's announcement troubled him. Was the wedding likely to exacerbate tensions, or ease them? After all, with the world's attention on Stoneden, what better time could there be to try to derail the project?

First up this this morning, however, he wanted to make a call of a more personal nature, to get some things off his chest.

He turned off the engine and put on his cap. 'I won't be long,' he said to Stuart, curled up on his rug on the passenger seat. The dog looked up at him expectantly, in case Clarence changed his mind about taking him inside with him. He patted the Airedale's head. 'Wish me luck.'

He knocked on the door, then flicked a flake of dark green paint from his knuckle, listening to the rustle of wind high in the treetops. The door scraped away from its frame and Madeline stood there in her overalls and plaits, her style unchanged in fifty years. He smiled broadly. 'Good morning, Madeline! Whatever you're cooking in there smells delicious.'

'Silverside,' she said, unsmiling. 'I flavour it myself with vinegar, salt, sugar, cloves and bay leaves. None of that pre-packaged, chemical-pumped rubbish here.'

'Very wise.' He maintained his grin. 'Well, then, would you mind if I came inside? I was hoping we might have a little chat.'

'Now's not a good time,' she said. A tiny tabby cat appeared at her feet, peeked at Clarence, then stepped back again out of view.

'I only need a few minutes,' he persisted, with his most disarming smile. He had things to say that should have been said long ago.

'No.'

'I see.' He felt his smile falter. 'Have you heard about the wedding?' he asked suddenly, hoping to break through her resistance with some happy news.

'What wedding?'

'Two very big-name actors, Ying and Oden—'

'Never heard of them.' Her eyes narrowed.

'—well, it's the greatest good fortune for Stoneden. They're very eco-conscious, globally aware, grassroots-activist types who believe in supporting the local economy and all that, I think you'd like them, and they've decided to get married here in our tiny village! They're so impressed with the efforts we've been making to restore Stoneden to what it was back when the likes of you and I were youngsters. When we knew everyone's name. When we knew where our milk came from . . .'

'Mine comes from Grayson's cows.'

'. . . When we could all support each other at times of illness, or bereavement . . .'

'Stop right there,' she said, holding up her weathered hand. 'Bereavement?' She shook her head slowly, incredulously. 'You of all people dare to stand here and talk to me of bereavement?'

Clarence swallowed, feeling the colour bleed from his cheeks.

'Because of you and your hip-swaggering charm, my brother's life was ruined, just like that.' She snapped her fingers in the air.

'And now that Burton is in the home, I should be free to sell this house, to help pay for his care and also give me some freedom in the last mobile years of my life. But you've gone and ruined that, too.'

'But this is the point, Madeline,' Clarence said, trying to regain some footing. 'This is the beauty of the Renaissance Project. It's because of people like you – no, it's *for* people like you – that we want to return the village to the way it was. We want to recreate a resident-led community of people who care for each other, where people have the option to stay in their own home because they know they will be safe and looked after.'

'Bullshit,' she spat, making him flinch. 'Who were you looking out for the night of that dance? Not me, not Burton and not your precious Ellie, either.'

She said the word *precious* with such venom it made him flinch.

'You were looking out for yourself, and no one else.' She paused, her chest rising and falling with anger, her jaw muscles working. 'This was *my* time,' she said, grinding out the words slowly and quietly. 'And you stole it from me.'

Clarence opened his mouth, desperate to make it all right. 'I'm sorry, Madeline, I truly am.' He wanted to say so much more, about what a good man Burton was, had always been, about what a champion she'd been all these years since, about his foolishness in his youth, the wisdom garnered in hindsight, the things he wished he could change.

But he didn't get the chance to say any of that because Madeline slammed the door in his face.

•

Madeline moved on shaking legs to the couch and sat down, feeling the fury coursing through her veins, blinking away tears with an impatient growl. She wasn't one for tears. It was just that Clarence had arrived unannounced and she hadn't been ready for him.

The cat jumped onto her lap and settled immediately. Madeline threaded her fingers through her fur and the cat began to purr loudly. She had an incredibly loud purr for such a tiny thing. The cat had, apparently, moved in, fully possessing every room in the house with her napping spots, claw-sharpening stations and precision knowledge of when the fridge door was about to open. Surprising herself, Madeline realised she didn't mind at all. In fact, she absolutely loved her. She hadn't allowed herself to love a cat since she was six years old and found a kitten crying on the banks of the Fahn one cold spring morning, tucked it into her jacket and brought it home. But her father had tied it in a sack and tossed it back into the river while Madeline cried and begged and screamed, watching helplessly as the bag sank below the surface.

Now, Madeline folded herself over the little cat in her lap and broke into sobs, grieving for the kitten she hadn't been able to save, grieving for her own young self who'd been scolded for being 'too soft'. This sudden surge of long-buried pain confused her. How could she feel such grief over something that had happened so many years ago? She let the tears flow.

Then she sniffed and wiped at her eyes, looking down at the purring bundle in her lap. There was only one thing for it and that was to love this little cat with everything she had. Madeline had decades' worth of unspent love to share. Why shouldn't this abandoned kitten be the beneficiary?

Firstly, she needed a name. 'What would you like to be called?' she asked softly. The cat pushed her head into Madeline's hand and rolled over, exposing her white chest, reaching her white-tipped paws into the air. 'You might have come from humble beginnings but that doesn't mean you can't have a fancy name. There are no rules.' She ran through options in her head until she remembered, with an almost physical blow, the name she'd once thought of giving a daughter.

She stroked the cat's ears. 'What do you think of Eirlys?' Eirlys was a Welsh name meaning 'snowdrop', and it had enchanted Madeline the first time she read it in one of her childhood books. It had sounded like pure magic.

The cat reached out and grabbed Madeline's hand and buried her face in her palm, purring even louder.

'Eirlys it is, then.'

Madeline sat there for a long time, not wanting to move the cat, enjoying their closeness, feeling her heart awash with the unfamiliar sensation of unbridled love.

It also gave her plenty of time to sit and stare at the thing she'd not wanted Clarence to see, the reason she wouldn't let him in.

•

Helge arrived on Sunday night, having had Regine and Elias for the weekend before returning them to Birgit and jumping on a plane to England, excited to be there when Darcy woke the next morning, though his prime motivation was to be here to take Olivia on a date on the one day of the week that he could: Monday. Darcy was in bed, though it had been a struggle getting him to sleep. He was counting down the time till he could see his pappa again, cranky that he had to go to school tomorrow, but somewhat consoled that Helge was staying till the wee hours on Tuesday morning, when he would catch an early flight back to Oslo and go straight to work. He would start late, but fortunately, his job had a fair amount of flexible time available to him.

'Hi,' Olivia said, grinning like a fool in the open doorway. The sight of him in jeans and a sheepskin coat made her heart beat faster.

'Hi.' He smiled down at her, a little crookedly, and she had to take a deep breath not to throw herself into his arms.

'Have you eaten?' she asked, closing the door behind him and leading him through to the lounge room.

He shrugged out of his coat and hung it on the back of a dining chair. He was wearing a bone-coloured long-sleeved knit top, and she could see the outline of his pecs.

'I ate on the plane.' He made no effort to take his eyes from hers.

Oh boy. If she listened to her primal urges right now, they'd be naked in the next ninety seconds. She grasped the back of the nearest chair to steady herself. He stepped towards her, lifted his hand and ran his knuckle gently down her cheek. She closed her eyes and covered his wrist with her fingers, feeling the warmth of his skin, and he huffed a little, a haughty breath of pleasure at her reaction to his touch.

'Scrabble,' she whispered, opening her eyes.

He tilted his head questioningly, and dropped his hand from her face. She kept hold of his wrist, then slid her hand down to his so they could thread their fingers together.

'Would you like to play Scrabble?' she said, her voice strengthening.

He eyed the stack of games in the corner of the bookcase behind her. 'In English or Nor*v*egian?'

She laughed. 'How about both? I'll play in English and you can play in Norwegian.'

He grinned at her. 'You're on.'

Somehow she managed to get through the evening without giving in to her physical desires. Once again she'd set up a bed for him in the lounge room, and this was where Darcy found him the next morning, racing downstairs and landing on his chest, making Helge *oomph* as a knee landed painfully in his ribs. They played together and then wolfed down the pancakes Olivia made for them, until it was time for Darcy to go to school. He asked if Helge could walk him there so he could meet Miss Finch.

Olivia kissed Darcy goodbye and smiled, warm all over, at the sight of her little boy holding his father's hand as they walked down the hill to school. For a moment, she thought she might cry. She pulled herself together, and headed for the shower so she would be ready to go out on her first proper date with Helge in eight years.

Helge opened the passenger door of her van for her, and she slid into the seat, her blood humming with excited anticipation. He'd asked if he could chauffeur her today, and she'd readily agreed. 'Where are we going?' she asked, as he clicked in his seatbelt.

'*V*e are starting at Stow-on-the-*V*old.'

'Lovely. I haven't been there yet.' The car swooped down the hill and round the bend, heading along the river, and she spotted

Grayson on the opposite footpath, carrying a load of milk into Lance's store. He looked up, recognising her car, lifted his chin and smiled. She waved to him, but his smile faltered when he realised she wasn't driving. She felt bad, though she wasn't sure why. She wasn't doing anything wrong.

'Who is that?' Helge asked, turning onto the bridge over the river. There was a note in his voice that suggested jealousy, or suspicion.

'That's Grayson,' she said. 'He's the local dairyman and makes a delivery to the shop each morning.' She noted that she felt defensive of Grayson, or perhaps her friendship with him. 'He's lovely,' she added. Helge didn't respond.

Stow-on-the-Wold in Gloucestershire was a market town, the highest of all the Cotswolds villages, positioned at the junction of several major roads, which had led to its rich trading history. It was full of commanding stone buildings with shingled roofs and dormer windows, and long terraces of shops with the odd spot of colour – a bright blue door, a flower basket at an entrance. Olivia and Helge walked all over, then stopped to rest their feet and lift their energy with a coffee in Jaffé & Neale Bookshop and Cafe, breathing in the lovely smell of new books. They skipped the perfumery – though it was impossible to avoid the scents that wafted out the door as they passed – but stopped at the cheese shop, where they tasted more than was probably polite but made up for it with bags laden with cheeses from France, Italy and Switzerland as well as local cheesemakers. They ogled the jars of brightly coloured lollies in the Cotswold Sweet Company; Helge bought her a bag of milk-chocolate champagne truffles and she bought a fancy jar for him to fill with sweets of his own choosing, which included a significant amount of liquorice dynamites filled with creamy aniseed, something she personally detested but which made Helge grin like a little boy. They left the shop carrying their bags in one hand, and their free hands knitted together, the warmth between them shielding her from the cold day. It was a glorious morning.

They'd planned to drop in to a number of art galleries and she was touched that Helge remembered how much she loved art, but hunger had crept up suddenly. They took their bags back to the car then headed to The Porch House for lunch. They found a cosy corner in the atmospheric old pub and ordered a ploughman's lunch each, feasting on pie, sausage roll, quiche, pickles, cheese, ham and pints of beer.

'This is so yummy,' Olivia said, licking balsamic dressing off her fingers, grinning at Helge. Their knees were touching and neither of them was making any move to change that. He gazed into her eyes a moment, then slowly, so slowly, he leant in towards her. She moved to meet him, their lips locking together for the first time in eight years, for the first time since that tearful, heartbreaking farewell at the airport, Darcy in her belly, tying them together forever. Now, his lips felt even better than she remembered, soft and full. He tasted of salty ham and yeasty beer. She moved her leg up, wrapping her calf around the outside of his. For a moment, she forgot to breathe.

'I've missed you,' he murmured, pulling slowly away to drop small kisses on her jaw.

'Me too,' she whispered. She hadn't realised just how much she missed him until this moment. When she'd first seen him here in England, it had been all about Darcy, building her son's relationship with his father. But *this* was all about them, and what they might be in the future. Her pulse was racing. His hands were on her back, pulling her towards him. She'd been so right to come to England, so right to take this chance to be closer to Helge. Now that he and Birgit were separated, a surprising new opportunity had opened up for them.

'Let's go home,' she whispered, running her fingers through the small curls at the base of his hairline.

He groaned and peeled himself away, muttering something in Norwegian and pulling her to her feet. They headed for the car as fast as they could, their arms wrapped around each other.

It was a half-hour's drive home, and they held hands for most of it, Helge untangling his fingers from hers if he had to take a sharp corner. He talked to her the whole time, about Norway and the blinding sun as it bounced off snow-capped peaks and ski fields, about the particular beauty of rivers formed by melted glacial ice, about the Nordland train, which crossed the Arctic Circle, the scent of pine needles, and the gentle sunlight that filtered through forests in summertime. His words flowed over her like poetry, inducing feelings and sensations, while her mind was preoccupied with thoughts of what they were going home to do, calculating how much time they had before Darcy needed to be picked up from school, wondering if her bedroom was a mess, and whether Helge had condoms, because she knew she didn't, because she hadn't needed any in such a long time.

They stumbled entwined into the cottage, kicking the door shut behind them, his arms around her back, her hands around his neck. She walked backwards, letting him guide her towards the staircase. In passing, he flung his jacket onto the couch; her jacket dropped to the ground. His hands ran up under her shirt to her ribs, making her gasp. He smiled against her lips.

'You are so beautiful.'

At the staircase, she spun around and charged up the yelping wooden treads, pulling his hand. Together, they ducked under the lintel to her bedroom, smiling at each other in wonder. His eyes were focused on her face, her lips, her shoulders. It was exhilarating, his body so familiar and totally new at the same time.

'Have you . . . I haven't . . .' Between kisses, she tried to raise the issue of protection.

'I came to date you,' he said, dropping kisses along her shoulder.

'What does that mean?' she mumbled, lifting his shirt to reveal his toned abs and contoured muscles. 'You're gorgeous,' she said, admiring the expanse of golden skin. Words were beginning to fail her. 'Condom?'

'Pocket.' He lifted her shirt over her head and her long hair fell down the bare skin of her upper back. He slowed a moment, running his fingers through it, sending tingles through her body. 'Pocket,' he said again.

'Oh, right.' Her body pressed up against his, she slid her hand down over his glutes into his back pocket, her fingers digging around for the foil packet. Being this close to him, glued to him in this way, was the most delightful precursor of what was to come.

'God, I love you,' she said, without thinking. He bit her collarbone gently, making her groan.

'I wish you'd been here the whole time,' he said.

'Me too.'

He guided her backwards towards the bed and she sat on the edge, looking up at him, charged with attraction to him, charged with excitement for this moment and sadness for all they'd lost.

'I wish I'd had your help with Darcy for all those years.'

Her words made him pause. His brow lowered as he watched her, his chest rising and falling with his quickened breath.

'Sorry. I don't know why I said that.' She waved a hand, trying to shoo away the sudden change in mood. 'I didn't mean to . . . I'm not trying to make you feel bad.'

He dropped to the bed beside her and took her hand. 'I missed it all . . . everything. If I could change it, I *would*.' He leant his forehead against hers, rubbing his thumb over the back of her hand. 'I am lucky you *v*ere such a good mum to our boy.'

And there it was, the awful truth she'd been keeping from him: that the accident that nearly killed him was all her fault.

She took a breath. 'I need to tell you about Darcy's accident.'

21

Olivia had arranged for Darcy's sixth birthday party to be held at the playground opposite the white boathouse near the main street of Richmond. The boathouse rented out swan-shaped paddling boats and rowing boats to those wanting to meander slowly up Coal River towards the convict-built Richmond Bridge. Alternatively, bicycles could be hired to explore the heritage village at leisure. Olivia had invited Darcy's whole class, and the playground had space for the kids to run around, all twenty-two six-year-olds, plus their siblings, parents and even dogs.

Darcy's birthday was in August, and the day of the party was freezing but clear. The sun shone high in the deep blue sky, not offering enough warmth for people to shrug off coats and scarves but giving the day an optimistic air, as though winter would soon be broken. But by the end of the day, it wasn't winter that was broken, it was Darcy.

And Ma.

*

Olivia had begun planning two months earlier. She felt the pressure keenly, wanting him to have the best day possible and hoping he might forge a connection with his classmates that would carry over into the school playground. She began by sitting him down on the couch with her laptop and opening Pinterest to show him examples of cakes.

'Which ones do you like?' she asked, beginning to scroll down.

'Look at that one,' he said, pointing to a white unicorn cake with a tall, gold, spiralling horn and pastel-coloured icing swirls for the mane. She nodded. The unicorn was a popular cake, and she'd already made a few for clients. He giggled at the next one, pink pigs floating in chocolate mud. 'That's funny.'

'Would you like that one?'

'Nah.'

She kept scrolling while they considered Lego cakes, mermaid cakes, Paw Patrol cakes, Smartie cakes, My Little Pony cakes, lions, ladybirds, racing cars and monsters.

'That one!' he said, definitively, pointing at the screen.

She hesitated. 'This one?'

'Yes. I want that one.'

Granted, it was a magnificent cake, a work of art. It was based on the *Frozen* movie, which Darcy had discovered when he was five and promptly became obsessed with. She agreed that it was a great movie, but she also knew it was widely considered to be a *girls'* movie.

Darcy threw his arms around her. 'I love you, Mama!' He squeezed her tightly. 'I can't wait to see my cake!'

How could she refuse? It was his dream, and it was, after all, *just a cake*. Surely it wasn't that big a deal. She checked back in with him as his birthday approached, wondering if he'd changed his mind, but he was adamant. It had to be *Frozen*.

*

Olivia worked through the night to finish the cake. It had two layers, covered with thick fondant icing the same shimmering blue as Queen Elsa's dress, and white snow scalloped around the top of both layers. The figurine of Elsa was poised in dance on one layer, while the figurine of her sister, Anna, danced on the other. There was a plastic snow globe on top, enclosing her handmade Olaf snowman. A gold crown would go on the very pinnacle of the globe, and a net skirt around the base would finish it off. Olivia was hand-carving the white icing snowflakes and snow-covered pine trees when Ma came out of her room, perhaps disturbed by the lights on in the house.

'This is a mistake,' she said, her arms folded over her dressing-gown.

Olivia rubbed at her eyes, which were stinging with fatigue. Ma was a tall woman. Her short, wavy hair was flattened on one side, and her bottom lip pressed up into her top lip with worry, marionette lines reinforcing her disapproval.

'If we don't support his choice, who will?' Olivia snapped. She was sick of this argument. People attached so much judgement to cakes and movies and clothes. What did any of it matter? She wanted Darcy to be happy. If she and Ma didn't teach him how to know his own mind, who would?

'You overestimate people,' Ma said, giving her a good long stare.

'Maybe you *under*estimate them.'

Ma shook her head, as though remembering a hard lesson learnt. 'I found out the hard way that people can let you down when you least expect it.'

Olivia was momentarily distracted by this. What was Ma talking about? But she didn't get the chance to ask because Ma pushed on. 'I thought you wanted to help him fit in. This will only make him stand out more.'

'So what you're saying is you want him to *pass*, is that it? Hide who he really is?'

'That's ridiculous,' Ma said. 'He's turning six. He doesn't know his own mind yet. He needs your guidance. He needs you to protect him.'

'From what?' Olivia's voice was sharper than she'd intended.

'From other people. Learning to fit in, to assimilate, is a skill, a necessary one.'

Olivia waved her away, too exhausted to try to talk reason into Ma at two o'clock in the morning about a six-year-old simply being a six-year-old. 'I need to get this finished so I don't let him down. This is what he wants. We should respect that.'

The next morning, Darcy tore open his presents – Lego from Olivia, and from Ma a digital watch that played games – and they indulged in Darcy's choice of iced finger buns for breakfast. Ma washed hers down with black tea, directing her conversation towards Darcy, not Olivia, with whom she was stiff and cool.

They passed the next few hours playing games and building Lego, before packing the food, drinks, decorations, plates, cups and games into bags and into the car, ready to go. Olivia noticed that Darcy had slipped away. She found him in his room, sitting on the floor, pushing a train around on a track. He was dressed in long corduroy pants, a long-sleeved tee beneath a short-sleeved one, his jacket and beanie already in the car.

'Hey, Mr Darcy, are you okay?'

He looked up, but didn't smile.

She sat down on the edge of the bed. 'What's wrong?'

'I don't want the cake anymore,' he said, so quietly she had to lean towards him to catch the words.

'What did you say?'

He said it again and she felt the impact of each word in her chest, and her own resistance to accepting them. Yes, there was all the effort and the hours that had gone into making the cake – and it was a spectacular cake – but it was also the fact that he was backing out on something he'd wanted so much. And yes, it also stung that he was siding with Ma. Perhaps Ma was right.

'Did someone say something to you to make you change your mind?' she asked, as calmly as she could over the pulse of her rising anger. *Was it Ma?*

'Yes,' he squeaked, staring at her with the look on his face that meant he thought he was in trouble.

'It's okay. You can tell me,' she said, easing the sharpness in her voice. 'Who was it?'

'Ty.'

'Ty, from your class?'

'Yes.'

'What did he say?'

'He heard me say that I was having a *Frozen* cake and he started teasing me, saying it was a stupid cake.'

Olivia huffed. 'Well, that's a silly thing to say. He doesn't get to say what's stupid and what's not. He doesn't get to tell you what you like and don't like. He's not the boss of you.' She fought back mental images of herself inflicting violence on Ty. Darcy looked so sad. How dare that little bully ruin his day?

'It wasn't just him,' Darcy said, his voice louder now.

'Who else was it?'

'Devon.'

'Of course it was,' she muttered under her breath. Ty and Devon were two of the boys who had chased Darcy earlier in the year. They were both older than their years, prone to smutty comments and leers, whether influenced by older siblings or parents she didn't know. Darcy had never been exposed to the things those boys had been. He was still so innocent. Oh, if only he could remain like that, remain a child, for as long as possible.

She breathed out, trying to calm herself. As Darcy's mum, she'd been protecting him from the moment she first knew she was pregnant. It was her job to keep him safe. Recently, though, she'd read an article in which the author made the point that while a parent's instinct might be to protect her child from everything, she could never stop him experiencing pain. It was one of the hardest things to come to terms with. But given this reality, the only option was to help him walk into that pain and teach him how to come out the other side. It was her job to hold his hand as he went *through* the pain. It would be uncomfortable and painful for her too, but if that was her job than that was what she would do, starting today.

'Look, Darcy. Not everyone we meet in life is going to be our friend, even if we want them to be.' His brow crumpled as she spoke, as if she'd crushed his dreams. 'Not everyone will agree with your choices or respect you for them. But your duty in life is to honour yourself and your dreams. No one else will do it for you.'

'Huh?'

She'd lost him. Too many big words. She rubbed at her forehead, praying for inspiration. She looked up and there on Darcy's wall, next to a *Frozen* poster, was a colourful picture of Merida, the heroine of the movie *Brave*, drawing back her arrow, her wild red hair flying free.

'Today, you need to be brave,' she said. 'Today, you need to stand up for yourself and your right to like whatever you like and to celebrate your birthday your way. Do you think you can be brave today?'

He looked at her, then went back to running his train on the tracks. 'Okay,' he said.

She wished his voice was stronger, more convinced, but she'd take it as a start. She was going to help him to be whoever he wanted to be. Out of the corner of her eye, she saw movement in the hallway and turned to see Ma walking away. How long had she been listening?

The parents – nearly thirty of them, Olivia estimated – hovered around the picnic tables where the food was laid out, setting out chairs and blankets on the grass, opening thermoses of hot drinks. She noticed that they automatically formed smaller groups comprising those who were already friendly with each other. The kids ran off across the grass to the playground, to climb the ladders to the slides and swing from the rings and bars. Ma busied herself pouring cordial into paper cups and offering around trays of ham and cheese sandwiches while Olivia set up her cake. Several of the parents clustered around to admire it, pulling out their phones to snap photos, and a couple of mums enquired about ordering cakes from her.

'This is incredible!' said Tilly Anand's mum. Olivia had, regrettably, forgotten at least half the parents' names already. 'You must have been up all night.'

'I was.' Olivia laughed, holding aloft the cup of takeaway coffee she'd picked up from the bakery in the main street on the way.

'Well, it was worth it. He'll never forget this cake,' the woman said, picking up a handful of salt-and-vinegar crisps. Olivia liked her, and Tilly, who'd always been kind to Darcy.

Late by half an hour, Ty and Devon and their mums arrived together as a foursome. Olivia bristled at the sight of them, the way the boys punched and kicked the air, their loud, taunting voices. But she forced herself to greet them with a welcoming smile. The boys ignored her and the mothers grimaced disdainfully. Ty and Devon dug their hands into the popcorn and chips, shoving the food into their mouths as they ran off towards the playground.

'Nice cake,' Ty's mum said. It could have been a compliment if not for the sneer in her voice. She peered mockingly at Olivia through her thick fringe, her hands in the pockets of her jeans.

'It's amazing!' Tilly's mum said. 'You're so clever, Olivia. I wish I could do something creative instead of processing forms all day long.'

'My niece had one of those for her *first* birthday,' Devon's mum put in. She wore a black scarf with skulls and crossbones tied around her shaved head.

'Darcy only discovered *Frozen* last year at kindy.' Olivia tried to keep her composure. At kindy, all the kids seemed to love *Frozen* equally, and boys and girls loved dressing up in the gowns and dancing to the songs. 'He's a pretty typical kid in that he moves from one obsession to another. We've got good mileage out of it,' she added, with forced brightness. She looked over towards the playground, where she could see Darcy climbing the big rope spider net with Candice, who'd come dressed in an Elsa costume, taking her cue from the themed invitations.

Ty's and Devon's mums hadn't brought gifts, Olivia suddenly realised. She didn't care about the presents – birthday parties generated way too much stuff, and nobody could ever remember where the gifts had come from anyway – but it was telling that these two had chosen not to. Their resentment at being here was obvious from their sour faces and the sly looks they exchanged. Olivia wondered why they'd bothered to come at all. Neither of them had texted an RSVP, so she hadn't even been sure they'd turn up today, and she had no idea what their names were.

She smiled at them. 'I think I forgot to introduce myself. I'm Olivia.'

One nodded. The other said nothing.

Tilly's mum – Prema, *that* was her name – raised her eyebrows at their rudeness and shot Olivia a sympathetic look. Picking up a pikelet with jam and cream, she turned to start a conversation with Candice's mum. Olivia went to find the newspaper-wrapped gift to begin a game of pass the parcel.

As she carried it towards the playground, she heard raised voices and looked over to see Ty standing at the end of the slippery slide taking a swing at Darcy, who was trying to back up out of his reach.

'Hey!' Olivia called, horrified. She rushed towards them. 'Stop that!'

Ty was glaring at Darcy. Olivia looked over her shoulder to see if Ty's mother was watching her son, but she and Devon's mother were walking away towards the main street. Olivia would have to deal with this herself.

'He kicked me in the back,' Ty yelled, still glaring at Darcy.

'I didn't, it was an accident,' Darcy said, looking at Olivia, his eyes pleading. 'I just came down the slide.'

'Okay,' Olivia said. 'Darcy, how about you apologise for accidentally running into Ty.'

'Sorry,' Darcy said, still gripping the sides, trying to stay out of Ty's reach.

'Whatever,' Ty said, and charged over to Devon on the spider net.

Darcy gave Olivia a tremulous look, clearly shocked by the sudden attack. 'He hit me,' he said, wounded, rubbing his arm.

'He shouldn't have done that,' she said, feeling shaken herself. 'Are you okay?'

'Yes.' He slid slowly down to the base of the slide.

'Come on. It's time to play pass the parcel.'

She called the kids over to the picnic table, holding the wrapped parcel up high as an incentive for them to follow her and form a circle on the grass. Many of the parents gathered too, to watch the game. Olivia handed the parcel to Darcy to start it off and pressed play on her phone. *Trolls* music this time, to break up the *Frozen* theme.

At first, the game proceeded in the usual manner. Some kids held the parcel for too long and other kids yelled at them. Two kids had their hands on it when the music stopped and Olivia had to make a call. Each person who got the parcel unwrapped a layer of paper to find a chocolate frog as their gift, and Olivia had to focus hard to make sure that each of the kids got the chance to unwrap a layer. Then, midway through the game, Ty grabbed the parcel and jumped to his feet, roaring with triumph, and ran away to the playground, while Olivia called to him to bring it back. Devon ran after him, whooping and yelling, and then other kids followed. Darcy's face fell.

Beside Olivia, Ma *tsk*ed. 'Where's his mum?'

There was no sign of her. Olivia had no choice but to follow Ty to the playground herself to retrieve the parcel. By the time she got there, Ty and Devon had torn through several layers and were eating the chocolate frogs.

'Ty, stop,' she said. 'Hand me that parcel now.'

'Bitch,' he muttered, and threw the parcel on the ground.

Olivia gasped. Several kids squealed and told him off for swearing, while others ran back to their parents, shouting, 'Mum, Mum, Ty said a bad word!'

Olivia fought to stay calm. As she resettled the children to finish the game, she could feel her cheeks burning with rage at Ty, Devon and their AWOL parents.

The game ended, finally, taking its blessed time to get through all the remaining children, with Candice winning the ultimate prize of a kite-making kit. Ty and Devon returned from the playground in time to declare that it was stupid. Darcy's eyes widened in hurt.

'Let's do cake,' Olivia said brightly, putting her arm around his shoulders.

'Cake!' the kids squealed. Several parents collected their children and brought them to stand at the table. The shimmering blue and white cake in pride of place was stunning.

'I love this cake,' Tilly said, her hands held dramatically on either side of her face, and her evident delight soothed Olivia's shredded feelings a touch.

'Can I have the globe on top?' one girl asked.

Olivia brought Darcy to stand in front of the cake and then tried to light the six candles that she'd placed in the blue icing of the bottom row. Ma came to help shield the candles from the gusty breeze while she made several attempts.

Out of the corner of her eye, Olivia saw Ty's and Devon's mums sidle up to the group. Devon's mum screwed up her chip packet and tossed it towards a nearby bin. It missed and fluttered to the ground. She ignored it.

'Hurry up!' Ty demanded, and Olivia gritted her teeth.

The wind extinguished one candle after another, until a few of the more helpful parents gathered around with plates and shielding hands and finally all six were lit, casting a golden glow on cake.

'Okay, we got it. Happy birthday to you . . .' Olivia began the song slowly, giving everyone time to join in. It was awkward as they still had to shield the candles, but soon everyone was singing and Darcy was grinning, staring at the candles. When the song finished, one of the dads called out 'Hip, hip, hooray!' and Darcy leant forward to blow out the six flames.

Everyone had finished clapping when Ty said, 'I don't want a piece. It's a stupid cake.'

'Ty, that's enough.' Ma's voice cut across the gathered group. She had her hands on her hips and a fierce frown line between her brows.

'Well, it is! It's a *girl's* cake. He's a *girl*!' he taunted.

'That's not true,' Olivia said, at a loss for anything more effective to say. She didn't want to further ruin this moment for Darcy, but she couldn't let this brat tease Darcy in front of her, in front of everyone. She widened her eyes at Ty's mother, pleading with her to intervene.

'Ty, baby.' His mother smiled and shook her head at him as though he was just being a bit cheeky.

Then Devon joined in. '*Frozen*'s for girls. I don't want to eat it. Yuck. Girl germs!'

They were just words, Olivia tried to tell herself as she cut into the cake. Yet everyone knew the power of words, the insidious way they worked themselves into your mind and heart and stayed there for years to come. They were words of exclusion, of derision, of hatred, and it wasn't only Darcy they attacked; those words told every girl there that they were lesser, that there would always be something wrong with them.

Olivia was putting a piece of cake on a paper plate when the words came out of her mouth. 'Go away, Ty.' She meant to mutter them under her breath, but a sudden drop in the wind, combined with the shocked silence at Ty and Devon's behaviour, meant that everyone heard.

'What did you say?' It was Ty's mother, her voice loaded with anger and defensiveness.

Olivia closed her eyes momentarily, then straightened and faced the other woman. 'I think it would be better for everyone if you left now. Ty isn't happy here and he doesn't want cake and he's being rude and mean to my son and I'd like you to leave.' Her heart was rattling so hard and fast in her chest she could feel the tremor all the way to her hand, still holding the knife. She turned towards Devon's mum, who stood with her jaw dropped open in exaggerated shock, as if to imply that it was Olivia who was out of line. 'You too,' Olivia said to her, and nodded towards Devon.

'How dare you? Who do you think you are?' Ty's mother said.

Some parents quietly moved their children away. Ma stood squarely next to Olivia, the two mothers fixed in her stare. She reached out and pulled Darcy back towards her. Olivia knew that the confrontation was awful for Darcy to witness, but he'd been hurt too much already by this boy. It was his birthday party – he mustn't remember this moment as one in which his mother didn't stand up for him. Ty's behaviour was not okay, and she would not stand there silently, allowing it to go on.

'You wandered off and left your son here. He hit Darcy. He tried to ruin pass the parcel, and now he's being cruel to Darcy on his birthday, not to mention every other child here who loves *Frozen*.'

'You bitch,' Ty's mother said.

'Oh, yes, he called me that too,' Olivia said. 'I can see exactly where he gets it.'

Ty's mother lunged at the cake and smashed her fist into the top. Olivia jumped back in shock. Children squealed, and parents began to shout.

'Are you insane?' Olivia cried.

'My boy might have a bit of a mouth on him but at least he's not a faggot.' Ty's mother shook cake and icing violently off her hand, some of it whipping across Darcy's face. Ty and Devon shrieked with excitement.

Darcy burst into tears, broke away from Ma's hands and ran.

'Darcy!' Olivia dropped the knife and ran after him, but she was no match for a little boy sprinting flat out across the expanse of green grass, away from the party, away from the humiliation, away from the ugliness his special day had become, away from the hurtful words, towards home, she assumed. She wanted to call out to him but needed to save her breath, willing her legs to go faster and faster.

He got to the road well ahead of her. He didn't stop. He didn't look. Olivia screamed. The red car screeched, the noise tearing open the morning sky as if cracking open the dome of the snow globe, letting horror rain down on top of them all.

22

Helge was still naked to the waist but he was no longer touching her. He stood, his arms folded over his chest, his familiar broodiness darkening his expression.

'He flew through the air and landed in the gutter,' she said, suddenly cold. She reached for her shirt and slid it over her head. 'The sight of him . . . my God, the *sound* of him hitting the asphalt . . .' She couldn't finish.

Helge began to pace across the floor of her bedroom, his hands now resting on top of his head.

Olivia palmed a tear away from her cheek. 'Ma had the stroke that same night, while she was in the waiting room of the hospital. She fell, right there in front of me, unconscious.'

Helge grunted, still pacing.

'I tried to rouse her but couldn't. I called for help and a bevy of doctors and nurses arrived. They took her away for tests. She was wheeled past me on a gurney – her arm flopping out to the side. I thought she was dead.'

'But she *v*asn't,' he said, as if remembering back to that time and her frantic, teary phone calls.

Olivia shook her head. 'But she never regained consciousness. Sometimes I think it was the shock, remembering losing her own daughter, the fear of having to go through that sort of devastation again with Darcy. It was all too much.'

It was only after becoming a mother herself that she felt she could even begin to appreciate the magnitude of the kind of grief that followed the loss of a child, even if that child was an adult when they passed away. She hadn't appreciated it enough when she was younger, hadn't give due weight to what that had done to Ma.

'She died there in the same hospital while Darcy was waiting for surgery. I couldn't tell him right before he went to theatre, so I had to pretend, and then I had to tell him later.' She dropped her face into her hands.

Then she looked back up at him, steadying her voice. 'I'm so sorry. I should have listened to Darcy and left the cake at home. I thought I was doing the right thing, encouraging him to face his fears, not to back down, but I should have let him choose when he was ready to do that.'

'He could have died.'

'I know.'

'Your ma did die.'

His words were a slap in the face. 'I-I know that.'

They stared at each other a moment, then he picked up his shirt and shrugged it over his head. 'I *v*ill pick up Darcy from school,' he said, his voice hard and angry. He didn't look at her. '*V*e *v*ill stay out for a *v*hile, but *v*e'll be back in time for dinner.'

He left without another word.

They put on a pretty good show of solidarity for Darcy, she thought. He was swimming in happiness to have Helge pick him up from school and take him out for a nature ramble before dinner, to play with him and read to him before bed. He protested when they said he had to sleep in his own bed, rather than camp downstairs near the fire with Helge as he'd done last time, but Helge hugged him and promised to see him again as soon as he could. At last he was asleep, snoring softly upstairs.

'Are we going to talk about this?' Olivia asked, handing Helge a cup of coffee and setting herself down on the lounge.

Still sitting on one of the dining chairs, Helge took his time to answer. 'He could have died,' he said eventually. His face was drained of colour.

'Is this . . . are you only just realising this properly now?' she asked.

He shrugged. 'I guess so.'

'Look, I was wrong, I accept that. But I did the best I could. Parenting involves making dozens of decisions every day and I was doing it alone.'

He lifted his chin slightly. 'It *v*as a mutual decision for me to return to Nor*v*ay,' he said. '*V*e agreed. You didn't *v*ant to live in Nor*v*ay.'

She nodded slowly. 'That's true. I was a lot younger then. Maybe if I had my time over, if we had the same choice today, I would make a different one.'

They were silent a moment, and Olivia noted something growing and pulsating in her chest. Anger. 'But you had choices too,' she said flatly.

'*V*ot do you mean? I didn't have a visa to stay in Australia.'

'You didn't even try to get one.'

'My whole life *v*as on the other side of *v*orld.'

'And my whole life was in Tasmania.' She waved an impatient hand. 'Look, we made the best choices we could at the time.' She paused and realised she was clenching her teeth. 'What I'm wondering now, though, is why you never came to visit us once in seven years.'

A muscle flicked at the side of his neck, but he didn't speak.

'You're here now, but you could have come earlier, just once.'

His eyes flashed. 'And you could have come to me too.'

'How, Helge? I had a baby, then a toddler. I was a single parent. I was the sole trader in my business, which was my only source of income – an income that was lower than yours. It would have been easier for you to visit us than for us to visit you.'

'I had young children too.'

'Not for the first couple of years. And after that there was Birgit. You had two sets of hands, two people to make decisions, two people to share the load, two incomes.'

He glowered at her, but said nothing.

'It seems just a little too convenient that you're here now, to be honest.'

'Vot?'

She took a steadying breath. 'Don't get me wrong, I'm glad you're here, and Darcy is beside himself with joy. But let's face it, you're only here now because *we* took the leap and gave up our lives in Australia to come here, closer to you. So, yes, I'm sorry that I screwed up and Darcy got hurt.' Her throat threatened to close in on itself, the guilt still severe. 'You have no idea how sorry. But the fact remains that you weren't there. I can understand why you're angry, but to be honest, I don't think you've got much right to hold onto it for long.'

'I—' Helge stood, leaving his coffee on the table. He walked around the room, stopping in front of the fireplace for several moments, staring into the flames, his hands on his hips. She waited.

At last he sighed heavily and turned to face her. 'You are right.'

She flicked an eyebrow at him, vindicated. 'Go on.'

He smothered a fluttering smirk at her obvious satisfaction. 'I should have come to you. I have no excuse other than I *v*as young and dumb and I made the wrong choices. Now, I am changed.'

'I believe you,' she said, though her feelings were still deeply hurt. She didn't need Helge to dump guilt on her, she was more than capable of doing that for herself. 'I just thought you deserved to hear the whole truth, that's all.'

He nodded. 'Thank you.'

She was glad he knew the full story. If they were to have any kind of relationship, it had to be free of secrets. She just wished she felt better for having told him and that he didn't have to leave at four o'clock in the morning. She ran a hand through her hair, trying to shake off the tense atmosphere that lingered in the room. 'I think I might call it a night,' she said. She didn't want to risk ending up in bed with him now when it would be for all the wrong reasons.

Helge looked like he was about to protest, then nodded. 'I understand.'

She stood up and he wrapped his arms around her, holding her in a sad but determined hug. 'I had a great morning with you,' she said into his chest.

'Me too.'

'At least next time we can start with a clean slate.' She gave him a hopeful smile.

'Squeaky clean.'

'I'll come down before you go. I'll make you a coffee, okay?'

'Okay.'

They kissed lightly on the lips and she waved goodbye, ascending the creaking stairs, this time all alone.

The next morning, Grayson came through the door of Rambling Rose humming a tune under his breath.

'What are you singing?' Olivia asked, happy to see him.

'Morgan Evans. He's a country singer. Have you heard of him?'

'No. Not a big country fan.'

'Me neither, really. I like to cherrypick. He's Australian. You should look him up.'

'I might do that,' she said.

He put the crate of dairy products on the bench, and drew out a small posy of purple, yellow and white violas.

She took it, surprised and delighted. 'These are gorgeous. Did you grow them?'

He shoved his hands deep into his jacket pockets and grinned. 'I did – well, to be honest, I literally just threw a packet of seeds around near the house where the cows couldn't get to them and left them to it, so I can't claim too much credit.'

'Clever little seeds,' she said, gently touching the bright, velvety petals. 'I think it's amazing that whole plants, whole trees, can grow out of something so tiny.'

'I spotted them this morning as I was loading the truck and thought of you.' His face coloured, just slightly, and it made her speechless for a couple of seconds.

'Thank you, really. I love them.' She turned to find a small glass bottle and fill it with water, tucked the tiny stems into it and placed it proudly on her counter.

'Has Darcy recovered from his injury?'

'Yes, he's good,' she said.

'Glad to hear it,' he said. 'He's such a nice kid.'

'He really is.'

After a moment, he said, 'I saw you in your car on the way out of town yesterday.'

'Yes. I went over to Stow-on-the-Wold for the morning. Cute town.'

He nodded, and a silence stretched between them until she said, 'I was with Helge, Darcy's father.' She felt distinctly self-conscious as she spoke, as though she didn't want to let Grayson know because she didn't want to put him off. She liked him, as a friend if nothing else, though this posy of flowers suggested he might be hoping for more. She had to confess that she liked his attention.

'Helge and I met in Australia, but he left before Darcy was born,' she explained, unpacking the milk bottles from the crate. 'Before we moved here, they'd never met in person. Helge's started to visit us so they can get to know each other better.'

'That must mean a lot to Darcy,' Grayson said.

She smiled. 'He's so excited. It's been great for both of them. It's made the whole move over here worth it, just for that.'

'Is he married?' Grayson asked, straight-out. He softened it with a small smile, whether cheeky or self-conscious, Olivia couldn't tell.

'Yes, but he's separated. He and Birgit have two kids.'

'Huh.' He lifted his chin a little and gave her an appraising look.

'What?'

'Sounds like I'm still able to invite you over for dinner, then.'

She scoffed. 'Of course you can. We're friends, aren't we?'

'At least that,' he said, and winked at her, picked up his crate and turned to leave. 'I'll text you.'

'Okay,' she said, for want of any other sensible words floating to her brain. She put a hand to her cheek. It was warm and tight from smiling. That was one thing about Grayson, she'd noticed. She was always left with a smile on her face.

Several days had passed since Yoden's announcement that they would be holding their wedding in Stoneden and that Olivia would make their cake, and her days had become much busier. Each day this week so far, she'd fielded orders from a steady stream of new customers. Just today she'd taken orders for a sixtieth birthday party, a christening and a dog's birthday – the last order comprising two cakes, one for the human guests and one for the four-legged party attendees – all of them to be ready on the same weekend. Her little shop, too, had been packed with visitors, devouring her cherry brandy-drenched Black Forest cake and pikelets with jam and cream.

On Thursday, Rex Harrington arrived in the midst of a stream of customers, announcing a surprise health inspection, and proceeded to work his way methodically around her small shop with his trusty iPad, looking for hygiene transgressions. Olivia watched, embarrassed, as customers looked on. It must have been difficult for them to enjoy Bill Haley and His Comets rocking around the clock and savour mouthfuls of cherry curd and chocolate ganache while an officious man was searching for signs of filth and contamination. Of course, he found nothing of concern, and merely left after giving her a signed form, but she still felt shame creep up her body.

As she worked through the last hour of service, her mind drifted to the upcoming wedding. She couldn't wait to hear what Ying and Oden wanted for their cake. She wondered if they would have very set ideas or allow her some artistic freedom. Would it be a traditional cake, or something cutting-edge – requiring a chemistry set, a blowtorch and liquid nitrogen? If the latter, would she have the skill to make it? Or perhaps they would go the opposite way; she wouldn't put it past them to request a humble sponge cake with local berries picked from Stoneden kitchen gardens and cream cheese icing made from Grayson's cows' milk.

She washed dishes and wiped down benches, pausing to admire Grayson's flowers, which were still going strong, as she prepared the shop for tomorrow's trade. Then she slipped out of her navy button-down swing dress with white polka-dots and back into her overalls and skivvy and zoomed up to the school to pick up Darcy. There was one more thing she wanted to do this afternoon before they went home.

'What are we doing here?' Darcy asked, looking out at the lonely stone farmhouse.

'The lady who lives here, Madeline McCarthy, knew Ma when they were young. I'm hoping she might be able to tell us what she was like back then.' Olivia turned off the engine. 'Put on your coat.' She opened the door and the chill caught her in the throat. It wasn't anything she hadn't felt before in Richmond, but she could tell it would get even colder here in the depths of winter than it ever did in Tasmania. It was a different kind of cold. It was still only autumn, but the temperatures had peaked at no more than eleven degrees this past week.

Olivia knocked firmly on Madeline's door then tucked her hands into her armpits to keep them warm. Darcy hopped up and down on the spot, one hand clutching the paper dragon he'd made at school.

Madeline opened the door wearing a green tracksuit and sheepskin boots, her hair caught in a simple snag at the base of head today, rather than in plaits as Olivia had last seen her. 'Oh, Olivia,' she said, cautiously.

'I'm sorry to drop around without warning again – I really should get your phone number, shouldn't I?' Olivia said, smiling. 'And I'm sorry I don't have any cakes this time, but my customers ate every last crumb today. This is Darcy,' she finished, putting her hand on his shoulder.

'Hi,' Darcy said.

A tiny meow sounded from the hallway, and Darcy ducked down to look under Madeline's arm, which was still grasping the door handle. 'Aw, look, it's a tiny cat,' he said. 'It's okay. It's okay, little cat. We won't hurt you. We're friends.'

Madeline seemed distracted, disarmed even, by Darcy's gentleness. He crouched down on his haunches, trying to see the cat. There was another meow from inside.

'I had some more questions about Ma. Would it be okay if we came in?' Olivia asked, still smiling even as her teeth started to chatter.

'I don't think I've ever been so damn popular in this village as I have this past month,' Madeline grumbled, but nevertheless she stepped back and motioned for them to come inside.

'Thank you.'

Darcy crawled forward on all fours, following the small cat, possibly still a kitten, which scurried away into the lounge room. Olivia watched them a moment before looking around at the old farmhouse, as shabby and lived-in as she remembered from her first visit. She took in the sagging couch with its worn upholstery, the scuffed architraves, and the original raw stone walls, not rendered as in most of the other cottages she'd seen. Her eyes fell on a large rectangular object taking up most of the space in the lounge room. She was sure it hadn't been here last time. Several sheets were draped over it, falling all the way to the floor. She wondered what it was – perhaps a piano with its lid closed, covered to protect it from the dust?

'What's her name?' Darcy asked, crawling on his belly towards the cat, commando style. She'd taken refuge below an antique dark wooden buffet table.

'Eirlys,' Madeline said, her voice suddenly warm and proud.

'Here, Eirlys, here, girl,' Darcy said, clicking his fingers.

'Would you like some tea?' Madeline asked, abruptly.

'Yes, please,' Olivia said.

'Darcy, would you like tea?' Madeline asked.

'No, thanks,' he sang, his head disappearing under the buffet table.

Madeline went to the cabinet near the mysterious covered item and pulled out a tea set, carrying cups and saucers to the small kitchen. Olivia noted the unusual shape of the tea set, not round but hexagonal.

'Art Deco,' Madeline said, as if reading her mind, putting out two saucers with cups. 'And you can take the set with you. I don't need them.'

Olivia tilted her head, confused. 'Um . . .'

'There's only one of me and too much crockery. Absurd. It might as well go somewhere it can be used. I imagine you could put it to some use in your shop.'

'Yes, I could. Okay, thank you,' Olivia said, thrown by the unexpected offer.

Madeline filled the kettle and lit the hob, then ran hot water at the sink and swished it around in the teapot. She plucked a tea canister from a shelf and scooped heaped teaspoons into the pot. 'So, what do you want to know about Nora?'

Right. Straight to the point, then. Olivia had hoped to ease her way into the conversation, but clearly Madeline had no patience for small talk. 'I have a photo,' she said, digging into her handbag to find it. 'I was hoping you could tell me more about it.'

Madeline carried the cups and saucers over to the small table and set them down on the lace cloth. She took the black-and-white photo from Olivia, holding it at a distance to focus on it, before giving up and reaching for her glasses. She looked again, and her expression changed. Turning it over, she read the date on the back. There was a silence before she spoke. 'Goodness. I remember that dress well.'

'So you knew her, then, in 1966?'

Madeline raised her sparse eyebrows. 'Yes, I told you, we were friends.'

'I found this photo in Ma's things after she died. Recently, I was searching online for more information about her and found the same photograph.'

Madeline turned her head in surprise. 'On the internet?'

'Yes.'

The kettle whistled on the stove and Madeline moved to switch off the gas, still clutching the photo in one hand.

'It said the copyright holder was Burton McCarthy,' Olivia said, to Madeline's back. The older woman stilled, her shoulders hunched, as if expecting a blow of some kind. 'Do you know who that is? I know your last name is McCarthy but I didn't know if it was a married name or . . .'

'I never married,' Madeline corrected her. She poured the boiling water into the teapot and carried it and the photograph back to the table.

'Are you related to the photographer?' Olivia was excited now.

Darcy had enticed the cat out from under the buffet table with twitches of his paper dragon. The tiny bell on her collar tinkled merrily as she pounced. Snatching the dragon between her teeth, she ran away across the lounge room. Darcy giggled and followed her. She put the dragon down and waited, her tail flicking.

'Burton's my brother,' Madeline said.

Olivia waited, hoping for more details.

Madeline indicated that Olivia should sit, and then eased herself down into the chair next to her and poured the tea. She turned the cup in circles on her saucer while she thought. Across the room, Darcy was flicking the dragon from side to side for the cat to chase.

'Is Burton . . . still around?' Olivia prompted, as sensitively as possible.

Madeline raised her cup to her lips, staring into the middle distance. 'He is, though he's in a care home now.'

'I'm sorry to hear that,' Olivia said. 'Was he a keen photographer when he was younger?'

Madeline tapped the side of her cup with a thoughtful finger. 'Yes, he could have been quite good, I think, given the chance. He might have had a career as a professional, perhaps.'

'What happened?'

Madeline was silent for so long that Olivia began to wonder if she should repeat the question. She was about to speak, but Madeline got there first. 'He had an accident. He was crushed by a bull here, on the farm. He almost lost his arm. They saved it, but he never regained full use of it again, and he had permanent brain damage.'

'Oh, Madeline, I'm so sorry. That's awful.'

'It was.'

Out of the corner of her eye, Olivia noticed movement. Madeline must have seen it too, because they both turned towards the lounge room. The sheets that had been covering the mysterious item tumbled to the ground on top of Darcy and the cat, exposing the black object underneath.

Olivia stared at it, and her son sitting underneath it, then turned her head slowly to meet the older woman's eyes.

'Madeline, why is there a coffin in your house?'

Olivia arrived home to find a bouquet of pink roses and oriental lilies waiting at her front door. The aroma of the lilies was intense, seductive and sweet, and she smiled as she knelt down next to them.

'Are they from Pappa?' Darcy leant on her shoulder, peering at them.

'Let's see.' She plucked the card from the plastic holder and opened it.

I'm sorry. H x

She smiled and inhaled the heady scent again.

'Why's he sorry?' Darcy asked, reading the card over her shoulder. There was a worried note in his voice that made her heart squeeze.

She and Helge had to be so careful to get this right. Darcy's emotions were heavily invested in their relationship, whatever it was going to look like. His question was a warning bell for them both: they couldn't screw this up. Their son had to come first.

'Nothing, really,' she said, wishing she could think of something more reassuring to say. She couldn't tell him their argument had been about his accident. 'We were both sleepy and grumpy because he had to get up so early to catch his flight and we hadn't had any coffee.' She put her arm around him. 'Everything's fine. Come on, let's get these inside.'

They'd just closed the door behind them when her mobile phone *tinged*. The message was from Katrina.

Is it just me or is there far too much homework? It's driving me nuts!

It's not just you. Want to come over? The kids can do their work together and we can make pizzas. I've got bases in the freezer.

Be there in five. With wine!

Olivia put the flowers in a vase and turned on the oven. Katrina, Russell and Eloise arrived soon after, Katrina carrying bags of ingredients, Russell with two bottles of wine. Eloise skipped into the lounge, looking for Darcy, her long plaits swinging.

'Hey, Eloise!' Darcy called, thundering down the stairs. Olivia had given up trying to get him to slow down.

'This is the best idea ever,' Katrina said, dumping her bags on the kitchen table and taking out cheese and tomato paste.

'We should do this every Thursday night. It's more fun for them and for us,' Olivia said, lifting three wineglasses down from a cupboard.

'Agreed,' Russell said, opening a bottle.

'Nice flowers,' Katrina commented.

Olivia smiled. 'From Helge.'

'Ooh,' Katrina said, excited. 'Things are going well, then?' Russell glugged wine into glasses and handed one to Katrina. 'Thanks, babe,' she said. He winked at her.

'Yes, maybe, not sure,' Olivia said. 'They're apology flowers.'

'Ouch.' Russell sipped his wine and tilted his head towards the lounge room. 'That sounds like my cue to go and supervise the homework,' he said, excusing himself.

'What happened?' Katrina asked, taking a capsicum and mushrooms to the sink to wash.

'Long story.' Olivia groaned. 'In short, it was to do with Darcy's accident. I feel guilty, like I might have been able to prevent the accident from happening.' She took a gulp of wine. 'I wanted Helge to know everything. I couldn't have it hanging over my head.'

Katrina wrinkled her nose, as though assessing whether or not to press her for details now, but perhaps deciding to shelve that for another time. 'He didn't take it well?'

'It wasn't great, but it could have been worse. I did screw up. I'm not surprised he was angry.'

'But he wasn't even there,' Katrina said, starting to slice vegetables.

'That's kind of what it came down to, and he got that, and he apologised. But the moment was ruined.'

Katrina widened her eyes. 'There was a *moment*?'

Olivia grinned and felt herself redden. 'Very nearly. And you've no idea how difficult it was to stop that moment from reaching its . . . you know, climax.'

Katrina threw her head back and laughed. 'Oh no, what a waste!'

'Nearly eight years. That's how long it's been.'

'And you threw away your chance with *that* hot man? You're mad.'

Olivia took the pizza bases out of the freezer. 'You know what, though? It's actually my second bunch of flowers this week.'

'Who were the others from?'

Olivia tried and failed to suppress the smile that sprang to her lips. 'Grayson.'

'I knew it! He's been into you from day one.'

'He's going to ask me over for dinner.' She started spreading tomato paste over the bases.

'You must go. Let me know, and Darcy can stay over at our place. How long's this been going on?'

'There's nothing going on, really. Darcy and I went to his place for coffee. He brings me his dairy products each day. He's helped me out with the shop. We went for a walk . . .'

'Oh, that's right. The walk in the rain when you were chased by a bull. I suspected at the time that was a bit more than "just a walk". How do you feel about him?'

'I like him, a lot,' Olivia admitted.

'But . . .?'

'But Helge is Darcy's father. Darcy is crazy happy when Helge's here. If there's any chance that now is the right time for me to be with Helge, for Darcy to have his family together, then I need to be open to that.'

Katrina frowned and popped an olive into her mouth, chewing thoughtfully. 'I guess.'

'I need to be really careful about the choices I'm making. I don't want to rush anything, but I don't want to miss my chance either. And I have to think about Darcy's future too, what's best for him.'

Katrina sighed wistfully. 'Why is it that it never rains but it pours?'

'Beats me. But I came here to find a family, to find out where I belong in life. I can't not take this chance with Helge seriously. He *is* our family right now, and I still have a lot of feelings for him.'

'Trust me, *I* have a lot of feelings for Helge, and I don't even know the guy.'

Olivia laughed, but then added, 'The reality is that Grayson is an unknown.'

'Then get to know the unknown. You need to dive in with both feet,' Katrina said, pointing her knife at her. 'Do your researching and work out which one of these gorgeous men, if either, is the right one.'

With the fire crackling, the kids full of pizza and dancing to a playlist from Olivia's phone, and an empty bottle of wine on the table between the parents, Olivia told Katrina and Russell about her second visit to Madeline.

'She really has a coffin in her lounge room?' Katrina said.

'Yep. She's been painting it and lining it, and putting in a few of his things. She says it's the last big thing she can do for him, to prepare this coffin rather than letting strangers do it. She bought a plain wooden coffin and has done all the work to it. It's quite a piece of art, actually.'

Russell scratched at his beard. 'She's brave.'

'I wonder if Eli knows. That must be so sad for her, having cared for him her whole life, the last of her family.'

'I think she's sadder than she's letting on,' Olivia said.

'I'll talk to Eli. He'll go around and check on her.'

They were silent a moment, then Olivia spoke again. 'I have a photo of Ma from 1966, taken here in Stoneden. Turns out Burton took the photo.'

'Really? Can I see it?' Katrina asked.

Olivia fetched her handbag from the kitchen and drew out the photo, passing it to Katrina. She and Russell studied it, their heads close together. 'She was beautiful,' Katrina said. 'Look at those cheek-bones, her flawless skin, and that smile. Her eyes are lit up with joy.'

'They're practically sparkling, aren't they?' Olivia agreed.

Russell cleared his throat uncomfortably. Katrina whipped her head around to stare at him. 'What?'

'Nothing, really,' he said.

'No, what?' Olivia asked.

He made some ticking noises with his tongue, thinking, then said, 'She looks like she's in love.' He blushed.

Both Katrina and Olivia looked back at the photo. Olivia felt a swooping sensation in her chest. He was right. Ma seemed to glow as she gazed towards the camera. She inhaled sharply. 'Do you think . . . she and Burton . . . Could they have been . . .?'

'What did Madeline say?' asked Katrina.

'She said they were friends, that they all hung out together.'

Katrina frowned and turned over the photo to look at the date on the back. 'What year did Nora leave Stoneden?'

'Nineteen sixty-six.'

'Same year this was taken,' Russell said.

'Why would she leave if she was in love?' Katrina wondered.

Olivia riffled through her brain. Ma had said she had moved to Australia with her parents because work opportunities in the village were drying up, and everything she'd heard about Stoneden in the 1960s supported that explanation.

But something else was tugging at her thoughts.

She didn't often think about her mother, Laurie. Olivia was so young when her mother died that she had no memories of her, just a few photos that Nora had taken over the years, black-and-white baby photos, and a few weirdly coloured snaps from the 1970s and 1980s. When she did think about her mother it was in an abstract kind of way, this person who was important but of whom she had no real memories. But she knew that Laurie was nineteen years old when she gave birth to Olivia, which meant that Laurie herself had been born in 1967.

Nora's husband, Lawrence, had been more than ten years her senior. He'd left England to start afresh, away from the memories of his late wife, with whom he'd had no children. They'd had no more children after Laurie, and Lawrence had died from acute liver failure when Laurie was just five. His death had been the result of a rare allergic reaction to medication.

This was the story Olivia had been told.

But as she ran these scant details through her mind, she realised that the timing was very tight, the circumstances perhaps rather convenient.

She put a hand over her mouth, staring at Katrina.

'What is it?' her friend asked, still holding the photo.

It took Olivia several more seconds before she could speak. 'I think Burton might be my grandfather.'

23

Clarence struggled to remain upright on the uncomfortable three-seater sofa, a red studded-leather affair that was too tightly packed in the arms and back while too limp and saggy in the cushions.

'Here, take a cushion,' Bethan said, passing him a scratchy black woollen thing to prop him up, holding the baby in her left arm. Lillan was at yoga and Bethan was clearly at ease in the tiny one-bedroom flat. Clarence struggled to make sense of how the family lived here. The kitchen was barely a metre wide, the bathroom a few steps away from the stovetop. A four-tiered bookcase, stuffed with books, sat recessed into the wall behind this God-awful sofa, and the dining table was a sliver of wood against the wall above a couple of nasty-looking stools. The bed sat in a loft at the top of a set of terrifyingly narrow, wall-hugging stairs with no handrail.

'That can't be legal,' Clarence said, motioning to the stairs, which had been bothering him since he arrived twenty minutes ago. Arionna was already crawling. Any day now she'd be up those stairs – a fall from the top could be deadly.

'They've got baby gates, they just haven't put them up yet,' Bethan said, passing him the baby.

He held her up in the air, smiling at her and making silly *aboo aboo* sounds, while she giggled at him, two bottom teeth jagged white points in her pink gums. She smelt sweetly of baby lotion, and her fluffy romper suit had stains on the knees.

Bethan groaned a little with the effort of bending down to arrange a play space of sorts on the floor near the bay window, which overlooked the street. The flat was about a block away from Notting Hill.

Clarence blew a raspberry on Arionna's chest, making her squeal with delight and bounce up and down painfully on his thighs – she was a surprisingly dense little thing. He handed her back to Bethan, who had managed to get the lights flashing and the annoying tinny voices speaking on the plastic activity centre. Arionna quickly began pressing buttons to hear the sounds, spinning colourful wheels with rattling things inside them, and popping squirrels up out of plastic tree trunks.

'I know what you're thinking,' Bethan said, smiling. 'Why do the toys have to make so much noise? How can they raise a baby in this? Kids need room to run around and fresh air to breathe.'

'Am I wrong?' he countered.

'Well, if your project keeps going as well as it is, attracting celebrities, people will be flocking back to live in the village.'

Clarence grunted, watching Arionna grab a squishy snake and startle when it squeaked at her, her dark eyes widening. Then she giggled, and did it again. 'We'll be lucky if there is a project after this wedding,' he said.

'What?' Bethan stood near Arionna with her hands in the pockets of her stylish slacks, her smart blouse hugging her slim frame nicely. Her hair was short but with brushed volume on top, and she had wrinkles in all the right places – the kind of wrinkles that suggested she'd been laughing most of her life. No thanks to Clarence.

'Pepperworth's summoned me for a meeting later today,' he said. 'I've got a bad feeling.' It was funny that he could voice his fears so easily to her, when he hadn't even acknowledged them to Howard. Stupid pride again, probably. Bethan had already seen the worst of him. He didn't have to maintain any sort of front with her.

'What do you think he wants?' she said, her cheerful face suddenly determined and serious.

'Who knows, honestly? He doesn't need much provocation. The man has an axe to grind with me on behalf of his wife.'

'Ah, I see.' Bethan grimaced at him, then came to sit on the sofa. 'Oof,' she complained, and hauled herself back towards the edge, where it was more stable. 'You've not had a good run with the ladies, have you?' she said.

Clarence huffed and looked to the ceiling for a moment. He frowned – was that mould up there? He'd ask Howard to come with him next time and do a building inspection. 'I haven't always behaved well.'

They both watched Arionna squirm over to the window and press her little hands to the glass to stare outside.

Finally, Bethan said, 'I'm sure you'll work it out. You always do.'

He covered her hand with his in gratitude and gave it a squeeze. He'd never deserved her.

Chester Pepperworth delivered the blow over lukewarm coffee in a crowded cafe in Fahren Way. 'The council will be meeting soon after the wedding to vote on the dissolution of the Renaissance Project, and we have the numbers to win,' he announced with a delighted sneer.

'But the wedding will change everything,' Clarence said, lowering his voice in the hope that Chester would follow suit. You never knew who might be listening.

'Temporary madness,' Chester said, patting his mouth with a serviette. 'Before the announcement, the village was imploding with attacks on the imports.'

Clarence scoffed. '*Attacks* is a strong word,' he countered, while simultaneously reliving the menace behind the words painted on Raj's and Leanne's shops.

'Council believes those issues are only the beginning, that it is inevitable that the offences will escalate. We don't want to see a further breakdown in law and order, and we feel it is best to stop the dangerous project now, in order to protect our citizens. As for the wedding, it will be a shooting star, blazing for a moment across the media firmament and then gone.'

'Rubbish,' Clarence hissed. 'The wedding is the perfect chance to put Stoneden on the map and attract tourists to boost the economy.'

'Listen to yourself. That's exactly the opposite of what you were trying to achieve with the project. You wanted to return Stoneden to what it was in the Fifties – a quiet, insular, self-sufficient village. It was the tourism trade that you railed against. You cannot have it both ways.'

Was Chester right? Clarence paused, staring at his adversary till he could stand the sight of him no more. Surely, though, adaptation was the key to success – being flexible, open to new opportunities. Yes, he did want Stoneden to be a working village again, ideally one that didn't have to rely on tourism to prop up a handful of businesses while the residents had to travel further and further afield for substantial services and supplies. But going back to the 1950s wasn't the answer either, he knew that. There had to be a compromise, a new version of Stoneden that combined the spirit of the old village with the best of the modern world.

'Please don't do this,' he said heavily, hoping to appeal to some kernel of compassion in the small man across the table. 'Give us a bit more time.'

But Chester stood up and reached for his homburg. 'The deal is done.'

24

Clarence's apologetic call came through at midnight, and soon afterwards Olivia was dressed and stumbling bleary-eyed and somewhat grumpily down the stairs. All the key wedding people had been summoned to the manor immediately to meet with Ying and Oden's minders, who Clarence said had managed to slip unnoticed into the village in their silent, sleek, black car. Knowing that Olivia couldn't leave Darcy on his own, Juliet had offered to come over for a few hours.

'It's so generous of you to help out,' Olivia said, opening the door to Juliet's quiet knock and leading her through to the kitchen.

'Not at all.' Juliet looked tired around the eyes but was still smiling. 'As a vicar's wife, midnight calls come with the territory.'

'Though not usually to do the bidding of celebrities, I should imagine.'

Juliet snorted. 'No, this is a first.'

Olivia quickly downed a triple-strength coffee and showed Juliet around, whispering so as not to wake Darcy. Driving away down the hill, she was glad that she and Juliet seemed to have moved on from the awkwardness of the cake incident, but she was still annoyed at being dragged from her bed in the middle of the night by celebrity managers who clearly felt entitled to order ordinary plebs like her around.

As she neared the manor, though, her heart rate kicked up a notch, the caffeine taking effect, accompanied by a little thrill of excitement. This wedding would be the highlight of her career so far – and perhaps propel her towards even starrier heights. Maybe she might get to do the next royal wedding, if not in England then maybe overseas. Perhaps even in Norway. The thought was lofty, sure, but exhilarating. She'd had no idea anything like this might happen when she left Tasmania just two months ago.

A dozen or so cars were parked outside the manor, which was in near darkness, only slivers of light showing around the closed drapes. Her breath cast misty clouds as she crunched over the gravel. She was stopped at the front door by a tall man with tree-trunk legs in a dark suit who asked her name, and then repeated it without taking his eyes off her. She hovered awkwardly and was about to ask him what was going on when he nodded curtly and stepped aside. He must have been checking her name via some sort of headset, she realised.

She pushed at the door, which swung open quietly. A circle of people sat in plush chairs beside the fireplace, in various states of dishevelment. Clarence looked up and smiled at her, waving her over. She approached self-consciously. Was she the last one to arrive?

'Olivia, come join us.' He gestured to two unfamiliar people seated to his right. 'This is Ferdinand and Giselle,' he said, then gestured towards her. 'And this is Olivia Kent, our cake maker.'

The pair wore matching high-necked black tunics over black pants and black shoes. Their black hair was pulled back from their faces in matching severe buns, and they regarded Olivia through black-rimmed eyewear. They also clutched the same thick, leather-bound diaries on their laps. Olivia felt an unwelcome bubble of mirth making its way up her chest, but clamped it down quickly when she saw their expressions. She couldn't tell if they were glaring at her or if their faces were simply immobilised by botox. 'Hi,' she said uncertainly, and sat down.

'I think we're all here now,' Clarence said to Ferdinand, who passed him a list of names to check off.

Olivia looked around. She recognised about half the people in the circle. Viola was wrapped in a fluffy knitted shawl, her eyelids heavy. Olivia gave her a sympathetic smile as she tried to hide a yawn. Miguel was there, with Elena, Newton and young Lance. She was disappointed to see that Grayson wasn't there, but presumably he was one of the suppliers whose products would go through a central source, such as Lance's shop. Leanne looked the most alert, evidently quite used to being up in the middle of the night. Anthony Cabot sat beaming comfortably, as though this was the most normal way to spend the night. That left another half-dozen people whom she guessed were suppliers from nearby villages.

'Yes, all here,' Clarence said, passing back the list.

Ferdinand reached up to touch his ear and muttered something into his sleeve. Then he resumed his expressionless silence while the gathered villagers exchanged confused looks. The silence stretched into brittleness as people began to scratch and sniff and shuffle.

Then the heavy front door opened again, and Ferdinand and Giselle stood up. Everyone else turned to look as Ying and Oden walked in, hand in hand. There was a collective gasp and one or two stifled yelps from the circle, a smattering of nervous giggles and applause. Elena muttered something to herself in Italian and put a hand on her chest, clasping Newton's hand with the other.

Without any logical explanation, Olivia's own eyes filled with tears like some sort of hysterical groupie who'd just seen the Beatles walk in, or perhaps Ed Sheeran.

Ferdinand and Giselle showed the actors to their vacated chairs, then stood on either side of them, clearly signalling that no one was to approach. Olivia wasn't sure she could have stood up if she'd tried. Her legs had turned to cooked spaghetti. As her cheeks started to burn, she realised she was grinning – enormously.

The actors took a moment to settle into their seats. Ying wore a stunning full-length cream silk dress, the sleeves shot with shimmering silver. Cute dimples appeared in her rosy cheeks as she smiled warmly around the circle, acknowledging each of those present with her piercing dark gaze beneath long dark lashes. She radiated mystique, and breeding, and wealth.

Beside her, Oden crossed one leg casually over the other knee, his smile roguish within his unexpectedly luxuriant beard. 'Good morning,' he said in an upper-class British accent, and gave a hearty chuckle at the stunned faces staring back at him.

'Morning,' a few people replied, faintly. Olivia couldn't speak. She was starstruck, well and truly.

Oden adjusted the open-necked white shirt beneath his black jacket, revealing more tanned skin. 'We apologise for the ghastly hour of this meeting. We're aware that you all have families and jobs and lives you need to get to when the sun comes up, and so we won't take up much of your time now.'

'It's *absolutely* fine,' a young woman said, leaning forward in her chair. Several other people chimed in to agree. Realising she must look exactly like that woman, with her big smile and sparkling eyes and eager-to-please posture, Olivia made herself sit back in her chair.

'We wanted to meet all of you,' Ying said. 'You are the ones who will be making our wedding day dreams come true.' She put her hands together in prayer position at her chest and dipped her head gracefully, and several people mimicked the gesture. 'We also wanted to introduce you to Giselle and Ferdinand, who are our executive assistants.' The distinct lack of enthusiasm on both sides was embarrassingly evident. 'Due to our schedules, sadly we won't be able to discuss details with you personally, so you'll be communicating with them instead.'

Olivia gave an involuntary whimper of dismay, which she hoped no one heard.

'We have great faith in you,' Oden said, running a hand through his artfully messed-up hair. 'We're so impressed with the Renaissance Project and this village's efforts to rejuvenate a local economy.'

Olivia glanced at Clarence, whose eyes were fixed on the ground as he listened, his face red with pleasure and pride.

'You're leading the way,' Ying added. 'We hope that by holding the wedding here we can highlight the achievements of this village and inspire other towns to consider following your example.'

'Thank you for having us in Stoneden,' Oden said.

'Yes, thank you,' Ying echoed.

'Thank you for choosing us,' Clarence said, his voice a little gravelly.

'You made it an easy choice.' Oden smiled.

'We know some of you might feel a little nervous, even overwhelmed by the intensity of the attention this will bring to your village,' Ying said. 'We're here to assure you that we want the wedding to be fun and creative. We don't expect perfection.'

At that, Giselle cleared her throat and looked to the ceiling. Evidently she didn't agree.

Ying and Oden exchanged a glance, then Oden leant forward with his forearms on his knees, wrinkling his brow and lowering his voice. 'We do have one favour to ask, though. Well, two requests, actually.'

The circle of villagers inched forward on their chairs, listening attentively.

'We announced that the wedding would be at Christmas time.'

Olivia held her breath.

'But we want it to be earlier than that. We've decided to hold it on the last Sunday in November, about four weeks away. But we'd like you to keep the date a secret from everyone.'

'No one outside this room is to know,' Ying added, her sparkling eyes hardening.

'No, no, never,' the murmurs went up.

'We appreciate your discretion,' Oden said. He straightened up in his chair again, and there was a collective rustle as the rest of the circle followed suit. He clapped his hands together once, happy. 'So, we'll see you at the end of this month!'

With that, the pair rose, nodded their farewells, clasped hands and returned to their waiting car. Giselle and Ferdinand continued to glare mistrustfully around the circle. Ignoring them, the gathered locals slowly began to mutter and exclaim among themselves. Four weeks! The village was about to get very busy indeed.

Olivia was finishing a traditional fruitcake with thick white fondant icing and a yellow ribbon for a christening tomorrow when Grayson texted.

> Dinner tomorrow night? My
> place. I'll pick you up. ☺

Anticipation skittered up her spine. She quickly texted Katrina to see if Darcy could sleep over, and Katrina agreed immediately, attaching an animated GIF of Snoopy dancing in a circle. Then Olivia replied to Grayson.

Sounds great ☺

She had a big day ahead. Fridays were always busy in the shop, and she also had three special orders to make for the weekend. Four, actually, since the dog's birthday party consisted of two cakes. She was in the zone, totally focused on her work, not allowing herself to get distracted by thoughts of the wedding.

On Saturday morning, she had the gratification of presenting her creations to a series of delighted clients. The woman who came to pick up her mother's sixtieth birthday cake was thrilled. The cake was in the shape of a flamingo, with each individual bright pink feather, the eye, beak, long pale legs and a string of pearls around its neck crafted in fondant icing. It had been a lot of work to create but really rewarding. Olivia had taken several photos of it for her Instagram account and her lookbook.

The dog's owner was equally impressed with her English collie's peanut butter cake with whipped coconut cream topping and biscuit bones, and the triple-layered gingerbread cake with eggnog icing and lashings of salted caramel drizzled from top to bottom for the human guests.

'It's Lady's fifteenth birthday,' the woman said, her eyes going bright. 'We won't have her for much longer. We've invited all the people who love her, and a professional photographer will be there to capture the day.'

'That's amazing,' Olivia said. 'It's been a joy to make this cake for her. I hope you all have a wonderful day tomorrow.'

'Thank you,' the woman said, nodding and choking back emotion.

Olivia helped her load the cakes into her car. 'Give Lady a cuddle from me,' she said, waving her off. Not for the first time, she marvelled that something as simple as a cake could become the focal point for so much human experience and emotion, and represent the crossing of a threshold from one stage of life to another. It humbled her to play a role in these traditions. It reminded her why she loved her job so much.

She was standing in the bathroom, a hair band between her teeth, separating her hair into three sections to weave a long plait down her back, when Grayson arrived, his truck crunching over the stones in the driveway.

'That's Grayson,' she said to Darcy, who ran to open the front door.

'Hi, Grayson,' he called.

Olivia hurried to finish plaiting her hair and checked her make-up.

She heard Grayson at the door. 'Hey, Darcy.'

'Mum's in the bathroom,' Darcy said.

'Nearly done,' Olivia called.

'Want to play Guess Who?' Darcy asked him, closing the door.

'Sure.'

Olivia stepped out of the bathroom as they were setting up the game on the kitchen table.

'Mama, you look beautiful,' Darcy said, pausing to beam up at her. She was wearing her dress jeans with a new black asymmetrical long-sleeve knit she'd picked up from Wilhelmina's store. A gold chain hung down to her navel.

She walked over and squeezed him around the shoulders. 'Thank you.'

'I have to agree,' Grayson said, grinning at her. Then he motioned to the board. 'We're just going to have a quick game.'

'Take your time,' she said, loving very much that Grayson would jump in and play with Darcy. She and Darcy were a package deal.

'I go first 'cause I'm the youngest,' Darcy said.

'Sounds fair.'

'Hm . . . Does your person have yellow hair?' Darcy asked, seriously, like a miniature detective.

'No.'

Darcy flicked down several cards.

'Does your person have earrings?' Grayson asked.

'No!' Darcy leant his chin in his hand, staring at his array of suspects. She loved him so much it hurt, and that was what made this whole dating thing so tricky. As they played, she let herself enjoy looking at Grayson, so tall and broad, his farmer's fingers accidentally knocking down the wrong characters on his board. And when he lost, as he was always going to, he asked Darcy if he wanted to play again.

'Maybe next time,' Olivia interjected. 'Eloise is waiting for you, Darcy. Have you got all your things to stay the night?'

'I think so,' he said, jumping up out of his seat. As much as he obviously liked playing with Grayson, the lure of Eloise's company would win every time.

Grayson drove them down the hill to Katrina and Russell's place, and they delivered him there with minimal chitchat, Katrina waving them out the door and saying she would drop Darcy back to Rambling Rose at midday. Then Olivia and Grayson were alone, driving down the dark roads towards his farm.

'Hi,' Grayson said, sneaking a sideways glance at her.

'Hi.' His attention made her feel jittery – happy but nervous. Her mind jumped unbidden to Helge for a moment, and she wondered what he was doing this weekend with the kids.

It was only a short drive to his farm. As Grayson pulled up outside the house, lit up invitingly from within, Olivia peered out his window, noticing something new since her first visit. Next to the cow paddock was a tiny house on wheels, no bigger than a standard caravan.

'Oh wow!' she said. 'I love tiny homes. I've been fascinated with them for years. When did you get that?'

'Just this week,' he said, the truck's engine ticking down in the sudden quiet. 'Found it on Gumtree.'

'What are you going to do with it?' For now, the building had plain brown wooden planks for walls and a pitched roof, a door and a single window, but she could imagine it once it was done up, with a colourful exterior and window and door trims, curtains hanging inside. The possibilities were endless.

'Not sure yet. The people I bought it from built it themselves, but their plans changed. It's just a box, not fitted out inside yet.' He shrugged, looking a little self-conscious. 'It was a spur-of-the-moment thing, a new project to work on, and super cheap. The price alone made it impossible to pass over.'

'Well, I can't wait to see what you do with it. Let me know when you want to do a tiny house warming and I'll bake you a tiny cake. I'll even craft a figurine of Ruby.'

He grinned at her. 'That would be cool.'

They climbed out of the truck and entered the house through the unlocked door. It was beautifully warm inside, and she could smell wood smoke and something else amazing.

'What are you making?' she asked, laying her coat over the back of a chair.

'It's a surprise,' he said, shrugging off his own jacket.

'Can I help?'

'Absolutely not. Tonight is all about looking after you.'

25

Grayson returned from the kitchen carrying two pieces of pumpkin pie for dessert. They'd eaten on a rug in front of the fireplace in the lounge room, with lots of cushions and a low square table the perfect height for eating on the floor. The fire was crackling melodically. The evening's pumpkin theme had already lent itself to soup, which tasted great with sour cream and crusty bread from Leanne's bakery. That was followed by rosemary and lemon roast chicken, potatoes and, naturally, pumpkin, with gravy and vibrant green peas. Olivia wasn't a pumpkin enthusiast, but the man could cook, that was for sure. He'd gone to a lot of effort and it wasn't often someone cooked for her, so she wasn't going to complain. Besides, going by the number of huge green and grey pumpkins she'd seen stacked in rows along Grayson's kitchen walls, he needed to use them up.

'This looks amazing,' she said, taking the plate. The golden pie was served with a big dollop of thickened cream on the side.

'I have to confess I didn't make the pie shell,' he said, lowering himself back down to the floor and adjusting a cushion. 'It's rather intimidating trying to make dessert for a pastry chef, so I didn't even try. This one's from Tesco.'

'It's all incredible,' she assured him. 'I'm so full, though; I'm not sure how much of this I can eat.'

He smiled at her, and the flickering firelight danced across his glasses. She'd been surprised to see him put on his blue-rimmed specs, but they suited him, framing his gorgeous eyes, which had so much detail within the iris it was like looking down through water and seeing the changing depths of the ocean floor.

'All optometrists have glasses,' he'd laughed, when he saw her looking. 'But I usually wear contacts.'

She took a bite of the pie. It was sweet and creamy, with slightly too much nutmeg, but really good. Still, she was bursting. 'That is delicious but I will absolutely pop if I eat any more.'

He turned his spoon upside down in his mouth and sucked on it like a lollipop, which she found ridiculously cute.

'How did you end up with so many pumpkins, anyway?'

He chuckled. 'They're from my customers.'

She frowned. 'Your milk customers?'

He put the rest of his own pie down on the table between the half-empty bottle of white wine and the salt and pepper shakers, which were fire-engine red. 'I deliver milk to many older members of the community, a lot of them living out of town.'

'Like Madeline.'

'You know her?'

'We've met a couple of times.'

An interested smile tugged at the corner of his mouth. 'You talked about me?'

She grinned in response to his flirtiness. 'A bit. Anyway, go on. You were telling me about the pumpkins.'

'Many of these people don't have much money but they do love the idea of getting fresh milk from a local farm – that's one part of the Renaissance Project they appreciate. It's the restrictions on selling property that are hurting some of them.'

'So, they pay you in pumpkins.'

He nodded. 'Yep. I can't eat them all, so I feed them to the cows. They love them.'

'Then I guess they are kind of paying you, aren't they? They're giving you feed for your cows.'

He lifted one burly shoulder. 'Not really. Pumpkins aren't a staple for the cows, they're more of a treat. But yes, they're trying to pay in their own way.'

They were silent a moment and Grayson held her gaze for long enough to make her face flush. 'I've really enjoyed having you here tonight,' he said, his voice low.

'I've enjoyed being here. Thank you for making me dinner.'

'Pleasure. I'd love to do it again.'

'So would I.'

Grayson looked pleased at that, and shuffled towards her. 'Is it okay if I come and sit over here?'

'Yes.'

He kept inching towards her, making fun of the stiffness in his knees, which made her laugh, and she watched his body move closer and closer to hers. She took in the strength of his broad shoulders under his soft-looking tartan shirt, the curve of his hips sinking towards the floor, the straight outline of his thighs up to his knees. His woollen socks. The five o'clock shadow of whiskers on his jaw. The scent of nutmeg on him. The pressure of the air between them intensifying as he brought all of that over to sit beside her. She liked it all.

'I'm glad I moved to Stoneden,' she said.

'Me too,' he said, his voice husky.

She was suddenly aware of the silence in the room, the only sounds the occasional popping of the fire and the pounding of her pulse in her ears. Momentarily unnerved, she blurted out, 'Do you have any addictions?'

Grayson blinked, then burst out laughing. 'I think that's the most original question I've ever been asked on a date.'

She buried her face in her hands, her body shaking with giggles. 'I can't believe I just said that.'

'No, it's fabulous. People should be a lot more careful about who they're getting into . . .' he caught himself – before he said 'into bed with', she guessed – and finished, '. . . involved with.' He took a sip of wine, thinking, then placed the stemless glass back on the table. 'To answer your question: no drugs or alcohol or gambling or sex addictions, but, as well as my large collection of pumpkins, I have been collecting anchors for many years.'

She looked at him blankly. 'Anchors? Like, off boats?'

'Yes.' He pointed up above the fireplace. 'That's one.'

She followed his finger, staring up at a large mixed-media artwork on canvas. Black and white stripes formed the background to a red anchor with a rope twisted around it. She'd noticed it when she first came into the room but hadn't thought much of it, just taken it in as part of the generally masculine vibe of the room, with its dark brown leather couches, cowskins on the floor, and a wine rack made from horseshoes. Looking around the room now, her eyes fell on an actual anchor in rusty brown iron, about the length of her shinbone, propped up beside the bookcase.

'Yes, that one too,' Grayson said.

'What made you collect anchors?'

He shrugged. 'My grandfather was a sailor so I spent time on his boat as a kid. He gave me a real anchor for my tenth birthday and it seemed like something straight out of a pirate story.'

'How many do you have?' She was fascinated.

He turned his eyes to the ceiling, mentally counting. 'Including the big ones in the milking shed and the smaller ones around the house, the painting, the fridge magnets . . . I don't know. Thirty, maybe?'

Anchors – she could deal with that. 'You'll have to give me the tour sometime.'

'Your turn,' he said. 'Any addictions?'

'Hm, none of the usual ones, like pumpkins or anchors, but I would have to confess to marshmallows.'

He raised his eyebrows. 'Go on.'

'Only Pascall marshmallows, though.'

'Ah – this is what Darcy was referring to the other day.'

'Yes – sadly, I think I've passed my addiction on to him, but it's only for the pink and white ones.'

'Very specific.'

'It is! They have this dry coating that cracks and crumbles when you first put them in your mouth, but if you can restrain yourself from biting into them, they start to melt around the edges, and then they're silky smooth and stretchy, and when you finally can't stand it any longer and bite down, the flavour of the raspberry or vanilla comes out.'

'So, what, you eat whole packets of them?'

'Sometimes, yes,' she confessed. 'Once I start I really can't stop. I also love them in hot chocolate or melted over a fire, but I think they might be best frozen.'

'Frozen?'

'Yep. Put them in the freezer and they go cool and chewy. So good!'

'You're going to have to introduce me to these wondrous things.'

'It's terrible if I need to use them in a cake, though. I eat at least as many as I use.'

He smiled at her, then looked down at his jeans and tugged at the seam a moment. 'Would it be okay if I kissed you?' He raised his eyes to hers. 'You know, after what we were talking about the other day, with my sister and all she went through, Me Too and all that, I want to do the right thing. I want everything to be really clear. I'm doing my bit to lift the standard.'

She nodded, impressed. 'Yes.'

He scratched at his jawline. 'Yes, you understand what I'm saying, or yes, it's okay if I kiss you?'

She grinned at him. 'Yes, it's okay if you kiss me.'

'Good.' He moved even closer and she held her breath, waiting. But then he paused, inches from her lips. 'So we're really clear,' he said, his voice rough with desire, his breath warm on her cheek. '*Enthusiastic consent* is the catchphrase of the moment. In that spirit, do you think I could get a bit more than a *yes*? Any chance I could get a *hell yes*?'

She leant in towards him and grasped the front of his shirt. 'Hell yes,' she whispered, and pulled him towards her.

Their lips met. He was warm and nutmeggy and all sorts of wonderful, and it was just as well she was already sitting on the floor, as she'd gone weak at the knees.

Olivia woke early the next morning. She hadn't slept much since Grayson dropped her home last night. They'd spent a long time kissing in the doorway like teenagers, before he'd finally groaned and pulled himself away, blowing her a kiss as he climbed back into his ute. She smiled as she remembered it, glad they hadn't done more at this stage than kissing – okay, a *lot* of kissing – but enough to know they definitely had chemistry.

It was dark and the house was quiet, Darcy still at Katrina's, but Olivia knew she wouldn't go back to sleep. She climbed out of bed and pulled on her hummingbird-patterned dressing-gown and slippers. Downstairs in the kitchen, she switched on her phone – 7.30 am – and put the kettle on to boil. A text message was already waiting for her from Grayson, who must have been up for milking.

Can't wait to see you again.

Smiling, she replied:

Same. Give Ruby a kiss for me.

She made a plunger of coffee. Waiting for it to brew, she planned what she might bake for the shop today. It was cold enough out there to warrant some seriously stodgy comfort food. Perhaps a molten cake, moist chocolate cake around oozing warm caramel sauce.

Her phone *ting*ed again. Grayson had sent a photo of one huge brown eye framed with long lashes.

Ruby bids you good morn.

Good morning, Ruby! She's gorgeous.

She'd just sent off that text with a *swish* when an email came through. It was from Ferdinand with instructions for Ying and Oden's wedding cake. With shaking hands she opened it, read their request, and jigged on the spot with excitement. Oh, this was going to be fun.

With Darcy out of the house, Olivia was able to leave for Rambling Rose earlier than usual. On a whim, she drove first to Madeline's house, raindrops splashing heavily on the windscreen. She pulled up outside and cut the engine. The lights were on inside the house, as she'd known they would be, a lifetime of rising early still ingrained in the older woman.

She thought about Madeline preparing that coffin – painting it, varnishing it, lining it with quilts, and putting in photos of her parents, and finally a small brown teddy bear that Burton had had since he was a toddler. As Olivia had listened to Madeline describing the process of putting the coffin together, she'd felt great sadness but also admiration for her courage and her commitment to her brother, right to the end.

She knew that now wasn't the time to ask Madeline about Burton and the possibility that he was Olivia's grandfather, but after learning how close Ma had been to them both, she wanted to be there for her, somehow. The least she could do for Madeline was to be a friend, the kind of friend Nora would have been. She got out of the car and ran up to the front door.

Madeline opened the door to her knock, wrapped in a dressing-gown. She looked pale. 'Olivia,' she said, sounding surprised. 'Come in.' She had a fire going already, and the little cat was licking its paws on the couch.

'I'm on my way to work but I was thinking about you. I wanted to check that you were okay,' Olivia explained.

Madeline eyed her, wrinkled her nose, then said, 'Whisky?'

'That good, hey?'

Madeline grunted, and poured out two nips of whisky. They sat on the couch with the cat between them, Madeline's gnarled hands rhythmically stroking Eirlys's soft fur.

'I went to see him last night. He's no longer conscious. They said his time is nearing.' She shook her head in disbelief. 'I've been awake most of the night, waiting for a call.'

'God, Madeline, I'm so sorry.' Olivia fought the urge to ask to see Burton, a man who was quite possibly her grandfather, the man Ma had loved. It was too late, she knew.

Madeline stared down at her hands. 'I've cared for him my whole life.' She turned and considered the coffin for several minutes in silence. Olivia sat beside her. In another time and place they might have been watching a sunset.

'My whole life's been about him,' Madeline said at last, not bitterly, not regretfully. Her tone was one of surprise and loss, as she let go of Burton and also this long chapter of her life. 'He's been my life's work.'

'A commitment to be proud of.'

'It's been a small life, but still a lot more than many get.' They sipped their whisky quietly for a few moments. 'He never went anywhere, you know, never past London. His death will be the biggest journey of all.'

Olivia let that sentiment sink in, then raised her glass. 'To Burton.'

Madeline's hand shook as she raised her own glass to meet Olivia's, and they sipped their drinks to the sound of the crackling fire.

26

The day arrived for the school bazaar. It started at two o'clock on Tuesday, at the end of the school day, which was perfect for catching all the parents and carers doing school pick-up, and it was fortunate that Olivia only had to walk up from her shop, because cars lined the streets in every direction, and parking would have been impossible. The clouds were low and grey, and the air was damp and the kind of cold that sank right into your bones. Still, the concrete quadrangle between the school buildings was packed with colourful stalls and trestle tables displaying second-hand toys and clothes, books and bric-a-brac, as well as local produce and homemade foods. Olivia walked through the crowd, holding the large cake box high above the heads of children rushing around with their faces painted to look like tigers or pandas or dragons.

She'd made a tall column sponge cake, the size and shape of a top hat, flavoured with lavender water from her special box of fragrant waters and covered with a white buttercream icing, around which she'd tied a ribbon. Dried lavender flowers were sprinkled on top and around the base. Cathy Finch had said she wanted a show-stopper, and Olivia was pleased with what she'd made.

A smiling Juliet was manning the cake stall, dressed in a faux-fur coat, a velvet skirt and elegant black button-up boots. 'Hello!' she sang, waving Olivia over. 'My goodness, that looks beautiful.'

'Thank you.' Olivia placed the cake on the table and admired the mounds of cupcakes, pastries, pies and biscuits in plastic containers or covered with cling wrap, all precious things made lovingly by parents. Except, perhaps, for the chocolate scroll cake at the end. She eyed it suspiciously. It looked like a supermarket cake removed from its plastic packaging to masquerade as homemade.

Juliet took two pounds from a woman and handed her a box of shortbread, then turned back to Olivia. 'How much are you putting on your cake?' she asked.

Olivia hesitated a moment, weighing up what seemed reasonable for a cake like this against the community spirit of simply raising some cash. 'Fifteen pounds?'

Juliet barked a laugh. 'No! Crazy woman.' She gave Olivia a jovial wee hug. 'That's not nearly enough for a cake like that. All the funds are going to the arts program, you know.'

'Oh, I see.' No wonder Juliet was so keen to raise money. Just then a dreadful noise erupted from the far end of the quadrangle: squeaking clarinets, shrieking violins and the uncoordinated banging of drums. The older students were practising their band instruments – or perhaps they were actually performing. It was difficult to tell.

'What about twenty-five pounds?' Juliet suggested.

'Do you think?' Olivia said uncertainly. 'I wouldn't want to price it out of reach.'

'Nonsense. There're still a few people around here with money. Besides, we only need one buyer. In fact, let's make it thirty pounds. Then someone can haggle us down if they want to, or we can change the price later if it hasn't sold.' She scribbled the price on a yellow tag and stuck it to the box.

'Olivia, that cake is gorgeous!' Cathy Finch arrived at the table, her face painted like a giant, sparkling butterfly, its wings spreading out above her eyebrows. She read the tag. 'Thirty pounds? Not enough,' she said, firmly. 'Thirty-five at least.'

'I agree,' Juliet said, taking her marker pen and writing a new tag.

'Oh, no,' Olivia began, but Cathy held up a hand to silence her.

'Forty, then,' she said, and then pealed off a flurry of tiny fairy claps.

'Mum!' Darcy charged over. His face was painted like Toothless, the dragon from his favourite movie, his blue eyes peering out from a totally black face, rows of huge white teeth painted around his actual lips.

'Wow, look at you.' Olivia bent down to hug him, deftly avoiding the sticky toffee apple he was carrying in one hand. 'Hi, Eloise,' she said, putting her arm around the girl, whose now green face was painted like an alien, with a third eye between her brows and another two waving up towards her hairline. 'You look fabulous!'

Eloise roared and bared her teeth.

'Eek! You two are totally scary.'

They giggled in satisfaction.

'Is your mum here?' she asked Eloise.

'Over there,' Eloise said, pushing back her fair hair and waving a hand towards the bookstall, where Katrina was looking through books.

'Come with me!' Darcy said, tugging on Olivia's arm. 'I found something.'

'Okay,' she said, lurching after him. Darcy had found a black and red scooter in a pile of bric-a-brac, second-hand but in good condition, for five pounds.

'Look!' he said, bouncing up and down. 'Can I get it?'

'Sure, great idea,' Olivia said, pressing a five-pound note into the seller's hand. As they wandered back with the scooter, she saw a familiar figure striding away from the cake stall, her hair wrapped in a scarf.

'Was that Mrs Wilson?' Olivia asked Juliet.

'Yes, I think she wanted to buy your cake for her weekly morning tea with her ladies tomorrow, but it was out of her price range.' Juliet frowned. 'I feel terrible now. She and her group of ladies do so much volunteer work at the church, cleaning and organising, leading the singing. We'd be lost without them.'

Olivia saw an opportunity. 'Here, I'll get it for her.'

'You can't buy your own cake,' Juliet protested.

'Of course I can. I'd only be spending money on other things. And it all goes to the arts program, remember.' Olivia pulled out her wallet, fat with the day's takings. 'Here, no arguments.'

Juliet looked pained, but took the money. 'If you're sure.'

'Trust me, I am. I need to make amends to her.'

Juliet gave her an enquiring look, and Olivia grinned. 'Long story. Look, Darcy and I will go and catch up with some people, then I'll come back for the cake.' She took the marker and wrote *Sold* on the price tag.

Olivia was woken the next morning by Darcy landing on her like a big dog leaping onto the bed.

'Mum, can we take out the scooter?' he said, wriggling around, his knees in her stomach. 'Can we?'

'Yes,' Olivia croaked, and he sprang up to a seated position on top of her. 'Hop off, baby, you're heavy,' she gasped, as the air was squeezed out of her lungs. Darcy flopped down beside her and she rolled towards him, pulling him to her. If only he could always be this gorgeous, cuddly, good-natured child. She never wanted him to grow up, never wanted him to leave.

'How long till we can take it out?' he muttered, his face pressed into her neck.

'After breakfast. On the way to school.'

'Aw, that's so long,' he complained, and sat up. His hair stuck out at crazy angles and there was a bit of muck in the corner of one eye, which she wiped away with her thumb. Without explanation, he jumped off the bed and left the room.

She stretched and blinked, trying to wake up. She really needed to teach Darcy how to make coffee. Either that, or get a machine she could set on a timer and place on the bedside table so she could down a cup before she even got up.

She reached for her phone and turned it on. A message was waiting for her from Katrina.

Burton McCarthy passed
away late last night. Funeral
should be in a couple of days.

Though she'd known it was coming, Olivia still felt the disappointment. The man who might have been her grandfather, possibly her ma's love, had left this world. But she swatted those thoughts away for now. Far more important was Madeline and the very real loss of her brother, likely the most important person in her whole life.

Thanks for letting me know.

She texted the news to Grayson, who said he'd take Madeline some flowers this morning while delivering her milk.

On the way to school, Olivia carried Darcy's bag on her back while he practised riding the scooter, one foot on the board, the other pushing himself along, then both feet on the board, until he started to wobble and had to put a foot down again. He shrieked with glee and she cheered him on, although her own heart felt heavy. Once they'd passed the graveyard he could ride along the narrow path beside the river. The swans moved slowly today, reflecting her mood.

She sat down on the short half-wall and watched as Darcy pushed himself along, the wheels rumbling on the damp footpath. She should get him a helmet as soon as possible. She was always conscious of the possibility of accidents these days.

Darcy came scooting back, too fast for her liking, though she tried to hide it. 'Look at you go,' she said, and clapped her hands.

'Did you see? I'm doing it!' he said. 'Can you take a video to send to Pappa?'

She took her phone out of her jeans pocket. Darcy scooted a distance away, then hopped off to turn around, shouting, 'Ready?'

'Ready,' she confirmed, lining him up on the screen.

'Can you do a slow-mo one?' he called.

'Okay.' She changed the setting to slow motion. 'Go!'

He flew along, his face bright and determined, then scooted to a stop in front of her, his cheeks red from the cold air. 'Let me see.' She showed him the video, and once he'd approved it, sent it to Helge.

'Come on,' she said. 'Time for school.'

She dropped him at the classroom, where Cathy proudly announced how much money yesterday's bazaar had raised. Then Olivia rushed home again, keen to surprise her neighbour.

She took the cake out of the fridge where it had sat in its cake box overnight, then placed it on a black slate board, which really made the lavender pop. She crunched carefully down her pebble drive, turned right at the gate, continued up the path, and turned right again at Mrs Wilson's gate. Several cars were parked in the street, but she didn't give this much thought until she was standing at the wooden front door and heard voices and laughter from inside.

'Damn!' It was only nine o'clock. Surely it was too early for morning tea? She shifted the weight of the cake to one hand and rapped the heavy doorknocker twice.

Chattering voices continued inside as she waited. 'Come on,' Olivia urged, jiggling her foot. At last the door swung open. Olivia offered an enthusiastic smile. 'Mrs Wilson, hi!'

The woman's face registered shock, then suspicion. She was dressed much more casually than on the previous occasions Olivia had seen her, in slacks and a long-sleeved shirt under a plain woollen vest. Her hair, usually covered, was unsheathed, revealing tight, steel-grey curls that suggested weekly styling at the hairdresser. She eyed the cake in Olivia's hand, opened her mouth to say something, then apparently thought better of it and closed it again.

'I'm sorry to bother you,' Olivia gushed. 'Juliet told me you were interested in the lavender cake that I made for the bazaar yesterday? I really wanted you to have it, so I bought it for you. I'd planned to drop it over before your guests arrived. I must say, I didn't expect them here so early. I hope I'm not too late?' she finished anxiously.

Her neighbour's features worked their way through a range of expressions, landing on appreciation. 'That is kind of you,' she said at last. 'These ladies work hard to clean the church each week. They deserve a little reward.'

'As do you,' Olivia said.

To her surprise, Mrs Wilson's formidable facade suddenly crumbled. Her hand went to her chest. 'Some of these women have dying husbands, absentee children, serious health concerns.' She stopped, and Olivia had the distinct impression that Mrs Wilson knew a little about at least some of those things. The woman cleared her throat and continued. 'But they soldier on, serving their community.'

'It's amazing how much of the world runs on volunteer labour,' Olivia said. 'It's largely hidden and unappreciated, yet it's often the thing that holds communities together.' She held out the cake. 'Please, enjoy.'

Mrs Wilson reached out and Olivia delivered the board into her arms, their fingertips brushing. 'Thank you,' the older woman said.

'You're welcome. And really, I am very sorry about taking your apples.' Olivia smiled, Mrs Wilson nodded her acceptance, and Olivia waved goodbye. Walking back to the street, she felt as if a weight had been lifted from her shoulders. She didn't like unfinished business or ill will with anyone, especially a neighbour.

Her phone began to ring just as she reached her driveway. Helge's name was on the screen.

'Good morning,' she said, a smile on her face and in her voice. She pushed open her front door and stepped gratefully into the warmth.

'*God morgen* to you,' he said.

'Where are you?'

'On the train to *v*ork. I've *v*atched the video of Darcy ten times.'

'He's cute, isn't he?' She gathered up her bag and left the cottage again, heading down towards Rambling Rose, a little late now that she'd been to Mrs Wilson's. Still, she could whip up some scones, pikelets and biscuits quickly enough, and make a cake after opening her door.

'I *v*ant more,' he said, 'of both of you.'

She paused midstride, hearing the plaintive, aching note in his voice. 'What are you saying?'

He mumbled in Norwegian, as though trying to set his thoughts straight. Then he said the words that made her heart nearly stop. 'Move to Nor*v*ay.'

'What?'

'Come here, *v*ith me, *v*ith Darcy. Let us be a family. Let's do it right this time. We have lost so much already.'

'I . . .' She had stopped walking and was leaning against the stone wall of the graveyard, entirely lost for words. Move to Norway?

'I know it is quick, and I know you have to do the cake for the super-*v*edding, but by Christmas, yes? *V*e could be together by then.' He was excited now, as if he could picture them all together – the three of them around a fireplace, presents under a tree, snow outside. She, too, found the image seductive. But it was too soon, surely?

'No more *v*asting time,' he urged. 'Life is short. Let us do this.'

27

Burton's funeral was at ten o'clock the following Monday morning. Grayson tucked himself in beside Olivia, giving her a smile. In spite of the sadness of the day, she was pleased to see him. He nodded to Katrina, who was seated on Olivia's left. Clarence was there too, standing beside Howard and his wife, a small woman with rosy cheeks.

Anthony Cabot led the small service inside the cavernous church, weak sunlight through the stained-glass windows casting rosy and indigo patterns across the stone flooring. Dust motes rose slowly, as if they themselves were tiny spirits rising to the heavens, and Olivia brushed away tears. As well as her sadness for Madeline, and her questions about what her own connections to Burton may be, she had been in turmoil ever since Helge had made his proposal. She'd asked him to give her some time to think about it, but five days had passed and she felt none the wiser.

She had only recently arrived in Stoneden, but already she felt a commitment to the project and the community. But above all was her commitment to Darcy. Should they move to Norway, give him the chance to build a real relationship with his father? But what if they went and it all fell apart? Then she would have lost not just Helge but this new life in the village, too.

Mrs Wilson and the other church volunteers were all present, dressed in black, smelling faintly of powder, and carrying the hymns loudly enough for everyone. In the front pew sat Doc Eli, wearing a suit that smelt of mothballs, his hair brushed especially neatly. Olivia couldn't begin to imagine how many funerals he must have attended in this village over his lifetime. He sat beside Madeline, who wore a black smock dress that looked to be decades old, her silver hair pinned up in a bun instead of her usual long plaits.

Olivia's mind kept flicking back to Ma's funeral. It had been a cold day, like this one, and Darcy was still in hospital, battling a post-surgery infection. She'd been torn between staying with him and going to the funeral; her dilemma had felt like a symbol of her life at that time, ripped in two by his accident. She'd sat in the pew, feeling bereft without her mother figure, her son ill, feeling the loneliest she'd ever been.

After the service, Burton was buried in a plot alongside his parents and grandparents. She watched Madeline throw in the first handful of dirt, heard the dull thud on the wooden coffin she'd painted and lacquered herself.

Olivia stepped forward and offered her a bunch of ivy leaves cradling thick bursts of white baby's breath. 'I'm so sorry for your loss,' she said, handing Madeline the bouquet, her throat pinched taut with reignited grief. They were trite words, yet they were all you could say in the face of the unfathomable abyss of loss.

Madeline looked at her steadily, the lines on her face deeply etched. 'Thank you.' She took the flowers, held them a moment, then let them drop onto the coffin. Others followed her example, the stark grave filling with colour and abundance.

Olivia stepped back carefully on the uneven ground, mindful of the other gravesites and headstones. Seeing the expression on her face, Grayson wrapped his arms around her. She let herself cry for a moment. 'Sorry,' she whispered into his chest. 'I didn't even know him.'

'Doesn't matter,' he said, rubbing her back. 'You know the feeling.'

Katrina joined them, and Olivia hugged her too. Anthony offered final words of condolence and support to Madeline, before leaving the gravesite, Juliet at his side. Others began to drift away after them.

'Is there a wake of some sort?' Olivia asked, finding her voice again.

Grayson shook his head. 'No. She wanted to be alone.'

'From what I understand, she's not much for socialising even on good days,' said Katrina.

They lingered there a few minutes longer, then Clarence strode towards them, his hair lifting in the wind. 'I'm sorry to interrupt.' He acknowledged each of them and shook Grayson's hand. 'Olivia, I'm wondering if you are able to come down to Viola's cellar for a meeting about the wedding?' His face relayed hopeful anticipation.

'Yes, of course,' she said, surprised but willing to attend. It was her day off anyway, as it was for many of the village's shopkeepers.

'See you in about fifteen minutes?' he asked.

'Sure.'

He farewelled them and went on his way, heading purposefully towards the lichen-licked graveyard gate.

After a moment, Grayson said, 'I heard on the radio on the way over that the wedding date's been leaked.'

Olivia's attention was suddenly laser-focused. 'Has it?'

'When is it?' asked Katrina, keenly interested.

'In a few weeks,' Grayson said. 'When I delivered the milk to the hotel this morning, their phones were running hot. I'd say they're already fully booked.'

Olivia shivered with a mix of excitement and anxiety. The craziness was about to begin.

'Let me know if there's anything I can help you with,' Grayson said.

'Me too,' Katrina said, hopefully.

'I will,' Olivia said, grateful to have made such good friends in this village. She would have to say something to them soon, tell them about Helge's proposal. It was just that the idea of leaving this place, even after such a short time, was surprisingly hard.

'I've got to go,' she said, and waved goodbye.

•

Clarence stood in front of the small group gathered in Viola's wine cellar, Howard seated to his right, noting how differently he felt today from the first time he'd delivered a speech down here. Today's group wasn't just imports, of course, but included all the local people involved in the wedding. The wedding that would possibly be the grand finale of his hopes and dreams for this village. Pepperworth had assured him the Renaissance Project was doomed the moment the wedding was over.

Chatter and bursts of laughter filtered down from the bar upstairs. News of the wedding date had zipped around the village and spirits were high. The hotel was already fully booked leading up to the wedding, and he was certain every pub and spare room in the Cotswolds would be filling by the second. The group in front of him was waiting expectantly for him to speak, sharing excited smiles and occasional whispers. Sitting opposite him was Olivia, still in her black dress from Burton's funeral. He stared at her a moment, struggling to believe that the whole project might have been for nothing. Seeing his expression, she cocked her head questioningly: *What's wrong?* He raised the fingers of one hand at her in reassurance, then cleared his throat. The group fell silent.

'Thank you all for coming. By now, most of the world will know that Ying and Oden's wedding is happening in just a few weeks. That means people are going to start arriving in the village and setting up wherever they can. The streets will be choked with traffic, the media attention will be relentless. Journalists will want to talk to you.'

He took a moment to check his tone, which sounded uncharacteristically downbeat. 'These are exciting times,' he said, lifting his voice with a practised smile. 'This is your time to shine as an artisan, and Stoneden's chance to shine on the world stage, showcasing the achievements of the Renaissance Project and demonstrating what can happen when citizens are willing to honour both their heritage and their future. When citizens are willing to make the difficult choices that serve the whole community and not just the rich.' There was a smattering of applause at that. Gosh, he was even beginning to believe it himself. The ceiling lights shone down brightly, illuminating the rich tones of the rows of wine bottles.

Looking around at the smiling faces, he briefly questioned whether he *really* had to tell them about Chester Pepperworth's threat. But of course he did. If he didn't, it might leak anyway, as things tended to do in small communities; as uncontrolled information, it would be far more dangerous. If he told them now, he could guide the narrative, though it would mean breaking some hearts, right when they should be riding their highest wave. But it had to be done.

'I have some other news,' he said, solemnly, and the noise once again ceased. 'I recently met with Chester Pepperworth.' He felt his jaw twitch when he said the man's name. 'He told me that immediately after the wedding his council will vote to bring an end to the Renaissance Project.'

There were exclamations of shock and anger, followed by a flurry of questions.

'What?'

'They can't!'

'But we only just got here!'

'What will happen to us?' Leanne asked. 'Will we be sent home? Back to Ireland?' She looked aghast.

'Will they take away our working visas?' Elena asked, grasping Newton's hand. 'Will they evict us from our cottage?'

'I'm afraid I don't yet know what it will mean in terms of those things,' Clarence said. 'What I do know is that politicians and councils are fickle beasts and there is *always* room to negotiate.'

The panic quietened slightly.

'This is what I suggest,' he said. 'For now, we forget them and focus on the wedding. We take this once-in-a-lifetime chance to create a show-stopping wedding. We show Pepperworth and his council that Stoneden will benefit both economically from the wedding *and* the goodwill it generates for years to come through increased tourism to our picturesque village. These are the things that matter to councils. Councils come and councils go. Pepperworth is here now but he won't be forever.' Clarence's voice was loud now, confident and, yes, arrogant. He *was* an arrogant bastard, but by God it had its uses. Someone had to be the one to believe in the impossible. 'This is not the end, it is only the beginning. We are the new Stoneden and we are here to stay!'

'Yes!' several people cheered. Others leant forward, nodding, their faces determined.

'I started out with a dream to save this village, and you answered my call. We're not done yet. Who's with me?'

The answering cheer would most certainly have been heard in the bar above, if not out on the main street of Stoneden itself.

•

Katrina was leaning against the bench while Olivia worked on a hummingbird cake for this morning's trade. Her friend wrinkled her nose. 'Ian's been messaging a lot. It's starting to get on my nerves. How many times can I say *I miss you too*?'

Olivia shrugged, distracted. It was Tuesday, and there were now less than two weeks to go until the wedding, a calendar counting down in her mind each day she woke up. With a muffin tray placed upside down on the bench, she was laying fine slices of fresh pineapple over each of the hubs. As they baked in the oven, the slices would wrap around the hubs, forming crisp pineapple bowls. When they had cooled and set, she would pry them off, upturn them and place them on top of the cream icing, like yellow flowers. It was an easy yet impressive decorating move.

'It's been hard for us both,' Katrina continued, helping herself to a slice of pineapple, 'but I think he needs to start trying to build some new friendships, you know? Anyway, Russell and I are fine. I'm not as homesick now and I feel like I've found my feet at last. Even though I wasn't totally enthusiastic about coming here, it might actually have been the best thing to do. Eloise is so happy, due in no small part to your adorable son. Do you know she gave him a friendship necklace?'

'Yes,' Olivia said. 'He was wearing it at breakfast this morning. He loves her.'

'They're so cute,' Katrina said, her hand on her heart. 'Maybe they'll get married one day and we can be mothers-in-law together.'

'You never know,' Olivia said, laughing. And then she remembered Helge's proposal, and her heart gave a pang at the idea of taking Darcy away from his best friend.

'What's the matter?' Katrina asked. 'Your face just went all scrunchy.'

Olivia slid the muffin tray into the oven, closed the door, and turned around to face Katrina. She took a deep breath and blew it out. 'Helge's asked me to move to Norway, to be with him.'

Katrina gasped, her mouth hanging open for several incredulous seconds. Then she regained the power of speech. 'When? What did you say? Are you going? What does Darcy think? What about the wedding? What about . . . us?' She pulled an exaggerated sad face. 'I mean, it's great, right, that's why you came here, to find a family. I just didn't think . . . it's a shock . . .'

Olivia laughed at Katrina's flustered reaction. 'Believe me, I know how you feel. It *is* a shock.'

'But a lovely one?'

'Yeah, I guess so. It's just . . .'

'Fast?'

'Yes! But then . . .'

'You have history, and a child together, and a sizzling attraction.'

'Definitely.' Olivia blushed, remembering kissing him in the pub and how close they had come to taking it further, and put her hand to her cheek.

'Have you made up your mind? Are you going?'

'Well, there's quite a bit going on right now with the wedding, and I need to keep my head firmly focused on that, but yes, I think so.' Olivia smiled nervously. 'Darcy doesn't know yet, though. I'll have to pick my time to break it to him. And first I need to be really sure.'

Katrina hugged her, hard. 'Oh, I don't want you to go – though of course you must if you want to, and I promise we'll still love you. I'll be horribly, dreadfully, drunkenly sad, but we'll just have to come and visit you in Norway.'

'I'll miss you too.' Olivia hugged Katrina back.

'Oh, don't, you'll make me cry.' Katrina released her and stepped back. 'What about Grayson?'

Olivia put a hand to her stomach, feeling ill, and let out a long breath. 'I'm not looking forward to telling him. It will make me very sad.'

Minutes after Katrina had left for the surgery, a tall woman with artfully dyed purple hair entered the shop backwards, pushing open the door with her backside, a crate in her arms. She wore a woollen jumper beneath oversized – possibly men's – overalls.

'Hi,' she said, spinning around. 'You must be Olivia.' She dropped the crate onto the counter, and Olivia saw that it was full of Seven Cows products. 'I'm Lucy.' She held out her hand to shake Olivia's, smiling as if they were already great friends.

Olivia shook her hand.

'I'm Grayson's big sister. Well, he's *my* little brother, actually. Ha!' She laughed from deep in her belly and her eyes – which had the same deep set as Grayson's – twinkled. It was impossible not to like her at once. Before Olivia could speak, she went on, 'Mum and I arrived last night. We've decided to camp out at his place until after the wedding. We're huge fans of Oden's.' She flapped a hand at her face as if the mere thought of the actor had set her on fire. 'I'm afraid I did a terrible thing and got Grayson drunk last night.'

'Oh . . .'

'He told me all about *you*,' she said, wagging a finger at Olivia.

Now it was Olivia's turn to blush. 'Ah, I see.'

'Gosh, we're happy to hear he's interested in someone,' Lucy said, leaning on the bench. 'He's been a mopey bastard for the past two years. Anyway, I gave him too much Drambuie – I like to pour long – and now he has a smashing headache and he mucked up something or other in the cowshed and needed to stay back and fix it and asked me to do deliveries this morning. I think he was a bit sad to miss out on seeing you, to be honest, but I jumped at the chance to meet the woman who's captured his heart.'

'His heart?'

'Oh, yeah!' Lucy reached out towards the hummingbird cake as if she were about to dip her finger into the icing, but pulled herself up promptly. 'Why waste time, right? None of us is getting any younger – well, not sure about you. What are you, mid-thirties?'

'Yes.'

'Pft! Still a baby. Trust me, once you hit forty it's like a time bomb goes off.'

Olivia couldn't help but laugh at this high-spirited, verbose sister whose lack of discretion was both alarming and refreshing.

'He loves your kid, too. Damon?'

'Darcy. Does he really . . . love him?' Lucy well and truly had her attention now.

'Totally sunk. Says he's just the sweetest kid, funny too. Grayson's a great uncle, the best. Trust me, your kid's in great hands.'

Olivia swallowed, lost for words.

Lucy tapped the side of the crate. 'Anyway, I'd love to stay and chat but I have to keep delivering the goods around town. I'm making dinner tonight, nothing fancy, just a good honest lasagne, but I always over-cater. You should come, and Darcy too, of course. Seven okay? Oh, no, wait, not with a little one. Mine are teenagers now, barely talking to me, they eat after I'm in bed most days, but if memory serves, five o'clock's probably better for his age, right?'

'Ah, yes, but—'

'No, don't bring a thing! See you tonight.' With that, she dashed away, leaving Olivia to blink slowly into the sudden quiet Grayson's sister had left behind.

28

Rambling Rose had a real tropical theme today, with the pineapple flowers on the hummingbird cake, a fluffy coconut sponge roll and a lime bundt cake. Olivia had matched her day's offerings with the soundtrack to *Blue Hawaii*. The movie was actually from 1961, not the 1950s, but it wasn't too far outside her usual musical repertoire, and she was delighted to notice how many of her older customers sang along to the title song.

When she'd finished for the day, Olivia packaged up half a leftover lime bundt cake to take to Madeline's. The golden cake – the eggs had been particularly rich in colour today – was drizzled with lime syrup and topped with cream cheese icing and lime zest confetti. The sharp zing of lime juice had been a relief from the dreary day outside, and she hoped it might have a similar effect on Madeline's spirits.

Madeline answered the door wearing her usual overalls, but for once she wore her hair down – long, fine and energised by static, it framed her face like a silver halo. She looked beautiful and vulnerable and small and striking all at once. She made a pot of tea and they sat down at the kitchen table, but Olivia was a little disappointed to see that she left her wedge of bundt cake untouched.

'Can I refresh your cup?' Olivia asked, reaching for the pot.

'No, thank you.'

'Have you had anything to eat today?' Olivia asked, checking the kitchen for signs of food preparation.

'I had some porridge.' Madeline's drawn, pale face brightened as the cat jumped up into her lap, purring.

'I could prepare something for your dinner, before I go?' Olivia said, letting her eyes drift to the empty space in the lounge where the coffin had been.

'I'm fine,' Madeline said, but not unkindly.

'Of course you are,' Olivia assured her. She accepted Madeline's declaration that she was fine for the moment, but she'd feel better if she knew there was some sort of organised care in place to keep an eye on her for a while. She made a mental note to speak to Juliet about it and they could organise a roster of sorts. She was happy to pop over regularly, and she was certain that others would be too.

As Olivia sipped her tea, she wondered if it was too soon to ask Madeline about Burton and Nora. Or perhaps now was a good time, offering Madeline the chance to talk about Burton and remember the years before his accident.

Madeline raised the hint of an eyebrow at her. 'What's on your mind? Spit it out.'

'Well, it's about Burton, actually. And Ma.'

That caught Madeline's attention. She regarded Olivia through watery eyes, her arthritic fingers continuing to stroke Eirlys. Olivia cleared her throat, wondering where to start.

'You're wondering if he's your grandfather,' Madeline said, taking Olivia completely by surprise.

'Yes, I am,' she said, her heart quickening. 'Is he? And are you my great-aunt?'

Madeline pursed her lips and screwed up her nose as if in disgust. 'No, I don't believe so.'

Olivia's shoulders slumped with the weight of her disappointment. 'Oh.'

Madeline straightened in her chair, the movement prompting the little cat to leap down and stalk over to the fireplace. 'Burton loved your grandmother,' she said, quietly, her eyes following the cat across the room. 'I thought they would marry. I *hoped* they would. But Nora had a different view.' She gave a hollow smile.

Olivia tensed. Had Ma done something to hurt Burton?

'Oh, I believe she did have feelings for him, of some sort,' Madeline conceded. 'Given time and the right circumstances, she may have grown to love him and accept a proposal from him. Unfortunately for all of us, she was . . . distracted.'

Olivia waited a few beats, letting Madeline's words sink in. 'There was someone else.'

'Yes.' Madeline folded her arms across her body and bent forward. Olivia looked at her anxiously – was she in pain, or just tired? She was wondering whether she should offer to help her over to the couch, or to bed, when Madeline spoke again.

'The night that it came undone, Burton witnessed it all. It was at the church dance. He was humiliated and stormed off. I went after him but he shouted at me and told me to leave him alone. Our father later said he came home in a foul mood and downed a few beers, which was quite unlike Burton. The bull was bellowing in the field and Dad reminded him that he was supposed to have moved the damn thing. Burton slammed his beer down and stormed off to the paddock in the dark. He was usually good with cattle, but that night something went wrong. From what he could remember and was able to tell us, he shouted at it, then shook a branch at it to hurry it on . . .' Her eyes widened, still unable to comprehend what had happened. 'Well, the bull saw red. It charged him and tossed him into the air. Burton crashed to the ground headfirst, and then the bull stomped on his arm too. That was that. The young man I knew was gone.' She stared at Olivia now, her eyes bright, her grief fresh. 'Such a waste. Such a terrible, dreadful waste.'

'I'm so sorry,' Olivia said, horrified and confused. 'I wish Ma was still here so she could . . .' What? Explain herself? Apologise to Madeline and Burton? Tell Olivia who her real grandfather was? 'Did Ma know about your brother's accident before she left the country?'

'Of course she did! The whole village knew. We all thought he was going to die for the longest time.'

'Did you and she talk about what had happened? Did she talk to Burton?'

'No. I was furious with her and didn't want to see her, and Burton was unconscious for weeks.'

'So she just left to go to Australia?'

'It's *why* she left,' Madeline said, anger still nipping her tone after all these decades.

Olivia frowned. 'She told me that her parents decided to leave because there was no work in the village, so they took an opportunity to start over in a new country.'

Madeline shook her head. 'The part about the work was true enough. But she was nineteen. She was going to let them go on their own and try to make a go of something here. But after that night she took the chance to flee, and I can't say I was sorry to see her go.'

Olivia sat for a moment, trying to reconcile the Ma she'd known - honourable, cautious, steadfast - with the heedless young woman Madeline described. She took a deep breath. 'Thank you for telling me. I know it can't be easy, especially so soon after saying goodbye to your beloved brother. I'm sorry if I've raised painful memories.'

'Oh, none of this is your fault,' Madeline said, dismissively. 'Nora was Nora and you are you. I still like you.'

Olivia gave a shaky laugh. 'I like you too.'

'I can't say for sure who your real grandfather was, but I do think there is someone in this village who might be able to help.'

Olivia straightened. 'Who?'

Madeline sniffed. 'I suggest you go ask Clarence what he knows and what he did.'

Grayson's mother peered at Darcy over the top of her spectacles. Darcy was lying, Olivia could tell. His chin was raised and he was trying not to laugh. Estelle narrowed her eyes at him, and his lips quivered. She looked down at the cards in her hand and at the pile sitting on the table between them, then delivered her verdict. 'Bluff.'

Darcy held his composure for a moment longer, until Estelle flipped over the three cards. 'Aha! What have we here, Darcy?' she asked. 'That's not three eights, that's one eight and two fours.' Darcy collapsed forward onto the table, laughing.

'Bad luck, Darcy,' Grayson said, delivering bowls of ice cream to the table.

'You didn't stand a chance,' Lucy commiserated. 'You can't outsmart a criminologist.'

'Retired criminologist,' Estelle reminded her, accepting a bowl from Grayson.

'Trust us, we never got away with anything as kids,' Lucy said, sighing dramatically. 'It was the most boring childhood.'

'That was simply a lack of imagination on your part,' Estelle retorted, fluffing up her short grey hair and pinning Lucy with a falcon-sharp stare.

Darcy stared wide-eyed at Estelle, his spoon paused halfway to his mouth. 'Are you a detective?'

Estelle licked her own spoon. 'Yep. Just like Scooby Doo.'

'Wow!'

'I'm not sure I can eat all this,' Olivia said. Grayson eased down next to her on the bench seat in the warm kitchen, smiling at her in a way that made her melt around the edges just like the butterscotch ice cream.

'There's always room for ice cream,' Lucy said, flicking her purple hair off her shoulder. 'It just slides around the corners.'

There would be no argument from Darcy, who was tucking in to it as though that lasagne had never existed.

'Never mind, Darcy,' Grayson said, gathering up the cards. 'You'll beat her next time, for sure.'

Next time. Olivia was speared with guilt for allowing Darcy to bond with Grayson. Would there be a next time? Would she even see Grayson again after tonight?

'So, Olivia,' Lucy said, sitting forward with a conspiratorial smile. 'Have you actually met Ying and Oden?'

Estelle stared at her too, waiting for the answer.

Olivia lowered her voice to a whisper. 'I have.'

Lucy and Estelle dropped their spoons, Lucy squealed, and they peppered her with questions.

'They seemed nice,' Olivia said, 'though it was the middle of the night.' She told them all about the secret meeting. Estelle and Lucy drank in every word about what the pair said, what they were wearing, how tall and thin and dewy-skinned they were in real life. Grayson chuckled every now and then, amused by their rapt interest.

'Will you be at the wedding?' Estelle asked.

'I will.'

Lucy pretended to faint. 'Do you get to talk to them?'

Olivia shrugged. 'Not sure. I doubt it, honestly. They were pretty clear that they're too busy to deal with us directly and we have to go through their two ninjas.'

'But you'll see them?' Lucy pressed. 'Up close? In the same room?'

'Maybe. Those of us who are supplying the goods and services are invited to stay, though not in the main hall. We'll have our own separate space to hang out and enjoy food and drink.'

'But the wedding cake won't be cut till much later in the evening,' Estelle said. 'You'll have the opportunity to go out into the hall and make sure it's perfect for that moment.'

'Yes, now that's a great idea.'

'Can you take photos?' Lucy asked.

'No, there are strict rules about that. They'll have their own media people on the ground, and the only local media allowed access are the Stoneden journalist, Ryan, and his photographer, Farzenah – though I'm sure Ferdinand and Giselle will have made them sign all sorts of forms about what they can and can't report on or photograph.'

She was enjoying this conversation. Estelle and Lucy were engaging and easy company. It made her think about Helge and his parents, whom she'd never met. She wondered if Helge had told his parents she was coming to Norway and how they would react. Would having her and Darcy based in Oslo make them want to stop travelling the world for a while and get to know their newest grandson? No, that was fanciful. Helge already had two children in Oslo and that had never stopped them. The thought of having a set of in-laws, by either marriage or de facto status, was daunting.

As they continued to fire questions at her, Darcy got bored and went to play a game on his iPad. Grayson joined him and they took turns racing each other through obstacle courses, shouting and cheering. After a while, though, Grayson got up and came back to the kitchen.

'Okay, I'm going to rescue Olivia from this interrogation,' he said, putting his hand on her shoulder. His touch sent a ripple through her body.

'Oh, all right,' Lucy grumbled.

'Spoilsport,' said Estelle.

'Honestly, look at you both,' Grayson admonished them. 'You, an environmental scientist, and you, a court criminologist who's put away some of the worst offenders this country has ever seen, and you've lost the plot over a pair of movie stars.'

'Oh, Grayson,' Estelle said, waving him away crossly. 'We can't be serious all the time. We need some frivolity to keep our sanity in this dark world.'

'Yes, Grayson, mind your manners,' Lucy sniped, in such a big-sisterly way that Olivia laughed.

Grayson turned to Olivia. 'Let me save you from these two. There's something I want to show you.'

'Oh, yes!' Lucy said, clapping her hands. 'It's a great surprise.'

'On my own, thanks,' Grayson said.

'Fine, then.' Lucy winked at Olivia, stood up and called, 'Darcy! Would you like to see the toads I caught today?'

'Okay!' Darcy said, putting down his iPad.

Grayson helped Olivia out of the bench seat, passed over her coat, and led the way out of the kitchen door and down the pathway. They stopped beside the tiny house. The darkness felt deep and velvety after the brightly lit kitchen, the night sky pierced with glittering stars. He stood looking down at her, his eyes glinting softly. 'I have a surprise for you,' he said, 'though my big-mouth sister already gave that away.'

Olivia laughed. 'I love her, and your mum. They're fun and welcoming.'

'Yeah, they are,' he relented. He reached out and took her hand in his. She knew she should take it back, that she should tell him now that she was moving to Norway to be with Helge, but the truth was that she liked him holding her hand. She liked him.

'I didn't know what to do with the tiny house at first, but then I realised it was perfect.'

'Perfect for what?'

'For you.'

'Me?' Baffled, she cast her eyes to the door, then back to Grayson. Did he think she and Darcy should live there in that house? 'What for?'

'I'll show you.' He grinned and used his free hand to push open the door, then stepped up into the darkness. She followed, holding his hand tightly. He guided her into the space and closed the door behind her. As he fumbled around in the dark, her eyes adjusted to the dimness, picking out a table and a bench but not much more. Then she heard a click and the room was illuminated by fairy lights strung all around the ceiling and cascading down the walls. She gasped.

'Obviously, I haven't painted the outside yet and I didn't want to fill it up with too much stuff, just enough to get you started.'

'It's amazing,' she managed to say, taking in the large easel set up at one end of the small space, the empty shelves waiting for paints and brushes, charcoals and pastels, and the long day bed below the window, piled with colourful cushions and throw rugs. Grayson went over to a chest of drawers, pulling one of the drawers out.

'These are empty at the moment. I don't really have any idea what you'd need, but when you do, you'll have somewhere to store them.'

Tears had welled in her eyes and she swiped at them with the back of her hand. 'It's gorgeous.'

His smile revealed how proud he was. 'I have to admit, Lucy helped with the throw rugs and cushions.' He scratched self-consciously at his jawline. 'It was a nice touch, I think. Oh, and I've left these walls bare so you can hang your artworks on them.'

She stared around for a moment in wonder. The art studio was utterly beautiful, and she was touched by his thoughtfulness. But she knew she couldn't accept it, or the meaning behind it. She had to say goodbye to him, though right now it seemed like the most difficult thing in the world.

She swallowed hard and took his hands. 'I can't tell you what this means to me,' she said. 'It's the most beautiful thing anyone has ever done for me.'

He leant down to kiss her and she let him because she wanted to kiss him, one last time. He rested his forehead on hers. 'You're welcome.'

She took a deep breath, and let go of his hands. The change in his face, his realisation that something was wrong, broke her heart. She took a step back. 'As much as I love it, though, I can't accept it.'

He shook his head, quickly, his smile returning. 'No, wait, God, I should have clarified. It's on wheels.'

'What do you mean?'

'I mean, you don't have to work here. I know things with us . . . we're new, and I don't want to pressure you. This studio is a gift from me to you, regardless of whatever happens with us. Honestly, I just walked out the door the other day and saw it and imagined you inside it, with your own space to work on your art. It felt right. But you can move it anywhere you want. I'll tow it for you, wherever you want it to go. It will fit in your driveway at your cottage.' He patted the wall next to him. 'This is yours, no strings attached.'

The fairy lights cast the room in a romantic golden glow, making it impossible to think clearly and practically. Olivia closed her eyes a moment, trying to steady her heart rate.

'You like it, right?'

'Without question, and I can't tell you how grateful I am that you want to support my dreams in this way.' She held up a hand to stop his next words. 'But I'm leaving.'

He jerked his head backwards, as if he'd just run into something. 'What?'

'Helge wants me and Darcy to go and live with him in Norway.'

Grayson's face dropped and he stepped back slightly. 'Oh.'

'It's a great opportunity for Darcy to live with his father.'

'And what about you? What do you want?'

'I . . .' She didn't know how to finish that sentence.

'Do you love him?'

She sighed, suddenly exhausted. 'It's complicated.'

'No, it's simple. Do. You. Love. Him?'

She stared up into his blue eyes, which were pinched with pain. She did love Helge, she knew she did. 'Yes,' she said. 'We didn't break up because we didn't love each other. We broke up because he lived on the other side of the world.'

'It didn't work the first time,' he said, slowly. 'Why do you think it will work now?'

His words speared straight into her deepest fear, and she bristled a little. 'Because he is different, I'm different, and I'm on the other side of the world now too.'

'Convenient,' he said, dryly.

'This is our chance to get it right,' she said. 'I'm sorry. I really am. If it wasn't for . . . You and I are . . .'

'It's fine,' he said, his voice heavy with resignation. 'I understand.'

'I'm sorry,' she said again, fighting back tears. She wanted so much to touch him, to hold him, but his shoulders were stiff and she knew her touch wouldn't be welcome. 'I'd better get Darcy home to bed or I'll never get him to school tomorrow. Will I see you at the shop in the morning?'

He blinked a couple of times before nodding. 'Sure, I'll be there.'

'Okay.' She gestured around the room. 'Thank you for this. It means the world. I wish I could accept it.'

She waited for him to say something, but he wasn't looking at her, instead crossing his arms at his chest and staring at an imaginary spot on the floor. When it was clear he wasn't going to respond, she left the studio, went back down the steps, returned to the house and said goodbye to Estelle and Lucy. As she and Darcy drove off into the dark, she was sad but certain she was doing the right thing.

29

In the countdown to the wedding, the streets of Stoneden filled with bumper-to-bumper traffic. Tents appeared, illegally pitched on the grass along the river. The hotel garden overflowed with rowdy drinkers day and night, huddling next to braziers for warmth. Every building in the village must have been photographed from every possible angle by tourists and visitors. Randolph Wilson and his fellow officers had been brought in from nearby villages to patrol the streets, policing the influx of people from all over the world and the direction of their lenses.

Every business in the main street was booming. Olivia's shop sold out of food every day and she had to turn people away at the door, even as they were photographing her, the now famous wedding cake baker. Clarence couldn't stop smiling. Even Chester Pepperworth had turned up for a strategic photo opportunity or two.

Ryan churned out endless articles for newspapers, magazines and online news sources. Although he and Farzenah were the only invited journalist and photographer in the village (apart from Yoden's own publicists and photographers), dozens of other journalists arrived, setting up tents and camping in vans. Days before the event, helicopters began circling, and barricades were erected to form exclusion zones around the streets in preparation for the arrival of the rich and famous.

Olivia and Helge spoke or texted almost daily, when she could snatch a minute.

'Have you told Darcy yet?' he asked.

Olivia squirmed, standing inside her storeroom for a few moments' quiet in between serving customers. 'Not yet.' She knew he was getting anxious about the delay in sharing the good news with their son. 'I'm not sure how long after the wedding I will need to be here to finish up, and as much as I'm sure Darcy will be thrilled to be moving to be with you, he will be sad about leaving Stoneden, and Eloise, especially. I'd like to delay that for as long as possible.'

Helge sighed. 'I know, of course. It's just that I'm excited too, and I want to share it with him.' He sounded a bit like a frustrated child himself, which made her laugh.

'Me too. But we've already waited years. We can wait a bit longer.'

'It feels like a lifetime,' he grumbled.

She looked forward to their regular chats, feeling herself growing closer to him each day. This also helped to soothe her sadness and awkwardness over Grayson. He continued to make his deliveries to the shop, and was as friendly and gracious as ever. Sometimes they discussed Madeline and how she was getting on. But although they both tried to pretend nothing had changed, she could see that he was hurt and there was nothing she could do about it.

One afternoon, she arrived home after picking up Darcy from school and found the tiny house parked in her driveway with a note on the door.

For you. No strings.

•

For their wedding, Ying and Oden had requested a Persian love cake. Olivia thought it was an inspired choice. The actors had first met on set in Iran, co-starring in an action film in which the characters fell madly in love while saving the day. The tabloids had gone crazy with leaked images of the two smiling and holding hands and even kissing. Olivia also loved the fact that the cake itself had a story attached to it. Several versions existed: the most popular was one in which a Persian woman had been madly in love with a prince for many years but could not get his attention. One day, she baked him a cake and filled it with enchantments – cardamom, an aphrodisiac; rose for the heart; lemon for hope – and won his affections forever. In another version, the prince rejected the woman, whereupon she realised she didn't need a man at all, took home the cake and ate it all by herself, revelling in her near miss. Olivia also liked that version, and it further confirmed her theory that there was indeed a cake for every imaginable life event.

She spent hours researching recipes online, which were as varied as the stories that went with them, and trialled different variations. Some used dried rose petals, some whole dried buds, some fresh flowers. Some used cardamom powder, some ground it fresh, some used none at all. Some used yoghurt, some cream, some neither. Some used lemon, some orange. Some used almond meal, some semolina, some polenta. Some used raspberries, some figs. There was a chocolate version that used pecans, not pistachios, and pomegranate juice instead of lemon or orange juice. The variety gave her great scope to make the cake her very own, which was a baker's dream. She'd been playing with ideas every day since she received the instructions from Ferdinand, and now she was pretty sure what she wanted to make.

She sketched several versions of how it might look, sitting on the couch at home after Darcy was in bed, watching her mental images take shape and colour before her eyes, feeling like an artist once more. Part of her longed to use the studio sitting in her driveway, but how could she? She'd have to hand it back before she left for Norway. Still, that feeling of being an artist again: Grayson had done that for her, at least in part, reminding her of who she'd always been, and she was grateful to him for that.

On the Monday before the wedding, when Rambling Rose was shut to customers, she made two full practice cakes, perfecting the oven's intensity and timing, to be ready in time for Giselle and Ferdinand to make a flying visit to taste-test them. Their jet-black attire and officious manner easily set them apart, and small crowds followed them down the street, chattering and taking photos, speculating on their role and purpose. When they entered Rambling Rose, an excited cheer went up and Ferdinand had to push the door closed hard against prying faces. Olivia already had blackout curtains hanging over the glass frontage to maintain secrecy. The assistants wasted no time on small talk, simply gesturing for the plates. After carefully forking in mouthfuls of cake, and nibbling at the additional decorative details, they stared at each other silently, apparently communicating telepathically.

Then Ferdinand turned to her. 'It's acceptable.'

'Acceptable?' she queried, looking from one to the other. Giselle was writing down notes.

'Yes,' Ferdinand confirmed. Then he pointed to the leftover cakes on her bench. 'Make sure you destroy those.' With that, they glided out of her shop and into the throng once more.

It was wholly underwhelming. Of course, she'd been hoping for something more enthusiastic to emerge from their static faces and snooty tones – *sensational*, *wonderful*, *delicious* or *perfect* would have pleased her – but she resigned herself to having to celebrate *acceptable* instead.

Sadly, she destroyed the cakes by smashing them into small pieces and drowning them with boiling water to make a slurry that would go down the drain, leaving no evidence that might be photographed to then be posted on social media. And if anyone was going to release the first pictures of the cake in progress, it would be her. Her followers on Instagram had grown to hundreds of thousands and she'd been strategically posting photographs that showed tiny elements of the cake – pistachios on a grey marbled background, or rose petals scattered across a black slate board. Every post was liked and shared a thousand times, newspapers around the world using the tidbits to write pieces on celebrity wedding cakes and wedding trends over the years.

On the Friday before the wedding, she closed the shop and kept Darcy out of school, the masses of people in the village making her nervous, making her want to keep him close. People were loopy with wedding fever. Traffic accidents were increasing, and there were arguments in the street and fights in the pub. She spent the day concentrating on nothing other than Sunday's wedding, and Darcy came with her everywhere she went. They checked in with Miguel to see how he was feeling ('Nervous'), Elena and Newton ('We have enough food to feed an army'), Leanne ('Aye, grand'), Juliet ('Tuning my best Rainer Leonhardt now'), and Viola, who was barely visible behind the stacked boxes of wines in her cellar ('Grayson's coming over to help me transport them all to the manor house').

Back at Rambling Rose, Olivia triple-checked her supplies of ingredients, using a calculator to make sure she really did have enough of everything, and confirmed the delivery of every item on her list of fresh ingredients still to come. She answered several snippy text messages and emails from Ferdinand and Giselle, assuring them once again that yes, she did know the cake was the showpiece of the event, right behind Ying and Oden themselves, and tried not to be infected by their frenetic energy.

On Saturday, with the shop closed again, she took the time to set out all her bowls and tools, her mortar and pestle and measuring spoons and dry ingredients, and cut the baking paper to fit the pans, then allowed herself to go home and rest before the big day.

Well, that was the plan. But as soon as she laid her head on the pillow for an afternoon nap, her mind began racing with thoughts of Helge, Norway, Darcy, Grayson, Stoneden, the wedding, the cake, the media . . . and Clarence. Giving up on the idea of sleep, she texted him, hoping that if she dealt with at least one piece of the many moving parts in her head now, she'd have half a chance of getting some sleep tonight.

Hi! I know you must be super busy today, but wondering if you have time for a cuppa? There's something I've been wanting to ask you. I'm at home with Darcy.

Always time for my favourite cake maker. Be there soon.

Great. Mind the crowds out there.

'Have Ying and Oden arrived yet?' Olivia asked, passing Clarence a cup of tea. They were sitting at the small table in the kitchen, Darcy in the lounge room watching *How to Train Your Dragon: The Hidden World*. Helicopters could be heard in the distance – media outlets filming shots of the Cotswolds.

'I'm not sure they'd tell me if they were,' he said, unzipping his pullover in the warm kitchen. 'I suspect they're somewhere within driving distance, but they've managed to keep their location under a tight lid.'

'Are you nervous?' she said, noting the furrow in his brow.

He paused, a half-smile on his face as if weighing up his answer. 'A bit. Only because of bloody Pepperworth, though, the great buffoon that he is.'

'Hm. The council meeting.' With everything that had been going on with the wedding and in her own life, she'd almost forgotten about Chester's threat to end the project. 'Do you think he'll get it through?'

'He's a determined man, sure. But if everything goes as well tomorrow as I'm sure it will, then I think it will be a difficult and unpopular decision. Pepperworth isn't stupid.' He tapped his temple below his thick brush of white hair. 'He knows elections are popularity contests.'

Olivia nodded, sipping her tea. No matter where she ended up, she hoped that the project would survive Pepperworth's campaign.

'Have you seen Madeline recently?' Clarence asked, changing the subject. 'I haven't seen her since the funeral.' His lips pressed together tightly, then he said, 'I'm not exactly her favourite person in the world. As much as I'd like to offer comfort, I fear I'd only be doing the opposite.'

Olivia placed her mug down on the red tabletop. 'It's funny you should bring that up, because Madeline said I needed to talk to you.'

Clarence looked at her questioningly. 'Oh?'

'You see, I found a photo.' She took the photo of Ma off the sideboard, and handed it to him.

He held it at a distance where he could focus, then blinked. 'Well, look at that.' His voice was soft, nostalgic. He turned it over. 'Nineteen sixty-six.' He shook his head, quickly, as though bringing himself back to the present. 'Your grandmother was a great beauty.' Now, his voice was tinged with something else, though she couldn't put her finger on what, exactly.

'The photo was taken by Burton McCarthy,' she said.

'Yes, I remember. I was walking down the road at that moment. I smiled at her and she smiled back just as it was taken.'

Olivia recalled her conversation with Katrina and Russell. *She looks like she's in love.* 'It was you,' she said.

'What?'

'For a while I thought she must have been in love with Burton, but it was you.'

Clarence went very still, aside from the finger tapping the side of his mug. He gazed down at the photo in his hand but said nothing.

'Madeline told me that something happened at a dance that year, that Burton went home, heartbroken, and had that terrible accident, and Ma left the village not long after.'

Clarence put the photo back on the table. He stared up at the ceiling, scratching his neck.

Olivia waited, then said, 'Could you please tell me what happened that night at the dance?'

•

Long-forgotten memories swam through Clarence's mind, and his skin fired with regret. He cleared his throat. How could he tell

Olivia what he'd done without making her hate him? But she had asked for the truth, and she deserved to know.

'Ellie and I . . .' He paused, catching her puzzled shake of the head. 'To me, she was Ellie.'

Her face changed, then, a dawning of understanding of their relationship – that they had been more than friends.

'We were only together for a short time, maybe a month. We kept it secret,' he said, and right there was the shame of it all. Ellie hadn't wanted to hide their relationship. She had wanted to shout it from the rooftops, but he'd convinced her that he just wanted to keep her all to himself for as long as possible, give themselves time to enjoy each other's company before the village tongues began to wag. Couldn't they just *be*? Really, though, he was simply keeping his options open, like he always did.

'Burton didn't know,' said Olivia.

'No,' he confessed.

'But he loved her.'

'Yes.'

She frowned, as though attempting to fit pieces of a puzzle together. She abandoned her cup of tea and crossed her arms at her waist, waiting. 'What happened the night of the dance?'

'The dances were always held at the church hall. I was there, standing with Howard and a group of our friends. We were young and stupid,' he said, flatly. 'We were all decked out in our new suits. I remember that the overwhelming smell of hairspray and Brylcreem made me cough once or twice.'

Olivia gave a small smile at that detail.

'The hall was packed, people dancing, or standing around the walls, disappearing into the cloakroom or out the back door for a sneaky drink away from the vicar. I had to shout over the band as I introduced the boys to Bethan.'

'Who was Bethan?'

'She was from Stoneden too, but she'd been sent away to an expensive boarding school. Her grandparents owned the biggest haberdashery supplier in this part of the country and her parents were set to inherit the whole thing. They were wealthy, they were connected, and they were the sort of people who could help me with my political aspirations here in the district.' He sighed heavily.

'I see.'

'I didn't think Ellie was coming that night. She must have changed her mind. One minute I was standing with the chaps, Bethan beside me, her hand on my elbow, smiling, looking like . . . like a princess. She was wearing a pale green dress with silver trim and sparkles, and a tiny tiara in her hair.' He smiled in spite of himself as he remembered how smitten he'd been. Bethan was beautiful and smart and kind and he'd honestly believed he was in love with her and they would make a good marriage match. But at twenty-one, how could you possibly know? 'Then I saw Ellie come into the hall, with Burton and Madeline behind her. Burton was . . . well, parties weren't really his strong suit. Couldn't dance to save his life,' he said, wincing at his own words. 'He had it tough at school when he was younger, and at home as well.' A lot like Howard, he thought. 'But he was happiest when he was working on the farm. A good man.'

His recollections were interrupted by a voice outside on a loud-speaker, instructing anyone who wasn't a resident to move out of the street. A truck reversed, warning beeps piercing the air, as workers installed barricades. Clarence waited for the noise to die down, then continued.

'Howard raised a hand in greeting, beckoning to her. She pushed her way through the crowd, making her way over to us, but I knew she hadn't seen Bethan. She was smiling at me, waving. I was just finishing up a story when she arrived, beaming, so happy to see me, and it made my heart lurch. She grabbed my arm. She said, "Can we talk? Let's go outside." She was pulling on my arm. I smiled at her, but didn't move. All I could think was that this wasn't supposed to happen. She was meant to be at home. I had no idea what to do. Howard tried to step between us, take her attention, perhaps draw her away from the circle. He was trying to help me, I suppose. He knew I'd moved on with Bethan and he was there to help, as always. Ellie looked at him, then at me, hurt and confused. Then she saw Bethan standing on my other side, her hand on my elbow, and the group fell silent.'

'Oh, poor Ma,' Olivia said quietly.

'I tried to smooth over the awkwardness. "You know the lads," I said to her, gesturing around the circle. She looked around and nodded, trying to be polite. And then Bethan stepped forward, smiling. She was such a kind person – she still is,' he corrected himself. 'She held out her hand to Ellie and introduced herself. Ellie reached for Bethan's hand, and I noticed her own hand was trembling, her face was pale with hurt. "Ellie."'

Ellie – daughter of mill workers. Perfect for Burton but not for Clarence.

He went on, 'Ellie stared from Bethan to me, fitting all the pieces together. Bethan slid her arm through mine and leant into me, looking up trustfully into my face, her smile bright. "So how do you two know each other?" she asked. And I said, quickly, "School. Ellie and I have been friends for years, haven't we?"'

He paused here, recollecting the moment as he'd done so many times over the years. 'I could see Burton, and Madeline too, looking between me and Ellie and Bethan. Madeline's face, confused, Burton's full of pain.' He went to pick up his cup of tea, but then slid it away across the kitchen table. Olivia was staring at him, waiting.

'"Yes, friends," Ellie said, and I could see she was trying not to cry. "Lovely to meet you, Bethan, but I must go." She turned and pushed her way through the crowd, running towards the door, Burton and Madeline behind her. At the door, I saw Burton reach for her arm but she threw off his hand and disappeared into the dark. Burton went to follow her, but Madeline grabbed his arm. I turned away then – I was focused on Bethan, worried what she might think. Burton's accident happened some time that night and Ellie never spoke to me again. She and her family moved to Australia a few weeks later and that was that.'

Olivia put her hands on top of her head and rested her elbows on the table for several moments. Clarence waited, bracing himself for her condemnation. Then she straightened and took a deep breath.

'My mother, Laurie, was born eight months after Ma left England,' she said. 'Do you think you could be my grandfather?'

He stared at her, a buzzing sound in his ears.

'I mean, were you sleeping with her in that month you were together?' she said, bluntly.

His face flared hot. He might have been a modern man in an unorthodox relationship, but he was still a child of the 1940s and talking about his sex life didn't come naturally. 'Y-yes.'

'Well, well,' she said. 'I'm not sure if I want to laugh or cry, hug you or shout at you.'

He stared at her, this young woman from the other side of the world who might well be his granddaughter. There was so much he wanted to say and so much he wanted to ask, so many apologies and welcomes, celebrations and commiserations. And then there was Darcy, sitting in the next room, who might be Clarence's great-grandson, and it was all too much to take in or make sense of.

'Perhaps you could do a little of each in turn?' he said at last, with some of his old cheekiness. This made her laugh, and he found himself grinning at her in wonder.

30

Olivia rose at three o'clock on the morning of the wedding and dressed in her most comfortable baking overalls. Juliet, bless her, arrived at quarter to four. She had offered to look after Darcy for a few hours while Olivia worked on the cake, then Katrina would take him for the rest of the day, and Juliet would go home and change into her wedding frock.

'Nervous?' Juliet asked now, looking surprisingly awake for this hour of the morning.

'Yes,' Olivia admitted, 'though not so much about the cake itself. I know I can do that. It's more the paparazzi and the crowds.'

'The roads are quiet at the moment,' Juliet reassured her. 'The police are patrolling the roadblocks, and only people with a resident's permit can get through. You're going to be fine.' She rubbed Olivia's arm. 'This is your day to shine.'

As Olivia stepped into Rambling Rose, any nerves fell away. She knew how to do this. She felt the invisible arms of her shop, her partner in this baking dance, embrace her as she slipped an apron over her head and set some music to play. Rather than her well-worn 1950s playlist, she put on Morgan Evans, the country singer Grayson had recommended. She liked his cheerful, poetic way of looking at the world, and enjoyed the reminder of Australia.

She whisked egg whites, then used a tiny brush to paint the liquid onto twenty-five perfect rose petals, before sprinkling them with sugar and setting them aside to dry on a rack near the oven. Next, she separated more eggs and beat the whites with a pinch of cream of tartar until they formed peaks, then gradually added castor sugar, beating it till it was completely dissolved into a glossy meringue. Using different-sized piping bags, she created two rows of meringue cones – the larger ones were smooth, while for the smaller ones she created a swirl – and popped them into the oven to bake. The sugary rose petals and the meringues would form part of the cake's finishing adornments.

By now, she was in the zone, humming along to the music, her hands knowing exactly what to do as she creamed the butter and sugar, then added eggs and saffron-enriched milk heated gently over the gas, and folded in the flour and chopped pistachios. She divided the batter into three tins to form the layers of her main cake; this would be flanked by two smaller versions, creating a trio of cakes. While the first lot of cakes baked, she began work on the rosewater whipped cream-cheese icing. She paused for a moment to take a photo of the precious rosewater from the Iranian family's farm in Tasmania, a lovely authentic touch for this Persian love cake, and posted it to Instagram before continuing.

The air was full of delightful aromas – the saffron, the rosewater, the meringues, the baking cakes. She checked on the rose petals, which were crystallising beautifully, and pulled out her presentation board, a slab of reclaimed wood from an old farmhouse in the district, stained with oils to enhance its natural hues, which ranged from dark chocolate brown to warm maple syrup. Then she set to baking the two smaller cakes that would accompany the larger one. She was confident these cakes were going to be fabulous, she only wished she could feel as assured of her own future. This wedding was a huge boon for her business, yet she'd only have to shut her shop soon after in order to move to Norway and start all over again under completely different circumstances, in a country where she didn't even speak the language. She might have found her grandfather here in Stoneden, only to have to say goodbye again, with no guarantee of an ongoing relationship. And then there was Grayson. Lovely, kissable Grayson with a warm, funny family. She turned out the layers of cake and drizzled the tops with lemon sugar syrup, hoping beyond hope that she was making the right life choices.

The ground floor of the manor house had been transformed for the reception, and the effect was breathtaking. Ying and Oden's people had crafted a glorious blend of English and Chinese traditions. Gold and silver silk curtains draped the windows. Dozens of tables covered with white tablecloths nestled together to form one long table in the centre of the room, long enough to seat a hundred guests, each place set with eighteen pieces of rose gold cutlery and five glasses, glinting under the soft lighting. More glassware ran down the centre of the table, holding tea lights and roses. Suspended from the ceiling was a canopy of tree branches woven with hundreds of delicate pink English roses. Large white paper parasols hung from the branches, threaded with fairy lights that cascaded down towards the tables.

The wedding table was set up near the expansive windows overlooking the green lawns, currently full of famous people in heels and top hats and eye-wateringly expensive suits and frocks.

Around the walls were food and beverage tables adorned with tall blue and white Chinese vases full of blooming roses.

'It's gorgeous,' Viola said. She and Olivia were hovering near a beverage table, taking in the hall's transformation. Giselle and Ferdinand were rushing around in their black uniforms, speaking rapidly into headpieces.

'It really is,' Olivia agreed. 'You look gorgeous too.'

'So do you!'

Viola was dressed in a lacy maxi dress, her soft hair pinned up with a white flower above her ear. Olivia was wearing a formal dress she'd ordered especially for the day. It was pale pink, overlaid with floral lace down the bodice and layered into the long skirt. It had a bateau neckline and elbow-length sleeves and she'd paired it with gold shoes with toe-crushingly high heels. Today was not the day to choose comfort over fashion.

'That cake is divine,' Viola said.

Olivia looked over at her elegant trio of cakes: pale pink cream-cheese icing, with meringues and shards of handmade white chocolate laced with pomegranate liqueur arranged like a crown around the edges, and soft pink clouds of rose-flavoured Persian fairy floss in the centre. The crystallised rose petals were scattered over the cakes and strewn liberally over the presentation board too. Next to the cakes she'd placed a small blackboard with *Ying & Oden* written in white chalk.

'There is a security guard standing there, literally assigned to watch over my cake,' Olivia said, looking at the tall, stern-faced man in wonder.

Viola nodded. 'Did you ever think you'd make a cake that required its own bodyguard?'

'Definitely not.'

As Viola moved off to check on the ice supplies for the French champagne, Leanne arrived, smart in a black suit.

Olivia gave her a big smile. 'How are you going?'

'Aye, good. Well done, you – that cake looks incredible. You should be very proud.'

'Thanks. I am.'

'I hope all of this'—Leanne gestured around the room—'is enough to save us.'

'Oh, yeah, the vote.' Olivia sighed, saddened at the idea that even if she wanted to stay on here in Stoneden after the wedding, she might not be able to. They'd all worked so hard to get this far. It would be cruel for it to be taken away so soon. She'd come to love the people in this village as a big extended family. Even if she wasn't able to stay, she wanted them to be able to continue on.

'I don't want to go back to Ireland,' said Leanne.

'Why did you come here to Stoneden?' Olivia asked. 'What made you want to leave?'

Leanne glowered. 'It was my husband's family. You've no idea. So big. So bossy. Exhausting. Interfering mother-in-law, drunk father-in-law, gossiping sisters-in-law, everyone over all the goddamn time. But I could never say anything. Always had to keep the peace and hold my tongue. Keith thinks the sun shines out of every one of them. I had to escape to survive. We've been the happiest here we've ever been.'

'Huh. Seems like this project has rescued people from all sorts of situations.' Olivia felt for Miguel, too, an honourable man who'd taken on responsibility for his brother's family, but who might lose the home he was preparing for them before they even arrived. 'You never know. As Clarence said, it's not over yet. There's still hope.'

Leanne lifted her eyebrows. 'Let's hope they don't have a fat lady singer to end the night, then.'

Olivia chuckled, then raised her hand in greeting as Ryan and Farzenah arrived, the young photographer wearing a long gold dress with a matching hijab. Ryan nodded to her, and he and Farzenah walked around the room, quietly discussing what to photograph. He pointed to Olivia's cake and the bodyguard standing next to it, and Farzenah moved over to snap some images.

Anthony and Juliet Cabot were next to enter the room, Anthony smart in his new charcoal suit with matching waistcoat and holding his Bible, while Juliet carried her cello. She looked beautiful in a glittering royal blue floor-length dress with enough volume in the skirt to accommodate the positioning of her instrument. They both looked elated. Juliet caught Olivia's eye and gave her a thumbs up to let her know that all was well with Darcy.

Suddenly, Giselle rushed at Olivia and Leanne, her arms open wide like a large crow. 'Out the back now,' she said, her lips moving but no other features of her face. 'Ying and Oden are on their way.' She clapped her hands at them, and Olivia flinched in surprise, but she and Leanne did as instructed and headed out through the kitchen towards the sitting room that had been set up to host the suppliers.

The kitchen was in an uproar, white-hatted chefs yelling across the rows of tiny plates holding asparagus spears wrapped in pink slices of ham off the bone, and quail eggs with lemon verbena, laid out on trays and waiting to be delivered by tuxedoed waiters. Elena and Newton were there, tasting sauces and lifting handmade pasta from drying racks. Olivia was so happy for them, but she kept walking, not wanting to disturb them. She saw Miguel plating up cheese boards with tremendous precision. He looked up and winked at her, beaming with pride.

They continued through to the sitting room, which had its own cosy fire and trolleys of food and drinks. Olivia pulled her phone out of her clutch bag to message Katrina.

How's everything going?

Great. Darcy and Eloise are playing weddings. Maybe one day . . . ;)

Give him a hug from me

Will do. He's asking to stay the night. Is that okay with you? It's fine with us and will give you time to enjoy the wedding.

Sure! Thanks x

The room slowly filled with artisans and suppliers who had been rounded up and herded away by the grim-faced Giselle and Ferdinand. A beaming Clarence arrived at her side, looking dapper in his suit.

'Hi,' he said. From his slightly dazed smile she could see that he was still struggling to process the startling news that he might be her grandfather. She knew how he felt.

'Hi, yourself.'

'The cake looks incredible,' he said. 'Perfect.'

'Thank you.'

'You've done the whole village proud. I'm quietly confident that our success today will save the project.'

'I do hope so, really.'

He was about to speak again when a short, stocky woman suddenly stepped between them. Startled, Olivia took a step back. The woman stood and glared at her with an unnerving set to her jaw. She looked familiar, but Olivia couldn't place her.

'Olivia Kent, right?' the woman demanded.

'Yes,' Olivia said, cautiously. Her eyes flicked to Clarence's and he frowned slightly, also trying to work out what was going on.

The woman was dressed casually in jeans and boots and a yellow cardigan and didn't appear to be part of the service team. Was she a crazed fan of Ying and Oden? Olivia cast her gaze around the room, searching for Giselle or Ferdinand, maybe even security.

'I'm Adele Bellington,' the woman stated, staring at her expectantly.

Olivia looked back blankly, which seemed to enrage her further. 'Adele from Stroud Specialty Cakes,' she hissed, pulling a piece of paper out of the pocket of her jeans and holding it in front of Olivia's face.

'Oh God,' Olivia whispered. It was a printout of a photo showing a large cake with white icing, sprinkled with rose petals. It had been taken at the wine and cheese night. It was Adele's cake, the one Olivia had bought from her on the day of Darcy's accident. It looked to have come from Ying's Instagram account. Olivia looked at Clarence, who appeared to be trying to put the pieces of this conversation together.

'How did you even get in here?' Olivia asked desperately, looking around for security. She feared she knew exactly what Adele was here to do, and that was to ruin Olivia's career and reputation and, with it, the viability of the Renaissance Project. All around her were smart dresses and suits and professional hairdos, high heels, hats, even a silver cane or two, but no sign of security. 'The roads are blocked . . .'

'My brother's a guard here,' Adele said dismissively, and pushed the photo into Olivia's face. 'You passed off my cake as your own. You're a fraud. Ying and Oden hired a fraud and I am going to make sure the whole world knows.'

'Now hold on a moment,' Clarence began, obviously having caught up with what had happened.

Olivia held up her hand to push the photo away. 'There's been a mistake,' she began.

'Oh, oh, a mistake!' Adele screeched, her voice piercing through the excited chatter in the room. An abrupt silence fell. Olivia felt the weight of every pair of eyes on them.

'Adele, I assure you I never once claimed that cake as my own,' she said.

'I found this photo online. It looked familiar and when I went back through my orders I matched the dates. A cake maker never forgets her cake. You passed it off as your own.' Adele waved the picture in the air again. 'Now you're set to go down in history as the amazing cake maker for this celebrity wedding, when it could have been me!' she shrieked. 'It *should* have been me.'

In that moment, Olivia understood. She had been chosen to make the cake for the wedding not by virtue of her talent, but purely because she was part of the Renaissance Project. If Olivia hadn't moved to Stoneden and opened a cake shop, Ying and Oden might have looked for their cake maker in nearby towns, and they could well have chosen Adele. The photo of the misattributed cake would only have added fuel to the fire of Adele's resentment.

'Hold on a moment,' Clarence said again, trying to calm things down. 'There was a lot going on at that wine and cheese event, which is where this photo was taken. The vicar was excited over the announcement of the wedding – we all were,' he said, smiling, cajoling. 'He may have suggested the cake was Olivia's, but she's telling the truth. She never once said it was. Lots of people took photos of the cake that night, thrilled about Stoneden's involvement in such a big event. We can't control what people put on social media.'

Just then, Ryan and Farzenah walked in. Olivia felt as though she was watching it all in slow motion, the unravelling of this day, her career, her reputation, and the hopes and dreams of the villagers who were counting on today being such a success that Pepperworth's council would have no choice but to permit the Renaissance Project to continue.

'Look, Adele, could we go somewhere else to talk about this?' Olivia asked, eyeing a door near the fireplace, desperate to get away from all the listening ears.

'No, we can*not*,' Adele spat out each syllable. Olivia was certain there was not a single person in the room who wasn't watching this blow by blow.

Ryan walked towards them with his voice recorder in his hand, obviously eager to capture a story in progress. Olivia closed her eyes, wishing that when she opened them she would be back in Richmond. Her eyelids fluttered open. Ryan was standing at her side.

'What are you going to do about this?' Adele flapped the photograph at him.

'What's going on?' Ryan said, taking in their faces and the photo Adele was holding. He flicked the switch on his recorder so the red light flashed.

'Ryan,' Olivia began, swallowing hard. 'There's been a big misunderstanding, something we need to clear up.'

'I can save you the time,' Adele said. 'This woman is a fraud.' She paused, clearly enjoying the look of surprise on Ryan's face. 'This cake from the wine and cheese night'—she showed him the photo—'was made not by Olivia here, but by me.'

'Yes, I know,' he said. 'That's why we didn't run the photos.'

'Yes,' Adele said, fervently. 'But many people shared photos on social media, claiming the cake was made by Olivia, and no one refuted that.'

'In hindsight,' Clarence said, gravely, 'we could have tried to track down any photos and correct the mistake. But photos get shared and circulated and copied and it's nearly impossible to find the original source, or even to locate each one. I'm sorry you've been hurt by this.' He sounded genuinely regretful.

'Too little, too late.' Adele turned back to Ryan. 'Are you going to publish this story or not? If you won't, it will be the next journalist I meet when I walk out this door.'

To Olivia's surprise, Ryan switched off his machine.

'What are you doing?' Adele demanded. 'Are you really turning your back on the biggest story of the day?'

Ryan pressed his lips together, thinking. 'Yes, I am.' He looked at Clarence. 'Seems I'm Team Renaissance after all.'

'Big, big mistake.' Adele spun on her heel and left the now silent room.

Clarence brought Olivia a glass of brandy and she downed it quickly. She felt numb, battered. It was over – her career, her reputation, the Renaissance Project, all because of a stupid misunderstanding.

'There's still hope,' Ryan tried to reassure her. 'It's a flimsy story.'

'But it's still a story,' Clarence conceded, glumly. 'And today of all days, the world's media is dying to report on anything at all to do with this wedding.'

'I can write pieces to refute the story, give our side,' said Ryan. 'Everyone knows social media is the Wild West. Olivia's done nothing wrong.'

Olivia wasn't so sure about that, but she gave him a grateful nod and turned to make her way through the crowd of people, desperate to get away from all the curious eyes.

She managed to convince the guards at the entrance to the grand hall that she had to go in there one last time in order to remove a ribbon that might interfere with the ceremonial cutting of the cake. Inside, she walked close to the walls, stepping carefully so she didn't trip in her high heels, but she was unable to resist glancing up towards the bridal table where Ying and Oden sat.

Ying looked divine. Her wedding dress was sleeveless with a high-collared Asian-inspired neckline, and the pale blush fabric was intricately embroidered with tiny flowers. It looked heavy, and regal, and insanely expensive. Olivia would be happy to bet that was one item at their wedding that hadn't been made locally. Beside her, Oden looked dashing in a loose suit and an artfully unbuttoned shirt, and he was clean-shaven for once.

As Olivia reached the table where the cake was displayed, Ying looked across and saw her. With a warm smile, she lifted her champagne flute in gratitude. Olivia found herself sinking into a curtsey. She felt a fleeting moment of happiness, before she remembered what was going on right now outside the walls of the manor, as Adele poured her tawdry tale into the eager ears of any journalist who would listen.

She fussed around the cake one last time, making sure the ribbon was tight on the cutting knife, that all the flowers were perfect, fluffing one or two and removing a petal that looked a little tired. She stood gazing at it for a moment, letting it sink in: this cake, which should have made her career, might have instead destroyed it.

31

Clarence farewelled her out in the designated staff car park at the back of the manor. He lay a comforting hand on her shoulder. 'Don't worry about the cake. We'll sort it all out in the morning.'

'Sure,' she said, sounding more confident than she felt. She climbed into her van and rolled slowly out of the car park, stopping a couple of times for security guards to check the permit on her dashboard with their torches, then made the short distance home, pulling into the driveway behind the tiny house. With equal parts dread and desperate curiosity, she turned on her phone and checked her social media feeds for any sign of Adele's success in sharing her story.

Twitter was already awash with the hashtags #cakefail and #Yodenscandal. There were several unanswered calls on her phone from numbers she didn't know – journalists, she assumed. Text messages had come in, too, from people who must have found her number on her business page, asking for her comment.

Stepping out of the car, she switched off the phone and stood quietly a moment, watching her breath forming white puffs in the cold night air, letting the chill seep right into her bones. This definitely wasn't the end to the day she'd been hoping for, but at least for now she could go inside, lock the door, and collapse into bed.

She awoke to knocking. The sound floated in at the edges of her consciousness, filtering into her uneasy dreams, slowly dragging her to alertness. She sat bolt upright, her heart hammering. Who would it be? A journalist? Giselle and Ferdinand? Adele, back for another argument?

No, wait, the streets were still blocked off. It had to be a local.

Oh God, it might be Katrina. Had something happened to Darcy? She flung off the covers and raced down the stairs in her pyjamas, her hair flying loose, then yanked open the door.

Grayson was walking away down the path, but he turned around at the sound of the door. His jeans and jacket were mud-splattered, his whiskers unshaven, his hair mussed, and his eyes so full of *worry*. For her.

'You're here. I'm so glad you're okay,' he said, running his eyes over her body as though checking her for soundness. Then again, she wasn't wearing a bra, and the frigid morning air had hit her hard. His eyes snapped back to her face, and she crossed her arms over her chest.

'Come in,' she said, and quickly shut the door behind him. She pulled a soft angora shawl off a peg on the coat rack and wrapped it around herself.

'Are you okay?' he asked, putting a hand on her shoulder.

Touched by his concern, she felt dangerously close to tears. 'Is it that bad? I haven't had my phone on since last night.'

'I know, I've been calling.'

'I had a lot of missed calls from unknown numbers.' She looked around for her phone but couldn't remember where she'd left it. 'Show me what they're saying.' She held out her hand for his phone.

He hesitated, then reached into his pocket, pulled out his phone and swiped the screen to a Twitter feed.

Australian blow-in steals England's prize

Hack cake maker from the sticks fakes her way to the country's most coveted baking assignment

Stoneden project doomed

Cheap knock-off

Fake cake

Yoden duped

Poor Ying. Poor Oden. We love you Yoden!

Rambling Rose is CANCELLED!!!

Boycott

Olivia Kent is Cancelled!!!!!!!

She gasped. 'Cancelled?' She thrust the phone back at him, unable to read any more vitriol.

Grayson slipped the phone back into his pocket. 'Would you like a hug?' He held out his arms, giving her a sympathetic smile.

She nodded, tears brimming, and stepped into his open arms, resting her head on his chest while he held her, just tightly enough. He smelt faintly and comfortingly of cows and earth. 'You're going to be okay.'

She took a deep breath and stepped back, reluctantly moving out of his embrace. 'I know. It doesn't seem possible right now, but I do know it. I've been through worse.'

He nodded encouragingly. 'This will pass. It's shit, don't get me wrong. But this is not the end of the world, it's not the end of your business, it's not the end of you. You know that, right?'

She wiped away an errant tear. 'I do. Thank you.'

'People in this village, your friends, they still love you.'

'You think so?'

'I know so.'

'That's good, because I love them,' she said, her tears starting afresh. 'I came here looking for family and everyone has become just that. Katrina, Russell and Eloise, Clarence, Elena and Newton, Leanne, Viola, Miguel, Raj, everyone in the main street, dear old Madeline, Anthony and Juliet, even Mrs Wilson, they've all found a place in my heart.' She swallowed down the lump in her throat. 'And you too.'

Her words hung in the air for a moment, until Grayson said, 'Is there something I could do for you, right now, that would help?'

'Um . . . yes, actually. Could you please help me find my phone?'

His denim-blue eyes smiled. 'Let's do it.'

They searched the cottage, every room, downstairs and then up, under every pillow. Finally she found it on the edge of the sink in the bathroom. She turned it on, dreading the string of beeps that would follow, and carried it back to her bedroom, where Grayson was perched on the edge of her bed.

'I found it,' she said, as the beeps began.

Grayson arched his brows at the noise. 'Would you like me to stay with you?'

She would, very much. She was just about to say so when her phone sprang to life in her hand, the screen lighting up with a familiar name.

'It's Helge,' she said, biting her lip, unsure what to do.

'It's fine, answer it,' Grayson said, standing up. 'Message me later if you need anything.' With a final squeeze of her arm, he left, the spiral staircase yowling with every footstep.

She swallowed her disappointment and answered Helge's call.

'Oh, Livvy, are you all right?'

'I'm fine,' she said, almost believing it.

'*V*ot happened? Is it true?'

That made her pause. 'Which part?'

'That you faked a cake?'

'Of course not! How could you even think that?'

'I don't, of course,' he was quick to assure her. 'I'm just trying to *v*ork out *v*ot's happened, that's all. Who is this *v*oman, Adele Bellington, and *v*hy is she saying these things?'

Olivia sighed and fell heavily to the edge of her bed. As she told him the story, her phone continued to vibrate with incoming calls and messages.

Helge listened and sympathised, earnestly. 'Such bad luck,' he tutted. 'Everything blown out of proportion.'

'Exactly,' she said, rubbing at her eyes. She was exhausted and needed a shower.

'But soon you *v*ill be here,' he said. 'You can escape the madness and start over in a new country where no one knows you. You can open a new store with a new name if you *v*ant to. Or maybe do something totally different. A new you, yes?'

'Yes, maybe,' she said, suddenly longing to be in Norway, somewhere she could hide away for a while, disappear into a new culture, a new landscape. Maybe she could even have a bit of a break. She still owned Ma's house in Richmond, but if she sold it she would be able to take a holiday and spend it with Darcy, for the first time in his life. She could help all three of them to connect. It all seemed very appealing indeed. 'I've got to go,' she said, softly. 'But thank you so much for calling. It means a lot.'

'It's the least I could do for my future . . .' He trailed off, and she wondered what he'd been about to say – *wife? partner? love?* 'My future,' he said again. 'You, Darcy and me.'

'Don't worry,' Katrina said, passing her a cup of tea. 'I've been stalking Adele online and there are quite a few people who have some nasty things to say about her.' She waved her hand in the air. 'This will be over before you know it.'

'If I'm ever in hospital I hope I have you by my side,' Olivia said. 'You have a terrific way of making me believe everything you're saying.'

'Trust me,' her friend said, grinning, 'I'm a nurse. This won't hurt a bit.'

Olivia laughed properly for the first time that day, and sipped her tea. By the time she left – dragging Darcy away from Eloise's dress-up box of tutus and swords and monster masks – her worries had eased.

She and Darcy stopped in at Clarence's house on the way home. As he set out biscuits that Raj's wife had made, he told her he'd heard from Ying and Oden.

'Really?' she said, spluttering into yet another cup of tea.

'Really.' He smiled, kneeling down with the poker to adjust a log on the fire.

'What did they say?' She leant forward on the couch, her foot nudging the snoring dog. 'Sorry, Stuart.' She rubbed his belly with her toe and he rolled over onto his back to encourage her to continue.

'Well, it was relayed via Giselle, of course.' He rose slowly, his knees the last to straighten. 'She said Ying and Oden wished to advise us not to concern ourselves with the media frenzy. They are well used to it. Ying is sorry she shared the photo of the cake from the wine and cheese night, which someone had posted and tagged her in, and which had been incorrectly attributed to you. She said she should have checked the source first. She said to tell you she loved the cake very much.'

'She said *very much*?'

'Yes.'

Darcy finished his biscuit, put his plate on the coffee table, then went to lie on the carpet beside Stuart, rubbing the dog's ears. She could see he was tired from his largely sleepless night spent laughing and playing games with Eloise, as Katrina had described it: *Like a pair of chattering gibbons all bloody night.* Olivia wondered if they'd be able to have a dog or a cat in Oslo with Helge.

'Well, that's great news,' she said to Clarence as he eased himself down into a chair. 'But how do you think all of this will affect the district council's vote this week? Do you think the wedding has helped your case, or has "cakefail" ruined it all?'

Clarence frowned. 'A bit of both.'

'But if you were a betting man, which way would you go?' she fretted. Even if she wasn't going to be here, she wanted the project to go ahead.

He thought a moment, then shook his head. 'Too close to call.' His attention drifted to Darcy, and his grumpy expression softened. Olivia was touched by the faraway, amazed look on his face as he regarded his possible great-grandson. It was beautiful to watch, and she felt a moment of sadness to think that they would have to part again, so soon after finding each other.

'How would you feel about coming with me to see Doc Eli this week?' she said suddenly. Clarence's attention snapped back to her.

She inclined her head towards Darcy, then pointed to herself, then to Clarence. 'To see if we can find out for sure, officially.'

He blinked a couple of times as he caught her drift. 'Yes,' he agreed. 'I'd like that very much.'

Darcy went to bed early that night, exhausted after his sleepover and with his belly full of roast chicken, potatoes and peas. Olivia was perched downstairs on the couch, her laptop on her knees, researching real estate in Tasmania, trying to get a sense of what the market was like, should she feel the need to sell Ma's house anytime soon. But when an email arrived with the subject line *Representing Adele Bellington*, she opened it, her heart in her mouth.

The email was from a London lawyer, advising Olivia that his client planned to sue her for intellectual property theft, fraud, and damages due to loss of future earnings. If Olivia wished to move this on swiftly, he said that Adele was open to negotiations to settle out of court. Either way, he said, she would need to get herself a lawyer.

She felt the blow like a kick to her gut. She closed her eyes for several long moments, feeling the swell of adrenaline in her blood, the acceleration of her heart, the shaking in her hands. Then she took a long, deep breath.

She would be okay. She felt the helping hands of everyone in this village ready to lift her up, felt the roots that ran through her, deep into Stoneden's earth. This was her village. It had survived collapse to rise again, and so would she.

32

Madeline sat on the couch, staring at the empty space where the coffin had been until so recently. She was still untangling her feelings about Burton's death. So many feelings, so little logic behind any of them. Eirlys was in her lap, purring; she waved a paw in the air, as if demanding attention. Madeline ran her fingertip down the little cat's chest and rubbed her furry belly, and that was when she noticed it. Several large lumps. *Kittens.* Sometime soon, her house would be full of kittens, running around, stealing socks, climbing curtains, eating from her best china plates. She laughed out loud, then started to cry – she seemed to be crying all the time these days – holding the little cat close, her warm body and rumbling purr the best balm in the whole world.

A few minutes later, a car door slammed outside. Hastily wiping her face, Madeline got up to investigate. When she opened the front door, Eirlys skipped out past her into the cold afternoon air, and ran straight to Darcy, who was holding onto Olivia's arms and standing on her feet as they walked. His giggles pealed through the air, while Olivia grunted with the effort. She stopped and toppled him gently off.

'You're too heavy for me now,' she said. Spying Madeline at the door, she held up a hand to wave.

Darcy scooped up Eirlys and rubbed his face in her fur. 'Hi, Madeline,' he called.

Madeline was surprised by how happy she was to see them. 'How was the wedding?' she asked, as they reached the door.

Darcy put Eirlys down and the cat galloped back inside, Darcy running after her.

'It couldn't have been more perfect,' Olivia said, 'except for the media storm that followed.' She rolled her eyes dramatically. 'Have you heard?' Her hair was scraped up messily into a bun, her face bare of make-up, a woollen scarf around her neck. She looked worn out, but still somehow focused.

'No, what happened?' Madeline beckoned Olivia in and shut the door behind her. 'Would you like tea?'

'Love some, thanks,' Olivia said, taking off her coat. 'Would you like me to make it?' She was already moving towards the kitchen, as if they'd known each other for years, rather than just this autumn.

'All right, then.' Madeline took a seat at the dining table, content to watch her.

'I'll come back to the media circus later,' Olivia said, opening a drawer to look for a teaspoon. 'First I have two other pieces of news I wanted to share with you.'

'Oh?'

'I spoke to Clarence, about Ma.' Olivia stopped fussing in the kitchen and looked warily at Madeline. 'We're fairly certain he's my grandfather.'

'I did wonder,' Madeline said, eyeing Olivia evenly. Gosh, she didn't envy Olivia that conversation.

Olivia spooned fragrant black tea into the pot. 'We're going to see Doc Eli about genetic testing. From what I've read online, I would only have twenty-five per cent of his genes, so a test wouldn't be conclusive, but it would still be interesting.'

'I wish there was an easier way,' she said, her heart aching for this young woman who had already lost so many members of her family.

Olivia went to fetch teacups and saucers from the good cabinet, stepping over Darcy, who was stretched out on the floor with Eirlys. Madeline watched eagerly to see which pieces Olivia would pick. Whichever they were, she'd send them home with her today. She returned with a hideous set of 1970s off-white cups with an orange floral pattern and brown rims. Her aunt Phyllis had given them to Madeline for her thirtieth birthday. She'd never liked Phyllis or her tea set. Maybe she wouldn't inflict that particular set on Olivia.

Olivia poured boiling water into the teapot, then brought the teapot to the table and eased herself down. 'Well, Clarence is certain enough to claim me and Darcy as his own, and it feels right, you know?'

Madeline nodded, her eyes encouraging. It did feel right, she had to agree.

'I keep thinking about Ma, though. Clarence told me she'd asked him that night at the dance if they could go somewhere to talk. I can't help wondering if she knew she was pregnant, if she'd gone there to celebrate the news, only to have her heart broken.' Olivia bit her lower lip, her face pinched with pain.

For Madeline, the thought that this was true was sad indeed. What a horrible turn that night had taken for them all. Her guest continued, absent-mindedly scratching at her arm while she thought it through.

'I wonder about her and Lawrence. I can't quite believe that Ma would trick him into marriage, so I have to believe that he knew her situation, that he was willing to help her because he had lost his wife, was childless and needed to start a new life too. She always spoke so well of him. I'm sure she was deeply grateful for his support.'

'Yes, I imagine she would have been,' Madeline said. 'Those were different times, that's for sure. It would have been very difficult for her to be on her own with a child, even if she'd had her parents' support.'

Olivia's eyes widened. 'Her parents! I wonder if they knew, if they convinced her it was the best thing to do, if they even somehow made the match during the voyage to Australia.'

Madeline let out a breath she'd not known she'd been holding, her feelings towards her old friend shifting shape, holding only sympathy for her right now.

Olivia lifted her shoulders high then let them drop. 'And maybe the reason she changed her married name back to her maiden name was that she hadn't really wanted to be married, or maybe she felt guilty, like she'd trapped him and then she could set him free, or maybe she felt she didn't deserve his name after he died. I have no idea, and the reality is I will never know the truth for sure.' Then her face brightened. 'But it does look as though I might have found some family after all.'

Madeline smiled. 'I'd say you found a whole village,' she said.

A shadow passed across Olivia's face then. 'Yes, well, the other thing I need to tell you about is the Renaissance Project,' she said. 'The district council is meeting tomorrow to vote on the future of the project. There's a strong chance they'll shut it down.'

It was the oddest thing. The news should have made Madeline happy, and until recently she would certainly have enjoyed watching Clarence's pride take a knock. The end of the project would release her financially. Yet it would surely mean that Olivia and Darcy would be sent away. Where would they go?

The idea left her feeling concerned and, blast it, close to tears, again.

'If that happens, you'll be able to sell this place,' Olivia said, gazing at her steadily. Madeline tried to say something, but nothing came.

Olivia smiled at her, encouragingly. 'You'll be free at last.'

'I see,' Madeline managed to say.

Darcy arrived at the table, the cat slung purring around his neck. 'Can I please have a cup of tea too?'

Madeline touched Eirlys's head, then patted Darcy's shoulder. 'I'd be sad if you didn't.'

The idea of not being able to sell this house had kept her burning with rage for the past year. Now, though, she wondered why. Where was she going to go? What would she do? Olivia and Darcy were Nora's kin, and they'd come to Stoneden to build a life where Nora had grown up, and maybe for that reason alone Madeline wanted to stay here and watch over them, even if only on behalf of Nora, who couldn't do it herself. She was surprised at her depth of feeling for them, but there it was.

'Surely, though, that's not a decision to be rushed,' she said tentatively, her voice croaky. 'Is it an open meeting?'

'It is,' Olivia said, looking surprised.

'Then I should like to be there.'

•

Olivia lay in bed late that night, unable to sleep. There were many things that should have been keeping her awake – a pending lawsuit and the threat to her career, the district council meeting tomorrow and the possible end of the Renaissance Project, Norway and Helge, telling Darcy about her decision to relocate them to another country, closing down her business and leaving Stoneden.

All those things were there, humming in the background, but strangely, it was Madeline who was front and centre. If tomorrow's meeting resulted in the cancellation of the Renaissance Project, Madeline would finally be free to sell up and move away, just as she'd wanted to before the project prevented it. But where would she go? Madeline was all alone. How could she possibly leave Stoneden now? Olivia didn't think for a moment that Madeline was incapable or fragile, but the idea of her new friend being out in the world alone, of Olivia not being able to visit her and watch out for her, made her anxious, feeling as though she'd failed, somehow.

Then she realised that buried beneath her concern for Madeline was apprehension over her own act of abandonment in leaving this place, leaving these people she'd come to care about so much. *Her* people.

She was about to get up and attempt to sneak down the surly stairs – she certainly wouldn't miss these stairs in Oslo – when her phone lit up beside her. It was Helge.

Are you awake?

Yes ☺

Can I call you?

Of course.

She waited, twisting a corner of the sheet around her finger, until he called a few minutes later.

'Hi,' she said, a smile in her voice. Amid all the confusion, Helge was the light, the place she was headed to, the new horizon, the safe harbour. She was so glad he'd called.

'I didn't *v*ake you, did I?'

'No, couldn't sleep.'

He didn't respond, and the silence grew heavy with foreboding. 'What's wrong?'

'I needed to . . . there's something . . .' He sighed heavily into the kilometres between them.

'What's wrong?' she said again, firmly.

'It is Birgit.'

'Has something happened? Is she okay? Are the kids okay?'

'Yes. Yes. And yes.'

Dead air hung between them again, but she fought the urge to fill it, her gut churning, dread clawing up her chest.

'I didn't *v*ant to tell you like this,' he said finally.

'Tell me what?' she said, trying not to snap.

'I should have *v*aited till the morning,' he muttered to himself, then groaned, took a deep breath, and spoke clearly and precisely. 'Birgit is pregnant again.'

'A-again?' Her mind raced to catch up, doing the maths, not wanting her thoughts to go where they seemed intent on going. 'Is she seeing someone?'

After a lengthy silence, he said, '*Nei*.'

'Then whose baby is it?' She was sitting bolt upright on the edge of the bed now.

'She only just told me. She *v*anted to make sure it *v*as going to last, you know. She didn't think there *v*as any point in upsetting me if she didn't have to. She is three and a half months now.'

'Helge, is it *your* baby?'

'Yes. I'm sorry.'

'But you said you separated in March.' She forced herself to lower her voice so as not to wake Darcy.

'*V*e did. But these things aren't straightforward. *V*e slipped up. Just once. And all it did *v*as show us it *v*as really over. I know this is a*v*ful timing. But this changes nothing bet*v*een you and me.'

'How can you say that?'

'I visited you in September. By then, Birgit and I *vere* over, completely, and *ve* both knew it. This is just . . . just . . . really bad luck,' he said, sounding exhausted from talking, shocked and drained.

Olivia dropped her head into her hand. If Birgit was three months pregnant, the 'slip-up' had happened before Helge's first visit to Stoneden. He and Birgit were over by then – not by much, sure, but who was to say what an appropriate length of time would be? Their separation might have been coming for years. She could appreciate how a 'farewell moment' could happen. The fact that microscopic pieces of genetic material had made a baby was, indeed, bad luck. He and Birgit already had two other kids; now they would have three. They would all always be in each other's lives, regardless of the number, yet it felt like a new, rather large, complication in the puzzle of divorce and childcare agreements for them and, by extension, her and Darcy too.

'I still *vant* you here just as much as before. You and Darcy are my future and I can't *vait* till you arrive. But I had to tell you as soon as possible. I don't *vant* to keep things from you. *Ve* need to be honest with each other about everything, like you *vere vith* me about Darcy's party. I'm sorry, truly. I know it's not perfect. I'm not perfect. But I do love you.'

She was nodding along silently. 'I know you do.'

'This is a big shock. Please, can *ve* talk more tomorrow?'

'Okay,' she agreed, hollowed out and lost for words.

'Please, try to keep the big picture in mind – you, me and Darcy, together at last.'

'Okay.' She disconnected the call and flopped back against the pillow, not expecting sleep to come easily anytime soon.

33

The district council meeting was held on Wednesday afternoon at the town hall in the village of Burnbell, fifty minutes' drive from Stoneden. Darcy was at school, most of the shops in the main street of Stoneden, including Rambling Rose, were shut especially for this afternoon's event, and by the time Olivia and Madeline arrived, it was almost standing room only. The council members were seated behind desks arranged in a U shape, with Chester Pepperworth in the centre, dressed for duty in a suit and tie, with a neatly pressed matching pocket handkerchief. He stood up to set out the agenda of the meeting, reminding everyone that the reason for the assembly was for the council to vote on the continuation, or not, of the Renaissance Project. After the initial formalities, members of the public would be invited to speak, and then the sitting council would vote on whether the Renaissance Project should continue beyond the one-year trial phase.

As he spoke, Olivia and Madeline claimed two of the remaining seats. Olivia cast her eye around the crowded room, her gaze quickly landing on Grayson, who was standing on the other side of the room, his back to the wall, his arms folded across his chest, his chin raised. He was strong and determined, and she couldn't help but smile at his commitment to the village. He must have felt her attention on him, because he suddenly turned his head to meet her gaze. She raised her hand in greeting and he nodded at her and Madeline, a softening around his eyes and an easy smile suggesting that he was pleased to see them both. She was stabbed with a sword of regret.

She was going to miss him.

There were many other familiar faces, including Elena and Newton, Wilhelmina, Lance, Raj and Sally, Leanne and Keith, and Miguel. Katrina and Russell were both there, seated next to Eli; evidently they had decided this meeting was important enough to close the surgery for the afternoon. Randolph Wilson was there, and his aunt sat in a row with all her church ladies - a strong showing for the anti-Renaissance team, Olivia reflected glumly, noting that Fern, Georgio, Roger and Guy were also present.

Anthony Cabot was sitting quite literally on the edge of his seat; Juliet, glamorous as always, had her hand on his knee, as if to steady him. Olivia spotted Howard sitting on his own a few rows behind them. In the front row, Clarence was seated next to a stylish elderly woman with long sleek curls, who was wearing an expensive emerald pantsuit.

'That's Marina Haines,' Madeline said quietly, following Olivia's gaze. 'Long history there.'

Clarence looked around then, and Olivia waved. He beamed at her, whispered something to Marina and nodded towards Olivia. The older woman looked back and smiled at her warmly, and Olivia felt moved by this further evidence that Clarence had wholeheartedly embraced their newly emerging family connection. It helped to ease the discomfort that lingered from the conversation with Helge last night.

In the light of day, she could see that Helge was right that the baby really had nothing to do with him and Olivia. He'd not cheated on her. They hadn't even been in a relationship at that time. He and Birgit had simply been unlucky – if that was the way they wanted to look at it. The same could have been said of her and Helge eight years ago – they'd been unlucky. Except it wasn't. Unplanned and unexpected, yes, but also the greatest gift, something she hadn't seen coming but which had changed her for the better in a million ways. Darcy had changed her, and Helge's new baby would change him too, even if he couldn't see that yet. That was life, wasn't it? One emotional tsunami after another. Huge, unexpected events that crashed through and wiped the landscape clean, so all you could do was pick up the pieces and rebuild, never the same again, though hopefully stronger.

Around the outside of the room stood Ryan and Farzenah, among numerous media representatives, some with video cameras. This meeting was a big deal, and – thanks in part to Yoden's wedding – not just to the local community. The eyes of the world were watching, once again. Olivia saw Chester pull a handkerchief from his pocket and dab at his brow; clearly he was conscious of the weight of the attention.

Chester began by reviewing the history of the Renaissance Project to date, the agreements set in place by the previous council, the complaints his newly elected council had received about the myriad ways the project had upset particular residents, a reminder of the graffiti incidents (he left out the rat, for which Olivia was grateful), and for balance mentioned the recent celebrity wedding.

As the meeting went on, the crowd began to clear their throats and shuffle their feet. Olivia felt the tension in the room rising, and she impulsively slipped her hand into Madeline's and gave it a squeeze. To her surprise, Madeline patted her arm reassuringly and squeezed her hand in return. Even if they were on opposing sides, it felt good to be standing here together, facing whatever decision would be made.

At last, Chester wrapped up the boring procedural bits. He cleared his throat. 'I now open the floor for general discussion.' Dozens of hands shot into the air. 'I remind you that your words will be recorded and entered into the minutes as an official historical record.' No hands were lowered, and Chester turned to Fern and Georgio, who both had their hands in the air. 'Please, Mr and Mrs Paddinson,' he said warmly.

'You go,' Fern said, pushing her husband to his feet.

Georgio gave a lengthy statement about the financial impact the restrictions of sale had had on people's freedom and economic future, and said he hoped council would see sense and vote to end this ridiculous project immediately. There were a few shouts of *hear, hear.* Guy (supported by Roger) rose to his feet next to give a similar testimony, followed by several other disgruntled landowners.

It was heartening, though, to see how many people got up after them to praise the diversity and energy the imports had brought to the village. Anthony Cabot delivered a succinct but powerful mini sermon about the importance of a thriving, working village, a tight-knit community who would be there to support each other in times of need, a return to the values on which Stoneden had been built. Juliet addressed the council too, describing how the school had been reinvigorated by the influx of children from around the world, and how their new cultures and ideas had enriched the lives of their classmates. These new pupils, she affirmed, were very much a part of the community now, and it would be a disservice to both the new residents and the established ones to send the imports away. 'Let them stay,' she pleaded.

To Olivia's surprise, Ryan stepped forward next. He held aloft a massive three-ring binder. 'These are media clippings from around the world.' He delivered the binder to the table of councillors. 'Here, take a look and pass it on.' The first councillor put on her reading glasses to peruse the clippings. 'These articles are merely the tip of the iceberg: this project has attracted worldwide interest in Stoneden, and it has been almost universally praised as an example of community-led change.'

The councillor flicking through the clippings was nodding, as though impressed. Watching Ryan, Farzenah smiled proudly.

'What about the cake maker's scandal?' boomed a voice. There was a collective intake of breath, followed by a few titters among the crowd. Everyone turned to see who had spoken. Howard rose to his feet.

'Howard?' Clarence called out, standing up, his face pale. 'What are you doing?'

Very slowly, Howard turned to look at him, a small, nasty grin spreading across his lips. 'Bringing this show to an end.' Another gasp whipped around the room.

'It wasn't a fake cake,' Olivia objected, letting go of Madeline's hand to raise her own.

'What are you talking about?' Clarence asked, ignoring Olivia, his gaze fixed on Howard, his best friend of more than sixty years.

Howard waited a beat before he next spoke. 'It was me – the rat and the graffiti.'

The room erupted with ripples of shocked conversation, some cheers, some shouts of anger. Ryan was still on his feet, staring at Howard with a look of dawning realisation.

Clarence gaped at Howard. '*You* did that?'

'That I did,' Howard said.

'What are you talking about?' Clarence asked, his face red. 'I-I don't understand.' He looked around to find other Renaissance Project faces, seeking answers. Grayson shrugged, equally baffled. Anthony Cabot's jaw was slightly unhinged, a deep frown line between his brows. Juliet's hand covered her mouth. Clearly, Clarence wasn't the only one blindsided.

Howard shook his head and a look of pure disgust crossed his face. 'You, Mr Big Shot. I'm talking about you. Flying through exams without studying. Captain of the cricket team. You had girls falling at your feet. Any job you went for, you got. It was you who had not just a wife but a mistress too.' There were a few snorts at that, accompanied by tuts of outrage. 'Then another wife and still a mistress. Now a single man living it up and *still* with a mistress.'

A hubbub broke out. Several people turned in their chairs and craned their necks to get a look at Marina, still seated beside Clarence. She didn't look the slightest bit embarrassed or ashamed; she merely looked back at Howard with something akin to disgust on her face. Chester sat back with his arms folded, enjoying the show, clearly pleased as punch by this display of divisiveness. Finally, the councillor sitting on his left took up the gavel and banged it several times on the sounding block to restore calm. She gave him a meaningful look.

Clarence stood tall, squaring his shoulders, and spoke into the sudden hush. 'Marina is *not* my "mistress". She is the love of my life,' he said. Beside him, Marina continued to sit still and calm, her gaze directed unflinchingly at Howard.

But Howard wasn't finished. 'It was you who got the big redundancy payout from your cushy government job. It was you who travelled to Europe for summer vacations. It was you who appointed yourself president of the Renaissance Committee.'

'That's . . . I *offered* to be president and everyone agreed,' Clarence objected.

'That's how you see it,' spat Howard. 'No one is game to even try to take you on.'

There were some nods around the room then. Fern and Georgio couldn't wipe the smiles off their faces.

Clarence reeled in shock. 'You . . . absolute plonker!' he growled, finding his voice once more. He clenched his fists at his sides as he began to put the pieces together. 'To be clear, it was you who painted that disgusting slur on Raj's door, and you who broke into Leanne's bakery and defaced her shop?'

Heads bobbed and weaved as they tried to locate Raj and Leanne in the room. The toyshop owner stared in shock and betrayal at the man he'd thought was his ally. Leanne's face was a swirl of thunder. She looked ready to punch the guy.

Howard smirked, unfazed. 'Surprised?'

'You put that rat in Olivia's shop?' Clarence frowned. 'But you're terrified of them. How many times in our childhood did I have to save you from Roy Hobson when he was flinging rats at you?'

Now it was Howard's turn to blush. He puffed his cheeks out, clearly mortified at having been publicly reminded of that. 'Well, little Howard doesn't need you anymore.'

Clarence said quietly, 'I can't believe you would do that to our new residents. To Olivia, Raj and Leanne.'

'It was never about them!' Howard yelled. 'This is about me. For once, it's about me. You never saw me as anything but your sidekick.'

'But we . . . we decided about the Renaissance Project.'

'*You* decided, not me. You were like a train that couldn't be stopped.'

'But why would you put all that work into it, only to try to sabotage it?'

'For the mere pleasure of seeing you fail.'

Clarence put his hand on his heart, Howard's words obviously striking him deeply. Marina lay her hand on his arm, checking that he was okay, as though concerned he was in medical trouble. 'I'm fine,' he said quietly. The room was deathly silent now, no one moving or talking. The conversation had taken a turn no one had seen coming.

'Howard, what did I do that could possibly have led to this?' Clarence asked, his voice quieter now, broken by sadness.

To Olivia's surprise, Howard flicked his attention towards her, then back to Clarence. She turned to Clarence, who had also followed the shift in Howard's gaze, and he frowned, trying to piece the puzzle together.

'You knew,' Howard began. 'You knew how I felt about Ellie.'

Olivia gasped. Clarence jerked his head back as he caught the words.

'You knew I was going to declare my feelings but you seduced her anyway.'

Now the crowd began to murmur and whisper, devouring this salacious gossip.

'But . . . she was your friend, that was all. I'm sorry, Howard, but she didn't love you.'

'She never got the chance,' Howard said, his voice flat now, like a deflated balloon. 'How could she ever see me when you were there, taking up all the space, making her fall in love with you?'

Beside Olivia, Madeline had stiffened, her chest rising with sharper breaths. Olivia squeezed her hand.

'I couldn't talk as well as you, dance as well, dress as well. But instead of helping me, coaching me, facilitating some conversation to get us started, or even directing your attention somewhere else to give her a chance to see the real me, you had your fun with her then moved on with Bethan. The result, as you know, was catastrophic for many.' Howard nodded towards Madeline. Then, having run out of steam, he left, his cap in his hand, a growing wave of chatter filling the hall behind him.

Clarence folded at the knees, sinking back down into his seat.

'Are you okay?' Olivia whispered to Madeline.

Madeline nodded, blinking away tears. 'Yes.' She took a deep breath and let it out slowly.

Olivia was shocked, picturing her grandmother at the centre of so much attention from the young men in the village, yet only having eyes for the one who didn't want her, who dismissed her devotion in public, forcing her to strike out on her own into an unknown future. It must have been such a brutal blow to her heart. At the same time, Olivia could see how it had made her strong, had made her protective of her family, had made her so cautious of trusting other people in the world, of not taking anything for granted. 'Oh, Ma,' she whispered, wishing Eleanora Kent had taken the time to tell her everything before it was too late. Instead, she'd held her cards close and left this world without sharing her story. Olivia made a promise to herself not to ever do that with Darcy, to share the good, the bad, the shameful and the hopeful at every stage.

A grim-faced Randolph Wilson stood up and followed Howard from the room. Olivia assumed he would be asking Howard to go down to the police station to make a full statement. Would charges be laid? The room was in an uproar. Leanne was in tears, and Anthony Cabot sat shaking his head as though in despair. Katrina turned around, her eyes huge as they sought out Olivia's.

What the hell? she mouthed.

Clarence looked broken as he stared vacantly at the door through which Howard had left. Marina put her arm around him gently.

'Order!' the councillor called, hitting the block three times in a row. 'Order, please.'

The room finally quietened. The woman turned to Chester and nodded, inviting him to speak.

Chester cleared his throat, working to smother the grin on his face. 'Right,' he soothed, then waited a few more beats before continuing. 'Howard's objections to the project have been recorded in the minutes.' He paused as if trying to decide what to say next, but couldn't stop himself from adding, 'I believe that his extended testimony illustrates precisely why the project should be shut down today. The project's own administrators cannot even form a united front.'

More shouting and objections flooded the room. Order was called again. 'I'd like to hear the rest of what Mr Baker was saying before the interruption,' said the councillor to Chester's left. Chester frowned, then dipped his head reluctantly.

'Thank you,' Ryan said to the woman with the gavel. He pointed once again to the large binder of media clippings, and looked directly at Chester. 'These articles from around the world overwhelmingly praise the vision, insight and leadership *this district council* has shown in restoring a village on the brink of collapse.' Chester shifted uncomfortably in his chair. 'Struggling communities around the world have started up online petitions, asking their own councils to adopt similar projects. I put forward this binder as evidence of the great precedent Stoneden has set for the revival of villages across the globe. For this reason, I argue that it is vitally important for the project to continue until the end of the first year's trial period, at least. Ending it now would be premature and near-sighted.'

Ryan nodded to the councillors. As he sat down, murmurs and discussions sprang up around the room. The councillor next to Chester leant over and whispered something urgently in his ear, until he held up a hand to halt her words. 'Ah – Mrs Wilson,' he said loudly, gesturing to the woman with a relieved smile.

Olivia's heart sank as Mrs Wilson lowered her hand and thrust herself purposefully erect. Her church ladies looked up at her expectantly. The woman looked elegant in a powder-blue skirt suit with a diamond brooch sparkling on her lapel. She spoke briefly, but calmly and with authority.

'From the beginning, I was staunchly opposed to the Renaissance Committee and this project,' she said, and paused. Her next words made Olivia gasp in astonishment. 'But I now believe that we have all benefited from the revived sense of energy, momentum and youth the project has brought to our village, as well as many new, *good* neighbours. I confess that I was wrong. I agree with Reverend Cabot and declare that I am in favour of the project continuing.' The church ladies clapped loudly in support. Mrs Wilson cast a quick glance at Olivia before resuming her seat. Still in shock, Olivia grinned at her and mouthed, *Thank you.*

Chester's scowl only deepened when Eli stood next, speaking into a respectful hush. 'I'm eighty-three years old and I've lived in Stoneden my whole life, serving the community from births through life until deaths. But I can't continue to do it on my own for much longer. The village needs new blood, it needs a new generation with energy, vision and commitment, and it needs a secure future. If we want services to continue here, such as those my clinic offers, we need to build something that can attract and sustain professionals. In my opinion, the Renaissance Project is the only viable way to ensure that happens.' He sat down, and Katrina hugged him, Russell reaching across to pat him on the shoulder.

Chester opened his mouth, but then Madeline raised her hand and rose to her feet. Olivia and Grayson looked at each other in surprise.

Madeline's voice quavered slightly as she began to speak. 'I have also lived here my whole life. I was also opposed to the project. I, too, have changed my mind. A project such as this is ambitious and brave and few people could pull it off.' She turned to nod at Clarence. 'It was always going to have teething problems. Our challenge now is to move through those inevitable obstacles and come out the other side, something I know Stoneden can achieve, given enough time. I have been very grateful to receive much community support during some difficult times recently, including from some of our newest villagers.' She smiled at Olivia and reclaimed her seat.

Several councillors nodded. Chester was looking more and more uncomfortable as the tide of support continued, drowning out the objections. At last Chester stood once more.

'All contributions from the floor have been recorded.' He paused. 'Before we vote, I did want to invite just one more person to speak. Clarence? Are there any last words you'd like to say?' Olivia couldn't be sure, but she thought Chester's offer might have been given out of a tiny amount of grudging respect for his opponent's efforts thus far.

All eyes turned to Clarence, who looked pale and smaller, as if the stuffing had indeed been knocked out of him. He took a moment to consider, then stood and said, quietly, 'Thank you, but I don't think I have anything to add that the villagers themselves have not already said. I would only like to thank the council for giving this project a chance. It has been a tremendous honour to lead Stoneden up to this moment. The rest is in your hands.'

The two men eyed each other for a moment, then Clarence sat down and took Marina's hand.

Chester adopted a more formal tone. 'Before we the council vote, some of my colleagues have asked for a show of hands from the floor to indicate your support for or opposition to the project. This show of hands is not binding or official, and the decision will be made by council. So, without further ado, if you are in favour of the project continuing, please raise your hand.'

Hands shot up all over the room.

'Yes!' Olivia whispered, jiggling in her seat. There was a clear majority in favour. Still, she reminded herself, the vote wasn't binding in any way. It was all down to the councillors.

Chester nodded, his nose wrinkled as if he'd just smelt something unpleasant. 'Thank you. You may lower your hands.' More noisy chatter among the crowd. More banging of the gavel. 'We will now take the official council vote.'

Olivia put her hand to her stomach and reminded herself to keep breathing.

'All in favour of continuing the Renaissance Project, please raise your hand.' Chester kept his hand firmly on the desk in front of him.

There were twenty-one members of the council seated at the desks. Olivia scanned the hands in the air, counting furiously, but before she could finish the cheers went up. Thirteen hands. They'd won.

The room was in chaos, with some villagers whooping and cheering, others leaving quickly through side doors in anger, or sniping their displeasure to eager journalists. Olivia met Clarence's eye and held up her hands, clapping him. *You did this*, she mouthed.

His face sagged with relief, then he mouthed back, *No, we did this.*

Then she turned to Madeline and hugged her. 'Come on,' she said, 'let's go get Darcy out of school and celebrate.'

34

By the time Olivia and Madeline arrived back in Stoneden, a street party was in full swing. They broke Darcy out of school early, as many parents were doing, and he walked between them, holding their hands. A lump rose in Olivia's throat as she remembered doing this with Darcy and Ma back in Tasmania.

They joined Katrina, Russell and Eloise down by the river. 'We won!' Katrina cried, jumping up and down, her smile as wide as the horizon. Russell, too, looked delighted. There were hugs all round, Darcy and Eloise shrieking with joy, swept away by the festival atmosphere.

'Apparently Howard is still at the police station,' Russell said, in an aside to Katrina and Olivia.

'What do you think will happen to him?' Olivia asked.

Katrina waved a hand dismissively. 'Everything he did was minor. He didn't hurt anyone. I doubt much will happen to him at all.'

'That's true,' Olivia said. 'But my rat! Oh, the shame of it. I could shake him.'

Although the afternoon was cold and grey, the streets were still festively decorated from the wedding, with fairy lights and banners. Music was playing, braziers were glowing, Mrs Wilson and her ladies had set up tables with cakes and slices, and the pub was rolling out hot food and cold beers.

Clarence was strolling down the street, hand in hand with Marina, peering around cautiously, as though expecting another nasty surprise to jump out at him. What a terrible blow for him to have been betrayed so publicly by his oldest friend.

Juliet had found a fiddle and was leading an impromptu musical group in a high-spirited Celtic-style jam.

As she looked at the happy, smiling faces, at her excited little boy running around with Eloise, Olivia realised that this felt like home, more like home than she could ever have imagined when she'd packed up and left Tasmania. And she knew, for more reasons than she could count, and for a whole lot more she couldn't articulate, that she didn't want to go to Norway.

'Can you excuse me for a bit?' she said to Katrina. 'I just need to pop into the shop for a few minutes.'

'Of course. We'll watch Darcy,' Katrina said.

'Thanks. I'll be back as soon as I can.' Olivia hurried across the street, hunching her shoulders against the wind, and enjoying the smell of cooking popcorn coming from Lance's shop. At Rambling Rose, she slid her key into the lock and stepped inside. She pulled down the blinds to shield herself from the festivities and prying eyes outside, sat down at one of the tables and took out her phone.

'Hi.' Helge answered on the second ring, sounding relieved.

'Hi.'

'I'm so glad to hear your voice.'

She swallowed hard. 'I'm not ready to move to Norway,' she said, as steadily and clearly as she could over the emotion she was feeling.

'No, no, don't say that. Nothing has changed . . .'

'I have. I've changed. It's not about the baby, it's about me. This is my home now. I belong here.'

Helge was silent for so long she had to ask if he was still there.

'Yes, I'm here.'

'I'm sorry.' She wiped at a tear that slid down her nose. 'Darcy and I are part of something here, and we love it. Stoneden's been good for us and we're good for Stoneden.'

'I know there has been a lot going on *v*ith the *v*edding and the media, you can take your time, think it over. There is no need for a hasty decision now, one you might regret later.' He sounded desperate now.

She took in a long, deep breath. 'I've learnt that you can rarely say anything for sure, but right now, I don't think so. It's just not . . . right. It's *almost* right,' she hurried to add. 'So very, very close to being right. I will always love you, Helge. Darcy adores you and I'm so happy you and he have started a wonderful relationship. You will always be welcome here whenever you want to come. And we will go to visit you too. I so hope we can still go there for Christmas this year?'

She heard him swallow. 'Of course.' It broke her heart to hear the depth of sadness in his words. But she knew that their time had passed.

'When I left Tasmania to come to Stoneden, all I wanted was to find a family again, and I have, and you are a huge part of that. What you and I have right now is good, and strong, and I want to keep it that way forever.'

'Forever?'

'Forever – not together, but forever with each other. Does that make sense?'

He sighed. 'Yes.'

'Thank you for offering us the world, but we already got it when you walked into our cottage and got splatted with cream.'

He snorted, gently.

'You became a very real part of our family that day and you're stuck with us now,' she added, trying to keep her voice from breaking. 'We're not going anywhere.'

She wasn't sure how long she'd been sitting at the table, the phone still clutched in her hand, when she saw it – the rat. It scurried along the wall and disappeared behind the counter.

'Gotcha,' she muttered, placing her phone on the table and rising to stalk it into the storeroom. Outside, darkness was falling. Someone had set up a microphone in the hotel garden and speeches were being made, cheers and clapping erupting every now and then.

Olivia stood at the door and flicked on the light, illuminating her shelves full of supplies and pans and tools. Fleeing the bright light, the black creature scuttled across the floor and tucked itself in a corner behind a box.

'You're not getting away this time,' Olivia warned it.

She grabbed an empty plastic cake carrier in her left hand and a spatula in her right. As she crept forward, she formulated a very basic plan: she would place the plastic container on one side of the box and reach around the other side to tickle the rat with the spatula. She only hoped the rat would run into the container and not simply scale the box and run straight for her head. That didn't bear thinking about.

She took a deep breath to steady herself. With a miraculously fluid motion, she extended her left arm to set up the plastic container, and simultaneously flicked the rat from behind with the spatula. Just as she'd hoped, the rat shot forward, and she slammed the container down, trapping it inside.

'Woo!' she shouted, shaking with adrenaline, pressing down firmly on the container as the animal raced back and forth, banging against the plastic sides, looking for a way out. Then it froze, staring at her with bright, terrified eyes.

'It's all right,' she said. 'I'm not going to kill you. But you can't live here anymore.'

The shop bell rang as the door opened. She thought she'd locked it behind her, but apparently not. 'Hello?' she called from her position on the floor. She didn't dare move in case the rat escaped. God, what if it was Rex Harrington, here for another unscheduled inspection? Was this the end of Rambling Rose after all?

'Hello?' To her relief, it was Grayson.

'In here,' she called.

He stopped at the doorway and then peered over her shoulder. 'Well, look what you've got.'

'I just caught it,' she said, grinning up at him in triumph.

He smiled back, leaning casually against the doorframe. 'What are you going to do with it now?'

'I've no idea,' she said, and laughed, slightly hysterically.

'Would you like a hand?'

'Yes, please.'

Grayson tore the base off a cardboard cake box and slid it under the container, Olivia emitting a couple of squeals as the rat zoomed around inside the plastic. He then folded up the edges and firmly taped the cardboard to the sides of the container, and together they slowly turned it over, the rat's claws scrabbling inside.

'I'm happy to let it go at my farm, if you like,' Grayson said, taking a knife and carefully poking a few air holes in the cardboard. 'It won't get up to too much mischief. I have a pretty healthy family of hawks that live in the trees – they'll take care of it if it makes itself a nuisance.'

'I guess that's better than us killing it,' Olivia said, suddenly feeling sorry for the rat.

She wrapped a towel around the container so no one would see the rat when they carried it out, leaving some gaps over the air holes. 'That's all I need, a viral photo of me carrying a rat out of my world-famous cake shop!'

They both washed their hands thoroughly at the sink. 'Did you see Darcy out there?' she asked.

'Yeah, Eloise has made a grass chain for him and put it on his head and they're dancing around to Juliet's Celtic music. He looks like a woodland nature sprite.'

'Those two are so adorable together.' She smiled, secure in her decision to stay in Stoneden. She couldn't take Darcy away from Eloise right now. He needed her, and she seemed to need him too. Their relationships were just as important as her own.

'I wanted to come and say goodbye.' Grayson cast her a sideways glance.

'You're leaving?' she said, turning to face him.

He scoffed. 'No, I'm not leaving. Ruby would never speak to me again.'

'Oh,' she said, understanding. 'You mean you came to say goodbye to me.'

'I didn't want to miss seeing you before you left. I figured once the wedding was over you'd take your chance and go straight to Norway . . . and Helge.'

'Ah.' She waited a moment, studying his face. The way his fair eyelashes framed his beautiful blue eyes. The way the light from the storeroom highlighted the soft whiskers on his face. She wanted to reach out and trace her fingertip along the lines across his forehead. 'I'm not going,' she said.

'What do you mean?'

'I've told Helge I don't want to go. He and I . . .' She lifted a shoulder and let it drop. 'We had our chance. We've had multiple chances. He and I have Darcy and that's good and important, but it's not enough to build a life on.'

Grayson started to smile, then quickly wiped his hand across his mouth to stop it, as though not entirely sure of what she was saying. 'Mm, yeah, that's important. I mean . . .'

She stopped him mid-sentence by grabbing the front of his jacket and pulling him down towards her. 'Would it be okay if I kissed you?' she whispered, her face millimetres from his.

He stared at her for several seconds. She could feel his heart beating under his jacket, and her own heart kept time. Someone was playing a guitar out in the street and a singalong had begun. Grayson's next two husky words set her skin on fire. 'Hell yes.'

He held her face gently between his hands and they took their time, kissing for what felt like an eternity. She allowed herself to melt into him, feeling all the stress from the past few days fade away, here in this moment. She wrapped her arms around his waist, and his arms were around her back, pulling her close so they were pressed together, staring into each other's eyes. She smiled, happy, certain she was in the right place at the right time, exactly where she was meant to be.

'I'm glad you decided to stay,' he said, his voice roughened with longing.

'Me too,' she said. Reluctantly, she peeled herself away from him, missing the feel of his body the moment it left hers. 'I really need to get back to Darcy.'

'Sure, of course.' He stepped back, but she caught his hand and held it.

'Come with me?' she said.

His grin made her heart dance. 'Absolutely.'

Together they walked out of Rambling Rose, holding hands. She locked the door behind her – the rat could wait an hour – and slipped the key back into her coat pocket and her hand back into his, and they wove through the joyful crowd until they found the others, clustered around a brazier outside the hotel. Katrina leant happily against Russell, a pint of beer in her hand. Madeline sat in a chair, holding a glass of something that looked like whisky, her cheeks red from the excitement or the alcohol or maybe both, her foot tapping to the music.

'I'm back,' Olivia said.

Katrina's twinkling eyes swept between Olivia and Grayson. 'So I see! Are you back for good, then?'

'Yes.'

'You're not going?'

'Nope. I'm staying.'

Katrina thrust her glass into Russell's hand and threw her arms around Olivia. 'Oh, thank God. We would have gone to see you in Norway, but I'm so happy you aren't going. It would have broken Eloise's heart – and mine. Thank you!'

'Going?' Madeline said. 'Where are you going?' Her brow furrowed with worry.

'Nowhere,' Olivia assured her. 'Absolutely nowhere.'

Darcy skipped over from where he'd been out on the road, choosing a cake from Mrs Wilson. 'Mum, look!' He pointed along the street to where Raj was juggling at least three colourful balls and Miguel was playing a guitar, singing something in Spanish, while Eloise danced at his feet, spinning and leaping about, and people clapped and cheered.

Olivia pulled Darcy close, her hand on his chest. Raising a child really did take a village, and she felt so lucky to have found this one.

Epilogue

Olivia, Darcy and Grayson were in London for the day, on their way to Oslo for baby Mathilde's first birthday party. The city was putting on its best late-spring weather, with bright blue skies, carts selling flowers on every street corner, and people sunbaking in Hyde Park. Olivia and Grayson were in the back seat of the blue paddleboat, providing the muscle power to steer along the Serpentine, while Darcy lounged in the front, life jacket on, soaking up the sun. Olivia had had to ask Grayson to pedal more slowly so she could keep up, or they'd end up going in a circle.

The waterway was busy with paddleboats and rowboats. Small waves slapped against the side of the plastic boat, and geese bobbed past, giving the occasional nasal honk.

'Do you ever miss Tasmania?' Grayson asked suddenly.

'*I* don't,' Darcy said, sliding down even further in his seat.

Olivia smiled at the back of Darcy's head. It was true what they said, that you were only ever as happy as your unhappiest child. These days, Darcy was almost always smiling. He and Eloise were still best friends and had recently started making short films together, capturing life in the village, using an iPad and a tripod, the latter a gift from Clarence for Darcy's eighth birthday .

She thought about Grayson's question. 'I don't think so. I still miss Ma, of course, but not Richmond, or Tasmania, no. Not yet, anyway. Maybe when more time has passed, I'll want to go back.'

'If you do, I'd like to go with you,' Grayson said.

'Of course,' she said. There wasn't a version of the future she could think of that didn't include him, or Stoneden and its other residents.

Katrina had kindly offered to look after Olivia and Darcy's two cats, Bluey and Moo, brothers from Eirlys's litter. Katrina had joked that she and Russell were expecting the arrival of their own litter very soon. 'Not actually a litter, though,' she'd said, grimacing. 'Just one baby in there, thankfully.'

Russell and Grayson had formed a partnership, with Russell officially investing in Grayson's farm, doubling the size of his herd and allowing him to diversify to include free-range hens too. Seven Cows now had a sister business, Seven Hens. Having someone else to share the load had made Grayson's life easier – meaning he could finally take short breaks to travel with Olivia to Norway, or beyond – and Russell and Katrina were happy that Russell had been able to quit his job working for someone else's farming business and start his own venture, firmly settling them in Stoneden for the long haul, with no plan at this stage to return to New Zealand.

The Renaissance Project had easily won its bid to continue after the twelve-month trial period was over. In a unanimous vote, Clarence had been chosen to continue leading the committee. Since then, the district council had lifted restrictions on land sales, appeasing the grumpiest resisters, while the council still worked to attract new residents to the village. It was paying off: their projections for the next five years were positive.

International media interest in the project remained high, and since Yoden's wedding, Rambling Rose had gone from strength to strength. Olivia had had to take on two apprentices to keep up with demand. Fortunately, Adele Bellington had soon realised that she had a slim-to-nil chance of winning her lawsuit, and in the face of potentially crippling legal fees, had perfunctorily withdrawn her legal proceedings. Olivia had sent her a bunch of flowers and written her a card, again apologising for the misunderstanding, but she'd never heard anything back.

She had a great relationship with Clarence, talking most days and sharing dinner at least once a week. He and Marina had recently made the surprising decision that after all those decades they would in fact like to get married. Olivia was excited about making the wedding cake. 'It will have to be something unconventional,' Marina had said, smiling. 'Like us.'

With the project's success, Doc Eli had finally felt he could retire. Two new doctors, a husband-and-wife team, had moved to Stoneden with their children, who were slightly older than Darcy and Eloise. Katrina had remained with the surgery, but she confessed that she missed working with Eli. 'They don't make them like that anymore,' she said.

Miguel's family had finally arrived from Mexico six months ago. They were loud and hilarious and Miguel swung between loving the chaos they brought to his life and looking stressed and harried and grumbling that he needed tequila. 'Just like any other parent, then,' Olivia had reassured him.

Elena and Newton's daughter, son-in-law and grandchildren had moved over from Italy, and embraced the opportunity to work in the restaurant. 'We're building this for them, for their future,' Elena had said, proudly.

The clamour around the project had been less positive for Leanne, however; after enjoying more than a year without her husband's family, she had been dismayed when they applied to move to Stoneden as well.

Howard had left the village with his wife soon after the council meeting, without making any attempt to contact Clarence, and promptly listing his house for sale as soon as the restrictions were lifted. Clarence had taken his former best friend's betrayal hard at first, but he took comfort in his new relations, his work on the Renaissance Project, and then the arrival of his grandson Mikey, with Lillan – who promptly opened a fashion boutique – and baby Arionna, now a bubbly, bright bundle of toddler goodness. The young family had been lured to Stoneden by the success of the project, as well as the open spaces and the chance to work from home.

After a lifetime of caring for her brother, Madeline might have been expected to enjoy the opportunity for a well-earned break. Somehow, though, her home had turned into an unofficial animal rescue operation, the paddocks a temporary home to horses, cows, donkeys and sheep, while her house was full of stray cats and dogs. Grayson and Russell had volunteered their time to fix up fences and gates and to clean out the old milking shed and turn it into stables. Olivia had taught her how to use the internet and social media to help find homes for the animals. Although Olivia had worried it might all be too much for her, Madeline assured her that she hadn't felt as healthy or as motivated to get out of bed in the morning in many years.

Their paddleboat drifted past an outdoor wedding in progress on the banks of the river. Darcy turned around in his seat at the front of the boat to face them. 'Are you going to get married?'

'That's an interesting question.' Olivia swung her head to look at Grayson, laughing.

'Not today,' Grayson said, unperturbed, above the swish of the paddles through the water.

'Can you have a baby?' Darcy asked.

'There are no plans for that,' Olivia said decisively.

'Aw,' said Darcy, disappointed. Eloise's excitement about the baby's pending arrival had spilt over to Darcy, and he'd said a few times that he wished he had a little brother or sister to play with. 'Yes, but if you had one you'd probably fight all the time and then you'd wish you were an only child,' Olivia had explained. 'Everyone wants what they don't have.'

Next to her, Grayson had fallen quiet. She glanced over at him and he gave her a reassuring smile. She felt the tug in her belly. He would have been such a great father. She'd asked him about it before, wondering how he felt about not having kids of his own. 'It's okay. Some people get to be uncles,' he'd said. 'And we have Darcy.'

'Besides, you've already got three siblings,' Olivia reminded Darcy now. 'That's why we're going to Norway.'

'But they don't live with us,' Darcy sighed, dramatically.

She reached forward and rubbed his shoulder in commiseration. 'Did we work out what time we had to leave for the airport?'

'Three o'clock,' Darcy and Grayson said together.

For the weekend, she'd booked an apartment not far from Helge's place on the eastern side of the city, a short walk to the pier where the christening party would be held. Birgit, Elias and Regine would be there, of course, along with Birgit's new 'man friend', as Helge called him, and other family and friends. Helge had primary custody of the kids these days, as Birgit's new job as a lifestyle photographer involved lots of travel. As far as Olivia knew, Helge wasn't seeing anyone himself, but she didn't like to ask.

Now she blinked in the glare off the Serpentine. Her legs were aching from pedalling. 'I need to stop for a bit,' she said, taking her feet off the pedals, feeling the burn in her quads. 'Phew!'

'I'm not tired,' Darcy said.

'Cheeky,' she teased him.

The three of them floated along in silence, the boat bobbing up and down, a duck on the water beside them tucking its head under the surface to have a look, then coming up and shaking droplets off with ease.

'I've been thinking,' Grayson said, his hands resting behind his head.

'Mm?' She turned to look at him, and he met her gaze evenly. From his expression, she sensed he had something momentous to say, and nerves flitted in her belly. Surely he wouldn't propose to her here, in front of Darcy, without talking to her first?

'I've been thinking about us, and how good we are together.'

Her heart rate quickened. 'We are.'

'I think we can join forces and do something great together.'

She waited, breathlessly, the sounds and sights around her fading away. He grinned at her, his eyes crinkling at the corners.

'Would you do me the honour of becoming my business partner?'

She blinked. 'What do you mean? You already have Russell.'

'Russell and I have Seven Cows and Seven Hens. But I think there's something else that I can do just with you. I've been watching Stoneden growing and I can see where the village is headed. There's a service missing that I think you and I can fill.'

'Which one?'

'Flowers.'

'Hmm – you're right,' she said.

'I've got the land to grow them and you already use lots of flowers in your business. Miguel sells them too, but has to order them in. Seems to me there's a gap in the market.'

She started nodding as her excitement grew. 'That's true. And even if I couldn't be a florist myself – though I'd love to give it a go – Rambling Rose is the perfect location to bring in a florist.

I already supply the cakes for all the big events; this way I'd be able to diversify my services, maybe even move into full event planning.'

'See, I knew you'd know what to do.'

'Yes,' she said, leaning across to wrap her arms around him. The boat lurched, making Darcy squeal and laugh. 'Yes, yes, yes. I'd love to be your business partner. It's absolutely perfect.' She kissed him, sunbeams falling onto her face and shoulders, drenching her with optimism.

Darcy sighed. 'Can we go now?'

Reluctantly, she and Grayson stopped kissing and put their feet back on the pedals.

'Let's go,' she agreed. 'We're on our way.'

Acknowledgements

This story was inspired by a trip to the Cotswolds in 2015. Stoneden, and many other villages mentioned in this novel, are fictionalised locations inspired by composites of villages we visited on that trip, as well as pure imagination, while a few places that are mentioned, such as Burford, the Slaughters and Stroud, are obviously real. This is the beauty of fiction.

Thanks to my dad, sister and nephew for accompanying me on that UK trip and eating my 'illegal' apple crumble, and continuing to eat it with Bailey's Irish Cream long after we ran out of regular cream. To any residents whose apples I picked, my apologies.

Thank you to Terry and Brian from the Cotswolds, who made me a cup of tea and told me stories about what life was like in the 1950s, which gave me the spark of inspiration to use my magical writer's pen to bring a village back to life in this piece of fiction.

I am so very grateful to my dear friend Kate Smibert for joining me on boot-camp writing retreats in the hills, where we did so much brainstorming for this book, and also for the best cake story

I have ever heard, which sadly didn't make the final cut but gave me a great laugh.

Thank you to Katey Thew-Thin from Buttercups Cupcakes in my hometown of Cooroy, for meeting with me to share what life as a cake maker is like. Katey's cakes are gorgeous and you should definitely buy them if you have the chance.

Thank you to Ali Watts, my publisher at Penguin Random House, whose structural advice is always perfectly on point, to everyone at PRH who works on my books at every level to get them out into the world, to my editing ninja, Clara Finlay, for always pushing me to dig so much deeper than I think possible, and to Kathryn Knight for guiding the book through the system.

Thank you to my agent, Haylee Nash, for your ongoing enthusiasm and support, and to my rights agent, Natasha Solomon, for seeking new readerships for my work. Thank you to Mr Murray for a fabulous array of unique Irish sayings. Thank you to fellow author and romance queen Rachel Bailey for some emergency romance surgery. Thanks to Holden Sheppard for an enlightening chat, and to several participants in the Nash Agency Writers Retreat, including Rachael Johns, Inda Ahmad Zabri and Alex Adsett, for helping to brainstorm an entire plotline . . . which I later deleted in full. I promise you, though, Harry is not lost and will return.

My great-grandfather came to Australia from Norway. Alas, I speak no Norwegian. Any errors in translation may be attributed to Google Translate.

My deep gratitude and love as always to my husband, Alwyn, and son, Flynn, for being my biggest support and cheerleaders, and to my fluffy friends who sit by my side and warm my lap while I'm working.

Most importantly, thank you to my readers, who keep reading and cheering me on from the sidelines. I write for you.

Book club discussion notes

1. Olivia moves Darcy to the other side of the world in the hope of finding a family for him. Discuss the ways in which she does and does not succeed.

2. In your opinion, is the idea of the Renaissance Project unrealistic or ingenious?

3. What was the intention behind the saboteur's actions?

4. What do you think it really means to be part of a community?

5. Darcy's birthday party is a potent scene in the book. What do you think of the behaviour of the children and the adults involved? What do you think makes people act so cruelly?

6. In what ways does Olivia support her son?

7. Which male love interest did you prefer – Helge or Grayson? Do you think Olivia made the right choice?

8. Discuss the transformative power of friendship in the novel as it plays out for both Olivia and Darcy.

9. Discuss Clarence's determination to restore the village when he doesn't seem capable of mending the rifts in his own family. Is there something ironic in this attempt?

10. What are the trademark characteristics of Josephine Moon's novels? Which book of hers is your favourite?

Persian love cake

GF

Ingredients

Cake

200 g unsalted butter, room temperature
150 g caster sugar
4 medium eggs, room temperature
12 cardamom pods, ground in a mortar and pestle (discard the pods, keep the seeds to grind) ***or*** 2 tsp ground cardamom (see note)
275 g ground almonds
75 g rice flour, sifted
25 g arrowroot flour, sifted
zest and juice of 1 unwaxed lemon
1 tbsp rosewater
1.5 tsp baking powder
pinch of salt

Drizzle topping
2 tbsp caster sugar
juice of 1 lemon
1/2 tbsp rosewater

Icing
250 g icing sugar
3/4 of the juice of 1 lemon
1 tbsp rosewater
extra cold water

To finish
chopped pistachios
dried rose petals
fresh edible flowers from your garden or purchased specially (optional)

Method

1. Preheat the oven to 160°C (140°C fan forced). Grease and line a 20 cm round cake tin.
2. Using an electric beater, cream the butter and sugar together in a mixing bowl until combined.
3. Add the eggs and beat until combined.
4. Add all remaining cake ingredients and mix well on low speed.
5. Pour the mixture into the cake tin and bake for 45–50 minutes, or until a skewer or fork poked into the cake comes out dry. Transfer to a cooling rack.
6. To make the drizzle topping, combine the caster sugar, lemon juice and rosewater in a pan and stir over a gentle heat until the sugar melts and a syrup is formed.
7. Poke holes in the top of the cake and slowly drizzle the syrup over the surface.

8. Allow the cake to cool. Make the icing by combining the icing sugar, lemon juice and rosewater and beating until smooth and thick. If it's too thick, gradually thin it out with alternating additions of lemon juice and water, 1/4 tsp at a time.
9. Pour and smooth the icing over the cake, allowing it to drizzle down the sides.
10. Finish with decorations of your choice on top, such as rose petals and ground and/or chopped pistachios.

Note: Some people find the taste of cardamom too strong. You may choose to leave this spice out, or play with the amount you include (perhaps using only four pods, or 1/2 tsp of ground spice, for example).

Four generations of women – one special recipe for adventure.

Award-winning jam maker Aggie is determined to take her Barossa Valley cafe to new heights. She has put the pain of unsuccessful IVF treatments and a broken relationship behind her, and is focused on the many wonderful possibilities life still holds in store.

When an invitation to travel across Australia on the Ghan for her mother's seventieth birthday comes her way, she is at first apprehensive. But the trip offers a precious opportunity to spend some quality time with both her disgruntled mother, Valeria, and her distant daughter, Holly, as well as her meddling great-aunt, Myrtle. The four generations of the family, all single women, will be reunited at last.

As the iconic train chugs its way beneath majestic desert skies, Aggie's difficult past resurfaces, her business comes under threat, and long-held family rifts reignite. To complicate things further, she's distracted by the attentions of a handsome younger man on his own search for meaning in some of the country's most remote and magical places.

By the bestselling author of *The Cake Maker's Wish*, this is a sweet and soulful story about women being there for each other through the stickiest situations. It celebrates the joys and sorrows of life, and reveals the essential ingredients of the true recipe for happiness.

You've been given the gift of life, now go live it.

Gabby McPhee is the owner of The Tin Man, a chic new cafe and coffee roasting house in Melbourne. The struggles of her recent heart transplant are behind her and life is looking up – until a mysterious customer appears in the cafe, convinced that Gabby has her deceased husband's heart beating inside her chest.

Krystal Arthur is a bereaved widow, struggling to hold herself and her two young boys together since Evan's death, and plagued by unanswered questions. Why was her husband in another city the night he died? And why won't his spirit rest?

Krystal is convinced that Gabby holds the clues she needs to move towards a brighter future. Gabby needs Krystal to help her let go of her troubled past. The two women must come together to try to unlock the secrets in Evan's heart in order to set free their own.

By the internationally bestselling author of *The Tea Chest*, this is a profound and moving novel about the deeper mysteries of love and loss – and the priceless gift of life.

'This book is a gift in itself.'
Herald Sun

'Reading a Josephine Moon novel is always a delicious treat.'
Goodreads

'Part mystery, part romance and all heart, Moon has crafted a great novel about the power of friendship, love and second chances.'
QWeekend